HARD RIDDEN

By the same author

The Savannah Lady, The Book Guild, 2003

HARD RIDDEN

Iris Button

The Book Guild Ltd
Sussex, England

First published in Great Britain in 2005 by
The Book Guild Ltd
25 High Street
Lewes, Sussex
BN7 2LU

Typesetting in Baskerville by
Keyboard Services, Luton, Bedfordshire

Printed in Great Britain by
CPI Bath

A catalogue record for this book is
available from the British Library

ISBN 1 85776 859 0

1

They were galloping at a fast pace through the fields and over the hedgerows. Major loved to be out and about on sunny spring mornings like this, the sky so blue and the air so fresh in his flared nostrils. His sharp ears were pricked and his large brown eyes were bright, his head nodding like that of a rocking horse, as he kept up the steady pace. His chestnut coat gleamed and his ginger silky mane and forelock flew back from his beautiful head and shiny neck.

Miss Emily on his back let him have his head as they came to a high hedge. He lifted his forelegs, and they flew through the air together, landing safely on the other side.

He had carried Miss Emily for four years, and they had ridden this same path nearly every day. He stretched his long slender legs across the last half mile of the open fields; they were heading for the woods and almost home. As they entered the shady trees in the woodland he slowed his pace a little, but she urged him on, following the grassy path; the overhead shade of the trees felt cool to his now sweating body as the pale shafts of yellow sunbeams filtered through the leaves. He loved the sound of dry twigs as they snapped and crackled beneath the thud of his hooves, and the feel of the soft dewy springy grass as his hooves crashed down, crushing the toadstools and shy violets that peeped through the damp and tangy-smelling earth at the base of tall trees.

They galloped on, still at the same fast pace, past bushes, the leaves falling to the ground as the shiny chestnut body brushed them. They followed the grassy woodland path and they were nearly to the last stretch. The open meadow lay before them – they were almost home. She saw the low bough before her and ducked to the left side of his neck, but it was too late! He struck his majestic head on the large low-lying bough hanging from a huge oak; he faltered, his forelegs

1

crumpled beneath him, and he felt Miss Emily tumbling heavily over his neck. He was lying on his side on the grassy path, and he saw her lying in front of him. Then a terrific pain shot through his head, he huffed, and his body shook, and his soft brown eyes slowly closed, then everything went black.

Emily, stunned and winded for a moment, sat up slowly and winced as she rubbed her elbow then adjusted her riding helmet. She had hit her head hard and her head hurt, but luckily the helmet had saved her a nasty bump. She looked at Major through dazed vision. He lay very still. She got up slowly, first onto her knees, and then stood for a moment, shakily trying to get her breath back and looking down at him. She knelt down beside him. His eyes were closed. He had knocked himself out, and there was a gash bleeding above his left eye. She put her hand on his soft silky mane, stroking him gently and ran her hand down his cheek, then whispered his name close to his ear. He was motionless. She ruffled his mane in her hands and shook his neck. There was still no reaction. She shook him again and slapped him hard on the shoulder and spoke sharply to him, 'Major! *Major! Wake up!*' She slapped him again and shook him. He was still motionless. So still! Uncannily still... It was then with an appalled shock, her blood racing in her ears, she realized that he must be dead... He couldn't be dead; it was impossible. She felt for a heartbeat but did not find it. The woodland around her seemed so silent and still as if the whole world had come to a sudden stop. She shook him violently, tears rolling down her cheeks. 'MAJOR! MAJOR!' she screamed. Her voice echoed through the quietness, then her shoulders sagged as every ounce of her strength seemed to leave her. She sobbed quietly and bitterly, her cheeks streaked with black mascara.

Suddenly she heard the sound of her own voice echoing through the trees as she shouted hysterically, 'Major, Major. GET UP! GET UP, PLEASE!' The words faded away to a tiny whisper. Through misted tears she whispered, 'Major.' It was almost a whine. 'Major, Major,' she moaned, rubbing her cheek against the hardness of his head. 'Please.' It was a hushed breath as she shook her head gently. 'PLEASE! GET UP,' she pleaded through anguished tears as she fell forward, her head on his neck. She sobbed bitterly and loudly, knowing that she would never ride on his back again, her beautiful, beautiful friend was dead...

A tingling shiver ran down her back and through her arms, and although she herself felt limp and lifeless, her fists closed tightly like a clamp over the horsehair, scrunching up his mane. She beat on his neck, hoping to revive him, but there was no movement, no life. He looked so peaceful with his eyes closed. There was just the eerie stillness of death.

Emily looked from left to right, peering at the dense greenery and at the thick trunks of the trees through misty glazed eyes and hoping help would come, but knowing that there was no one there. No one. Any other day she would have been with her friend Jenny, but today she was alone. Oh, how she wished that Jenny was there with her now, to help her bear this agony with whispered words of comfort. She had never felt so alone in all her life. She didn't know what to do, she had never had to cope with death before. What should she do? She wanted to run deep into the woodland and get lost and to shake off the terrible feeling of guilt, but she knew she must stay here with Major, never to leave him. She could not leave him, not here in the woods, not here, not all alone with the trees looking on and whispering. She was sure that they were scolding her for riding him so hard. Her mind was in a whirl, but what was she to do? She wanted to stay with him, but she knew that she couldn't just sit here. She must go home, she must tell her mother, she must get help. She must make a big effort, but her knees felt weak as she tried to get up. She reached out and leaned on the mighty oak for support, and then she fell back on her knees again, resting her head on Major's neck and sobbing bitterly into his mane.

Major rolled himself onto his feet and stood up. He shook his beautiful head, his mane splaying out around him. He swished his silky tail and snorted as he pranced around, nodding. He felt light-headed; he could not think what had happened. But there, at his feet, was the body of a beautiful chestnut horse, and Miss Emily was on her knees stroking its head. She spoke sharply for it to get up, and then she was crying bitterly, the tears rolling down her cheeks and dripping onto the side of the horse's face.

3

Major stomped his feet about in the grass and snorted, trying to get her attention, but Miss Emily did not look up. He looked down at her. She was sobbing and so upset, with her head lying on the face of the horse, and through her tears she was saying, 'I'm sorry, I'm sorry. Oh Major, Major, I am sorry. I should not have urged you on. Oh, Major, what am I to do? It was my fault, it was, it was.' She took off her black velvet riding hat, and her long blonde hair fell over her eyes and mingled with the horse's mane, curling round its ears and over its eyes. The horse had a gash on its forehead. There was blood and now it was on Miss Emily's hair. He was puzzled. She kept calling the horse Major, but that was his name... He nudged at her shoulder with his nose, but she did not turn round. He nudged her again and again, but still she did not respond. He became alarmed. What was the matter with her? What was the matter with him? Had he lost his sense of touch? He nudged her again, then, suddenly, with a great shock, he realized that the body of the horse lying with Miss Emily was his body and that he must be ... DEAD ... that he must be a ghost ... though he wasn't quite sure what a ghost was.

He nudged her again. He did not feel anything and neither did she. He did not know what to do, and he felt helpless, unprotected. He was afraid. What would he do without Miss Emily's guidance? He looked down onto the body of the great horse, which lay very still with the large gash on its forehead. He sniffed at the deep-red blood that had oozed from the open wound; his nostrils smelt nothing. He felt a deep sadness, for the beautiful chestnut coat had only an hour ago been brushed to a brilliant shine by John the stable groom. John had polished the leather saddle, too. It was still in place. He remembered when it was new, and they had had to wait months for it to arrive, and when it was put on his back Miss Emily had looked at him so proudly, patting him and saying how handsome he looked. He remembered her walking up to him, pulling on her gloves, and adjusting the peak of her helmet before she mounted his back. He remembered the smell and the squeak and the crunch of the new leather and felt its softness on his back. He remembered her adjusting the leathers on the stirrups and settling herself, and saying to John that she must buy a new bridle to match. He remembered the smell

4

of the saddle soap on the old bridle as it was put over his nose. It was there now with the horse's tongue hanging over the bit. He remembered the squeeze of her knees and the softness of the rein in her hands, the signal, he knew, to move off.

Today she was dressed in the same beige jodhpurs, but now they were covered in brown earth and grass stains, and the heavy green roll-necked sweater had twigs and leaves clinging to her back where she had fallen. The short brown leather riding boots though, still had the brightest shine. Less than an hour ago she had given him a pat before climbing into the saddle. They had walked out of the yard happily, as they did most mornings, calling good-bye to John and then to her mother, who had come into the yard as they were going through the gate, calling to Emily to be careful.

They had trotted slowly and then cantered across the field. Galloping across another field, the feeling had been invigorating. He felt happy and free, and they were on their way back through the woods with the strong smell of the earth and the greenery and the wind in his face ... and then?

Looking down at the scene, he hung his head. He knew that Miss Emily would never ride on his back again; she would never smooth her hand down his nose, never pat him and tell him he was a good boy, and offer him a carrot; she would never touch his silky mane again; he would never hear her laughter! But then he pricked up his ears, and, although he did not like to see Miss Emily crying for him, inside he suddenly felt exhilarated. His nostrils were still flaring, his mane streaming out away from his neck as if a strong wind was still blowing, and his silky tail swished... But there was no wind, not now. Everything around him seemed calm and still. The trees seemed a brighter shade of green and the grass fresher, glistening with dew, and there were flowers that he had not seen before, and the air seemed clean and cool. He looked at the oak tree, and the low bough hanging over the woodland path. It must have fallen in the night. His gaze fell again on the horse lying on the ground, and he knew it had once been his body. He swished his tail and knew without sadness that he was dead. He had been so happy at the moment of his death that he would go on for ever being happy and he would never ever be sad. He would be alone now, but his beautiful silky mane and tail would for ever be flying in the wind. His heart was filled with joy. He felt no sadness, so why was Miss Emily crying?

Emily sat for ages, cuddling Major's head. She sniffed back her tears, wiping her eyes with the back of her gloved hand. She took off her glove and felt the satin-smooth hair on his strong jaw. She felt weak and exhausted; she knew it was no use just sitting here, but she was afraid to leave. With a big effort, she got up unsteadily again and started to walk away, slowly at first, dragging her boots, then turning to look back at the great chestnut body, as if expecting him to be standing. She walked slowly through the trees as if in a dream, seeing huge tree trunks and shafts of sunlight. The woodland seemed like an enchanted forest. She heard the leaves rustling on the trees, the birds singing, the swishing of grass as rabbits dashed into the undergrowth away from her. But although she heard all these everyday sounds, it was as if her ears were numb and deaf. There was a feeling of emptiness, hollowness. A feeling that hung so heavily over her, but a feeling she could not define. A feeling that she had never felt before, a feeling of utter despair as if she was the only person left in the whole wide world. She walked very slowly at first, still turning at intervals, hoping and expecting him to be standing behind her. Then suddenly she burst into tears and began to run like the wind, not knowing that the ghostly Major was one step behind her all the way.

As she went rushing into the house to tell her mother the terrible news, Major was wandering back to his stable, unseen by John Carter who was sweeping up the yard.

2

Emily still felt sad. She thought she would never get over the loss of Major. Three months had gone by. She was standing at the stable door, blaming herself for what had happened. Snowball, the pure-white cat, jumped up on the half door and waved his tail under her chin. She stroked his back gently and rubbed her face against his soft furry white head. 'Oh Snowball, I didn't mean it. I wouldn't hurt you, I didn't mean to hurt Major. I loved him. Do you think that he will ever forgive me for urging him on?'

She had been back to college. The teachers, knowing of her terrible experience and the trauma that it had caused her, tried to understand, but no one knew exactly how she felt, Emily found it difficult to concentrate on her lessons, and Miss Tilbury, the headmistress, had phoned her father and said that Emily was not doing well and could she come and see him. She had come to the house and explained that several of the teachers had spoken to her, saying that Emily spent most of the time in a daydream, gazing out of the window with a far-away look in her eyes and, when asked a question, would reply with some nonsensical answer and say that she was sorry that she had not been listening. Then there was gym. Emily had no energy. Mrs Swanson, the trainer, said that Emily had been good at netball and had been team captain, but now she would stand while someone threw the ball at her and she would not even attempt to move her arms to catch it. Miss Tilbury had said that Emily would not talk to her friends or to the teachers, and she had noticed that she didn't even eat.

Mike and Liz Peters had listened to Miss Tilbury, and Mike explained that they were also worried about their daughter, and that she was still suffering from shock, and that Dr Gibbons had given her medication and said that she would eventually come to terms with it, but he could not say how long it would take, that they must realize that it was going to take some time.

It did take time. It took months for her to feel even a little better. She could not shake the guilty feeling that she had killed Major. She would never get over it. She knew that every single minute of every waking hour his beautiful head would fill her mind and his soft brown eyes would seem to look deep into hers. So deep and so real that she would say out loud, 'I'm sorry', and tears would fill her eyes. She wanted to curl up into a ball and hide her face so that she could not see the fingers she imagined people were pointing at her...

She couldn't eat, and she lost weight that she could ill afford to lose. She couldn't sleep, even though Dr Gibbons had given her sleeping pills. She was tossing and turning until the early hours, then dozing and waking in the night with cold sweats, her hand tangled in her hair. Then she would gradually realize that it was a bad dream, that the hair was not his mane, and she would get up and sit by the window until dawn, imagining him, and expecting him to come trotting into the meadow... He never came.

She went into deep depressions, moping about the house, especially at weekends. She sat for hours in her room, with Snowball curled up on her lap. She stroked his back, not even conscious that he was there. She had days off from class and cried from morning until night, and then went to bed exhausted and then could not sleep again. Dr Gibbons had given her stronger tablets to help her through the crisis, but after taking the tablets she could not wake up, and when she did she felt drowsy and depressed all day. She would stand leaning over the stable door in a dazed state, blaming herself. If only she had let him slow a little as he had wanted to and not urged him on. Oh, if only she had not urged him on... She shook her head slowly.

Jenny Ellis, her friend who lived at Mayberry Farm, about a mile away, saw her every day at school, and phoned her again in the evenings. She came to see her on the days she did not attend school. She and Jenny used to ride out together at weekends and all through the school holidays. They saw each other nearly every day, and Jenny had tried to get her to come and ride one of their horses on the farm; they had four. She and Major had spent quite a lot of time at Mayberry Farm, practising jumping in the paddock, and she and Jenny would ride around the farmyard and then out across the fields. But Emily had not been near the farm since the accident. She could not bear to see Jenny riding Henry, or even to touch a horse. She could not bear the smell of horses. She had completely given up, telling Jenny that she could not be trusted to ride one of their horses ... she could not be trusted anywhere near a horse, she had killed Major with her carelessness. Jenny had said that it was all nonsense, and that Emily had always been very careful, loving Major with all her heart, and that it had been just a terrible accident, and it could have happened to anyone.

Liz said to Mike that Jenny was good for their daughter. She was the only one who could keep her going, she said she always seemed more cheerful when she came off the phone after speaking to her friend.

Emily had not spent much time at college in the last year, and now they had broken up for the summer term, Jenny had phoned the night before as usual to say that she would pop over and keep her company in the morning, but only if she wanted her to come. She didn't like to push it too much. Emily, who had seemed a lot better lately, agreed that it would be all right.

Emily leaned away from the stable door, wiping a tear from her eye, as she heard John saying good morning to Jenny down by the paddock. She felt a pang of foreboding as Jenny came riding into the yard on Henry with another horse on a leading rein. Henry was a large bay horse with a black shiny mane and a white splash down his nose and a swishing black long-haired tail. The hooves below his four snow-white socks clip-clopped on the cobblestones as he moved at a smooth walking pace. Even Jenny, who was tall and slender, looked like a tiny doll sitting in the middle of his huge back, her long dark hair tied into a ponytail with a red ribbon bobbed up and down on her shoulders under the black helmet in rhythm with Henry's nodding head and jaunty step.

'Hi Em!' she said brightly. 'I've brought old Webster. Hope you didn't mind.'

Webster had belonged to one of her three brothers who were now all married and living away from home with farms of their own. Her father kept the horses for when the grandchildren came to visit, which was about every two or three weeks. He exercised the horses himself when he had the time, often with the help of his wife, Carol, who rode out most days with their groom, Anita, a young woman of twenty-five, who was jolly and round, and about four foot nothing. Anita had muscled arms and legs like an all-in wrestler's, which she got from humping buckets of water and lifting bales of hay. How she ever rode a horse was beyond them all.

'How are you feeling today?' asked Jenny, as she handed the leading rein to John. She slipped her boots out of the stirrups and slid the long way down. 'I thought I might tempt you into a ride. Will you come with me, Em?' She waited. Emily made a quick intake of breath, and a strained look appeared on her face. Jenny had tried asking her several times, but had never gone so far as to bring a horse with her. Jenny saw the look on Emily's face. Was it longing or envy, seeing her with Henry? She was sure that Emily did want to ride, but was afraid to say yes. Each time she had been here to Rosemary Lodge she had cycled. This was the first time that she had ventured out with Henry, and she had taken a chance in bringing old Webster with her. The strained look on Emily's face faded. Jenny looked hopeful.

'Will you come for a ride, Emily? Please?' she pleaded, squinting her eyes with a smile, and clenching her even white teeth together, inwardly wincing, hoping that she had not upset her friend. 'Just a quiet walk. You might like it. It's a lovely day. You know old Webster... He's quiet. It's hard work to get him to trot.'

Emily smiled, screwing her face up, and clenching her fists at her side. Looking at Henry reminded her of the days when they used to ride out together. She wrinkled her nose. 'No, I don't think so, Jen. Thanks. I don't really want to. But thanks anyway.' She stretched out her hand and stroked Webster's nose, giving him a gentle pat on his neck. Jenny glanced at John, with a look of hope and expectation. Emily was actually touching a horse.

Emily saw the look and took her hand away sharply from Webster's neck. He flinched, lifting his head.

She shook her head. 'No, I can't trust myself. I wouldn't want to hurt Webster.'

'Oh, Em, don't be silly. You can't hurt Webs, he's a tough old boy, and you can't keep blaming yourself for what happened; it was an accident, it could have happened to anyone.'

'I shouldn't have urged Major on.'

'Oh, Em,' she sighed, sounding depressed, then her voice rose. 'Look! We have been riding together for years. You love horses. You didn't hurt Major... It was an accident, Em... It could have happened to me... To anybody... Look...! Think of all the horses on our farm; you have ridden them all, including old Webster here.' She glanced at him lovingly. 'You love being on the farm, you know you do, you love horses. You love riding. Think of all the horse shows we have jumped in together. Think of the fun we have had. You and Major were great. It was an accident, Em. Don't keep blaming yourself. You can't just give up riding like that. And besides, he wouldn't want you to, he would want you to ride and be happy, wouldn't he? Perhaps even get another horse in time, but you can always ride one of ours, you know that. You could school it your own way. Dad would only be too pleased to have one exercised every day, you know that. Please, Em, come for a ride with me, just a gentle walk.' She wrinkled her nose. 'I don't really want to go on my own. Please?' She smiled, holding her head on one side, and looking into her friend's face. 'Old Webster will be disappointed. Won't you Webs?' She put on a silly voice. 'He got all dressed up in his bridle and saddle, and now he has nowhere to go. Shame, isn't it, Webs? She doesn't want to ride you, poor old boy.' She looked into his face. 'It's awful to be unloved, isn't it, Webs? Never mind, I love you.' Webster snorted, as much as to say 'who cares?' as she gave him a friendly pat.

Emily smiled and patted his neck again. 'Sorry, Webs, I love you too, but not today.'

Emily's mother came round into the yard. She was surprised to see two horses.

'Morning, Jenny,' she said, smiling cheerily. 'I didn't hear you come up. Going for a ride, Emily?' She looked at Jenny hopefully. She was more than surprised to see Emily stroking a horse.

11

'No.'

'I have been trying to persuade her, Mrs Peters, but she won't come. I brought Webster with me. He is very quiet, but she won't come.'

There was a pause. Liz looked at her daughter for a long moment, and then at Jenny. She knew it was no good pressing Emily.

'Do you girls want a cup of coffee? I have just made one and I have just taken some scones out of the oven.'

It took the pressure off all three of them, and they followed her into the kitchen, leaving John with Henry and Webster. He was happy as he had not had a horse to look after for months.

The girls sat at the table, as Liz gave them mugs of coffee and set out a plate of scones, a dish of clotted cream and strawberry jam. Mrs Porter, the daily lady, came into the kitchen and said hello to Jenny. Liz asked her to take a mug of coffee and a couple of scones out to John. The radio was playing some pop music. Liz turned it off as the girls sipped the coffee thoughtfully. Then Jenny broke the silence.

'There is a gymkhana over at Foxhead Hall on Saturday. I thought I might get Dad to run me down there, and if I take the mobile phone, I can call him and he can pick me up when I am ready. I know that Mary Clark is riding. I met her in the village shop. She said she's entered at four o'clock with Derek Milner, Dominic Hadley and Maria Martinez. I don't think I will go too early. I might watch Mary ride. It won't be a very big event.'

Emily looked thoughtful. 'Why didn't you enter Henry?'

'I was too late. All the entries had been taken in. I didn't know about it. It was Mary Clark who told me, but I wasn't, all that keen anyway. It's only a small event, starts at twelve and finishes about five... Do you want to come?' There was a pause.

'Yeah! I might!' Liz raised her eyebrows at Jenny.

'Yes, go on, go with her Emily,' her mother encouraged gently. 'It will be nice for you to get into the swing of things again. You will enjoy it, won't she Jenny?' Liz felt she was treading on eggshells. It had been like that for months whenever she spoke to Emily about riding.

Jenny nodded. 'Oh! I will be so pleased, Em, if you came.'

Emily thought for a moment, 'Yes, all right, I'll come, and I think I might go for a little ride with you on Webster.' There was a pause again as Liz and Jenny exchanged glances and Liz sighed silently with relief.

'Good!' Jenny was all smiles. 'Good, Em. I am sure you will enjoy it. But we can turn back again if you change your mind, can't we?' She looked at Mrs Peters.

Liz nodded, eyebrows still raised, and filled the coffee cups again. The tension between them all seemed to ease. They were chattering just like old times. After the coffee, the girls went out into the yard. John was also surprised to see that Miss Emily was going riding with her friend. She automatically took up the rein and turned Webster's head, following Henry out of the yard.

They walked off. Liz and John watched them go.

John stood with his hands on his hips. 'That girl is good for her, Mrs Peters.'

'Yes, I know, John. She seems to do more that I can do. Do you want to come in for another cup of coffee? I still have one in the pot.'

He followed her into the kitchen, and they sat at the table talking about Emily and Major.

He was so slow ... oh so slow! Emily kept trying to push him on, but he just plodded on at a gentle pace, following Henry who was way ahead. They had ridden behind each other most of the way. Webster couldn't keep up, but Jenny and Henry had waited. Emily kept thinking of the fiery gait of Major. They rode without speaking, and they did not go near the woodland. Emily rode most of the way in a trance. Her thoughts were only of Major. Then they were back before she realized. They had been gone only for half an hour, but it was enough.

John took the bridles as they dismounted. He gave the horses some water, talking to them all the time. It felt good to him to have horses there again. He hoped that Miss Emily would start to ride again and maybe get another horse. That would suit him fine. As the girls walked off into the kitchen, he was smiling to himself.

13

'How did you get on, darling?' asked Liz.

'Oh, all right. But he was so slow, wasn't he, Jen? I kept trying to push him on.'

Jenny nodded with a chuckle. 'Yes, he is. But never mind; it gave you a ride out and gave him a bit of exercise. Anyway, if you go slow, you can see the scenery; if you ride too fast you don't see anything!' She clenched her teeth, sucking in air and clenching her fists under the table. She wished she hadn't said that. But it was too late, it just came out. Luckily it passed unnoticed, and they finished their coffee and went out into the yard again.

Jenny stayed there for a while, then afterwards she took the two horses back home to the farm. She phoned Emily the next morning, asking if she would like her to come over again. She was pleased when Emily agreed. This time Jenny brought Tammy, a fourteen-hands chestnut. Emily had ridden her before. She had a little zip in her when she was asked to go. Emily sat gingerly on her back and rode her so carefully as if she would break. Jenny was pleased all the same that she had at least got her friend out of her solitude. She had noticed a difference in Emily over the last couple of days. It was as if a cloud had been lifted from her, and she did seem a lot more relaxed. It was true.

Emily did feel a lot happier, but pictures of Major kept coming into her mind. The colour of his mane seemed to be continually in front of her eyes ... but it felt good to be in the saddle again. She had a funny feeling, though, when they entered the woods, a feeling of awareness. She could not explain it, although she mentioned it to Jenny several times.

'I feel he is here, Jen, all around me. I feel he is watching me, waiting to take revenge ... I didn't mean it, Jen, honestly I didn't, I didn't mean to.' She was shaking her head. They reached the spot where it had happened and at the thought of him lying there the tears began to flow again. She wiped them away with the back of her gloved hand.

Jenny leaned out of the saddle, gripping on to Henry's mane and took her friend's hand. 'It's all right, Emily. Come on, cheer up. He doesn't blame you; he doesn't, really! Come on, Em, let's trot.' She sat back in the saddle, tightened Henry's rein, and clicked her tongue. Henry began to trot, and Emily

14

and Tammy followed. With the breeze in her face, her tears soon vanished.

Later she told her father about her feelings in the woods. 'It's as if he is still there watching me, Daddy. I can't shake it off. It was my fault, and he knows it. He slowed down, and I urged him on. Oh, Daddy, I loved him so much.' She blew her nose into a tissue and wiped the tears away from her eyes. Her father took her into his arms, and he was talking gently into her hair.

'I know, darling, don't cry. It's over, over, it was an accident. It wasn't your fault. You mustn't keep blaming yourself!' He shook his head. 'I know it is terrible to have lost such a beautiful friend, but these things happen. I think they must be sent from God to teach us a lesson in life, to show us the right way. Maybe now you will not ride so recklessly, and we have to be thankful that you just had a few bruises... You could have been killed you know.' He held her away from him, looking into her tear-streaked face, the mascara black and smudged around her moist eyes again. 'It could have been your head that struck the bough... You know that, don't you? And I know that it's hard, but a horse can be replaced but we could never replace you.'

'Yes, I know.' Emily took a breath and pulled away from him, her blue eyes now red and swollen. The tears would not stop flowing. She sniffed and put a tissue to her eyes. 'But I loved him so, Daddy, and now I have to live with the guilt for the rest of my life. I know it was my fault. It was! It was. And I am sure he thinks so too.' She put her face in her hands and burst into floods of tears again, then rushed out of the room and up the stairs to her bedroom, throwing herself face down on the bed, sobbing bitterly.

Her father followed her. 'Oh come on, Emily, cheer up.' He put his hand on her shoulder and gave her a little friendly shake.

'He is waiting for me, I know he is, Dad,' she sobbed. 'I know he is, and I didn't mean to hurt him, really I didn't!' Mike sat on the edge of the bed, smoothing her hair. There was nothing he could do but just let her cry it out.

15

3

Major wandered round the paddock, as he had done for years, but now he was unseen. He watched Miss Emily as she came into the yard to talk to John and, finding he was not there, called out to him. John had now become the full-time gardener, even though Albert Mason still came in once a week to cut the lawn and then tidy up the flowerbeds. He had told Mr Peters that he was getting a bit too old for the heavy digging, so John did the digging when it needed to be done. There had been nothing much to do in the stable yard for the last year or so, except sweep up leaves, which seemed to be a full-time job, so he had more or less taken over as the gardener. He didn't mind. He was happy working for Mr Peters, he had been there for five years, ever since Miss Emily had got Major. Before that he had a job at the golf club cutting the greens and doing general handyman jobs. That's where he had first met Mike Peters. They happened to be chatting, and Mr Peters had said that he had got a horse for his daughter and was looking for a groom. John had said he used to be a groom in a racing stable in Newmarket, but it had got too much for him driving forty minutes every day to get there in the morning. The yard started at four-thirty, and although he was fit he was fifty and not getting any younger, so he had taken a temporary job at the golf club until he could find another in a stable. Mike had offered him the job; he was eager, and he was more than pleased when he found that the stable at Rosemary Lodge was barely ten minutes' walk from his house. Four years he had looked after Major and had seen Emily growing up. She was now almost seventeen and a young lady really. He enjoyed his work, pottering around the yard being his own boss. But, like Miss Emily, the loss of Major had saddened him greatly. He missed him, and for the last year even Henry had not set foot in the yard. But he still took pride in his job, and he kept the yard clean. John was not a man to sit around; he had to be busy all the time.

Major watched Miss Emily. She was leaning over his stable door facing him and looking into the empty space. The concrete floor was now scrubbed clean by John and smelled of disinfectant. His bridle still hung from a nail by the door, and she fingered a few ginger hairs that had got stuck in the buckle. She didn't want to take them out. She had told John not to even clean the bridle. She wanted it to stay just as it was, smelling of Major.

Normally when Miss Emily had visited his stable and had come to ride him she had been bright and cheerful and he had been raring to go for a canter through the fields and the woods. He had liked the woods. He had liked the smell of the fresh morning air, the earth and the trees. But now he noticed a sadness in her eyes. They seemed to stare at something that was not there. She was different. She was slow and dreamy, and he didn't know why. He watched as she put the leather bridle to the side of her face, her eyes closed as she slowly swayed from side to side. Her eyes opened, and he saw that they were glassy with unshed tears.

John hesitated at the corner of the yard for a moment, watching her, not wanting to impose on her privacy. She stiffened and sniffed, blinking away the tears as she heard him come into the yard behind her.

'Morning, Miss. Did you call me?'

Morning, John,' she sniffed, turning to him and lowering her eyes, hoping that he would not notice. 'Yes, morning, John.' She brightened, putting on a smile. 'Would you drive me over to the farm to see Jenny?'

'Yes, of course.' He almost sang out the words. Nothing was too much trouble for John. 'Bit chilly, this morning, isn't it, Miss?' He looked up into the sky. 'Bit cloudy, too, but I think the sun is trying to come through.' He looked away. He could see that she was still a bit tearful. He did not want to upset her more. He knew how his own daughters had felt when their Labrador had been run over and killed in the lane. It took them a long time to get over it. They had now got a new Labrador, but they still talked about Bobby.

Emily cheered up a bit, looking up at the sky. 'Yes, it doesn't look too bad, does it? I think I will walk over to the farm and get a bit of fresh air. Thanks anyway, John.'

17

'I'll drive you, if you like, Miss.'

'No, it's OK.'

She walked back into the house to tell her mother where she was going. Liz was just putting the phone down. She looked round with a big smile as Emily came in. 'That was Daddy.' Her voice rose slightly. 'He says he has a lovely horse for you to look at, and if you like her, he will buy her for you.'

'Her!' Emily said almost with a sneer. She lifted her top lip, her eyes squinting and frowning.

'Yes, it's a mare...' The look on Emily's face said it all. 'Well! You don't have to go if you don't want to. But Dad thought that you would be pleased, and so did I.' She was surprised at her daughter's fierceness. 'I'll call him back and tell him that you are not interested.' Liz felt let down. Mike had sounded so pleased, and she had said that Emily would be thrilled, but she had not expected a frown and rejection. She reached for the phone again. 'I'll ring Dad back, and stop him coming home. He is probably busy in the office anyway.'

'Oh!' Emily bit her bottom lip and clenched her fists; she looked doubtful. 'What has Daddy arranged then, is it ... I mean, she ... coming here, or have I got to go and look at it, her?'

'Well! Dad said he would come home lunchtime and pick you up, but I can phone him back and tell him not to come.' She had her hand on the receiver.

'Where is it then?' asked Emily bitterly.

'Over at Wickerbrook Hall. Sir James Bartram has a mare which he wants to sell.'

'Oh!' she raised her eyebrows with a disgusted look, and turned to go out. 'I am going over to see Jenny.' He walked to the door then turned back. 'If we go ... can I ask Jenny to come with us?'

'Of course! Why not?' Liz sang out the words airily so delighted was she that Emily had reconsidered. 'You can discuss it together. You would like her opinion, wouldn't you?'

Jenny was excited about seeing the horse and about going to Wickerbrook Hall; the house was said to be fabulous. 'It will be an experience anyway,' Jenny told her mother, and Carol had to agree. They had lived in the village all their lives and had never been to Wickerbrook Hall, even though there had been horse events and garden fêtes there from time to time. For some unknown reason they had just never been. Carol got Jenny an early lunch.

She was dressed in jeans and a sweater the same as Emily, when they arrived to pick her up. Neither of the girls had much to say on the twelve-mile journey. Mike turned into the long shingled drive through an avenue of tall conifer trees. Wickerbrook Hall loomed up in front of them, a large grey stone house with more long narrow windows than they could count. There was a fountain in the centre of the large oval lawn, with a cherub pouring water from a pitcher onto delicate pink waterlilies and their flat fan-like leaves. The contrast between the yellow shingle of the drive and the bright green of the neatly edged cut lawns that swept away from the house was striking. They got out of the car, closing the doors quietly, as if to make a noise in this garden would be a crime and some terrible disaster would befall them all. They walked up six wide grey stone steps, which stretched between tall Georgian pillars, to the large imposing front door that was arched and studded with iron bolts and an enormous black iron-ring door handle. Above this was a stone canopy that covered almost to the end of the steps.

Mike pressed the brightly polished brass button on the bell, but there was no sound, except the twittering of the birds. Emily took a deep breath to quell the nervous butterflies in her stomach and looked wide-eyed at Jenny, who seemed to be holding her breath. She could feel the tension in Emily and was sure that she would say no to the horse whether it turned out to be good or bad. They waited for what seemed like ages. Eventually the door was opened by a young and pretty housemaid, who looked like a doll in the huge doorway, dressed in a black dress and frilly white apron and mop cap. Emily sighed with relief. She had half-expected to see a large Victorian woman in a black dress and a white starched pinafore like she had read about in Dickens, who would look down on them from a great height and would turn them away, telling them not to darken her doorway again.

But instead, before her father had said anything, the young maid smiled.

'Oh, you must be Mr Peters, and you have come about the horse.' She pointed the way round to the side of the house. 'Sir James is there waiting for you. Just drive through the green gate and turn to the left; it will take you to the stables.' She smiled at Emily and Jenny as Mike Peters thanked her, and they began to walk back down the steps. They drove as instructed and stopped at the back by the covered stable yard. Getting out of the car they heard pop music playing on the radio. Emily's butterflies were beginning to fade. It wasn't such a stuffy place after all. To her surprise, the yard looked shabby. She had expected more from a stately hall such as this. The cobbled stones in the yard were old, probably hundreds of years of horses' hooves had trampled over them. There was straw in the cobbled grooves where it had not been properly swept. The stables, of which there were about eight, looked as if they were falling down. Buckets and brushes were piled in a corner, near to a heap of steaming horse manure. The water tap was dripping, and a stream was running between the cobbles carrying bits of straw. The place looked deserted and dilapidated. Two horses, their heads hanging over the stable doors, looked forlornly at them.

'Hello!' Mike called out a little hesitantly. He was about to call again when two black Labrador dogs, followed by a tall man, came bounding out of the end stable towards them barking a warning. They stood quite still as the dogs circled them. The man called the dogs to order, and they stopped, wagging their tails in a friendly way and walking around them sniffing, as if to make sure that these strangers in their yard were no threat.

The man was tall, well over six feet in height, well built with broad shoulders and thick muscled arms. He was obviously a stable groom from his appearance: a green checked shirt, blue jeans and brown riding boots that had not seen a polish rag in months. He was aged about middle forties to fifty. His fair hair was thinning, but his round and rosy face had a boyish grin. He came towards them, a shovel in one hand, and stretched out the other to Mike Peters and shook it warmly.

'Hello.' He smiled at both the girls. 'Sorry! You caught me

20

doing a spot of mucking-out. Have to keep my hand in you know,' he beamed. 'And someone has to do it. I'm Jim Bartram. You must be Michael Peters.' Emily was surprised. This was James Bartram, *Sir* James, mucking out his own stables. She always thought that Sirs wore navy pin-striped suits and never got their hands dirty. Emily's father smiled and shook hands with a friendly nod.

'Mike is good enough. I am sorry if we are a bit early.'

'No! Not at all, old boy. I just didn't realize the time, that's all. It goes so quickly. In fact, I was just doing a spot of tidying-up before you came to look at the old girl, but one always seems to get caught on the hop, doesn't one? Always the way, isn't it?' He chuckled in a companionable, friendly way. They smiled back.

Sir James Bartram was not at all what Emily had expected. She had imagined a much older man, grey and pompous, as she imagined all Sir-somebodies to be, living in such grand houses. But he had turned out to be, as she would have put it, a 'nice guy'. He had a nice smile, he was friendly, and he was normal, much to her surprise.

'Well, she is all ready for you,' he nodded, looking from one to the other of the girls, not knowing which was which.

'This is my daughter, Emily.' Mike put a hand on her shoulder, and this is her friend, Jenny Ellis. They both ride quite well.'

Sir James Bartram smiled and nodded to both the girls, then turned a gentle gaze on Emily. 'I was very sorry to hear of your tragic accident, Emily.' He screwed up his pale-grey eyes and shook his head gently in sympathy. 'Your Dad told me about it over the phone. It is very sad to lose a lovely animal which you love and trust. It is like losing one of the family...' He gave a sympathetic nod of his head, then took a breath. 'But anyway,' he said cheerily, clapping his hands quietly together, 'I am sure you could get to know and trust this old girl every bit as well.' Then he added, 'But, that's only, if you like her, of course. But she is a peach really, just needs loving care, that's all. She's almost human, knows every word you say to her. She belongs to my daughter,' he went on, as he moved towards a stable and stroked the ears of a grey horse which was looking over the stable door. He fitted a head collar on and patted the neck, then opened the door and led the old-

and weary-looking grey mare out into the yard. Its hooves clip-clopped slowly as if it had not got enough strength to walk. Jenny looked sideways at Emily, their eyes met, they were both thinking the same... It can't be... Then they relaxed as he led the old mare into the stable which he had just cleaned, saying, 'Come on, Bumble, in you go,' and gave the grey mare a friendly pat on the back. 'Harris will come and get you in a minute.

'She's a nice old girl, had her for years, knows every word you say; she just needs someone to give her a nice gentle ride, she is twenty-five you know, a good age for a horse... Well, come on, let's have a look, shall we? And see what you think.'

Emily's heart sank. He came out of the stable still holding the door open. 'Come on.' He waved his head sideways. They all moved to follow him, thinking he wanted them to go into the stable with the grey mare, but he pushed the door closed, walking past it two doors up, and called out.

'Harris!'

'Sir!'

'Bring the old girl into the yard, will you?'

'Sir.' The voice came back again.

'Come this way.' He beckoned with his forefinger for them to follow. 'Harris will bring her through.' Emily took a breath and glanced round at Jenny as they passed the grey mare. There was a look of despair on both their faces. He led them through a black newly painted door, and they found themselves in the most magnificent covered stable yard that they had ever seen. The ground was covered in red tarmac, and each stable was of red brick, and in each open stable door they could see that there were red tiles on the floor and the stables were padded so that the horses could not injure themselves and there were copper strips along the half doors so that they could not be nibbled. The yard was covered by a roof of high arched oak beams, and Casablanca fans were fitted for those rare hot English summers. It was perfectly clean and smelled of new paint, and at least twenty of the most beautiful horses' heads nodded to them over the half-open doors.

Emily, Jenny and Mike were shocked into silence. The girls looked at each other in amazement, and Jenny clasped Emily's hand and gave it a secret squeeze. Emily glanced at her and sighed. Jenny knew what she was thinking. It was surely not going to be the old grey mare, or was it? But Harris had not yet appeared.

'This is marvellous,' said Mike Peters, looking around him, his eyebrows rising in admiration.

'Yes, I am glad it turned out this well.' Sir James nodded, turning round in a circle and looking at the new surroundings that he was now getting used to. 'Yes, it has come on well. It has only just been finished, about two weeks now, but it has taken for ever to get there. We have had to make do with the old stable next door, and we have had makeshift stables over there in the field for the last year. Good job the winter was not too bad. I thought it would never come together, but we are almost straight now.' He nodded his head towards the black painted door. 'And I think old Bumble...' He nodded again, meaning the old grey mare they supposed. '...in there will die of fright when she sees this.' She hasn't been in here yet. She belongs to my daughter. We bred her from a thoroughbred mare. She has been a wonder in her time, won everything, every show she was in, even won at Wembley, the best show-jumper we have ever had. And she is still pretty good, lovely nature. You would like her.' He raised his eyebrows with a nod.

'We are about to start work in there next week.' He nodded again towards the old yard. 'Have to have it done while the builders are still around. Once you let them go, it's hard to get them back.' He chuckled. 'Do you jump or show, young lady?' He raised his eyebrows again at Emily.

'I did a lot of jumping,' said Emily with a smile. 'But I only went to local shows, gymkhanas and that sort of thing, nothing big, but Major was a good jumper; we have won quite a few rosettes and a couple of cups.' He noticed the sadness come into her blue eyes. She paused for a second. 'And Jenny has, too.' She turned to smile at her friend. 'Her father has Mayberry Farm, and we have ridden together many times, haven't we, Jenny?'

'Mayberry. Oh yes, they used to have some good horses over there. I remember seeing a young lad ride. I think his name was Tom Ellis. He did well. It was some time ago though.'

'Yes, that was my brother.' Jenny's brown eyes widened. 'But he doesn't ride much now, since he got married.'

'Oh, he's married is he...?'

'Yes and he's got two children.'

Sir James looked up. 'How time flies!'

They all turned as a groom came into the yard leading a very beautiful sleek black horse, complete with saddle and ready to ride. A girl in jodhpurs and jacket and helmet came into the yard and went into one of the end stables, followed by another groom leading a chestnut. They watched as the black mare clip-clopped its dainty hooves on the red tarmac, and swished her black silky tail. With head held high and proud, ears pricked and alert as the groom adjusted the stirrups and saddle, and patted her neck, the horse stood perfectly still and composed.

'Well,' – Sir James rubbed his chin, turning back to his three guests – 'as I said before, I think you will like the old girl. She is a perfect lady; in fact, I don't think she knows that she is a horse! She's used to young girls. She belongs to my daughter Louise ... I have three daughters. They have all ridden since they were children, all grown up now though.' He thought for a minute, then smiled. 'Lovely girls. Beth and Sarah both moved away, but are still riding, and not yet married.' He smiled at Jenny. 'Louise is still here though. She loves mucking about in the stables. Pity you missed her; she would have told you all about the old girl. She has not long gone off with a couple of the grooms to exercise the horses. It's been taking us all day while this stable block has been in progress. We have been in a right muddle, I can tell you.'

Emily found it difficult to concentrate on what Sir James was saying. She was watching the beautiful black mare. She could see that she was in tiptop condition by the way she pranced on her dainty hooves.

'Louise will tell you she is a perfect lady,' Sir James went on. 'You wait until you ride her. Come on, I expect you are anxious to try the old girl out.' Sir James smiled at Emily, but she did not see him. Her eyes were glued to the beautiful black shining coat and long slender legs.

'Emily?' Her father jogged her arm with his elbow.

'Oh yes,' she said, finding it hard to tear her eyes away from the beautiful mare. 'Oh yes, yes!' She was not sure what the question was, but she was saying 'yes' anyway.

24

'Well, come on then. I'm sure you are eager to have go. Harris?'

The groom nodded as if to say OK. 'Yes, Sir James.'

'Come on.' He gestured with his arm for them to follow. He moved towards the gleaming black mare. He patted her neck, then turned to Mike, saying casually, 'Lovely, isn't she? I have just had her shod.' He ran his hand down one of her long slender forelegs. 'Vet says she's fit and trim.' He stood up.

'Well, come on, Emily.' He encouraged her gently but impatiently. 'You want to ride her, don't you?' He took hold of the bridle. 'Harris! Give the young lady a leg up.'

For Emily it was as if time stood still. She was rooted to the spot. She looked at Sir James, swallowing hard, and her eyes flew open wide. A quick intake of breath. One hand went to her open mouth, the other to her breast.

'You mean this ... this is the mare we have come to see?' She swallowed hard again, then looked at Jenny, and then at her father, her mouth still open, and then a smile of utter disbelief and amazement; it was beyond her wildest dreams. It was love at first sight.

Sir James frowned then raised his fair eyebrows. He looked bewildered. 'Well, yes, of course...' His voice was as light as air. He sounded surprised. 'This is Black Tulip.' He swung his arm up and patted the beautiful black shining neck. Then he chuckled, seeing the surprise on the girls' faces.

Then, suddenly realizing, he said, 'Oh, I am sorry, I just naturally thought you knew that this was the mare when Harris brought her round.'

'Well, err...' Mike Peters's voice caught in the back of his throat with a little cough. 'I think we all thought it was the ... um ... grey...' He nodded his head sideways towards the next-door stable yard through the black painted door.

'Oh! Good heavens, no!' exclaimed Sir James with a hearty chuckle. 'Oh dear me!' He put his hand to his forehead. 'I am so sorry if I gave you that impression.' He looked a little embarrassed. 'Good God, what must you have been thinking? Oh dear, ha, ha. Come on then, up you go. Harris, help the lady, give her a leg up!' By now Emily was feeling enthralled, and both Jenny and Mike had grins from ear to ear. Sir James was still chuckling to himself.

25

Emily quickly reached up for the reins and grabbed hold of the saddle, putting her left foot in the stirrup as Harris grabbed the sole of her right boot and hoisted her up. She settled herself in the saddle, then collected the reins as Harris took hold of the bridle and led her out into the paddock, then let her go. 'Go on, Miss, give her a whirl. I promise you she is perfectly safe.'

Sir James led the way to the paddock, Mike walking beside him, Jenny following behind. Jenny was still looking round at the magnificent stable yard and at the gorgeous heads that nodded over the half-yellow stable doors. They came out from under the high arched beams and across the black tarmac drive: there in the paddock Emily was cantering round and round with ease. The horse looked fabulous.

'Yes,' Sir James was saying again, 'she belongs to my youngest daughter, Louise, but she is now riding Pico over there in the corner.' He flicked his thumb back over his shoulder to the end stable, where a majestic dapple-grey head with silver mane was nodding. 'He is a top-class jumper, and Louise takes him everywhere. They go all over the country, as she did with Black Tulip, of course. But Tulip is not only a jumper she is speedy, too. I would say even faster and better than Pico, but Louise likes to chop and change quite often. Oh, look at Emily.' He nodded to Mike. 'She rides very well.'

Emily was cantering around the paddock. She felt like an angel on a winged horse, still bewildered at the thought of riding this beautiful animal, but then she thought that Daddy could never afford it and she must make the best of it while she could. She had fallen instantly in love with Black Tulip, just looking at her was enough, but to actually ride such a beautiful creature had been beyond her wildest dreams. Major had been handsome but never as attractive as this, and she wasn't only beautiful she was easy to ride.

'Dad! She is wonderful,' she called as she sailed by, taking the low and medium-high fences twice more. Then she came to a stop by the gate. Black Tulip put her head over the fence and Jenny reached up to pat her. Emily slid down off her back and patted the glossy neck. 'She is great, Dad,' she said keenly, her breath coming in short pants and her face beaming with delight. She felt afraid to speak too loudly in case the dream vanished.

'Do you want to have a ride, Jenny?' she said enthusiastically. Then to Sir James, putting her hand to her mouth: 'Oh, I am sorry, Sir James. Can my friend have just a little ride? Would you mind? I know she is dying to have a go.' She added quickly, 'She does ride very well,' just in case Sir James was in any doubt.

Sir James smiled. 'Yes, of course, of course, go on have a go,' he said to Jenny.

Jenny was delighted. Harris helped her up, and they watched her trot then canter round and round the paddock taking the jumps.

'Oh, she's wonderful, Dad. I should love to have her.' Emily turned to Sir James. He was watching Jenny, amazed at the skill of these two young girls. 'How old is she, Sir?'

'Nine, nearly ten. And sixteen hands.'

'Oh!' She nodded with a smile, and then turned to look at Jenny, still cantering round. Mike saw the look in her eyes.

He smiled at Sir James. 'I really wasn't expecting anything quite so grand.' They were reasonably comfortable and able to afford a good price, but he didn't want to go way over the top, and he knew that this was going to cost him a bomb. He looked at Sir James. 'What are you asking?'

Sir James was watching the delighted Jenny, as she got into a rising trot and went smoothly around the paddock, taking the jumps with ease. He turned slowly to face Mike Peters. He was usually a good judge of people, and he had a good feeling about these people. He felt for the girl, who had loved and lost. He knew that if he sold this beautiful mare to them that they would take good care of her and that meant more to him than just selling a horse. He wanted her to be loved as his own daughter had loved her, giving her every minute of her spare time, and he felt sure that the Peters were that sort of people. There had been others to look at the mare, also caring people, but he had a gut feeling about the Peters and when he had that feeling he was rarely wrong.

'Well...' He rubbed his chin. 'I was asking thirty-five...' He bit the inside of his mouth, waiting for the reaction.

'Thirty-five thousand!' Mike's voice was hardly audible. He pursed his lips and blew a silent whistle, with the slightest flicker of his eyebrows, as he considered. He looked at the horse, and looked back at Sir James. In his mind he reckoned it a reasonably fair price, a bit steep perhaps, but the horse was immaculate, and he knew that Emily wanted it, and she had been sad for so long... He wanted to see her riding again and enjoying her life...

Sir James also saw the love on Emily's face, and as she looked at Black Tulip, he had an uncanny feeling in his bones that this girl and this horse were made for each other. 'Tell you what, I'll let you have her for thirty.'

'Done!' Mike didn't hesitate. His face transformed into a huge smile as he put his hand out to shake Sir James's. Both men thought that they had struck a good deal: Mike had saved five thousand pounds, and Sir James Bartram considered that the horse would go to loving and careful owners. The look on Emily's face brought tears to Mike's eyes. His daughter stood open-mouthed, looking from her father to Sir James. Tears of happiness sparkled in her blue eyes. The thought of owning this beautiful animal was a dream come true.

'Oh Daddy!' she cried, giving him a hug and a kiss. 'Oh, Daddy!' She turned excitedly to the paddock and squealed across to Jenny, 'She's mine, she's mine, Jen.' Jenny took the last jump and then rode over to the fence and dismounted. The girls clasped hands, hugging each other with joy as Harris Freemore took hold of the bridle and led the horse away. Emily did not want to let her go, and tears of happiness welled once more in her eyes.

Sir James said, 'You can have her vetted if you like, but there is really no need. I had the vet here only yesterday. He checks all my horses regularly and they are all sound. 'It's Keith Hadley. I'll give you his number. You can give him a bell if you like. Or you can call your own vet of course if you want to.'

'No, I think your word is good enough for me, Sir James.'

Sir James smiled. 'When would you want to take her?'

'Now!' said Emily. 'Can we take her now, Dad?' She was so excited, she was not even thinking.

'Just a minute, Em,' her father laughed. 'We can't take her yet! Do you want to put her in the boot of the car? We have to get a trailer first, perhaps in a day or two...' He looked at Sir James. 'We usually hire a trailer if we need it. Emily could usually walk to most events, and the horse she had was very good on the road.'

'Well, I can deliver her for you, if you like,' said Sir James. 'I can have Harris or one of my guys drive her over this evening, if it suits you, of course. You don't live very far away, do you? Or old Ben is not doing very much; he can come.' He turned to look as an older man came walking into the yard with a wheelbarrow, then Harris followed with a big seventeen-hands bay hunter which he took into the empty stable third from the end. The name over the door said 'Boris'. Another groom came into the yard, looked around and then walked out again, and Harris walked back past them with a nod as much to say goodbye.

'Well, all right,' Mike agreed. 'I would appreciate that; you see, we have never had much need of a trailer.'

'Do you want a horse box?' Sir James frowned. 'I have one you can borrow for a while if you like. I have a small one out the back that takes two horses. It's got small living quarters, too: a little kitchen and a calor-gas oven, even a loo,' he chuckled. 'It's quite easy to drive. I had it custom-made. We have had it a couple of years, three to be exact. Louise used to drive it, but we have got a bigger one now and a full-time driver. They take it everywhere, practically live in it. So you are quite welcome to the smaller one. It is just standing there doing nothing. Been there for months. Never really thought about it until now.'

Mike Peters considered for a second. 'Well, do you want to sell it?' He knew it would not be rubbish, even though he had not seen it.

'Well, I hadn't really thought about it to tell you the truth, but I suppose you can have it. Come and have a look. Your daughter can't go around showing off the beautiful Black Tulip without a carriage to take her in, can she?' He chuckled again. 'Tell you what! I'll send Harris over with it this afternoon, and you can keep it and drive it around a bit, see what you think, OK?'

'OK! Thanks!' Mike was a bit bewildered. They went to look at the horse box. Emily and Jenny both thought it absolute luxury, only ever having had a trailer before, knowing how difficult it was to get changed before an event and keep clean with just the trailer to change in.

Driving back in the car, the girls chatted excitedly all the way, saying they were going to hack out and jump in Jenny's paddock. Emily was saying that she would enter much bigger shows than she had done before because now she would be able to go further with the horse box and Jenny would be able to bring Henry, and she wouldn't have to bring her own trailer any more as they could go to the shows together.

'You will have to learn to drive, Em,' Jenny giggled. 'I'll take lessons, too, and then we can share the driving.'

'Oh yes, that's a good idea.'

Mike took his eyes off the road for a second, looking in the rear-view mirror. 'Oh no, Em! Don't tell me you will be wanting a car next.' The girls laughed.

'I think you will have to do a paper round, Dad, and make a bit of money.'

4

Major, unseen, had been wandering around in the paddock all morning. When he came near, rabbits scattered and rushed for their burrows in fright, and the birds flew to higher branches in the trees for safety, their animal instincts telling them of his presence. Although he was alone now, he still felt happy within himself. He suddenly broke into a gallop and went at full speed round the field, jumping a couple of poles that John had laid up against the fence. He stopped and shook his head, splaying his silky mane. He felt young. He was eight; he would always be eight. He nodded his head, and then stared out towards the woodland, thinking of the lovely days he had spent with Miss Emily on his back, and how they had galloped through the woods. He decided he would go again, so he cantered towards the hedge and jumped and then galloped off across the open field, heading for the woods as he had done on that fateful day in the spring. On and on he went, and he came to the tree with the low bough, and he ran right through it. He stopped with an impetuous skid and walked back to the tree and nudged it with his nose. It amused him that his nose went right through, and he did it again and again. And then he walked right through the large trunk of the tree. This was fun, for now, if he wanted to, he could run straight through the woods and the hedges; he didn't even have to jump. He raced on and came out of the woods and across the field once again, scattering the wildlife. Slowing to a trot on the last few yards, he walked around the garden and into the stable yard, where John was shovelling leaves into a wheelbarrow.

Something made John stop, look up and around him. He went back to the job, but had a strange feeling of not being alone, of being watched. He couldn't understand it. He looked around the yard and again went back to his job. He thought he heard the clip-clop of hooves on the cobblestones and stood for a moment, expecting to see Miss Jenny on Henry turn the corner into the yard. He waited ready to take the bridle but she didn't come. He must have imagined it! He was about to lift the leaves into the wheelbarrow, when he thought he heard a huff. John stood up, straightening his back. He hadn't imagined it; there had been a noise. He put his hands on his hips and stood looking around the yard. He was quite alone, but he was sure that he had heard a horse. He thought he could even smell a horse, but knew it must be his imagination, surely. He went to the side gate. Maybe Miss Jenny was outside the yard gate with Henry, though he couldn't think why she should be. He unlocked the gate and looked out. There was no one there. Once again he went back to his job. Lifting the shovel again, he turned his back on the unseen Major and bent to scoop up a few more leaves. Major stood there looking at him. Dipping his head he moved his feet. Again John stopped and looked round quickly. It *was* the sound of a horse's hoof that he heard. He went to check, looking in all the stables. He knew it was silly; most of them were full of straw and shavings which had been there for a year. Major's old stable was the only one which was empty. Miss Emily had wanted it that way. The clip-clopping came again, as Major walked into his stable. John took off his cap and scratched his bald head.

What was the matter with him, was he getting old and hearing things? The only sounds now seemed to be the birds whistling in the trees and Mrs Porter chinking cups in the kitchen. It was about time for her to bring him out a mug of coffee. In fact, he could do with a drink to straighten him up. He raked his ear and shook his head, then listened, but there was no other sound. He went back to work. Soon after Mrs Porter arrived with a mug of coffee and two biscuits on a tray.

'Oh thank you, Mrs Porter. Just what I need. He took the mug and biscuits from the tray.

'Nice morning, John. It's so peaceful and quiet out here, isn't it?' She looked up into the trees. There was just the sound of leaves rustling gently and the birds twittering.

'Oh, what was that?' She turned her head, clutching the tray to her large bosom. 'They must be back with the new horse!' She walked off in the direction of the kitchen.

'NEW HORSE! His own voice echoed loudly in his head. He frowned and sipped at the hot coffee, taking it into the tack room and sitting down. It was then that he heard the car coming up the drive.

Twenty minutes later Emily and Jenny came round into the yard. It obviously had not been Henry that he thought he had heard. The girls were smiling with excitement and eagerness. Miss Emily seemed a completely changed person to when he had caught her moping around the stables this morning. She was bright and alert as she had been before, and talking about horses as if nothing had happened, telling him about the new horse that they had been to see and that was going to arrive in the evening. Dad had bought it and they had both ridden it, and it was all so wonderful.

Emily asked him to get Major's old stable scrubbed out. It was already clean, she knew, but she wanted it to be fresh, with new shavings. They still had plenty stacked in the other stables. He wondered if the sound he had heard earlier could have been a premonition, although nothing like that had ever happened to him before. It was uncanny.

He listened with interest as Emily and Jenny went on and on about the new horse. He sat down on the edge of the tack room table listening while he sipped the now much cooler coffee and then asked questions. Was it a mare or a stallion? How many hands and how old? What colour and what was its name? John was pleased to see Miss Emily actually smiling with joy again. It had been a long time since her blue eyes had shone. She had carried a heavy burden for the last year, and now suddenly the black cloud seemed to have lifted. He felt as excited as the girls were. Another horse to look after. He loved horses, and had always hoped that there would be another one at some time and he could give up helping Al Mason in the garden. He much preferred the stable work.

The girls spent the rest of the afternoon, wandering around the yard and the meadow, not really doing anything, both of them totally unsettled. Finally they went to Emily's bedroom

33

and played a few CDs. Neither of them could really concentrate on anything much, and Emily kept going to the window and looking out to see if the horse box was coming. Jenny felt as excited about it as Emily. Soon they would be able to ride out again together as they had done before. Since the accident she had just been riding around the farm and mostly on her own. Henry, she thought, must have missed his rides through the woods, too, and he probably missed Major. She wondered whether Henry knew that Major had gone for ever. She supposed that he did. Animals had their instincts. The music suddenly stopped. Emily had switched it off.

'Let's go down, shall we?' Emily looked at her watch. She had been checking the time about every fifteen minutes for the last three hours. She glanced out of the window again. 'She should be here soon.'

They walked down the stairs through the kitchen and out into the yard. John had finished the stable. It smelt of mild disinfectant and fresh shavings, but he wasn't there. Emily stood in front of the stable with mixed feelings: sadness for the loss of Major and joy for the beautiful mare that was to take his place. Major could see her and Jenny, as he hung his head over the door. A shiver went through both of them, but neither mentioned it.

'I hope Black Tulip will be happy in here, Jen. It's not as glamorous as Sir James's yard, is it?'

Jenny shook her head. 'No, but she is going to get such a lot of loving care from you that she won't even notice. And Sir James said that he had only just got the new stable block ready, so she hasn't been used to so much luxury, has she?'

Emily wrinkled her nose. 'Yes, I guess you're right. Oh, Jen, I can't wait, I'm so excited.'

Jenny felt the same, she looked at her watch. 'She should be on her way by now.'

Harris Freemore drove the horse box slowly and carefully through the country lanes. Young Denny Tompkins followed behind with the Range Rover, so that he could bring Harris back once he had delivered Black Tulip to her new owners. Although the horse box was smaller than the one Sir James was using at the present time, it still took up a lot of room on the narrow country roads, and he had to stop frequently, pulling right over to the hedgerows. Thankfully the roads were not too busy, even though at this time of the day people were coming home from work. From time to time he glanced down at the instructions that Mike Peters had jotted down on a scrap of paper for him to follow. He had never been to the village of Long Melford before, and as he entered the village he drove even more slowly, crawling along, looking at each house name. Then he saw 'ROSEMARY LODGE' painted in bold white letters on a post. He turned into the lane, drove a few yards and saw the name painted again on the open gates. He turned right, the wheels crunching on the long gravel drive. Ahead of him, to his right, was a large farmhouse, and to his left he could see a tennis court. He drove past the front door of the house to where a notice painted in black letters pointed to the 'STABLES'.

Harris Freemore slowly brought the horse box to a standstill, and Dennis Tompkins rolled the Range Rover to a stop outside the gates, switching off the engine, which quelled the radio that had been blaring out pop music all the way, and walked through the gate as John was swinging it shut.

Harris jumped down from the cab. He was short, thin and lithe, and could have been a jockey. He was wearing the beige jodhpurs and green checked shirt that was the uniform maintained by Sir James in the yard, but now he had donned a dark-green quilted puffer jacket. He smiled. He could see the girls were waiting anxiously.

'Evening,' he said cheerily. 'Sorry, I'm a bit late! I had to finish mucking out before I left.' He was talking while walking round to the back of the horsebox, and unlocking where he was joined by not only John, Emily and Jenny, but by Liz and Mike Peters. Everyone was looking forward to the new arrival.

Harris led the beautiful Black Tulip down the ramp, her long slender legs striding out with a loud clanking as the polished hooves came down the steel metal stays and into the yard. She was serene and composed, and, as he turned her round to face them, they all gasped at her sleek raven beauty. Emily went to her and patted her neck, speaking to her softly.

Jenny was patting the other side of her neck, and Liz took a snapshot of the whole happy scene.

'She is beautiful, Emily!' said her mother, coming closer to pat the black glossy coat. Liz was a little wary of horses, although she had got used to Major and often talked to him and patted him. She had never ridden a horse, though Emily had often tried to persuade her, but she could not resist patting this beautiful animal. Black Tulip's brown, almond-shaped eyes looked down from her great height at all the new faces looking up at her and seemed to be enjoying the attention.

John stood awestruck. To think he was to have this beautiful creature to look after! He made up his mind that the black glossy coat would stay that way for always.

'Where do you want her, Miss?' Harris asked Emily, after they had all made a fuss of her. He turned to John with a nod, 'She's very easy to handle.'

'Right,' John smiled, 'bring her over here. I have cleaned and scrubbed this one out. It's got fresh shavings on the floor.'

'Right, come on, old girl,' Harris said encouragingly, as he followed John and pulled gently on the bridle. Black Tulip walked a few elegant steps towards the stable, where John opened the door. Harris had her facing it, when suddenly without warning she recoiled, whinnied and pulled back, almost pulling the leading rein from Harris Freemore's hand. He was used to handling horses, but the sudden jerk almost took him off his feet. He hung on with all his strength. He shouted at her, but she whinnied again, rearing up, and flaying her forelegs in the air. They all stepped back in horror. Snowball the cat, who had been watching from the stable roof, ran for his life. With Denny's help, Harris pulled her down again, the two of them pulling back hard. As the mare backed up, she bashed her hindquarters against the side of the horse box.

'What's the matter with her?' cried Emily in alarm. Denny jumped to Harris's aid again, and they both struggled. Some of Sir James's horses were difficult, but he had never seen the beautiful Black Tulip like this. He stood holding the bridle now. Harris had her under control.

'I don't know!' Harris soothed and patted her, talking softly. He could see that her eyes were still wild and afraid. 'Come on, old girl, come on. There is nothing to be frightened about.'

Gradually she calmed down as he walked her around the yard a couple of times, though she shied a little, lifting her regal head, and sidling as she passed the stable.

Black Tulip was calm now, and Harris stood quietly with her. She stood patiently waiting for his command.

'Come on, old girl,' Harris coaxed kindly, easing her forward towards the stable, but she once more neighed, pulling back, almost rearing again.

John stepped forward to help, but Harris held her head firmly. He had been handling horses since he was a child. So had John, but Harris was a lot younger and he knew this filly. He had handled some very difficult horses, but Black Tulip had taken him by complete surprise. He had never ever seen her like this before, and she was never any trouble to box. For some unknown reason she did not like this stable.

'It's the stable she doesn't like,' said Mike Peters. 'She probably knows there has been another horse in there. Try her in the one opposite, John.'

'Well, that usually isn't a problem,' said Harris Freemore, 'but it's worth a try.'

'It's full of straw, Mr Peters. It will take me half an hour to clear it out.'

'Well, I think that is what we will have to do, John.'

'I'll give you a hand,' said Denny Tompkins, who had been standing watching and not really saying a word. 'Between the two of us it will get done quicker.'

Twenty minutes later and the job was done. Harris led the horse forward. To everyone's relief she walked into the stable quite calmly. Harris turned her round, came out and closed the half door. On the other side, the mare stood serenely, looking out over the door as if she had been used to this stable all her life.

Harris gave her a pat, saying, 'Good girl,' and Emily came forward and gave her a carrot. She and Jenny stroked her nose gently. She seemed quite composed.

'I wonder why she didn't like the other stable,' said Emily. 'Major was happy in there. I put him there because he could see across the fields.' She turned to Black Tulip. 'Now, you silly old thing, you can't see anything, only the yard.' She stroked her nose gently. 'But I suppose, if you are happy in here, you can stay. It's all right with us, isn't it, John?' She turned with a smile, glancing at Mum and Dad and Jenny, then she said to her mother with a smile, 'Lovely, isn't she, Mum!'

Liz smiled in agreement but looked anxious. 'Yes, as long as she is happy and calms down. I don't want her to throw you off. She was a bit jumpy just now.'

'Oh, no chance of that, Mam,' said Harris, coming forward to pat the black shiny neck. 'She is the kindest mare I have ever known, mild as a mouse. She's just like a mother to her rider; she would never throw you off. She will settle down you see. But I must say, Miss...' He turned to Emily. 'She is a bit nervous on the road, but then I expect you will use the horse box most of the time, won't you? See, look at her now, cool as a cucumber. Never seen her any different, have you, Denny?' He slapped Black Tulip with a friendly smile. 'Lovely old girl, aren't you?'

All at once she gave a small whinny, lifting her head, the whites of her beautiful brown eyes showing fear. She stomped her feet and kicked at the door, then backed up and hit her hindquarters on the back of the wall, kicking over the water bucket. John and Harris and Denny all moved forward to calm her. They did not want her to have an injury.

Harris was bewildered. 'What can possibly be frightening her?' He looked round for the answer, which nobody could provide.

'Blowed if I know,' said John, lifting his cap and scratching his bald head, a gesture he always did when he was uncertain.

'I've never seen 'er like this afore, 'ave you, Mr Freemore?' said Denny. 'Usually, she's so quiet, ain't she?'

'Do you think we should call the vet?' said Mike, a concerned look on his face. 'Maybe he can give her something to soothe her.'

'No!' Harris shook his head. 'I don't think she needs a vet. Sir James had her vetted yesterday. I was there. And she was fine this morning, and when you saw her earlier this afternoon, too. But, of course, you can call your vet if you like. But I think it is something here that's spooking her. Could be a sound that we can't hear or maybe a smell. Could be anything, but I am sure she will be OK. She'll settle down.' He nodded. 'It's just being in new surroundings, I would think.'

*   *   *

Major had had enough of this silly girlish behaviour. He walked out of his stable, right through the closed door, and out into the paddock, swishing his tail in disgust. Was this screaming nervous filly to share his yard? He swished his tail angrily. No way! He would spend the night out in the paddock alone where it was cool and quiet, where he could stand under the tree in the corner, the big old tree where he and Henry had stood in the shade on those rare hot sunny days when Jenny had ridden over and then stayed for lunch. It had also given them shelter many times during a heavy shower of rain.

Black Tulip's brown eyes rolled with fright, the white showing as she watched Major come out of the stable.

5

Later that evening, after the family supper, Emily said she was going out to see Black Tulip. She walked quietly out into the yard, her trainers making no sound on the cobblestones. The mare was calm, puffing out a soft breath and moving her head up slightly to acknowledge Emily. Emily gently caressed her cheeks and her neck, telling her she was a lovely girl. It was quiet and peaceful in the yard, just the twitter of a bird on a branch that overhung the yard.

Suddenly, for no reason, Black Tulip became agitated. Her ears flattened, and she lifted her head. Her kindly brown eyes became frightened, rolling back to show the whites, and she gave a slight whinny. Emily stepped back in surprise, hoping they were to get on together. Surely the horse was not frightened of her? Perhaps it was, as Mr Freemore had said, a certain smell. Maybe it was her perfume or her shampoo. Something made her turn quickly. A sound behind her? A clip-clopping of hooves? But no! There was nothing there, it must have been Black Tulip or just her imagination. All the same, the horse was clearly afraid.

It was unusually quiet. She had never noticed the quietness before. She looked up as a bird flew low overhead. She heard the hushed flapping of its wings and saw it disappear into the dense leaves of the beach tree. The sky was pale grey with the oncoming darkness. She liked the summer months, when it stayed light until about nine or ten o'clock. The smell of the hay always seemed more pungent, and the smoke from a bonfire across the meadow drifted on the cool still night air. Maybe she noticed the quiet because she had not been out in the yard at this time for so long. The moo of a lone cow somewhere across the fields came to her ears. It probably came from Mayberry Farm. She soothed Black Tulip with her hands and soft words, stroking her nose and her cheeks, and she seemed to respond, sensing the love and kindness that Emily conveyed. Emily turned round quickly as she heard a quiet clip-clop, and again there was nothing. She shivered. It really was eerie here in the yard. Black Tulip moved uneasily and whickered, lifting her head. Emily felt her skin creep. She had never felt that eerie feeling before, not here, not in her own yard. The yard was safe and enclosed with a happy atmosphere, so what was she afraid of? She thought she saw the quick swish of a tail. She blinked her eyes several times, but there was nothing there. She strained in the silence that seemed to rush noisily in her head, her eyes wide as she looked around the quiet yard, but there was just the two of them, her and Black Tulip. She turned back to the horse, her nerves strung as tight as banjo strings. She wanted to run back into the house, but she also felt that she could not leave Black Tulip on her own, not locked in a stable anyway. If there *was* anything out there, she should be free to run away. She smoothed her hand down Black Tulip's neck, and the feel of the satin black hair was comforting, not only to the horse but also to herself. 'We will go for a ride tomorrow, Tulip,' she said softly. 'You'll like that, won't you? I am dying to ride you. You don't mind if I just call you Tulip, do you?' The horse nodded slightly as if to say it was all right. Emily smiled. Tulip seemed calm again, and Emily thought that it was time to leave her and go. But then the horse was agitated again.

'It's all right, it's all right,' she said, but then jumped almost out of her own skin, as John came into the yard behind her.

'Oh! John!' She could hardly get her breath. 'You gave me such a fright!'

'Sorry,' he smiled. 'I didn't mean to creep up on you. I didn't know that you were out here.' His long green wellington boots had been silent on the cobblestones, but Tulip had sensed him coming.

'How is she doing? I said to Debbie. I just had to come over and take a look at her. Has she settled OK? Debbie said she would like to come and see her tomorrow, if that's all right with you. I told her how beautiful she was.'

'Yes, I think she is fine. She did get a little upset just now, but, yes, I think she is settled again. How long have you been here? Ten minutes?'

John came closer and patted her neck. She moved uncertainly again. 'No, I have only just this minute arrived. Why?'

'She was edgy, and I thought I heard someone or something here. There, there.' Emily soothed her. 'There's nothing to worry about; it's only John.' Her own heart was still fluttering from the fright. 'You will get used to him. He will look after you.' She stroked her nose again, looking at John with a smile. 'She is lovely, isn't she, John?' John was about to nod an affirmation when Black Tulip's eyes became wild and white again. She turned her head, looking down towards the paddock, and whinnied with fright. Both Emily and John turned quickly, catching their breath.

'What is it, John?' Emily's eyes were wide and anxious.

'I dunno.' He frowned, then walked to the end of the yard and looked across the paddock into the dusk. He came back and switched on the yard light. 'Couldn't see anything, probably a bird,' he said as he came back to where Emily was soothing Black Tulip.

'It's all right, my darling,' she was saying, patting her neck gently. 'It must be something more than a bird, John; something is really spooking her. And me! I'm sure there's something out there John; it's far too quiet. Do you think it's quiet, John? I mean, it seems unusually quiet. I know it sounds a bit stupid, but there was a panther-like creature lurking around the fields in Cambridge. I saw it on the TV news, but I don't know if they ever caught it.'

'Yeah! I remember reading about that in the newspapers, but it was a long time ago now. It's probably a bird or something she can hear. Quite possibly a rat got into the feed in the other stable.'

'No, John.' She shook her head. 'That wouldn't scare her, not like this. Anyway, she was scared this evening when she arrived, and Harris Freemore couldn't understand it, and neither can I. Major never spooked when he was here in the yard, did he?'

'No, but maybe it's because she's a filly and she's more highly strung.'

There was a pause. John was looking out into the paddock again.

'John...?'

'Yeah?' He turned and came back.

'John,' she said again slowly, pushing her blonde hair back from her forehead. He looked at her waiting, 'John, do you believe in ghosts?'

'Ghosts!' His grey eyes flashed. He stood for a moment looking at her, then looked down at his feet.

'Well, Miss...' He scratched the back of his neck. '...I don't rightly know. I really never thought much about it afore... Why?' He narrowed his eyes inquiringly.

'Well ... just before you arrived, Tulip got a bit agitated. It's very quiet out here, and I know it sounds silly, but I thought I heard the sound of a hoof in the yard, and it wasn't Black Tulip, and when I looked again I sort of glimpsed, or I thought I did, a horse's tail just swinging round the corner over there...' She hesitated. 'You know John, they say animals are psychic. I have heard it said that they never really leave their home...' There was another pause. 'And Tulip wouldn't go into that stable, would she? She fell silent again, before finally saying: 'Do you think that Major could still be here?'

John took a sharp intake of breath, making a hissing sound through his teeth. He was about to say something, then changed his mind. Then he said: 'Well! I don't rightly know, Miss, and I never really thought much about ghosts and things, but I suppose it could be possible...' He thought for a moment and rubbed his chin with his right thumb and forefinger. He took another deep breath.

'Well... It's like this, Miss... I didn't really want to say anythink... Sounds a bit silly really... But you know ... earlier today, it was strange. I was sweepin' up 'ere in the yard, and I was sure I 'eard 'ooves clip-cloppin' about but when I looked I didn't see nothin', there was no one 'ere but me... Birds was a twitterin', but that was all. I looked about in the stables, silly really, knowin' I was 'ere on me own.' He shook his head slightly pursing his lips. 'Twas when I was waitin' for you to comes back, that's when I 'eard it. I 'eard it twice, right give me the creeps it did... But I wouldn't 'ave mentioned it to you if you had not said anythink ... about ghosts. Wouldn't want to alarm you, or your Mum and Dad or anythink, mind. Only that you mentioned it, like... Ghosts, I mean ... and now the 'orse is 'ere, I wonder could it 'ave been a premonition.

43

You see I wasn't to know that you had gone to look at another 'orse. Seems funny, don't it?'

'I wonder if it could possibly be Major, John. Do you think it could be? Perhaps he is upset because I have got a new horse... Perhaps he's jealous.' She smiled nervously. Tulip seemed calm again. She gave her a stroke then walked over to the stable opposite where Major had once been. John follow her, ready in case anything untoward might happen, just in case something had managed to get into the stable that he did not know about.

'I 'eard the 'ooves before you come back. So if it is 'im, well, he didn't come back 'cause of the 'orse; he was 'ere before.'

'Animals have a sixth sense, John. Maybe he knew I had gone to look at a horse. He could be jealous.'

Emily opened the half door of Major's old stable, but the yard light only shone near the door, leaving the back of the stable in darkness. She peered into the gloom. The stable was empty. The shavings that John had put down at the back of the stall ready for Black Tulip had not been disturbed, and the water bucket was still as he had left it, just inside, near the door. Emily stepped cautiously inside the stable, and John stood holding the door open for her. It creaked in the silence. He would put some oil on it tomorrow!

'Major! Major!' Emily whispered nervously. 'Major, are you in here?' Her eyes were wide and expectant, her heart thumping in her ears, which were primed for the slightest sound. But there was a dead silence. Again she called. 'Major!' Her voice sounding a little bolder this time, although she didn't feel brave.

'Don't mess with it, Miss.' John sounded anxious.

From behind, across the yard, Black Tulip fidgeted and made small whinnying sounds, which made both Emily and John turn nervously.

Emily came out of the stable. 'Major?' She called a little louder, leaning over the door. A cold shiver went down her spine. 'Major! Major! Are you there? If you are, please give me a sign.'

John had a wary look. 'You know, Miss Emily, you shouldn't really be messing with this sort of thing.' He wasn't sure whether it was a lot of nonsense or not.

'But I must know, John. I have to know if he is still here, then perhaps I will be able to tell him not to be jealous.' She turned back to the stable. John pulled a face.

'MAJOR! MAJOR!' she called loudly. 'Are you there?' She was more confident now. 'If you are there... She waited a moment. '...Let me see you.'

They stood side by side, quiet and still for a few moments, waiting, listening hard for the slightest sound... Nothing. Then they heard a click, and both Emily and John started, John looking wide-eyed. Emily wished that her heart would not beat so loudly in her ears, it drummed out all other sounds, and she wanted to hear so badly. They stood stock-still, hardly daring to breath.

'What was that?' John whispered, as his hand tightened on the stable door. He answered himself: 'A mouse I expect, or a rat after the feed.'

Emily had a queasy feeling in her stomach; she was holding her breath, then a feeling of excitement came over her, and she said loudly, 'MAJOR, MAJOR!' Her voice, clear and sharp, echoed round the emptiness of the stable and the quietness of the yard. 'If you are there, let me see you!' The silence was electric, but at the harsh tone of Emily's voice, Black Tulip whinnied and kicked at her stable door, bringing John and Emily back to reality.

Major wanted so much for Miss Emily to see him. He put all his energy and thought power together, and tried his hardest to materialize. He could see them both looking into the stable, straining their eyes, but what could he do? Nothing.

He moved back in the stable and kicked over the water bucket. It went down with a clatter, just as John and Emily were moving away. They stopped! The water bucket was on its side, and water spilled out over the floor.

'How on earth did that 'appen?' John's pale-grey eyes darted from side to side.

Emily peered into the stable, expecting to see Major, but knowing that if she did she would probably run or even faint.

45

John was beside her, but all they saw was the bucket, rocking gently, and the water seeping out over the floor.

'The bucket fell over, that's all. I expect it was the vibration as I closed the door.' John tried to sound quite normal, so as not to alarm Emily, but he was really feeling quite uneasy himself and he was sure he had not convinced her.

Emily took a step nearer to the door. 'John...' There was a tremor in her voice. 'You didn't shut the door ... it's still ajar.'

John froze. His thoughts were the same as Emily's. Major was trying to communicate! But it couldn't be. He was a sensible man. No! There was no such thing as ghosts; there had to be a logical explanation.

'Come on now.' He did not touch the bucket. John closed the stable door shooting the bolt across the outside. 'I think it's time that you went in, and I ought to be getting off home. Debbie will be wondering where I've got to.' He put a comforting fatherly arm round Emily's shoulders, and guided her out of the yard and round towards the kitchen door. 'Now you go in, my girl, and think about riding that lovely Black Tulip tomorrow. Jenny is coming over in the morning, isn't she?' And I will be here and have Black Tulip all brushed and saddled up ready for you at seven o'clock.' He gently pushed her towards the door.

'You go in now, there's a good girl. I'm off now. Good night! And don't start worrying. See you in the morning.' He started to walk away. 'Go on! Go in now,' he urged, then turned towards the gate. 'Good night.'

'Good night, John... Thanks.' She put her hand on the handle of the door as he turned to go, but did not go in. She heard John go back into the yard to switch off the yard light. A little later came the sound of the small yard gate closing and a key turning in a lock.

She took her hand off the door handle and walked back to the yard, slowly and quietly, peering cautiously through the half darkness. She heard a clink and quickly switched on the light. She heard Black Tulip fidgeting. The light had disturbed her. She went to her, speaking softly and stroking her nose to calm her. All the time she kept part of her back to the stable and looked over her shoulder for fear of something coming up behind her. 'It's all right, Tulip. Good girl.' She knew that it

46

must feel strange being here for the first night in a new stable, and alone, too. She was used to having other horses near. But Emily was sure that she would get used to it in a day or two. Apart from the sound of Tulip's breathing and gentle snorting, there was nothing, but she felt nervous. She wanted to go and look in Major's stable, but her feet seemed rooted to the spot. Besides, she felt safer standing close to the great black horse. She must do it! She started cautiously across the yard to the stable opposite, desperately afraid of the shadowed corners of the yard. As she got to the centre of the yard, she stood quite still, as if suspended in space, listening, then quickened her pace almost to a run, reaching the stable door as if it was a safety line. She peered cautiously into the darkness of the stable.

'Major,' she whispered. There was a clink. The same sound she had heard before. Where did it come from?

'MAJOR!' Bolder now. There was a clop, and she felt a chill run through her. Tulip began to dance about and kick at the door. In the light she saw Black Tulip's eyes roll back with fright.

'MAJOR!' Emily demanded quite loudly. 'MAJOR! Now just you stop upsetting Black Tulip, do you hear me?' She listened. 'You are making her frightened, and I will get really upset with you if you don't stop it! Do you hear?' She peered again into the empty stable. 'Major! Are you there?' She was sure that he was, but whether he could hear her she was not sure. 'Major, Major! Now you be a good boy and...'

Suddenly her father's voice came through the darkness, making her jump. 'Em! Are you all right? What's going on? Who are you shouting at? We can hear you in the kitchen. Who's there? Are you all right?'

'Yes, I'm OK, Dad. See! Now look what you have done,' she said to the empty stable. 'You've got Dad all upset now.' She had not realized that she had been shouting that loudly. 'Now you just listen to me, Major.' She pointed her finger, speaking quietly through clenched teeth, her tone threatening. 'If Black Tulip knows you are here, and she can see you, you talk to her in horse talk, and tell her that she is welcome here and that she will be well cared for, and *don't you dare frighten her again! Do you hear me?*' Her voice rose now, high-pitched with anger.

47

The kitchen door opened and she saw a stream of light shine out into the meadow. Her father came round into the yard.

'Emily!' He stood for a moment, his head raised looking and listening, then walked nearer into the yard, surprise on his face as he saw his daughter talking into empty space.

'Em?' he enquired curiously. 'Emily? Who are you talking to? Is John still here?' He was sure that he wasn't. He came nearer. 'Whoever were you shouting at, Emily?'

'Major, he's in there!' She spoke matter-of-factly, as if it was a natural answer to the question. She did not turn towards her father.

'Major?' Mike reeled, his mouth open in surprise. He peered incredulously into the stable, not knowing what to expect. It was dark and empty, of course.

'Emily, are you all right?'

Liz's voice called out from the darkness.

'What is it, Mike? Is the horse playing up again? Is John still here?' He didn't answer her.

'Mike?' Came the worried voice again.

'No! John's gone.'

'Shall I call him then?' He did not answer. She came out of the kitchen closing the door behind her.

'It's not her fault,' Emily was saying bitterly. 'It's him.'

'Who? John?' said her mother, coming into the yard. 'What's happened? What's he done?'

'No, not John! It's Major!' Her tone was sharp. 'He keeps upsetting Black Tulip, and I have just told him off.' She turned with annoyance to look at their surprised faces.

'Major?' said Liz, looking at the stable. 'Major! Where?' She glanced anxiously at Mike.

'He's in there,' said Emily with disgust. 'He keeps clopping his hooves, and he knocked the water bucket over when John was here, and John said that he heard him clopping around in the yard this afternoon.' There was a pause.

'Don't be so silly, Em.' Mike looked at his wife. Then he added gently, as if he was telling her something that she did not know, 'Major's dead, darling. He is not here any more.' He opened the half door and walked in. 'The stable is empty.' He saw the spilled water and the bucket on its side, then looked at his daughter with a frown. 'It's empty, Emily; there

48

is nothing here. It must have been the wind that knocked the bucket over.' He came out closing the door and shooting the bolt on the outside.

'Dad, there is no wind out here, and certainly not inside the stable!' She was exasperated. 'I tell you *he's there.*'

Liz looked into the stabled. 'Emily? Darling! There is nothing there, how could there be, its been empty for over a year. What are you talking about? It's probably a rat scratching about.'

'Well, who knocked over the water bucket then?'

'Well, how should I know, darling? I expect John didn't put it down properly, and it has toppled over and he didn't notice. Or maybe Snowball is in there. Have you called him?'

'Major did it, Mum. John was here, so was I. It just went on it's own, for no reason. Honestly.'

The bucket suddenly rolled across the floor of the stable. The clatter on the concrete made them all jump, and they looked cautiously into the empty gloom.

'Good God!' said Mike. 'How did that happen?'

Emily smiled. 'There I told you so. I'm not crazy.' She flung her hand out. 'It's Major, he's a ghost.'

'What?' said her mother in alarm. 'A ghost! He can't be... No Emily, it's your imagination. Major is ... dead.' The word came out in a whisper.

'Ghosts usually are, Mum.' Emily chuckled with relief.

Liz peered into the stable cautiously again, her eyes wide. She felt nervous and was ready to jump back.

'Do you mean he rolled this bucket across the floor?' she said in disbelief. 'The wind just caught it.'

'There is no wind, Mum, and, in any case, it's not windy in the stable, look!' She spread her hands. 'The night is still. There is just the slightest movement in the air, not even enough to move a leaf.'

'I don't believe it... It fell over.'

'No, Mum, it *is* Major. That is why Tulip is so jumpy. She knows he's there. Animals can sense these things, and I think she can see him, and it frightens her, and I have just told him off. *Haven't I?*' she added sharply into the empty stable.

'Don't you remember when Black Tulip's eyes followed something earlier this evening, and Harris Freemore wondered what she was looking at? None of us saw anything, did we?'

49

'Emily?' Liz's voice was hushed, she looked at Mike with alarm. 'Mike do something.'

'What can I do? We all heard the bucket roll, and no one touched it. Maybe a mouse or a rat ran across the floor... Come on, let's go in and have a cup of tea. It's getting late.'

'No, Dad! I have to stay and find out.' Emily leaned over the stable door. '*Major, please*, move that bucket again! MOVE the bucket! MOVE THE BUCKET, MAJOR!'

Mike turned to go. 'Oh, come on, this is ridiculous.' He moved away. Then they heard a clop.

Liz was so alarmed she gasped loudly and grabbed at Mike's arm.

'Come on, Major,' Emily cried encouragingly. 'Come on, there's a good boy, move the bucket. Please, Major, move the bucket.'

Suddenly the bucket was suspended in mid-air. The bucket was moving towards them. Emily stood back afraid, but then stepped forward with a sudden feeling of great joy.

'Major!' It was a tearful whisper. 'Major, you did it!' Her eyes blurred with tears. 'Major!' Her voice was hushed. The bucket hung over the stable door, and Emily took it in both hands and held it where it was. For a moment she felt a power holding it, then suddenly it went limp and she was holding it up on her own. It was not imagination.

All three looked at each other, mouths open in amazement, mystified at what they had just seen. Liz felt faint, but she was not the fainting kind. Mike stood with his hand clamped tight across his mouth, his eyes wide and unbelieving. They stood rigid, not daring to move. Until Emily whispered 'Major?' And put her hand up to where she thought his nose would be.

'Major? You are here, aren't you?' Tears of joy and sadness rolled down her cheeks.

In the silence of the yard, Liz wiped a tear from her eye and leaned against the stable wall; she felt if she didn't have some support her legs would buckle under her.

'Oh, Mike! Mike! What are we going to do?'

Mike was staring at Emily. He was speechless. He had seen the bucket move with his own eyes, but found it hard to comprehend.

Emily stood back, sniffing back the joyful tears and wiping her hand over her eyes. She put the bucket down.

50

'There you are, I told you so.'

Black Tulip gave a small whinnying sound. Emily went over to her and spoke softly. She called across to Major. 'Now you just stop frightening her, Major. Come over here and tell her you are sorry, and that there is no need for her to be afraid.'

Black Tulip stepped back deeper into her stable, as if something *was* coming towards her. She half reared, hitting her head on the roof. Emily went to her, worried in case she had gashed herself, but it was all right. A few soft words with soothing hands calmed the mare down. 'There, I told you there was nothing to worry about. Major won't hurt you. He was kind and gentle, and I loved him, as I love you. Please don't be afraid of him.' She stroked the long black nose and put her cheek against it. 'There's a good girl.' She looked up as the horse lifted her head. Tulip's eyes were still fearful. Emily turned to the empty space, lifting her hand she stroked the air. She felt nothing, but she said, 'Good boy, Major.'

Mike and Liz Peters watched their daughter in awed amazement. Liz wondered if Emily needed a doctor, she was acting so strangely. She linked arms with her husband. He felt her trembling.

'Mike! What are we to do? I'm scared.' Her voice dropped to a hush, then rose again: 'What can we do?'

6

The next morning, Debbie cooked John his usual bacon and eggs and toast. His two daughters, Angela and Susan, both came down to the breakfast table at about the same time in their housecoats.

Their mother asked if they would like a cooked breakfast.

'Yes please. The bacon smells good,' said Susan, who was thirteen. With a big grin, she pulled out a chair opposite her father.

'What about you, Angela?'

'Oh! No thanks, Mum,' Angela said emphatically. 'It's far too fattening.' She was seventeen and extremely aware of her figure. She yawned sleepily, as she sat down at the table, her left hand propping up the side of her head. She yawned again. 'Besides, it's too early for fry-ups and I am tired.'

'Tired!' said her father. 'You have only just got up. Why did you get up so early if you feel tired? You should have a few early nights, my girl. What have you got to do today?'

'Nothing much.' She grimaced sleepily. 'I might go into town, and meet some friends. School holidays are boring. I'll just have a cup of coffee, please, Mum.'

'Bored! A young girl like you!' Every day for Angela was boring, John thought, that was her problem; she had nothing to keep her occupied but coffee shops. Debbie put the coffee in front of her. She seemed really too lazy even to pick up the cup.

'Well, if you want something to do, why don't you come up to the stables with me? I can find you a job.'

'What!' She was aghast. She sat up straight. 'And ruin my nails! In all that muck and grime! Oh, no, thank you!' She was appalled. She looked at the blue nail varnish she had put on only last night and raised her eyes to the ceiling in utter disgust.

John ignored the snub. 'We've got a beautiful new mare up

there. You should see her; you're really missing something.' He nodded with a smile as he got up from the table. 'Well I must get a move on; got to get this beauty brushed and saddled up by seven o'clock.' He moved to the door, taking his old jacket off the hook behind the door and put on his flat cap. Giving Debbie a kiss, he said, 'I'll see you later. Come up and look at this fabulous mare if you get a chance.'

Debbie nodded eagerly. 'Yes, I would like to. I'll come up with you tomorrow morning. I have an early hair appointment this morning. Wendy couldn't fit me in at my usual time.' John nodded with a smile and looked at his wife. Her light mousy hair always looked nice. He wondered why she bothered with the hairdresser, and although a little plump and not really beautiful, he loved her. She was always clean and smart and on the go cooking meals for them and keeping the house spotless, and happy to be doing it, always pleasant and contented with her life, the same as himself. He wondered who Angela took after, certainly not either of them.

John was going up the hall to the front door.

'Have a great day, Dad, mucking out the stables,' called Angela, a little sarcasm in her voice. She thought stable work was lowly, most of her friends' fathers worked in offices. One was a jeweller. How glamorous was that. She didn't talk to her friends about her father. How could she tell them that he was a stable lad? If she was asked, and only if she was asked and could not get out of it, she would say that he was in charge of horses, implying that he was in charge of a large racing stable. She left it to their own imagination.

'It would do you good, my girl, to put your mind to something other than coffee bars,' her mother snapped back, clearing the dishes off the table and putting them into the dishwasher.

Behind her back Angela gave her mother a look of contempt.

'I would like to come and see the mare, Dad,' called Susan brightly. 'Can I?'

Angela sneered at her sister. 'Creep.'

'That's enough, Angela!' Debbie said sharply.

'Yes, you can come when you like,' John called from the hall. Bye.' He grinned to himself as he shut the front door, and walked to the front gate. His girls were so different; Susan always so willing and Angela always had that edge in her voice.

Angela, was a snob, *That* came from mixing with too many fancy girls at college. He shook his head, muttering to himself, 'Teens is a funny age.' He closed the gate and walked up the road to Rosemary Lodge. Angela, he thought, was so different to Miss Emily and Jenny Ellis, who were about her age. He guessed it was having the responsibility of animals. Angela thought more about her nails and her blonde hair, and sitting in coffee shops in the town with her friends. If the truth were only known, she was bored with being at school, and more bored at home. Nothing seemed to please her. It was that in-between age, growing up, but not yet grown up, and he would be glad when school started again to keep her mind busy. Her school reports were good, she worked well, but how she ever concentrated and got good results he could not imagine.

Now Susan, she was a completely different kettle of fish. So good-hearted. She would almost be willing to help with anything; she would love this new horse when she saw it. He just hoped that she would never want one of her own; he could not possibly afford such a great expense, and if he could, it would cost him double. Angela wouldn't let Susan get away with that. *She* would want a car. She had already hinted that all her friends had cars for their seventeenth birthdays, and he supposed on her next birthday he would have to buy her one. What a trial that would be! He certainly would not offer to teach her to drive; there would be more rows than enough.

He walked on, deep in thought, turning up into the lane and into Rosemary Lodge. He looked up at the sky. It was blue after the rain in the night and he hoped that it would not rain for a week or so as Mr Peters had asked him to put a coat of green paint on the woodwork. Smarten the old place up a bit, he had said, specially now we have a new horse. John didn't think a horse would notice if the stable was painted green or left brown. He could make a start this morning rubbing down the old brown paint that had been there for years.

When John arrived in the yard, Emily was already there dressed in blue jeans and blue sweatshirt; she was talking to Black Tulip.

'Mornin', Miss Emily,' he called, coming through the small side gate and locking it behind him again. 'You're up and about early this morning, beat me to it.'

'Morning, John.' She couldn't wait to tell him all about the events of last night. She followed him round, talking all the time, as he got his brushes ready and put the head collar on Tulip. He began to brush her, walking from side to side of the horse, Emily beside him. When she got to the bit about Major and the bucket, he stopped and looked at her in amazement.

'He didn't... Lifted the *bucket* ... I can't believe it... Bit scary that... *God, really!* You *all* saw it! I can't believe it.' He shook his head with a half smile and a frown.

'Yes. Mum and Dad were here, too. It's fantastic, isn't it?' Her eyes were wide with excitement.

'Sounds so, but I would 'ave to see it to believe it. Not that I doubt what you say, of course, Miss, but you know what I mean. It would have to be seen to be believed, wouldn't it?' I mean, you know, ghosts and all.' He went to the side and gave Black Tulip another quick once over, then went to the tack room and came back with the bridle, saddlecloth and the saddle. Emily took the bridle and fitted it on while John fixed the saddle.

'Well, I know how it sounds, John, but it happened. Ask Dad!'

He was pulling hard on the girth when Jenny came round into the yard on Henry.

'Morning, Em! Lovely morning, isn't it? But did you hear the rain in the night? Oh Black Tulip looks great. Bet you can't wait to ride her.'

Emily ignored all the good mornings and began telling her, with great gusto and excitement, hardly stopping to take a breath, about the night before and Major being there in the stable. 'I have been dying to tell you. I was going to phone, but it was getting late and I knew you would be here this morning.'

Jenny looked at her open-mouthed. She, like John, could not believe what she was hearing. 'You mean, he actually picked up the bucket!' Her eyes nearly popped out of her head. 'And *gave* it to you. I don't believe it... Were you scared? I know I would have been.'

'Well, I must say it was a bit scary at first, but then I told him off for scaring Tulip, and told him to talk to her, and he must have done because she calmed down. I don't feel so bad about it this morning, but I must say last night out here in the dark it was a bit scary. My mum almost fainted, and her face was as white as a ghost.' She laughed, putting her hand to her mouth. 'I shouldn't have said that, should I?' They both giggled.

Jenny looked across the yard at Major's stable, peering in as far as she dare. 'He won't frighten Henry, will he?'

'No, I don't think he's there at the moment,' said Emily. 'Tulip would soon tell us, and I looked into the stable earlier and called him, but there is nothing there. Perhaps he has gone now. In a way, I hope so...' She put her head on one side. 'And yet you know, in a way I don't.'

'Oh Em ... I don't know what to say.' Her eyes were wide and a little fearful, but there was a sort of excitement there, as she looked at Major's stable. 'Can I come over tonight and see if it happens again?'

Emily nodded. 'Yeah, if you like.'

'Black Tulip is ready for you now, Miss,' said John.

Emily mounted. So far she had only walked Tulip around the yard and cantered around the paddock, so this was an exciting morning for them. Jenny had already mounted Henry again and they were about to ride out, when Emily's mother came to the corner of the yard to see them off.

'Good morning, Jenny.' She looked up at both the girls with a smile, rubbing her arms against the slight chill of the early-morning air. 'Where are you going, Emily?'

'Oh, not far, just across the field and into the woods.'

Liz nodded. 'Well don't be too long, and please don't go galloping like crazy.'

'Oh, Mum, don't worry. We'll be OK, won't we?' She looked at her friend.

'Well, this is your first time out on a new horse.' Liz sounded a little worried. 'How is she this morning, anyway?' She reached up and patted Tulip's neck. 'Did Emily tell you about last night, Jenny?' She patted Henry. She didn't like to think he was neglected.

'Yes!' Jenny raised her eyebrows. 'Sounds a bit scary.'

'It was, Jenny. Very scary.'

'She seems fine this morning though. Come on, Jen. Bye, Mum.'

They started to walk away. Liz watched them until they were way across the fields and almost out of sight.

'They'll be OK, Mrs Peters.' John had come to stand beside her. 'They know what they're doing, Mam.'

'I hope you're right, John.' She unfolded her arms. 'I hope that horse doesn't rear and throw her off. I suppose Emily told you about last night?'

'Yes.' John nodded. 'Sounds a bit eerie, don't it? I felt it was a bit eerie meself, when I was 'ere earlier in the day. I ain't too 'appy 'bout ghosts, are you, Mam?' He grimaced.

'Well, no, John, but it happened. What do you mean when you were here earlier in the day?'

'Well, it were yesterday, when I was workin'. They went off to see the new 'orse. I didn't know that, of course.'

'They went to Wickerbrook Hall,' Liz volunteered.

'Yeah, well! It was then, like, I 'eard this clip-clopping of 'ooves.'

He told her about when he was sweeping up the leaves and how he had thought it was Henry. 'Well, I wouldn't 'ave said nothin' but out 'ere last night with Miss Emily, well, it gave me a bit of a turn, I can tell yer. The water bucket rolling over like that.'

'Mmmm, it certainly was eerie out here last night. I have been awake most of the night worrying about it.'

He grimaced. 'Might never 'appen again. Though, the 'orse seems 'appy enough this mornin', and I don't think there is anything to worry about.' He looked about warily as if checking.

'I hope you are right, John,' she nodded. 'I really do.' She walked away back towards the kitchen door, folding her cardigan across her chest and her arms around her body against the chill of the morning air.

Major was in the paddock. He saw them go off trotting across the field making for the woods. He followed at a slow trot some distance behind; he did not want to spoil Miss Emily's first day, and he did not want her to give him another scolding. He hoped that Black Tulip understood him now. He did not really mean to frighten her, he could not help being the way he was... He supposed that she could see him, but he was

57

puzzled to know why Miss Emily could not. He had heard the word 'invisible' when Miss Emily had been talking to John in the stable yard one day, about a television programme about a man who could not be seen... He pricked his ears. Yes, that must be it; he was invisible, but whatever that meant, he did not feel any different. He was still feeling happy inside. He followed them into the woods.

The first ride out on Black Tulip was a success. Emily and Jenny had cantered most of the way, and Black Tulip had been easy to ride. She was just as Sir James said, a lady, and almost human. Emily and Jenny rode out every day for the rest of the week, Emily and Tulip getting quite used to each other. Major, unseen, followed them.

On Saturday morning, John had just finished saddling up Tulip when Jenny arrived and the girls went off happily as usual. John was getting on famously with his stable painting. He had almost finished, but today he could not do anything because it was drizzling.

It had rained heavily through the night, and the morning was cool. A watery sun filtered through the leaves of the dense overhead branches, as Henry followed Tulip over the winding grassy path through the woodland. The air smelled of damp mouldy earth, and there was the soft sound of rain droplets still dripping from leaf to leaf. The fresh bright-green grass smelled sweet as it was crushed by the heavy tread of hooves, and twigs snapped and crackled quietly into the soft turf. Violets peeped through the grass half hidden under their own leaves as if too shy to show their faces. Sturdy toadstools pushed their way up through the grass and wet brown bark. The air wafted up through the trees as they walked on, scented with the rich, pungent smell of soil and musty wood moss and wet sweet grasses. A soft breeze rustled the leaves high above them, and the birds called loudly to each other. A wood pigeon fluttered its wide soft brown wings and flew high into the trees, disturbed by the hushed sound of horses' breath.

It was then that Major came up alongside Henry. He shied so suddenly that Jenny was taken by complete surprise and he took off through the trees. She shouted out in alarm, and although she was used to handling him, she tried in vain to pull him up or to turn his head. Still he went on and on, racing in a frenzy deep into the trees. She struggled with the reins, clinging on for dear life, as branches and leaves swept across her face. Luckily, seeing the low ones coming towards her, she ducked her head halfway down Henry's neck. She came to a clearing and managed to turn his head, and he slowed almost to a stop, huffing and puffing, his eyes wild and rolling, his head shaking up and down and sideways. Then he lifted his head, neighing in a frenzied high pitch, as Major came into his view again, and he raised his forelegs, twisting and turning his great brown body like a performing circus horse. As Jenny loosened the rein, he came down on all fours and he began to back up. She tried to calm him by patting his neck. She tried to urge him forward, but he kept backing away. Before she realized it, his back legs were sinking into soft and boggy ground. She tried kicking him, urging him forward and bouncing up and down in the saddle, with anxious cries of 'Come on, come on Henry.' She slapped his hindquarters with her crop, but he was sinking deeper. She could hear Emily shouting her name.

'Here, Em! Here!' she shouted in alarm. 'HERE! HERE! QUICK!' She was hysterical. She could hear Tulip thrashing about though the trees, but she could still not see them, and Henry was sinking deeper, his nostrils flared and his eyes wild and white with fright. He neighed and whinnied, crying for help. It was a pitiful sound and a pitiful sight to see the great horse struggling, fighting for his life.

Emily turned this way and that, trying to follow the sound of Jenny's anxious cries. They were in a part of the woodland where they had never been before. The trees were dense, and there were cruel thickets of wild blackberry barring the way. Emily's voice echoed through the quiet woodland: as wood pigeons disturbed by the noise flapped their wings and flew through the leaves with anguished cries and Black Tulip was turning this way and that trying to find a way out, disturbing the birds, and scattering the woodland creatures into the dense undergrowth.

'Jenny! Jenny! Where are you?'

'Here Em! QUICK, QUICK!' she screamed. 'I'm sinking. I'm sinking.'

Black Tulip could hear Henry's frightened call for help and she turned urgently, pushing her way through the undergrowth. Suddenly they broke into the small clearing, and Emily screamed in alarm as she saw Henry struggling, his back legs sunk nearly up to his haunches in the bog, his forelegs, flaying out trying to get a grip on the more solid ground in front of him.

'Kick him, Jen. Kick him!' Emily shouted anxiously. Jenny kicked but Henry sunk deeper. 'NO! NO! WAIT! Wait a minute, wait a minute! Keep still, keep still, Jen. Try not to move. He's getting in deeper.' Jenny did as she was told, her breath coming in short anxious puffs.

Emily saw a long branch lying in the undergrowth. Jumping down from Tulip, she pulled at the branch. It was entangled with the grass that had grown over it for years. She pulled and pulled and eventually it came free. Still holding on to Tulip's rein, she stood the branch up against a tree then put her foot in the stirrup and heaved herself back up into the saddle. She leaned down to retrieve the branch.

Tulip was facing Henry. Emily pushed the branch towards Jenny, who grabbed at it with her left hand. Emily began to back Tulip up gently, and as Jenny urged Henry forward, he managed to get one of his back legs free. Even with the great strength in his powerful haunches, he could not muster enough energy to pull himself out of the sucking mud and his leg went back with a loud plop, splashing mud in all directions.

'Pull, Em, PULL!' Jenny screamed through gritted teeth. Suddenly the rotten and decaying wood snapped in half, and both girls almost lost their balance.

Henry was frantic again. His eyes were white with fear, and he twisted his large brown body, trying to free his back legs and hindquarters.

Emily dismounted again but still kept a hold of Tulip, who was agitated and stepping back. 'Throw me your belt!' Jenny didn't ask why. She struggled to get the belt from around her waist with one hand, as Henry continued to baulk. She threw the belt at Emily's feet, and Emily buckled it to her own belt. She mounted Tulip again and rode as close as she dare to the boggy ground. She threw one end of the belt to Jenny who luckily caught it first time. Both girls got a good grip, winding the end around their hands. Tulip was very close to the edge, but then Emily began to back her up again slowly. They both strained, almost pulling their shoulders from their joints. The leather held, but the buckles began to break away from the stitching, and Jenny was now standing up in the stirrups to ease the weight on Henry's back. But in this position she found she could not get a proper hold on the leather, and she sat down again heavily. Henry neighed piteously, floundering about, nodding and twisting his head, his eyes wide and terrified and his nostrils flared. He managed again to get his left hind leg free, then suddenly the pulling between the girls seemed to get stronger, and, with Jenny kicking and urging him on, he got both forelegs onto solid ground. Suddenly he leaped forward with a frenzied whinny, and his back legs came free from the mire both at the same time. He was up on solid ground – both horses and girls – were exhausted. Jenny was breathless. Her chest was heaving and her whole body shook like a jelly. She looked at Emily, trying to thank her. They were sitting side by side and head to tail in their saddles, still holding the belts between them as if afraid to let go. The buckles were now almost severed from the holdings and hanging on by a thread. They tried to calm the sweating horses by patting their necks and talking gently to them, but they were still agitated, prancing and tossing their heads. But the girls seemed in control again, and gradually the horses began to calm a little.

'Thanks, Em. I didn't know we had so much strength between us. What made you think of the belts?' Jenny let her end of the belt go, and it slid through her stiff, chafed fingers as Tulip turned round.

Emily, every bit as exhausted, managed a smile of utter relief. 'I saw the belt thing done in a cowboy film, but I didn't know that it would work.' They both chuckled breathlessly ... relaxing into their saddles but still shaking like jellies.

'But it did work, thank God. Did you notice how we suddenly seemed to get a boost from behind, as if something was pushing Henry forward?'

Emily was about to reply when Black Tulip began to whinny in fright, her large brown eyes rolling back. Henry, too, was backing towards the bog again. Both girls struggled with the frightened horses once again. Then they suddenly froze. A shiver ran down Emily's spine. Ahead of her was a chestnut horse. It was as if time was standing still; even the frightened and fidgeting Henry seemed to calm for a split second or two. For there, standing in a clearing between the trees, stood Major, his chestnut coat gleaming as if he had just been groomed, his head high, his soft silky mane streaming back, his tail swishing behind him and his bridle and saddle polished to a high shine. His soft brown eyes looked at them keenly.

'Major?' It was no more than a sigh. 'Major?' Emily leaned slowly forward, as if he was drawing her to him. She felt cold, and a tingling feeling ran right through her body. Tears of joy and sadness ran down her cheeks. But then, before her eyes, the stallion began to fade, then simply wafted away. A vaporous mist hung in the air like the steam that rises from a horse that has been ridden hard and then in a second disappears into the atmosphere...

They stared for long minutes into the quiet green dampness of the woodland. The horses were calm now, and Henry huffed and crunched on the bit. A deathly silence hung in the air. Even the birds had stopped singing...

Emily remembered a similar silence from the day of the accident. In her mind, she saw Major lying on the woodland path, and she saw herself on her knees sobbing over the great chestnut body. The lifeless eyes were only half closed...

She was holding her breath, and she let it out slowly, as from the corner of her eye she saw Jenny looking at her.

'It was Major!' she whispered softly, hardly daring to speak. 'Did you see him, Jen?'

Jenny nodded slowly, as if she were deep in a wondrous dream.

The girls made their way back through the dense tranquillity of the woodland. Each was silent, deep in her own thoughts. When they reached the yard, John looked up with raised eyebrows. Liz was just coming out with a mug of coffee for him. She gasped at the muddy state of Jenny and Henry.

'Goodness me! Have you had a fall, Jenny? Look at the state

of you. What on earth has happened?' Her voice rose with anxiety and alarm.

Emily was the first to dismount. She went quickly to her mother, dragging Tulip by the rein behind her.

'Mum! Mum!' she sobbed, dabbing her eyes with the back of her gloved hand. 'What do you think? You'll never guess! We saw Major!'

Liz gasped. 'Major! What!' She frowned, and John glanced at her quickly over the stable door.

Emily turned to her friend, who had dismounted from Henry and was putting up her stirrups. 'We saw Major, didn't we Jenny?'

Jenny, still in a daze, gave a nod and walked round and put up the other stirrup. Finally she said, 'Henry took off when a pigeon flew up and scared him. It's unusual for him to shy like that. He is always so reliable, even on the road. He's virtually bomb-proof! You can trust him with your life... But he just took off...'

Emily interrupted: 'It wasn't a pigeon, Jen. I bet it was Major. Henry saw him, and it probably gave him a fright. I expect Black Tulip saw him, too, but she seems to have got a little more used to him now, though she is still a bit jumpy.'

'Do you really think so, Em?' Jenny brightened. 'Henry has never done anything like that before. I couldn't stop him, Mrs Peters.' She shook her head. 'He just went wild, didn't he, Em? I've never known him to spook before.' She patted him lovingly.

'I'm sure it was Major. I bet that's what happened. That's why Henry was so scared. But he did help to pull you out of the bog, didn't he, Jen?'

'What bog?' John frowned, with a quick sharp look at all three. He took Henry's bridle and tethered him to the stable door, and then did the same with Tulip.

'There's a bog in the wood,' said Emily. 'I never knew it was there. We always keep to the path, but when Henry took off he just ran straight through the trees and straight into it.'

'Yes, it was lucky I managed to turn his head when I did. If we had plunged forward, we would have been in so deep we would never have got out. I expect the ground is soggy from the rain last night.'

'Yes, but not enough to make the ground boggy like that, surely?' said Liz, looking at John.

Emily went on to tell her mother and John how she had pulled Jenny and Henry out by buckling their belts together.

'That was ingenious, Emily!' Liz sounded surprised. 'How did you know how to do that?'

'I saw it in a film,' she smiled. 'And it really worked, didn't it, Jen? Tulip was struggling backwards, and Jenny and I were holding the belts between us, and we were hoping that the belts would hold, and then suddenly we seemed to gain immense strength, didn't we, Jen? You said it was like a boost from behind, and I am sure now that it must have been Major helping.'

'Major!' said Liz and Jenny together doubtfully.

'Well, you said you felt as if you were pushed out from behind, and he was there, wasn't he?' She looked at John and then at her mother, and then back at Jenny. 'Well, Henry couldn't have got a boost from anywhere else, could he? He was up to his tail in mud.'

Jenny seemed miles away. 'Well, yes.' She sounded doubtful. 'But I don't know if...'

'Well, for goodness sake, Jen, we saw him, didn't we?' Emily looked alarmed, her eyes searching Jenny's face. 'Didn't we, Jen? You did see him, didn't you?'

Jenny nodded slowly, as if in a trance.

'Mum! He was standing before us in the trees.' Emily's voice rose, and her blue eyes shone with excitement. 'He looked just like he always did. He was real.' She turned back to her friend. 'It was real, wasn't it, Jen?' Alarm bells rang in Emily's head. She hadn't imagined it, had she?

'Yes, I saw him, but the whole thing just seems so unbelievable. And it was so quick. Quick as a flash.'

Emily turned with excited enthusiasm. 'His coat was all glossy, Mum, just like it used to be, and his mane was blowing in the wind. He seemed to be galloping ... his tail was swishing ... it was all so real, wasn't it, Jen?' She was talking so quickly, and getting more excited. 'And he looked straight at me like he always did...' Her voice choked as a picture of Major's big soft brown eyes came into her mind, and tears rolled down her cheeks. 'Oh, Mum, I didn't mean to do it.' She put her

64

arms round her mother, clinging to her tightly and sobbing. Liz enclosed her in her arms.

'He stood in front of you?' asked Liz, looking over Emily's head at Jenny.

Jenny was nodding slowly. 'Yes, just like he used be, saddle and bridle and everything, just like he... He was real.'

Emily drew away from her mother. She was glad to hear Jenny mention the saddle and the bridle. She raised her eyebrows. 'You really did see him, Jen, didn't you? You saw him just like I did. I didn't imagine it, did I?' Jenny had seemed so vacant a few minutes ago that Emily thought that she was just saying it to please her.

But Jenny was nodding. 'Yes, he was really real, and I think he must have pushed Henry to safety... He must have done. You see I couldn't get off Henry's back. It was thick with mud and green slime and ... oh, it smells awful.' She looked down at her clothes and pulled a face. 'Henry was struggling for ages, then all of a sudden, he just seemed to jump forward, just like he was pushed. One minute we were stuck fast and then next we were out. So if it *was* Major, then really he saved us both because we were getting in deeper and deeper, weren't we, Em?'

As she nodded her head, Emily looked up into the beautiful face of Black Tulip and gave her a pat. She had such kind eyes, and she loved her dearly! But Major would always be there in her heart. She sniffed, wiping a stray tear from her eyes and listened to what Jenny was telling Liz and John. '...I don't know how long we were there. Do you, Em? And then it just seemed to happen, we were out.'

To Liz and John the girls' story sounded so unbelievable, but the mud splashed on Jenny's boots and jodhpurs, on her face, hands and hair, and caked on Henry's legs, belly and haunches, seemed proof enough.

7

It was September, and the girls were back at college. Emily was now back on form, and Miss Tilbury was pleased to hear from her tutors that she now had full concentration and was doing well. Emily rode Black Tulip every morning and evening, but only in the fields, she did not go near the woods. She spent most of the time practising jumping over the poles which John had fixed up for her in the paddock. The rest of her time was taken up with homework; she had quite a lot to catch up on.

Jenny came over at the weekends. She walked mostly at the edge of the fields or on the grass verge. There was just a small stretch of road to walk on. Sometimes John would box Tulip and drive Emily over to Mayberry Farm. Tulip, though calm and composed, was nervous on the road, especially when the odd car came a bit too close round the corners of the country lanes.

This Saturday they had spent the day riding round the farm and jumping in the paddock. Finally they had helped Anita to clean out the stables, singing along to the latest pop group playing on the radio until Jenny's father had come round and shouted at them to turn it down.

After mucking out the stables, they went into the house and up to Jenny's room where they both had showers and changed their clothes. They came down to lunch starving. Jenny's mother, Carol, had cooked a chicken casserole. They were joined at the table by Jenny's father, Kevin Baily, a young farm-hand, Anita, Jim Spencer, another groom, and old Bill Stanton, who had been farming at Mayberry for thirty years. Eventually, of course, the conversation got round to Major and his ghostly activities. Young Kevin said it was a load of nonsense, but Bill said that it could be true for he had heard of such a story before about a dog that carried on barking in the garden after he died.

Animals never left their homes, he believed. They went on to talk of haunted castles and old houses, and of Pennydeck Manor in the next village, which was said to have the ghost of a grey lady who walked through the garden with a small white dog or appeared at a bedroom window. It was said that the dog had been trampled to death by a horse that had gone wild, and the grey lady saw it happen from the window. There had been sightings by guests at the manor until very recently.

Then it was all forgotten, and Carol got up and started to clear the table. The girls helped, glad to get away from the conversation. Then they went out into the yard, while Anita was already back at work. They saddled up their horses and rode them around the farm, keeping to the farm tracks.

With the winter coming on, the evenings got darker, but Emily had so far managed to ride Tulip every day. She had also been getting up an hour earlier in the mornings and riding before breakfast. At that hour it was still dark, and she rode just around the paddock and out across the field and back, before going to college. Major seemed to have gone. In a way she found this sad, but really it was a relief. She felt glad that he was now at rest.

She came into the yard and jumped down. Her face was rosy from the chill morning air, her breath coming out in clouds of white steam. John took the bridle and led Tulip away. He quickly threw a rug over her, saying, 'Come old girl, don't want you catching cold!' Emily smiled at the way he was talking to the horse as she went into the tack room, took off her scarf and hung up her crop, ready for the next time. She heard her mother calling to her from the kitchen.

'Emily, you're wanted on the phone.'

Emily turned and walked towards the kitchen, taking off her black velvet riding helmet. She slipped off her gloves before picking up the receiver. 'Hello?'

'Oh, hello. Emily Peters, is it?' The jolly hockey-sticks voice came down the line, loud and clear. 'Louise Bartram. You know, Sir James's daughter.'

'Oh, yes!' Emily grimaced, hoping it wasn't about Black Tulip. She had not met Louise Bartram, but she had seen her at horse events and knew her face. She always seemed very efficient. She was about twenty, three years older than Emily, small and slim, with dark hair pulled back in a ponytail.

'Hello, Emily!' The ultra-confident voice boomed out again. 'Thought I would give you a bell. I was wondering how you were getting along with the old gel. Is she behaving herself?' Emily detected a smile in her tone.

'Oh! Yes, thanks; she's wonderful. I have just come in. I ride her every day, and she is going well, thanks. I love her. I think we love each other.' She smiled into the receiver.

'Splendid, splendid. Yes, I loved her, too. She's a nice old gel.' Emily thought she sounded just like her father when she said 'old gel'. 'Yes, I miss her a bit! But I am quite satisfied with the old boy that I have now. Tell you why I rang...' Emily could not help imagining her standing at the phone in jodhpurs and thick polo-neck sweater, green wellies, or maybe riding boots and puffer jacket, just as she had seen her at shows.

'...I wondered if you might care to participate in our charity horse event? It's not until next spring, March actually! I'm in charge of recruiting!' She sounded as if she was trying to gather an army. 'Father is organizing the event for riding for the disabled. Jolly good cause, of course. It will be a bit of everything as you know! Showjumping, showing, showing in hand, dressage, gymkhana, pony rides, you know the usual thing, and of course all the sideshows, including a dog show. You get the general idea, do you not? ... eh?' She did not wait for an answer. 'Well, just hoping that the jolly old weather will be fine in March, but one just has to take pot luck, doesn't one...? Can't tell seven months in advance! What! Eh, ha, ha. But I thought you might like to enter the old gel. She jumps very well, you know. Well, I expect you have found that out by now, eh?' She tittered. 'Have you been to many shows before? With your other horse, I mean? I was sorry to hear about your accident, with ... err ... Major! Wasn't that his name? I am sure that I have seen you jump at shows. I remember the name – Major! Father told me about it, frightful business... Frightful...'

Emily had to smile. 'Yes, I have been in shows before, but only small gymkhanas; nothing big or exciting. But Major was a very good jumper. We won quite a few rosettes and cups, but I couldn't go too far; we didn't have a horse box then. Dad used to hire a trailer if it was necessary.

'Yes, yes, I am sure he jumped well. Yes, I remember seeing you. Very sad that; to lose an old friend so tragically.' There was a few seconds' lull in the conversation. 'Well, I expect you are enjoying the horse box now. It's quite comfortable, isn't it?'

'Well, we haven't been anywhere special yet. My groom drives me over to a friend. Normally I would walk; it's not far. But Black Tulip is not so good on the road, is she? But we haven't been anywhere with the box yet apart from that.'

'Yes, I used to find she was a bit nervous in traffic.' There was a pause. 'But anyway, I'll send you the forms then, shall I?' The voice was clipped.

'Yes, please. And one for my friend, Jenny Ellis. I know she will want to enter.

'Oh good! Good! Want to get as many as I can. Who? Jenny who? Oh! Ellis, yes, OK.' Emily knew she was writing it down.

'Jenny Ellis, at Mayberry Farm.'

'Yes, yes, right; got all that. Good, look forward to seeing you, and of course Black Tulip. Bye now.' And then the line went dead.

'What did she want?' asked Liz, who was coming into the kitchen with a basket full of clothes for Mrs Porter to iron.

'It's a horse show that Sir James Bartram is organizing. I'm entering Black Tulip. I must tell Jenny she can enter too. Miss Bartram is sending the forms.'

'Getting a bit late for horse shows, isn't it? And too dark, surely!'

Emily was dialling Mayberry Farm. 'It's not till next March, Mum... Oh, hello!' It was Anita. 'Can I speak to Jenny, please?'

There were a few days left for practising in November. The frost was thick on the ground, and the mornings were dark, damp and cold. Jenny was able to get some practice in the evenings as the farm was lit up, but Emily could not ride Black Tulip over there, and for the sake of an hour it wasn't worth John boxing her up and driving them. Sometimes a watery sun would brighten the day, but without warmth, and then thick grey cloud and snow flurries would sweep across the fields and hedgerows on a bitter east wind. Towards the end of the month the wind dropped, and there was thick freezing fog.

Emily caught a cold and had to have a week off school. Her mother would not let her out in the yard in the dampness. John walked Black Tulip around the paddock in the morning and put her on a lunge during the day.

The following Monday morning the weather was no better, but Emily was going to school. She had gone out to talk to Tulip, but she did not ride. The fog was too thick. She spent about twenty minutes with Tulip, and then it was time to leave. She was wrapped up in a thick jacket and woollen scarf. As she walked to the end of the lane, the freezing fog closed in around her, so thick she almost had to feel her way. The familiar trees which she passed every day and the uneven stones in the lane were invisible as she made her way carefully and slowly, turning left when she eventually found the end of the lane and walked a few yards to the invisible bus stop. She stood waiting for the school bus. She stamped her feet. Her boots were warm, but the cold and dampness seeped in everywhere nipping at her toes and her gloved fingers. The tall trees that usually waved their branches and whispered on the breeze were now bare and motionless like shadowy monsters with a hundred twisted arms ready to grab at her. In this grey and silent world her imagination ran wild. She thought she saw people coming out of the mist, large animals like buffalo rushing towards her... There was no escape. She knew that somewhere out there in the denseness Major must be lurking and several times thought she saw him, a vague outline in the fog.

Suddenly she heard the hum of an engine. Dull orange lights came out of the greyness, a car driving slowly. As it came nearer she saw the driver, a man in a business suit leaning hard over the steering wheel, peering with intensity at the blank unknown space ahead of him. She wondered how far he would have to go. Her father, too, was out there somewhere on the road. He had left an hour earlier and may not yet have reached the office in Cambridge. She looked at her watch. The bus was ten minutes late. She decided that she would wait half an hour, and then go back home. Five minutes went by and then she heard the sound of a heavy engine grinding slowly. To her relief large dull beams of light shone though the gloom, and the school bus drew up alongside the pavement and stopped. The driver, Mr Canley, whom she saw every morning and knew every pupil by name, wished her a friendly 'Good morning, Emily!' Jenny was already on the bus; she had got on two stops before. They sat together as the bus crawled along in the thick swirling fog.

The three-week Christmas break was well into its second week. Emily woke early. She lay in bed. Today seemed different, though she did not know why. The world outside her blue velvet curtains seemed quiet. Normally she could hear the odd car pass at the end of the lane, and the birds were usually singing. She supposed that it was frosty again; it had been like that all the week. She gingerly put her arm out of bed. The air felt cold despite the central heating, and she quickly put it back under the covers again. She snuggled under the covers for a few more minutes, then decided she must make a big effort to get up. She flung back the bedclothes, jumped out of bed quickly, straight into her slippers, and grabbed her warm red dressing-gown that she had left on the arm of the chair, wrapping it round her. She went to the window and pulled back the curtains. It was foggy again; she could not see ten yards! Oh, England was drab and dreary at this time of the year! She did not know which she hated the most, the fog or the snow. Either way, it wasn't pleasant to ride in, and she wanted so much to ride Black Tulip. She hadn't been out with her for a whole week. Although Tulip had grown a thick coat to cope with the winter weather, it was too cold for her to stay out.

She went down to the kitchen. Her mother was making coffee, and it smelled good. Her father was having a cooked breakfast. He was just saying that he hoped he could get into the office with the weather so bad. A week or so ago it took two hours to do a thirty-minute journey.

John opened the kitchen door, just to say that he had arrived. The freezing air and swirling fog swept into the warm kitchen, and Mike Peters told him to come in quick and shut the door.

'Do you want a cup of coffee, John, before you start in the yard?' Liz was automatically getting another mug from the shelf. She knew he wouldn't say no. John never refused a cup of coffee. In fact, she seemed to spend her life making coffee for everyone.

'How bad is it out there, John? I haven't been out there this morning.'

'It's pretty bad, Mr Peters. You can't see a hand in front of yer face, its that bad. 'Ope it clears tomorra. Got me sister and brother-in-law and their three kids comin' down from London for Christmas. 'Ope this weather gets a bit better, then the kids can get out into the garden. Don't want 'em running round the 'ouse all day!'

'Yes, I've got *my* sister and *her* husband and family coming on Christmas Day,' said Mike. 'Luckily they are only about fifteen minutes away. They could walk if it's this bad, but hopefully, it will clear during the day.' He finished his breakfast, then left the table. 'Well, I must be off.'

'Mike!' Liz was surprised. 'You're not really going out in this! Are you?'

'Well, I have to *try* and get to the office, darling! Can't let a little bit of weather stop me.'

'But it's like pea soup out there. You'll never see to drive.'

'I have to try. It's probably just worse here in the village. It's bound to be better on the main road.' He kissed her on the cheek, and then kissed Emily, and went out into the hall to put on his overcoat and scarf. They heard the front door close, and then the garage door opening and the car engine roaring into life.

'He's crazy!' Liz shook her head as she cleared the table.

'It's pretty bad out there, Mrs Peters,' said John. 'I don't think he will get very far.'

'Oh well, John,' Liz sighed. 'I can't stop him; if he says he's going, he'll go.' Liz gave Emily some coffee and toast, and began to clear the rest of the breakfast things. John was still standing by the back door with his coffee mug. He drained it and said he must get on, although he did not know what he could do. He had fed Black Tulip already and broken the ice in her water bucket before he came in. A hinge needed fixing on the tack-room door, and he would give the saddle and bridle

72

another good polish, sweep up the yard and salt it to clear the ice. Thanking Liz for the coffee, he went out of the back door.

Two minutes later, Mike came back, rubbing his hands and making shivering noises. 'It's impossible out there, can't see a thing, much worse than a few weeks ago, but I'll try again later. Any more coffee, darling?'

The fog lifted the next day. The weather, though still cold, was warmer than it had been, and the days were much brighter. The skies turned a pinkish grey, and an east wind swept across the open fields.

Two days before Christmas, Emily woke to find the whole world white. It had snowed heavily in the night, and drifts had piled up against the fence where the east wind had swept across the fields in the dead of night. Snow clung two inches high on the bare branches of the trees, smooth and flawless like the icing her mother had put on the Christmas cake. From the window it looked wonderful; she wanted to be the first person to make footprints in the crisp whiteness. She showered and dressed quickly in a thick sweater and jeans, and taking her camera with her she went downstairs and pulled on her rubber boots that were by the back door.

'Morning, darling. Cold out there!' Liz pulled a face as Emily walked out of the back door.

She smiled. 'Wonderful, isn't it, Mum. I will be back in a minute, just going out to wish Tulip an early Happy Christmas.'

'Wonderful?' Liz frowned. 'How can thick snow be wonderful?' She shook her head, but Emily had already gone.

She walked out into the paddock, her boots sinking deep into the whiteness. Looking back at her footmarks, she smiled: it was like being the first person on the moon. She made her way to the yard and to Tulip, who nodded over the half-stable door with friendly brown eyes as she approached. Emily stroked her black nose and told her that it was nearly Christmas, the first she was to spend here at Rosemary Lodge, and she gave her a few pony nuts and a carrot. Her soft lips sank into Emily's hand, and she munched with relish.

Emily spent most of the morning with John, helping to clear

the snow away in the yard. It soon got them both warm. Tulip watched over the stable door while John emptied bags of salt onto the cobblestones to stop it from being so slippery. The girl in the supermarket had said that it was in short supply. She had sold too many bags of salt, and now only two bags were allowed per customer, so he spread it thinly.

Christmas Day was bright. Overnight there had been another thick fall of snow, and a light-grey sky tinged with pink, promised more snow to come. It was the sort of day every child dreams Christmas Day to be – a fairyland of snow and bright sunshine. Emily showered and went down to breakfast with her parents. They had toast and coffee, and exchanged their Christmas presents, which had been put under the tree. Then she went out into the yard.

'Wrap up, Emily! It's cold out there,' Liz called, as if she didn't already know.

It *was* cold, but it looked so pretty. Snow topped the broom and the wheelbarrow; it edged the gutters and clung to one side of the drainpipe. The windowsills were imprinted with birds' feet. It looked like a Christmas card; all it needed was a horse, a carriage and a lady in a crinoline bonnet and muff; she had been sending out cards like this for weeks. She smiled as a robin came and perched on the handle of the wheelbarrow. She shivered. Mum was right: it was cold; it was freezing even in a big roll-necked sweater and anorak. But it had been years since it had snowed like this on Christmas Day, and it did look wonderful.

John came into the yard.

'Merry Christmas, John! It looks pretty, but it's cold.'

'Merry Christmas, Miss Emily. Yeah, it's certainly nippy. How's she doing?'

'OK, I think, but I have only just come out here.' The water bucket is solid ice. Could you break it, please? Thanks for coming up this morning, John. I didn't expect you, but I am grateful of course, but you shouldn't have bothered.'

'Oh, no problem, Miss; won't take long just to muck her out. No matter what day it is, Christmas Day or any other day, for animals it's all same; they still 'as to be fed and watered. Can't

74

feed themselves.' He had said this many times before. 'And in any case, I am pleased to do it, you know that.' He smiled and winked. 'Glad to get out of the 'ouse for an hour, got me sister and brother-in-law staying with their three kids, and there's paper up to the ceiling where they have opened all their presents. And Debbie is in the kitchen, battling with the turkey. I don't want to get involved. Looking forward to me Christmas dinner though!' He winked again.

She smiled. 'We have Uncle Ross and Aunt Pamela and my cousins coming for lunch, and Mum is in there now sorting out the turkey. Did you get some nice presents, John?'

'Yeah, got some new slippers and a tie, and aftershave and stuff. Did you?'

'Yes,' she beamed. 'All sorts. New dress, make-up, perfume and Dad bought Tulip a new rug. I'll bring it out after Christmas. She will be a very smart girl, won't you, Tulip?' Tulip nodded her head up and down, and both Emily and John laughed. 'I am sure that she understands everything I say. Could you bring her out for me, John, and hold her? I got a new camera, too, and I want to take some pictures of her in the snow.

John brought Black Tulip out, standing her in the yard while Emily took photographs of him holding Black Tulip and he took photos of Emily and Tulip. She jumped up onto her back and said she wished she could ride her.

'Well, you can,' said John, 'if you just take it easy. Just take her around the paddock a few times.' He saddled her, and Emily walked her around carefully, while John watched and took some more photos. They trotted round for just about ten minutes and got a little warmer, but Emily did not feel comfortable. She was afraid that Tulip might slip and break a leg. She rubbed her hands together. It was so cold her nose and her ears were bright red. She brought Tulip in, and John unsaddled her and rugged her up to keep her warm again. Her breath came out in great clouds of white steam as he turned her and put her back into the stable and she nodded over the door to him as if grateful. John grabbed the broom and started to clear the snow from the yard.

Emily said, 'No, John! It's Christmas Day, and there is no need to do it; it can wait.' She took the broom away from him, standing it back near the wheelbarrow, and there was nothing else he could do. So, wishing her a Merry Christmas again, he went off home to join his family.

Aunt Pamela and Uncle Ross, and their children, Gavin and Heather, arrived mid-morning. They hadn't seen each other for months, even though they only lived about fifteen minutes away. They shed their boots, coats, gloves and scarves. They had been trudging through the snow, which had started falling heavily again and still lay thick on the country roads.

'I could have brought the car,' said Ross. 'The local farmer has cleared the road up our end, but I thought it safer to walk. It will get worse towards the evening. The farmers are petty good, aren't they? Trouble is, these country roads are not wide enough for the snow plough, and they don't bother to grit them either, do they?'

'No, but the snow won't last long,' said Mike, always the optimist. 'Be gone in couple of days. Anyway, it's nice to have a white Christmas for a change. Now what will you have to drink?'

There was a lot of excitement as the two families exchanged Christmas presents, from under the Christmas tree sparkling with silver tinsel and lights. They sat round the roaring fire in the lounge gossiping. Mike was pouring drinks, and the smell of roast turkey was wafting from the kitchen. Soon they were sitting round the table, eating and drinking and pulling crackers. After lunch Mike and Ross enjoyed a cigar, and the aroma filled the house. Liz said she liked the smell, and it was special as Mike only ever smoked one on Christmas Day. Their enjoyment continued long into the afternoon and into the early evening, when they settled down with full stomachs and drowsy with wine in front of the fire to watch the television. Both the men fell asleep.

Emily was telling her cousins about Black Tulip. They were interested as they both had horses of their own. Uncle Ross was a gamekeeper on a large forestry estate, so they had plenty of places to ride. Emily said that she had to go out and feed Tulip and tuck her up for the night, and Gavin said he would like to see the horse. Emily led the way to the kitchen door, and they trudged out in their boots through thick snow to the

76

stable yard. It was freezing, specially after the warmth of the house, and the snow was still falling fast in big flakes. Heather said the golden glow from the kitchen light with the snowflakes falling in front of them made her think of a fairy-story, and she could imagine Santa Claus riding across the sky in his sleigh, with the reindeer galloping before him. Emily said she had feelings like that, too, and that Christmas evenings always seemed so much more magical than any other evening in the year.

Gavin, who was Emily's age, smiled. 'Come on, you two dreamers. You will have to wait another year for sleigh bells and reindeer flying across the sky. Santa came last night, remember! Come on, let's have a look at the horse. It's freezing out here.'

The girls giggled. Emily switched on the yard light and took them over to where Black Tulip was rugged up and warm in her stable. She went to get Tulip's feed, while Gavin broke the ice on the water bucket.

Gavin patted her neck. 'She's beautiful, Emily. How long have you had her?'

'Only since the summer, and she's wonderful. I've entered her for a show in March. It will be our first time out together, although she has been to lots of big shows before. She knows her way around, so she will probably teach me something!'

'Have you entered for Wickerbrook Hall?' Emily nodded.

'We've entered that too.' Gavin smiled. 'Should be quite a big day. I was with Louise Bartram the other night. There was a whole group of us. I belong to Young Farmers. You should join. We have some good evenings, and days out, too. Have you met her?'

'Louise Bartram? No,' said Emily. 'But I have talked to her on the phone. She's a bit jolly-hockey-sticks, isn't she? But very pleasant.' She smiled. 'Black Tulip used to belong to her. Dad brought her from Sir James.'

Gavin looked surprised. 'Oh, this is the horse. Of course, this is Black Tulip.' He spoke as if he knew the horse well. 'You know, Heather, I told you, Louise was selling the horse. She has Pico now, hasn't she?' He turned back to Emily, eyebrows raised, as if suddenly remembering. 'It must have been awful losing Major, Emily.'

Emily shook her head sadly. It's taken me a long time to come to term with it. I don't think I'll ever really get over it.' She shuddered. Gavin thought it was the cold weather until he saw the look on her face and the tears in her eyes. He glanced at his sister, flickering his eyes with the slightest nod of his head, and he and Heather both went back to patting Tulip and saying how lovely she was. He was glad the horse was there. He thought Emily was going to break down, and really start to cry, and he couldn't bear to see girls crying; it made him feel embarrassed, he never knew what to do.

Emily sniffed. Her nose was tingling, but she knew she must not let the tears fall. 'Yes, well... In any case, this is the first time that I'll have entered a show for a long time, and the first really big one ever. You see, we never had a horse box before, and I only ever took Major...' She faltered and bit her bottom lip. '...to local shows. We used to walk everywhere. But Dad bought a horse box from Sir James as well. Well, really Sir James lent it to us to start with, just so I could get around, but it's so much better than the old trailer we used to hire for special occasions.'

It was getting colder in the yard, and they moved to go in. Heather looked across the yard. 'Where is the other horse, Emily?'

She looked surprised. 'I haven't got another horse. Why?'

'Well, a horse has been round here. Look at the hoof prints in the snow. It must have been recently. It's still snowing, and they would have covered up by now.'

Emily looked, wide-eyed; the prints trailed from the paddock and stopped at Major's stable. She had a quick intake of breath. She didn't want to go into the story of a ghost horse. 'Oh, I expect John has been round and let Tulip out...'

'But surely,' said Gavin, 'the hoof prints would be on this side of the yard, when he put her back, wouldn't they? And why would he take her out on an evening like this anyway?'

Emily had to think quickly. 'I don't know. John does a lot of funny things. But, of course, you are right...' Emily considered for only a moment. 'Maybe the snow has drifted more on this side.' She shivered, then said quickly, 'Gosh, its cold out here, isn't it? Come on, let's go inside.' They walked into the warmth. The kitchen was welcoming, and her mother was there making

78

tea and offering them Christmas cake and mince pies. Nothing more was said about the hoof prints in the snow.

Mike was wrong. The last of the snow finally disappeared only at the end of January, melting into dirty brown slush that was thrown up onto the hedgerows by the slow-moving traffic. The grass in the fields began to show through green and lush in patches under a bright sunshine-filled sky, but there was no warmth. The freezing-cold weather continued though February, and the roads became icy again. March came. Buds sprouted and leaves uncurled on the trees after a long hard winter. Birds began to build their nests again, and rabbits came up out of their burrows and began to scamper about the fields, the first daylight they had seen for months. Shrubs flowered in the gardens, and bulbs pushed their way up through the damp dark soil to develop into yellow dancing daffodils, blowing their trumpets to awaken the new springtime and nearly losing their heads in the gusty March winds. Tulips stood proud and tall, bending away from the wind that undressed them of their petals, leaving black seed heads on sturdy green stalks. The sun shone, encasing the earth in its golden warmth and drawing it upwards. It was as if the whole world was being reborn, coming alive for another year.

8

Although the early-morning sun shone from the clear blue sky, a chill March wind swept across the paddock. A sudden gust almost took Emily and her mother off their feet as they walked into the yard to join John. He had boxed Tulip and Henry, who had spent the night in the stable next door, and was to drive them in the horse box first to Mayberry Farm to pick up Jenny and her mother, Carol, and then to Wickerbrook Hall. He had been up since the crack of dawn, preparing the horses for the show. He had brushed and plaited Henry's mane and tail, and then he had brushed Black Tulip until her satin coat shone like a mirror. He had just finished boxing them, when Emily and Liz arrived with the baskets of food and drink that would last them all day. The horse box was fitted with a small but comfortable living space: plush royal-blue seats were fixed either side of a small polished wood table that could seat four people; short pale-blue curtains hung from the windows and to one side was a kitchen, with a small calor-gas cooker and a sink. Under the small draining board was a fridge, and a tank that held enough water for all day. Liz had added a microwave oven, which was handy for heating snacks.

An hour later horse boxes were rolling in, one behind the other, through the farm gate at the side of Wickerbrook Hall. They were stopped by a bowler-hatted usher in a brown tweed jacket, who pointed across the field to the direction that they should take, then were waved into a parking space by another bowler-hatted usher.

When they arrived, there were already about seventy horseboxes. Emily thought Louise Bartram would be pleased with the turnout, and still they rolled in. They were parked around the perimeter of the field, facing the main arena. There were three other smaller rings, one for pony jumping, one for showing and one for practice. A dog show ring was set up some distance away.

Most people had their tack out and were giving their horses and ponies a last-minute grooming. The main-ring events would start early, and the jumping and showing and judging would go on all day until dusk. At the moment there was a hushed atmosphere in the field. Everyone was busy working: horses were being got out of the boxes; others being brushed and made ready for the first event of the day. In the practice ring, two girls were busy putting their ponies though their paces. A woman was setting up a caravan with an open side and a counter, and there was an ice-cream van travelling across the grass looking for a suitable place to park. Emily shivered thinking he would not sell too much, but, then, who could tell? People ate ice cream at any time.

As soon as they had parked, the girls jumped out and went round to the back to unload Henry and Tulip. Soon they were like everyone else, giving their horses water and a last-minute grooming. Liz put on the kettle and boiled water for coffee, to warm them all up, and Carol Ellis put bread in the toaster. A few minutes later they were sitting at the table having breakfast. John sat on the doorstep beside Tulip and Henry, who were tethered, a mug of coffee in one hand, a plate of toast balanced on his knee. Afterwards the girls helped him with the saddles and bridles. There was an announcement that the first pony class was to start jumping in fifteen minutes and would riders please make their way to the number two ring. Both Jenny and Emily had an hour before their class in the main ring. Another announcement came over the loud speaker: the showing of ponies was about to start in ring number one, and would the owner of car number SAL 425 please move it as it is blocking the entrance, thank you. And would Mrs Jennifer Higgins please come to the commentary box... It was going to be a long day.

Horse boxes were still arriving. Emily guessed that by now there must be over two hundred parked and still they rolled in. Louise Bartram had done a good job. The noise and the excitement was now building up, as spectators, wrapped in warm hooded anoraks, big scarves, trousers and jeans, and boots, came to watch the events, regardless of the chilly March wind that whipped across the field. The chill of the morning kept the horses and ponies dancing and prancing on long slender legs. With the excitement and the atmosphere, they were eager to be ridden and part of the scene.

The showing class got under way. The immaculately dressed riders paraded around the main ring in front of the stout middle-aged judge Mrs Jennifer Higgins, who was dressed in a short navy-blue jacket, silk floral dress, and a light raincoat that was a size too small for her and could not be buttoned up. She kept her hand firmly placed on a navy straw hat with orange flowers on the front, which the strong cold wind threatened to lift off her head. Her thick 60-denier beige tights wrinkled at the ankles as she bent and stretched and plodded about in sensible brown flat lace-up shoes in the long tufty grass wet from the early morning dew. She surveyed the group of horses and riders before her with a critical eye and finally selected the best six out of the nine riders. These she called to the centre, then after some long consideration, rubbing of her chin and bending of her bulky body to look at the horses' legs, she finally picked the best three. Then with even more careful judgment she picked the best one: a sturdy grey named Gallant, owned and ridden by Mrs Maddever, who received a red rosette, a silver cup and prize money.

The photographer took a photo of Gallant and the other two horses, Jerome and Mellow Bird, and then all three filed out of the ring, Mrs Maddever proudly carrying her silver cup and smiling at her groom as she took hold of the bridle and gave Gallant a pat and praise. The announcement for the next event came over the speaker, just as the pony jumping class came to an end in the next ring.

Emily and Jenny were busy giving the last finishing touches to Black Tulip and Henry, with John's help of course. They were oiling their hooves to make them shine when Louise Bartram suddenly came up, introducing herself and shaking hands with both of them. It was the first time that she and Emily had actually met, although they had spoken on the phone several times since she had first called Emily about the horse show. By the way she chatted though, you would have thought that they were long-time close friends. She nodded to John, and then said good morning politely to both the mothers, as they poked their heads out of the door of the horse box. John smiled as he heard the bold and confident voice. He had expected a large woman with a large bosom, but she was small and slim, wearing blue jeans and a red roll-neck sweater, her long dark hair tied back in a pony tail with a red ribbon. She was not particularly good-looking, though; he would have described her as horsey.

She reached up to pat Black Tulip, saying, 'Hello, old girl! Remember me? We had some fun together, didn't we?' Her jolly-hockey-sticks voice, as Emily always put it, was sharp and precise. Tulip flicked her ears in recognition. Louise smiled. 'She looks good. Getting on well together, are you?' Emily nodded with a smile. 'Good, good!' Louise moved her head in a confident masculine way, which reminded Emily of Sir James. Then she suddenly turned to Henry, reaching up to pat his huge neck, saying what a fine specimen he was. Then she announced abruptly that she would have to dash as she was riding Pretty Polly very shortly and had to get changed. Pico, she said, she was jumping after lunch. Both Jenny and Emily remembered seeing Pico the time they had gone to Wickerbrook Hall, the day that they had first seen Black Tulip.

Louise bid them a brisk good day and good luck, and turned on her booted heels, marching away with a wave of her hand. There were smiles all round and, Emily and Jenny said they would make a point of watching Louise and Pico after lunch.

They finished off their last-minute grooming and went into the horse box to change into beige jodhpurs and white blouses, and black ties and jackets. What a treat it was! Before, they had struggled into jodhpurs in the back of the car or even in the trailer, but now their clothes were on hangers in the cupboard and there was a small bathroom with a full-length mirror behind the door. Such luxury! Now they both looked exactly alike, except for their hair, one dark and one fair, neatly tied up and put into hairnets under their black velvet helmets. They looked very smart. Both mums gave them a last-minute brush across the shoulders, and wished them good luck before they each mounted and walked quietly side by side to the gate of the jumping arena. There Emily was given the number 107 on a white card and Jenny, 103, which they tied around their waists with long tapes so that the number was on their backs for all to see.

There were several competitors waiting by the ringside. Mary

Clark, a friend from school, was ready with a good morning. Derek Milner touched the peak of his cap. There, too, was ever-so-superior Dominic Hadley. You couldn't help but notice him, though it was a marked fact that *he* noticed no one; they had never even seen him smile.

It was quiet at the ringside, and the horses reasonably still, but fidgeting as horses do, anxious to get on with the job. Emily had butterflies in her stomach. Here she was, on a new horse, her first time at a big show and, indeed, her first time at a show in over a year. But she was confident Black Tulip knew her way around, and Emily knew that once they got into the ring it would be up to them both.

The class started. There were eight competitors. Mary on Coolie was the first to go. She rode into the ring wearing a brown tweed jacket and a dark-brown velvet helmet, a contrast to Coolie who was a pale-tan Palomino. Horse and rider trotted around the ring getting into a canter before the bell went for the start. Throughout she rode steadily but knocked down the second-to-last jump. The speaker bellowed out, 'Four faults, four faults,' as Mary slowed Coolie to a walk.

Next was Dominic Hadley, on Silverspoon, a sixteen-hands dapple grey. Dominic was about twenty. He sat tall in the saddle, his back poker straight. His black riding jacket with a split either side at the back fitted him well and flapped over the saddle as he rode. His handsome bronzed face, half hidden under the peak of his helmet, was confident and stern with concentration. He was there to do a job; he was there to win. Well, you couldn't blame him for that; they were all there to win. And most of the time he did win, and was smug about it, too. Emily and Jenny had discussed him many times, Emily saying he was cocky and stuck up, too full of himself. But he was known for his riding ability, and no one could argue with that. Even Emily had to admit to herself that he was a good horseman and popular with the spectators. Today, as he entered the ring, everyone clapped, but he looked straight ahead, a man in his own world, acknowledging no one. If anyone got in his way she was convinced he would probably ride right over them, probably wouldn't even see them with his nose stuck so far up into the air.

He trotted round, straight-backed, head held high. He was a

showman in every sense of the word; even his horse seemed to look down on other horses. They got into a slow canter and, as the bell went for the start, he quickened the pace, taking the first jump with ease and then the next and the next, horse and rider in perfect unison. He finished with a cocky satisfied grin, as would anyone who had just had a perfect round, Emily secretly conceded. He raised his arms in the air to his groom, who was waiting at the ringside, as the clapping spectators cheered him out. He stretched his lean body forward to pat Silverspoon on the neck as the speaker proclaimed, 'Clear round, clear round'. Emily noticed his eyes twinkle under the peak of his helmet and the hint of a smile as he looked at her in passing, shrugging his right shoulder with a 'what else would you expect?' sort of attitude. She could have knocked him off the horse, the conceited devil.

The next announcement was for Jenny Ellis and Henry. Jenny rode the great and powerful bay slowly into the ring. She looked like a child on his back as he sidled a little until she got him into position. Then into a trot ... then a slow canter ... until the bell went for the start and Jenny rode him round the ring once again before jumping the first red-and-white painted poles, which he took easily. Henry loved to jump. He finished all six fences, and to her delight the announcement of 'clear round, clear round' boomed out from the hidden voice behind the microphone. Emily congratulated her with excitement.

Next a very bumptious boy named Peter Smith, on Speedo Kid, went into the ring. He was so sure that he would get a clear round and went charging round like a warrior going into battle. He knocked the first and second fences flat, then belted on to the finish, the horse coming to a skid as if it had fire under its hooves. He rode Speedo Kid out of the gate, scattering people and riders standing near. The loudspeaker said, 'Eight faults, eight faults.'

Then it was the turn of number 104, Alex Freemore.

Jenny and Emily exchanged glances at the name. 'Must be Harris Freemore's son,' Jenny remarked. He was a thin stick of a man, aged about twenty, with a thin face and a long nose, and gaunt good looks. He had to wait for the fences to be put up again, and then he was off; he rode well but unluckily just tipped the last fence.

'Four faults, four faults!' came the announcement.

Penny Blythe on Jubilee was next. Unfortunately, Jubilee also knocked down two fences and refused the next, and, having been disqualified walked out of the ring. Penny was very disappointed and almost in tears, by the look on her face.

Then the announcer said, '107, Emily Peters and Black Tulip.' Her mother and Jenny's mother were watching at the rail, Liz with her fingers crossed. Emily walked into the ring. Black Tulip was composed, head held high, proud and confident. She preened on the spot for the spectators; she had done this many times before. Emily squeezed her knees, Tulip got the signal and they began to trot round. Emily quickened the pace by shortening the rein then easing on the bit, and Tulip got into a slow, smooth canter around the perimeter of the ring. A hush went through the crowd as the bell rang for the start and around they went again. Coming up to the first set of poles, Black Tulip jumped high and clear, and there was just the soft scrunch of the leather from the saddle and the stirrups, and the huffing of Tulip's breath as they went on to take the next jump. The third was higher, but they flew over the red-and-white poles with ease. On and on, until they had cleared all six jumps.

'Clear round, clear round,' came the announcement from the loudspeaker. Liz let out her breath and uncrossed her fingers, turning with a big smile to Carol, who was equally pleased.

'Well done, Em!' Jenny was overjoyed for her friend. Sitting on Henry's back, she leaned over and they clasped hands as Emily came by.

'Yes, she went well, didn't she?' She smiled at Jenny then leaned forward, patting Tulip on the neck, stroking her ears and telling her she was a good girl.

Next, Helen Clements had a refusal at the third fence, and the horse threw her off. She wasn't hurt but decided not to go any further.

Knowing that there had been three clear rounds and that they would have to jump again, Emily straightened her helmet, pulled her gloves tighter onto her hands and took a deep breath to compose herself. She and Jenny had agreed quietly that they were ready to take on the conceited Dominic Hadley and his equally conceited horse, Silverspoon. They waited for their names to be called, Jenny and Emily on horseback standing quite close together, and Dominic Hadley, with a superior sneer on his face, standing a little apart from them.

As she waited, people crowded round the main ring to watch the jump-off. In the background, horses were being ridden to classes or just finishing and walking away in all directions. Some of the riders looked pleased, winning rosettes, some disappointed, as their mounts had gone well, but not well enough. One ring had another showing class in progress, and, in another, jumping was just about to start. Elsewhere, children laughed as they watched clowns in brightly coloured suits, with white faces and red noses, making animals by tying long thin balloons into knots. Others let out screams and shouts of joy as they rolled and tumbled on a bouncy castle. On the far side of the field, children were enjoying pony rides, and there was a horse and carriage.

The caravan selling tea, sandwiches, hot dogs and hamburgers was busy. The smell of the onions wafted across the field and under her nose, making her tummy rumble; she promised herself a hamburger when she and Tulip had finished. To her astonishment, a long straggling line of people were queuing at the ice-cream van. Along the sides of the field, stalls and tents were now open for business, where people could buy anything from plastic water buckets, brooms and shovels, to new saddles and bridles and brushes and combs, saddle cloths and riding jackets, hats and boots, thick, warm anoraks to keep out the cold, and brightly coloured horse rugs. One tent advertised the skills of an animal painter: 'Your horse caught in paint by brilliant artist'. Louise Bartram had thought of everything!

Faces appeared and disappeared as the crowd swarmed like a sea of ants in the chill wind. Children mostly unseen carried an array of coloured balloons, bobbing and wavering on long strings above the heads of the crowds. Toddlers sat in push-chairs and buggies, faces smeared with ice cream and candy floss, or fingers sticky with doughnuts oozing jam. People crowded by in all directions, and horses and riders walked amongst them. Close to, now, were hundreds of spectators, leaning on or standing around the outer fences of the main ring, waiting for the jump-off to start.

Emily came back to reality as the bell sounded for the first jump off...

Major had been standing, unseen, by the front entrance gate in the field at Wickerbrook Hall since early in the morning. The horse boxes rolled in and around him and even over him. Two horses near the gate had shied, one rider managing to control his animal, but the other had pulled the young man handling him almost halfway across the field.

Major had followed John in the horse box when they set out from Rosemary Lodge. He looked out now onto the busy scene. He could see Miss Emily on Black Tulip waiting with Jenny and Henry from way across the field. He had always liked Henry. They had got on well together; they had walked and trotted and galloped and jumped together for years. And now he was watching them jump for the first time round, and he wished he could do it, too. He had been to many shows, and he had felt proud receiving a red rosette, especially when Miss Emily had displayed it over his stable door, and he had received more praise and extra carrots. But now those days were gone. Still, he was happy. He pricked up his ears: he could see that it was time for Black Tulip to win extra carrots and make Miss Emily very proud once again. He walked slowly over to the show ring, carefully standing a little way from the gate, away from the horses. Why couldn't he have a go, if he wanted? What harm would it do?

Emily wished Jenny good luck as her friend urged Henry forward. As he entered the gate, Henry shied a little. Jenny straightened him and scolded him, then told him gently, 'Come on, Henry! Don't let me down!' She trotted him and then got him into a canter. Henry, sensing Major behind him, took the first few jumps at speed, so as to get away, but it was when they came to the last jump that he saw Major out of the corner of his eye, as he came up alongside him. It gave him a fright and he misjudged the jump, just tapping his back hooves on the top of the pole. It rolled and hovered for a second and then fell, to aaaahs from the crowd.

'Four faults, four faults,' came the announcement.

Jenny came out of the ring, wrinkling her nose and a disappointed look on her face. But it didn't stop her from patting Henry; he had done his best, after all.

Silverspoon was the next to jump. Dominic Hadley adjusted his dark-blue helmet over his raven-black hair, and confidently took up the reins with his strong, bronzed hands. A secret smile of self-confidence played across his face.

'Conceited devil!' Emily muttered to herself.

He rode Silverspoon quietly into the ring, his rising trot so smooth, so perfect, the envy of every rider. For all her dislike of him, Emily had to admit that he was brilliant; there was no way that you could fault him. The bell went for the start, and horse and rider trotted round again, calm and composed, and then broke into a slow canter, in perfect unison. There was a low mumble from the crowd as the pace quickened and they easily took the first jump. A hush came over the spectators, all that could be heard was the clean crunch of polished leather and the thud of Silverspoon's hooves and the regular huffing of his breath as the pair took each jump smoothly. They finished to loud clapping from the spectators and the announcement of 'Clear round, clear round.'

He still wore the complacent look on his handsome face, and, as he passed Emily, a slight smile caught the corners of his mouth. He gave her a small wink and dipped his head as if to say, 'Beat me if you can.' His attitude puzzled her. She had ridden against him before, on Major, and she had come second, on more than one occasion. Emily just glared back. No one had beaten him, but he had never acknowledged the fact that she had done well to even come second. Most people shook hands after a jump-off, but he didn't even stay for a minute, so she had never had the chance to congratulate him for winning. He had always walked straight off, with that smug look that said, 'I've done a good job, don't bother me!' On the other hand, she supposed, he had every reason to be smug, for no one could deny he was a super horseman. Whenever his name was mentioned, people gathered round just to see him ride; they knew full well that he would win. He had no competition, except, perhaps, for his brother, Graham, who was equally as good but who never entered the same class. And then, as she and Jenny had agreed between themselves, they were both handsome.

The announcement came. It was their turn. Emily's heart leapt, and she had butterflies in her stomach. She took a breath; she had to get a grip on herself; she didn't want to let Black Tulip down. She knew she would be able to feel her nervous tension. She took another deep breath as she heard Jenny say, 'Good luck, Em.'

Emily spoke quietly to Tulip as she rode her gently into the ring: 'Now come on, Tulip, good girl, we have to get a clear round. Don't let me down now.' Tulip's ears twitched. 'We have to win this time.' Tulip knew what Emily was saying. She could feel the determination and the tension on her back as they walked into the ring. She trotted round once, and then she felt the firmly confident squeeze of Emily's knees as the bell went for the start. Emily tightened the reins a little as she cantered up to the first jump and then let her have her head. They flew over easily. The watching spectators were silent. Emily lifted Tulip high at each jump, and then she let out her breath, as the announcement echoed across the field: 'Clear round, clear round.' Then it was announced that there was to be a jump-off against the clock, between Silverspoon and Black Tulip.

'Well done, Em!' Jenny smiled. She was still mounted on Henry, standing near the entrance to the ring. John congratulated Emily, giving Tulip a friendly pat on the neck, and Carol turned to Liz, saying how well the horse had done.

Dominic Hadley sidled up on Silverspoon, with a rare smile. The horse circled, swishing his tail, as arrogant as his master.

'Well done!' he grinned, his eyebrows rising with an affected sneer. Emily could almost hear him adding, 'But you haven't won yet!'

It was a slight shock to her that he had actually lowered himself to speak to her. She lifted her chin, and her pink lips parted in a small gasp. Out of the corner of her eye she saw Jenny grimace with surprised amazement. Emily didn't get a chance to answer. The announcement came that the jump-off against the clock was about to start. Emily Peters and Black Tulip, the announcer declared, were to go first, adding some comment about letting ladies go first. Dominic Hadley inclined his head with a polite grin, his eyes twinkling, as if to say he agreed with the sentiment.

Emily tossed her head with tight-lipped determination, and then clicked her tongue and lifted the rein. Tulip knew the signal and walked serenely into the ring. Tulip was composed, knowing what she had to do, and was ready to trot when asked. Emily shortened the reins, quickening the pace and asking her to canter. The bell went, and over the first jump they went, and then the next and the next, flying high, and Emily could feel the power beneath her and the tension in the crowd. The only sound that of Black Tulip's breath huffing and her dainty hooves as they lifted and then thudded down onto the grass on the other side of the poles. Suddenly, as Black Tulip came to the next fence, Emily felt her flinch as she had done before in the paddock. Tulip lifted her head, but took the jump and was on her way to the next. 'No, Major! Don't! Don't!' Emily growled under her breath. She had guessed it was him, and at the sharpness of her voice, he slowed down, veering away and dropping back from Tulip's sight. He cantered right through the fence, unseen by the watching spectators, ploughing right through them. Then he came back into the ring behind Tulip as she cleared the last of the poles to a roar of applause from the crowd. Emily noticed as she came quickly out of the ring that some of the other horses, including Henry and Coolie, moved away uneasily, tossing their heads and whickering. Coolie gave a small whinny, but their riders did not seem to notice. Emily was worried and did not hear the time she had clocked.

Jenny was ready with congratulations, but saw the look of consternation on her friend's face. 'What's up, Em? You did so well, what's the matter?'

Emily spoke out of the side of her mouth, as she came level with Henry. 'Major's here ... I was lucky to get a clear round.'

'Really, Em!' Jenny looked about her fearfully. 'I didn't notice anything.'

'He nearly put Tulip off her stride at the second to last.' She also looked about her as if expecting to see him. Tulip was still a bit agitated, but soon calmed down as Emily smoothed her neck and patted her. 'I don't know where he is now, but he's here.'

A new announcement came over the loudspeaker. It was time

91

for Silverspoon to jump. Dominic was about to go into the ring, when for no reason, Silverspoon suddenly reared, neighing and flaying his forelegs. Horses and spectators near the gate moved quickly out of the way. Dominic Hadley was totally taken by surprise but, being an experienced horseman, managed to control Silverspoon after a few minutes. He rode him on into the ring, but the horse was still clearly agitated, tossing his head, his eyes wild and showing white. He shook his head, lifting it high as if trying to get the bit from his mouth and break free. It seemed that he did not want to go, but Dominic Hadley had him under control, urging him on with a slap of the crop on his hindquarters.

Emily glanced at Jenny, her heart in her mouth for fear that Dominic Hadley would fall. Only she and Jenny knew the reason for Silverspoon's behaviour. They looked at each other wide-eyed, holding their breath. What could they say or do? Who would believe that the ghost of a horse was in the ring?

Dominic Hadley got Silverspoon into order, the horse's head whiplashing from side to side in a frenzy. Finally, he managed to straighten him up and get him into a trot, as the bell went for the start, and he was now into a slow canter, coming towards the first fence... He jumped it clear and raced on to the second. Emily relaxed as he cleared it again, then raced on to the third.

At this moment, Tulip sidled, bumping into Henry, and lifted her head with a small whinny her eyes white with fear. Henry, too, stepped back, lifting his head. Emily felt the tension and held the mare firmly. She glanced at Jenny, who tightened her own grip on Henry's nervous movements. Emily felt sick as she watched Silverspoon falter at the third fence. She saw his eyes roll, the whites showing fear. He became frantically wild, shying away, whinnying, as if in pain. Emily clamped her hand rigidly to her mouth, every muscle in her body taut, seeing this beautiful animal so afraid. It was pitiful to watch. The magnificent Silverspoon was crumpling and cringing like a frightened mouse!

Dominic managed to get him over the third fence, but he knocked down one pole, and the horse raced wildly on to the fourth, as if galloping for his life. He refused the jump, veering away to the right, but Dominic straightened him up and urged

92

him on and they crashed right through the next jump, sending the poles flying into the air. Dominic was hanging half out of the saddle as the horse raced uncontrollably on to the next jump and refused again, flinging his rider right over his neck and onto the grass. Dominic lay flat on his back, still holding on to the rein, as the horse backed away wildly, pulling him to his feet. Luckily he was unhurt, and Dominic, determined that the horse would not get the better of him, managed to gather the reins and swing himself back up into the saddle, much to the approval of the clapping, cheering and gasping crowd. Patting and soothing Silverspoon a little, he rode out of the ring at a quick pace. He was clearly stunned and looked embarrassed as he caught Emily's eye. She was amazed to find that she actually felt sorry for this conceited devil, who, only a moment ago, had been full of his usual panache and egotism. The thought that she had won, and actually beaten the great Dominic Hadley, had not yet occurred to her.

But Dominic's trials were not over yet. As Charlie Fenwick, his groom, came to take the bridle, the horse suddenly reared in fright, neighing loudly and scattering onlookers in all directions. Charlie, too, ducked out of the way of the flaying hooves, and Silverspoon took off at a gallop across the show ground, with Dominic still on his back. There were screams and shouts as the horse charged in amongst the crowds. Dominic shouted frantic warnings, as horse and rider were weaving in and out of the terror-struck people. There was one terrifying moment when the horse jumped a buggy with a child in it being pushed by its mother, though, miraculously, no one was hurt. Finally, he took a high hedge near the parked horse boxes like a winner of the Grand National and disappeared from sight. There were sighs of relief and angry voices amongst the crowd in the wake of Silverspoon. They had never seen anything like if before. Emily glanced at Jenny and mouthed: 'Major'.

The announcer said that Silverspoon had been disqualified.

Just then, as the commotion was dying down, the contestants were called into the ring again. Unsurprisingly, it was Emily and Black Tulip, Jenny and Henry, and Mary Clark on Coolie, who stood in the middle of the ring and received their rosettes from the judge. Emily shook the judge's hand absent-mindedly, her eyes and her mind elsewhere, looking for Dominic Hadley and hoping that he was not hurt and lying in a ditch some-where. She was also expecting to see Silverspoon wandering around the show ground alone, and she felt responsible. She took the red rosette she was handed, and deftly stuck it into Tulip's bridle. Mary shook hands with Jenny and leaned over to shake Emily's hand and congratulate her. Then they stood with smiles while the photographer first snapped all three together and then snapped them individually. Black Tulip stood quite still, her head held high, and Emily felt so proud: the first time out together and they had done so well! It felt good having beaten Dominic Hadley, but she also had the uncomfortable feeling that she had not won fairly. She looked around her cautiously as Black Tulip began to prance and sidle. Her ears went flat to her head, and she shied away, recoiling back. Emily looked to her left and then to her right; she knew Major was near, but as usual she saw nothing. She patted Tulip to soothe her and felt her calm down, as Major walked away unseen.

The girls were very pleased with themselves, as they walked the horses back to the horse box, followed by John and their mothers. There were smiles and congratulations from spectators in the crowd as they passed.

'I felt sorry for that guy, Hadley,' Emily confided to her friend. 'He is usually so good, and so proud. I always wanted to beat him, but I didn't want to beat him like this. It wasn't fair, but what could I say? "Excuse me! But do you know there's a ghost chasing you?"'

Jenny laughed. 'Well, at least you'd get some reaction from him. I, presume he speaks English!' she said sarcastically. 'But I'm forgetting. He did speak to someone today. You! I think he was giving you the eye.'

'Don't be so stupid, Jen. Why would he give me a second look? He's too damned conceited to notice me or anyone else, for that matter.'

'But you like him, though.' Jenny lifted her eyebrows comically.

'No! I don't!' A smile caught the corners of Emily's mouth, though she tried not to let it show. 'He *is* good-looking though... Then, changing the subject, she said: 'But I'm really sorry I beat you, Jen.' She jumped down, handing the reins to John, and came round under Tulip's neck to give her a pat and a rub on the nose.

'Oh, I was pleased for you, Em. First time out with her. It just shows that all the practice pays off. And, in any case, someone has to win! Henry has won so many times before, and he didn't mind coming second, 'Did you, Hen?' She put on a silly voice and then kissed the velvet tip of his nose. 'But if they are going to keep beating us, we will have to go into another class, won't we? What do, you think, eh?' He huffed as if to say 'yes'. Jenny smiled across at Emily, then reached up to rub Henry's ears and stroke the side of his face.

They were silent for a while. Then Emily grinned and said, 'That Hadley guy felt so stupid, didn't he? You could see the look on his face.' She broke into a fit of giggles. 'I don't think anything like that has ever happened to him before. Oh dear, he wasn't so cocky then, was he? But I couldn't help feeling a bit sorry for him. I felt like telling him that it wasn't the horse's fault...

Jenny laughed. 'He didn't stay around long enough for you to say anything, did he?' They burst into fits of laughter.

'No, the last I saw was the horse's back legs going over the hedge and Hadley's backside, like a jockey's, on top.' The girls were doubled up with laughter.

John, who was close to them, asked them what the big joke was. But just as he did so Henry lifted his head and began to shy away.

Both girls stopped laughing and looked at each other. They stopped feeling afraid, however, and soon they broke into a giggle again as they went to pat their horses and soothe them with softly spoken words.

'Looks, like he's here again,' Jenny remarked.

'Yeah!' Emily nodded, still with a chuckle.

John looked up. 'Don't tell me it's Major?'

Later, leaving John in charge of watering the horses, the girls and their mothers wandered around the sideshows. Emily thought she spied Dominic Hadley going through the crowds, now on foot, but she was not sure; she did not mention it to Jenny.

The chill wind still blew across the open space of the field. And they were glad to get back to the horse box out of the cold for hot mugs of soup. It was well into the afternoon when the photographer came to deliver the photographs he had taken of them earlier that morning. He handed the large buff envelopes to Jenny, who was nearest to the door, and Liz paid him. The girls were anxious to see them. Jenny was the first to open her envelope. She smiled, as she handed the photos to her mother across the table. 'Oh look, Mum, they're good! What're yours like Em...?' She stopped in mid-sentence. 'Em, what's the matter?'

Emily's face was ashen. She was staring at the photograph, her mouth open. She slowly looked up at Jenny, handing her a photo, as if in slow motion. Jenny looked at the photo and gasped.

Liz was at the stove with her back to them but now she turned quickly, the kettle still in her hand. 'What's the matter?'

Jenny handed her the photo. 'Oh!' she gasped. 'Oh my goodness! John! John! *Quick!* Look at this!' She went to the door to call him. John stumbled in through the door, alarmed by the urgency of Liz's voice.

'Blimey!' He took off his cap and scratched his balding head. 'How did that 'appen?' Carol took the photo from him.

'He was in the ring with me,' said Emily, taking the photo from Carol and looking at the photo of herself on Black Tulip. There, standing a little to the side of her, was Major, looking quite immaculate, although he was somehow faded, almost grey. There was no doubting. It was him.

9

It was late into the evening and Liz and Emily were watching a film on the television, waiting for Mike to come home. He had left a note earlier in the evening, saying that he had to go to a business dinner and hoped to be home about eleven thirty.

Emily stretched. 'Are you tired, darling?' asked Liz. 'Why don't you go up to bed. It's been a very tiring day.'

'You're right, I am tired, but I don't think I can sleep. I want to show Dad that photo.'

'You could show it to him in the morning.'

'No, he won't have time to look in the morning. Anyway, I think I'll go out and see if Tulip's all right.'

'What *now*? At this time of the night?' She looked at the cut-glass clock on the shelf. It was almost eleven thirty.

'I know it's late, but I must go and see Tulip. I promise I won't be long, Mum.' She was out of the chair and almost to the lounge door when she stopped and said, 'We had a good day, didn't we, Mum?'

Liz nodded. 'Yes, darling. A lovely day, and I was very proud of you. I just wish it had been a bit warmer though.'

Emily smiled. 'Thanks, Mum. I am glad you were there to see us. I felt awful beating Jenny though!'

'But you rode so well, darling; you deserved to win! Especially as it was your first time out with Black Tulip.'

Emily hesitated for a moment. 'There's another reason why I feel bad, Mum. I think I only won because that horse went berserk ... I think that was Major's fault.'

Liz gasped. 'But you said nothing?'

'But what could I say, Mum? I can't tell anyone that the horse went crazy because of a ghost.' She took a breath. 'I really do feel responsible, but what can I do? What can I say? But anyway, I'm proud of Tulip and I am sure that we could win without the help of Major.' She walked out into the kitchen.

'Put a coat on Emily; it's cold in the yard,' Liz called from the lounge. Emily was already struggling into her anorak and boots, and she called back, 'OK, Mum.' Liz heard the back door close.

Outside, the night air was very cold, though the wind that had been so strong had now dropped. She switched on the light, and an orange glow filled the yard, making dark shadows in the corners. The empty wheelbarrow with a broom laying across looked like a large black animal with a long straight tail, and the empty stables with their half-open doors were gaping hollow holes of unknown depth. Tulip put her head over the half stable door to greet her visitor. Emily reached up to pat her satin neck, feeling her warmth and talking softly as she nuzzled gently at her hand. Somehow she felt safe knowing that the great horse was there.

She told Tulip what a clever girl she was, and fingered the red rosette that John had hung proudly above her stable. She reached up and put her arms around Tulip's neck and cuddled her. 'I love you, Tulip,' she said, and Tulip responded by blowing into her hair. She heard a slight clop of a hoof behind her, and turning quickly she added, 'Oh, Major, I love you too!' her voice echoing back eerily from every corner of the yard. 'Did you see us today?' she peered eagerly into the dark corners, trying to see if he was there. There was a huff. She turned quickly back to Tulip. 'That wasn't you, was it?' She listened. 'Major, I know its you making that puffing noise. I do still love you, I will always love you.' Tears welled in her eyes at the thought of his friendly chestnut face. 'You're in my photograph, do you know that? But you were very naughty today, frightening Silverspoon.'

Car lights shone through and under the wooden gate, she guessed it was her father coming up the drive. He parked the car in the garage, and she heard her mother open the front door to greet him.

'Emily did well." Liz smiled at Mike. 'She won a lovely cup. I was so proud of her, and Jenny came second, too.'

'Really!' Mike was about to step over the front doorstep. 'I wish I could have been there...' He stopped and looked over his shoulder. 'The light's still on in the yard, did you know?'

'Yes, Emily's out there talking to Tulip.'

'What! At this time of night?' He looked at his watch; it was gone midnight.

She smiled at him, raising her eyebrows. 'She loves that horse. I think she would sleep in the stable if she could. She has been waiting for you to come in.'

'Then I must go and congratulate her.' Mike started to walk back out of the doorway.

'Wait! I'll come with you.' Liz grabbed her coat off the hook in the hall, and came out, closing the front door behind her. It was cold, and she linked her arm through his, cuddling into him.

The side door was locked; John had locked it with his own key on his way out. Mike called out to Emily, and she went to the gate taking the spare key from a hidden nail hanging near the gate and unlocked it. She was surprised to see both her father an her mother standing there. His dress-shirt glowed a brilliant white in the stable light.

'Oh, Dad, we've had such a great day! Haven't we, Mum?' The excitement bubbled in her voice, as she gave him a peck on the cheek.

'Yes, so I hear!' He kissed her. 'Congratulations, darling, you won!' His voice rose with delight. 'Well done, Em! Great! I'm glad that Black Tulip did well. But wasn't it cold? It still is!' He shivered, drawing in a gasp of the chill night air through his teeth.

'I think we were so excited, we didn't even notice the cold,' said Liz, patting Tulip. Tulip gave a little whinny and stepped back, raising her head.

Emily had a wide smile. 'Yes, Tulip did do well, don't you think, Major?' She nodded excitedly to her right.

Liz and Mike looked at each other and then back at Emily, who was talking to the open space.

'Oh, I wish I could see you again, as I saw you in the woods. I still love you dearly.' She shook her head in sadness. 'But you must go away, Major. Please go away! I can't have you frightening Tulip again, and frightening other horses at the shows like you did today. *Please, please* go away.' She turned to her father. 'He frightened a horse today, and it went crazy, didn't it, Mum?'

Liz slowly nodded. 'Yes, it was frightening.'

She stopped suddenly. They all looked at each other as they heard the clop of a hoof. Liz stared open-mouthed at Mike, as they heard a huff. They all looked at Tulip. It wasn't her.

Tulip gave a whicker and shuffled her feet, and Emily smoothed her nose to console her. She swished her tail softly, then suddenly baulked back, jerking her head away from Emily and hitting it on the side of the stable door. Major had materialized right there in front of them!

There was a gasp from them all, Liz clapping her hand over her mouth to stifle a scream and gripping Mike's arm. They stared in utter amazement as their daughter stood between the two horses, one in the stable and one outside. Emily had tears rolling down her cheeks, as she reached out to stroke Tulip's nose with her left hand to reassure her, then put out her right hand to stroke Major's nose, but her hand was suspended in mid-air and she felt nothing but a shivery feeling. 'You must go, Major!' she sobbed. 'Please! I am so sorry. I don't want you to go, but you must, you must!' Her voice grew louder and stronger. 'Go, please, please...' Her voice went back to a whisper and her shoulders dropped as if she had suddenly lost all her strength, shaking and choking on the words. The big chestnut stood before all three of them, the big brown kindly eyes looking deep into Emily's... And then he began to fade. She reached out to him as if to stop him, but there was nothing there. For a fleeting moment he had seemed so real. She whispered through mingled tears of joy, sadness and guilt. 'Goodbye, Major. I love you, Major! I am so sorry... There was a long pause. Emily was holding her breath, her shoulders hunched with tension, and her father put his arm round her. Then in the quietness of the yard they heard a chink. It made them all start and look round.

Emily looked down through misty eyes. A few feet from her was a horseshoe lying on the cobbled yard. She bent to pick it up and felt a cold shiver go down her spine and a strong breeze whipped through the trees, blowing their hair and clothes. Then in a second the breeze was gone, and the night became still silent and cold, the chill seeping into their bones.

Emily stood holding the horseshoe. She wiped her eyes with the back of her hand to clear her vision. 'Look! It must be Major's,' she exclaimed in an amazed whisper. 'I'm sure it wasn't there before.' She frowned, shaking her head gently. For a moment she was doubtful. Black Tulip hadn't lost a shoe, she *was* sure, and if it had been lying in the yard earlier, John would have found it. She felt in her heart that Major was gone for ever now, leaving her a memento of his love. Perhaps he really had forgiven her. He must have known that she had not meant to take his life, but she would never rid herself of the guilt.

The quietness of the yard seemed more intense than ever. Her feelings were a mixture of high excitement and utter despair, and her parents seemed to have been frozen to the spot. Finally, Mike put his arms around them both, and the three of them huddled together. They felt the need for comfort, even though the scene had lasted but a few seconds. They knew, too, that they would never forget it. They parted as Black Tulip gave a slight whinny. Maybe it was her last goodbye to Major. Emily looked around the yard sadly, searching for even the smallest sign, but there was nothing.

Tulip now stood calmly with her head over the stable door. Major had gone. Emily stifled a sob. There was an emptiness in the yard, a tangible emptiness. She felt the stillness of the night, and a tingling ran through her body. There was nothing, nothing, nothing at all.

The three of them made their way out of the yard. Liz and Emily reached the kitchen door; Mike, a few steps behind them, hesitated, looking warily into the gloomy corners of the yard and around the garden and the paddock, before cautiously switching off the yard light. They heard Tulip give a slight whinny.

Inside, Emily grabbed a bundle of tissues from the box on the shelf and sat down, her elbows on the table. 'It was my fault,' she sniffled.

Her father stood behind her, his hands on her shoulders. 'Oh, come on, Emily.' He gave her a little friendly shake.

'It *was* my fault,' she mumbled into the tissue.

Liz also had a tissue to her nose as she poured tea into mugs and pushed one over to Mike as he sat down. She

101

gave Emily coffee, and in a few minutes Emily felt a little better.

It was very warm in the kitchen after being outside in the cold night air. As Mike took off his bow tie and dinner jacket, Emily told him all about the day: how Major had spooked the horse Silverspoon, and how embarrassed the rider, Dominic Hadley, had looked, and how she had felt equally embarrassed knowing it was a ghost.

'And Dad, you won't believe it,' she went on, 'but you should look at this photo.' She got up and took the envelope from the shelf, taking out the photo and handing it to her father.

'Oh yes!' said Mike enthusiastically. 'Yes, Em, this is a super photo. We must find a nice frame for this!'

Emily and her mother exchanged glances, waiting for the reaction, but there was none.

Emily walked round behind her father, looking over his shoulder. She gasped, for there was the photo that had been taken earlier in the day, and it was a picture of one horse and one rider, Emily and Black Tulip. She looked across the table.

'Mum! Look at *this*! He's gone!'

'Gone!' Liz came round the table. There was no sign of Major, and yet only this afternoon he had been clearly visible. Neither Liz nor Emily could explain it.

'You must have imagined it.'

'No, Mike! We all saw it,' said Liz, shaking her head. 'Ask John, he was there, and Jenny and Carol. And Emily said it was Major that put the other horse off its stride; it really went crazy, didn't it, Emily?' She explained all over again what had happened. But they could not explain the photograph.

'I don't think I can explain this horseshoe, either,' said Emily, picking it up off the table where she had put it and handling it with loving care. 'I am sure if it had been on the ground earlier, John would have picked it up, and I don't remember seeing it lying there when I first went out. It must be Major's. *It must be.*'

10

Over the next few months, Emily and Black Tulip entered many shows. She now had a whole tack room full of coloured rosettes and several cups and glass trophies in a glass cabinet in the lounge. They had a bigger horse box now that could take four horses. Mike had bought Pico from Sir James Bartram, and Emily rode both horses in turn and they were away at shows most weekends.

John was happy to have another horse to look after and to drive them all over the country. His younger daughter, Susan, went along to help, learning how to groom. She was getting interested in riding, and she was now riding at Mayberry Farm, where Jenny and Emily were giving her lessons. She had been plodding around on old Webster and had progressed to Tammy. Jenny's father was glad to have her there to help exercise his horses, and most days she rode out with Anita.

Susan enjoyed helping John, and now when they went out to shows she helped Emily and Jenny with their preparations, making sure that their clothes were immaculate, and sorting out the tack. If Liz and Carol did not go, it was Susan who took over the role of getting their lunch and making coffee. The four of them had become a good team.

When not at shows, John continued to spend a lot of time in the yard. Now that he had two horses to attend to, there was a lot more to do, and Pico needed a lot of grooming because of his dappled silver-grey colouring. John said trying to keep him clean was a job and a half, and so Mike had now employed Patrick Haynes, a young guy in his early thirties, to do the gardening and to give John a hand if he needed anything done. Patrick was young and strong and good at lifting bales of hay, so John said, and he could do it much quicker and easier than he could. John remembered when he was a young lad and working in a busy racing stables. He had thought nothing of lifting bales of hay and stacking them, he could still do it now, but he had to be careful of his back. Anyway, he was glad of a bit of help when it was needed, well, with the heavier stuff at least.

One Saturday, the team of four set out early in the morning for a show in Berkshire. It was about a three-hour drive. Summer rain poured all day, making the day warm and sticky, and the ground soggy underfoot.

Henry won his class and Jenny got a red rosette, but Tulip had not jumped well, coming only third. Emily was disappointed as she had worked hard with her, but she had obviously had an off day. Pico had jumped well but knocked down a pole and also come third.

John drove back through the hazardous rain, and they arrived home damp, bedraggled and tired, dropping off Jenny and handing Henry over to Jim Spencer, as Anita had now gone home. When they arrived back at Rosemary Lodge, Emily and Susan took the remains of the food, the wet towels, damp jackets and helmets out of the horse box, while John unloaded Tulip and Pico and gave them both a quick rubdown, fed and watered them, and put the tack away until the morning. Liz came out with hot tea while they worked, and Emily told her about her disappointing day. The conceited Hadley guy had won everything as usual and given her his raised-eyebrow look when it was announced that Black Tulip had eight faults; Derek Milner had come second. Louise had come over to commiserate. She, too, had had a bad round when a stirrup leather had broken, though she had managed to finish the course but lost on time on the jump-off.

John and Susan eventually left about eight-thirty, and Emily went into the kitchen. Mum had a hot meal waiting; she watched the television for a while and then went to bed feeling exhausted.

It was at the end of the week when Emily first noticed that Tulip was limping. It was only a week before another big event. She was in the yard examining the hoof, when John came through the side gate.

'Mornin', Miss... Oh! Got a problem?' He came straight over to her.

104

She nodded. 'Tulip's lame, but I can't see anything.'

John leaned over to look, then fiddled in his pocket for his glasses, and then came closer. 'Can't see nothin'. Better call the vet. Let him take a look at her. You've got all week before the Goldsborough show at the weekend, and she'll be right as rain by then.'

'Mmm,' she nodded, 'I think you're right, but do you think it's a bit early to call him yet?' She looked at her watch.

He turned his wrist over, looking at his own watch. 'No, six fifteen. He'll be up and about. Go and call him now!' She went off into the kitchen to look up the number. Luckily, she hadn't had to have the vet too often, and since she had had Black Tulip she had decided to change to the vet that Sir James had suggested.

'Good morning, Hadley Veterinary Clinic.' Vivienne Hadley, the vet's wife, had a Welsh accent. She said that her husband was out attending a sick cow, but she would contact him and give him the message. He rang Emily back within ten minutes and said that he had several calls to make, but would be at Rosemary Lodge by nine o'clock. In the meantime, Emily put Pico through his paces over the jumps in the paddock. He went well and gave her a smooth ride. She had also chatted to Louise Bartram and told her how pleased she was with him.

She and Louise had become quite friendly. They phoned each other regularly about the horses, sometimes just for a chat, and met each other at all the weekend events. Indeed, Emily's whole social life was flourishing. Emily and Jenny had joined the Young Farmers' Club, which met once a month in the back room of the Red Lion. Louise had been chairwoman last year. Parties were being organized and outings to farms and special horse events. Louise almost ran the whole show. Being a member meant that Emily also saw her cousins Heather and Gavin more often, as well as Mary Clark, Derek Milner and Alex Freemore. The Hadley brothers, too.

Last week she and Jenny had taken Tulip and Henry over to Uncle Ross's house on the Greenfurs End Estate and had a wonderful day, riding through the forest with Heather and Gavin. It had been marvellous with the heady smell of the tall sixty-foot pine trees all around them. Birds sang and called to each other high in the tree tops and grey squirrels scampered up the trunks. Surrounded by thick dense forestry, there seemed to be a feeling of great space. Sunbeams shot through the trees, sending shafts of golden light like giant swords being stuck into the ground. As they rode and talked, their voices echoed back at them through the trees. They watched as rabbits scampered into the undergrowth and a hare jumped high over the bracken and ran for its life. In a quiet glade, they saw two deer daintily grazing, and look up, startled, then sensing fear, darted off into the darkness of the pines, too shy to be seen.

Emily brought Pico back into the yard and jumped down, still holding on to his bridle. She put up the stirrups, then loosened the girth, giving his neck a friendly pat and telling him he was a good boy. John came to take the saddle, and then she handed the horse over to him to rub him down and water. Pico had done well. She had him entered for the Goldsborough show on Saturday in an early class, while Tulip was entered in the afternoon. She felt confident; she had two good horses so she stood a good chance. Tulip, though, was definitely the better jumper of the two and was capable of winning the Goldsborough Trophy. There would be some very good horses competing. They had to qualify throughout the year for a place at the Goldsborough. Both she and Jenny had qualified, and they were very excited and were putting in all the practice they could. There was still another week to go.

She left the yard, telling John that she would send him out a mug of coffee. Ivy, the daily lady, was standing at the sink. 'Good morning, Mrs Porter.' Ivy looked up, her plump face crinkling into a smile. She was always ready for a chat, rattling on in her London accent, hardly stopping for breath.

'Good morning, dear. Been riding, have you? Nice morning; a bit chilly though. I was just making a cup of tea for your mum and me. Would you like one? Oh, of course not, you like coffee, don't you, dear? Here.' She poured a cup of coffee and set it down on the table for Emily. 'Do you want some milk and sugar? Oh! No, you don't do you, dear?' She then got the teapot, warmed it with hot water, threw it away, and put in the teabags, bringing the kettle back to the boil and then pouring it into the pot.

'Mrs Porter, would you mind taking a mug of coffee out to John?'

'Yes, dear, course I will. Just let me make the tea and it can be brewing. Ooo! I've already done it, haven't I? Silly me.'

Emily smiled as she sat down at the table. She knew that if Mrs Porter went out to John she would be gone for some minutes, talking nine to the dozen.

Finally, she came bustling back into the kitchen. 'Well, now about this tea. Nice man, John, isn't he?' Emily smiled and nodded. She could guess that John hadn't got a word in edgeways.

Mrs Porter went rambling on about the horses and how lovely they were, and about the big show on Saturday, and whether she would need her new white shirt, and, if so, would it want ironing when she took it out of the packet? '...And you don't want to leave any pins in it, dear. Just give it to me and I will make sure that it is ironed and starched for Friday. I'll hang it in your bedroom, dear, shall I? And then you will know where it is. Oh, is that the phone ringing? Better go and answer it, dear!'

Emily was glad to escape into the hall, but Mrs Porter was already poking her head out of the kitchen door calling after her. 'Give your mum a call, dear, will you please? Tell her I've made a cuppa.'

It was Louise. Emily told her about Tulip being lame and that she was waiting for the vet. Louise was concerned, but said that Keith was a super vet, and, not to worry, he would probably have her fit for Saturday. 'And how's the old boy going? You're bringing him along, aren't you, eh?'

Emily smiled, telling her she'd entered both Pico and Black Tulip and would ride him in both classes if Tulip wasn't well enough to go.

'Good! Good! That's the spirit! He'll do well. Goes like a dream. Just let him have his head. Must say, I miss him, but Mystic Nights is coming along well. I think we're made for each other.' She laughed a hearty 'Ho, ho, ho'. 'What classes have you entered? We're not in competition, are we? I should hate to have to ride against Black Tulip, or Pico for that matter. Mystic Nights is good, but Tulip is something else. Anyway, best of luck. See you Saturday.' She rang off. Emily wondered why Louise had rung, she hadn't said. She had the feeling that Louise was regretting selling Black Tulip. She certainly was a super mare... 'Aah well,' as Mrs Porter always said, 'that's life...' She probably just phoned to see if she was going to the show, although she already knew that she was. Anyway, if she did have something special to say, she would ring back or she would tell her on Saturday.

John was busy in the yard rubbing down Pico's dapple-grey coat. Pico's sharp grey ears twitched back and forth, and his long silver tail switched slowly as he listened to John's voice. Suddenly there was a crash. Pico flinched, and, John looked quickly under his belly to see two bales of straw, which had been piled high in Major's old stable, come tumbling out of the door into the middle of the yard. Pico whinnied at the disturbance, but John patted him, telling him that it was all right. He gave him the last finishing touch, before putting him back into the end stable, next to the tack room, coaxing and saying gently, 'There we are then, all finished. Come on, my old rocking horse!' He came out and closed the half door, giving Pico a rub on the nose as he put his head over the door.

John went to pick up the bales. Patrick had obviously not stacked them well enough. Next time he must make sure he did a better job, he shouted out to him. He was somewhere around the garden. Patrick heard John's call and came into the yard to help. It took him about five minutes to stack them back, climbing up onto the bottom ones so as to fit them in. It wasn't easy because the bales were heavy and had to be lifted or rather dragged up above his head with John's help. John came out puffing, while Patrick closed the stable door behind him and shot the bolt. John thanked him, and Patrick walked off round the garden. John could hear him whistling the latest pop tune. It really meant nothing to him. All the music these days seemed to sound the same. One group was no different from another. *He* still liked the old songs, songs that he could hum to! Frank Sinatra was more his style, and Debbie's, too. But they still had to listen, when their daughters played the latest hits, John always said that people in Cambridge, twenty miles away, must be able to hear it. He went into the tack room and put a Sinatra disk in his CD player, and 'New York, New York' belted out. He turned the volume down a bit and came back out into the yard. He pushed at the stable door, just making sure that Patrick had closed it properly. He had hardly taken his hand off the door and started to walk away, when the door burst open again and two heavy bales of straw burst out into the yard. He took off his cap and scratched his head. Obviously they were stacked too high and not evenly balanced, so he called out to Patrick again. He waited a few minutes, but he didn't come, so he hefted them up on his own and stacked the two bales just inside the door on the floor where they could not possibly fall. Then he shut the top and bottom doors and shot the bolts. He was about to walk away when he heard a noise, and went to open the door again. Suddenly both doors burst open, and the same two bales flew out, hitting him straight in the chest and knocking him flat on his back.

Emily was just coming back into the yard. She saw John as he hit the ground and she ran to him. 'Oh, John, are you all right? Gosh, what happened?' She helped to push one of the heavy bales off his chest and gave him a hand. He got up slowly, a bit dazed.

John was clearly shaken but otherwise unhurt. Emily was still holding his arm as he got back onto his feet. She picked up his cap and handed it to him. 'Are you all right, John?'

He nodded, his breath coming in short bursts.

She looked at the heavy bales. 'Are you sure you are OK, John? What happened? Did they just fall out?'

'Well, I don't rightly know. Phew! Give me a right turn it did.' He put his cap back on. 'They came out with such a force. I've stacked 'em back twice. Patrick helped me, and I know I stacked 'em properly and I jest shut the door and out they flew again. You know, Miss, I don't like to say it, but, I think Major is back again.'

'What! Oh no!' Emily sighed, looking at the bales, the open stable door and then back at John.

'Well...' He shook his head. '...I keep closing that door, Miss, and lockin' it, and the bales keep flying out. These two were on the floor, they couldn't possibly have fallen out.'

Emily went to look in the stable. It was packed full of bales of straw almost to the roof, and it looked solid. It could not just have fallen down.

'Let's put them back, John. I'll help you. Do you really think that it could be Major? Let's see what happens.'

He grabbed at one end of a bale and Emily took hold of the other, and they lifted it back into the stable and put it down inside the door on the floor, and then went back for the other one. But before they had picked it up, the bale inside the door suddenly flew out again with great force, just missing them both.

Emily feeling both alarmed and annoyed went over to the stable and looked in, and then stood to the side in case another bale should fly out. 'Major! Major! Are you there...?'She waited and listened. John joined her. They stood either side of the half-open stable door, and heard a clip-clopping of hooves from inside.

'Can you hear that clopping, Miss? It's impossible. The whole floor is covered in straw bales. There is no room for a horse in there.'

A creepy feeling came over her. 'Oh, John!' She shook her head in despair, pushing her blonde hair back from her forehead. 'What are we to do?' Her blue eyes looked at him sadly, hoping for an answer, which, she knew, he could not give.

'Dunno!' He put his finger and his thumb to each corner of his mouth and his face twisted, as he wiped his mouth. 'I think you will have to talk to him again, Miss.' They stood together, waiting, looking at the stable door, but nothing else happened.

'I wonder what it is that suddenly triggers him off. What does he want?' John shook his head gently. He was puzzled. 'I dunno, Miss.'

'Well, I don't know what to do, John, I really don't.'

Between them, they put the two bales back and waited, but nothing happened. She took a deep breath and walked away, shaking her head, pushing open the kitchen door to tell her mother. Liz was obviously as worried as her daughter.

Emily phoned Jenny, and she felt better for talking to her. But Jenny had no answer about Major. She told her father. He couldn't believe it, and he was also at a loss about what could be done, especially as he said it seemed that whatever it was was becoming violent.

It worried Emily because Major had always been so placid.

She decided that she was going out to talk to Major again. As she opened the kitchen door, John was right outside. He was just coming to tell her that the vet was coming up the drive.

It was just after nine o'clock. He was right on time, driving his blue Ford van up to the side gate. He got his bag out of the back and rang the bell. John opened the gate, and he came through, stretching out a hand to Emily with a smile.

'Morning, I'm Keith Hadley.' Then pointing his thumb over his shoulder, 'And this is my son, Dominic. He is training to be a vet, so it is good for him to come along.'

Emily froze. There was a sick heavy feeling in her stomach as the dark and handsome young man beamed at her. Dominic Hadley... She had not made the connection; she felt uneasy, avoiding his eyes to hide her embarrassment, although he would have no idea why she should be embarrassed. She glanced up. His keen dark eyes seemed to look right through her, as if to say, 'Oh no! Not you again!' But he offered her a hand to shake and she took it.

'Hello, I'm Dominic Hadley! We have sort of met on several occasions, haven't we?' The roguish grin seemed fixed on his mouth. She had rarely seen him smile, but he flashed his even white teeth at her and raised his eyebrows. He was well spoken, educated, and a lot taller than she had thought, never having stood this close to him before. He was nearly always on a horse, with a black jacket and a riding helmet, which added to his height. But he still looked very smart in jeans and a grey sweater, the white open-necked shirt collar sharp beneath his tanned square jaw. Emily looked down, a little embarrassed, pulling her hand away. He didn't seem to want to let go.

Keith had his black bag in his left hand and then swung it into his right. 'Well, where's the patient? And what's the problem?' He sounded very efficient, but had a pleasant, easy manner. She liked him at once, but was not so sure about his son.

She led Keith towards Black Tulip, explaining that she had a limp and that she had just had her shod. John already had the head collar on her and was leading her out of the stable.

Keith watched her walk, and then patted her and said how beautiful she was. He examined the hoof, nodding, knowing what the problem was. 'What do you think, Dominic?' He

111

looked at John. 'My son is at veterinary college in Cambridge. I like him to come around with me when he is at home. It's all part of his training.'

Dominic went down on one knee looking and holding the hoof in his hand.

'There's something in there, a splinter perhaps. It will have to come out.' He ran his hand up the leg. 'The leg is hot and swollen. It's going to need a poultice and antibiotics, and she should not be ridden for a week or two. Perhaps just a short walk, maybe five minutes a day, no more.' He gave Emily a self-satisfied smile, blinking his eyes and raising his eyebrows with a complacent look and the slightest shrug of his shoulders.

'Cocky bastard' were the words that went through Emily's mind, as his brown eyes caught hers and she looked way quickly. He was looking at her now intently, with those brown and twinkling eyes. She hoped he could not read her thoughts; he seemed to be so cocky and clever about everything else, maybe he could mind-read as well. She was fuming. Vet! He hadn't an ounce of compassion in him!

'Good!' Keith nodded. 'You could be right; that's just what I thought. Let's have another look.' Bending down again to take the hoof in his hand, he got an instrument out of his bag and probed gently. Tulip was quite composed as John, holding on to the bridle, smoothed her nose, and Emily and Dominic looked on.

'I think she has a stone embedded deep into the hoof.'

They all looked on while he gently picked at the hoof. Emily could feel the pain in her stomach, but Tulip did not seem to mind. She stood quite still. It was as if she did not feel a thing, and then, suddenly, she flinched.

'Whoa!' said John.

'Aaah! There, look! There it is.' Keith took a large pair of tweezers and propelled the intruding object out onto the cobbled yard.

John bent to pick it up and held it in the flat of his hand. 'It's a small piece of rusty metal, a splinter.'

Small though it was, it had left a hole in the hoof, which was bleeding. Keith examined the fetlock; it felt hot and swollen. 'It's been there some time, as you can see. Look, the leg is swollen.' He ran his hand smoothly and gently down the

112

length of the slender leg. 'Have you only just noticed her limping?'

'Yes, just this morning.'

'It's a good job you called me. I can see that you have just had her shod.' He looked up at John, but Emily answered.

'Yes, last Friday.'

'Mmm.' Keith pulled a face. 'I hope you were not planning anything for the weekend. This is going to take a week or two to heal.'

'Oh, dear!' Emily put her fingertip to her mouth. 'I have entered her for the Goldsborough Show next Saturday.'

'Sorry!' Keith shook his head firmly. 'You can't take this mare. Don't ride her at all for at least a week. Don't even get on her back and I should keep her in as much as you can.' He looked at John. 'The infection is gradually travelling up the leg. Feel it.'

Emily put her hand on Tulip's leg. It felt on fire. He glanced at John and asked him for a bucket of warm water. John handed the bridle to Emily and went for the water. He had to go to the kitchen for the water as the tap in the yard was cold.

Keith bathed the underneath of the hoof in disinfectant and gave Tulip a shot. Then he gave John a bottle of tablets, and told him to give her two, three times a day. He would look in on her the day after tomorrow. He smeared the leg with soothing ointment then bound it in a bandage, and told John to put her back in the stable and keep her there. Just give her very light exercise after Wednesday, he said, maybe just a five-minute walk round the paddock a day, no more.

He watched her limp as John turned her round and walked her back into the stable and closed the door. Keith needed to wash his hands, and John walked across to the tack room with him to find him a clean towel.

Dominic, standing to the side of the stable with Emily, said to her, while stroking Tulip's nose: 'That's why you had a bad round at the Berkshire. I watched you. Terrible day, wasn't it? And now you can't go to the Goldsborough on Saturday! That's a pity.' He looked disappointed. 'I was really looking forward to the challenge.' He winked with a devilish grin. 'Not the same performance as before, of course. I think on that day, Silverspoon must have taken a fancy to your mare, here.' He

113

inclined his head to the side and he lifted his eyes to where Black Tulip nodded quietly over the stable door. 'Made him go all of a quiver, you did,' he said to the mare, smiling and stroking her nose. 'Otherwise you wouldn't have done so well, old girl.' The grin was still there. He patted her neck, then turned to Emily.

'I must congratulate you, though. Well done!' He said it as if she had performed a miracle by beating him. He bowed his head, as if he was bestowing a great honour on her, and he raised his dark eyebrows with a lordly mocking superiority. 'But I have never had any trouble before with Silverspoon, and I haven't had any trouble with him since. It's a shame that Black Tulip won't be able to make it. We were quite looking forward to the challenge at the Goldsborough, and, of course, getting our respect back. Being beaten by a gir... a *lady*.' He corrected himself, and a cynical smile touched the corners of his mouth. Emily knew he was referring to her and not the mare. 'Does nothing for his ego. Or mine.' He sort of grinned – it was more a sneer – then rubbed his hands together and clapped once quietly. 'Anyway, it was just unfortunate for us, and I'd say just pure luck for you, but I don't think it will happen again.' He half-smiled, and nodded. 'Not too soon, anyway. You were just lucky! You will always have to be prepared to take second place while I'm around!' The grin got slowly wider, and then fixed, and the keen brown eyes looked straight at her.

Her pink lips gasped open. Prepared to come second! She looked for a snappy answer but nothing came. Was she hearing this? He was joking, wasn't he? He never even thought that she tried. She was just lucky. Why was he so bent on provoking her? She knew he was cocky and arrogant, but this was unbelievable. She stood, eyes wide, mouth open, listening as he went on:

'Anyway! We have never been beaten in a fair jump-off yet...!' He waited. Surely he was enjoying playing with her?

With a quick intake of breath, Emily composed herself and said quietly, 'Are you insinuating that it wasn't a fair jump-off...?' In her heart she knew full well that it wasn't, but she couldn't tell *him* that. 'Well, you've got a nerve! It's not my fault if you have a randy horse that can't keep his mind on the job...' Sparks flew from the blue eyes. 'And anyway, if he has an eye for the girls, then you must agree he has good taste.' She looked at Black Tulip lovingly. 'She is rather attractive, don't you think?' She stroked Tulip's nose. It was her turn to wait for a reaction.

'Mmmmm!' he nodded slowly. He folded his arms with a tight-lipped smile, squinting his eyes to scrutinize Black Tulip. He leaned back, turning his gaze from the horse onto her. He moved his eyes from her boots to her jodhpurs, then rested his eyes for a moment on her breasts and then on the icy-blue eyes that stared straight at him from the beautiful face framed by the silver-blonde hair. 'Yeah!' He nodded with a pleasant smile. 'Yeah. I'd say, *very* attractive... And sexy, too.'

She swallowed hard, looked away, then swung her head back sharply to stare back at him. She wanted to retort, but nothing came to mind. She hung her head in anger.

'I'm sorry!' he dipped his head to her level and looked up from under his brows. 'Do I embarrass you?'

She stood for a moment, breathing heavily, clenching and unclenching her fists, not knowing how to answer. She felt she wanted to slap his face, although she would never dare. 'I ... I was talking about the horse,' she finally said haughtily.

'Oh!' In mock surprise, he jumped back. 'So was I! What else?'

'Do you take the mickey out of everyone or is it just me?'

'Mickey?' he blurted out with mock astonishment. 'I wouldn't do that! And certainly not out of you.' The smile was still there, mocking her.

She tossed her head, and pushed her fringe away from her forehead with pink polished fingernails. She changed the subject. 'Anyway, I shall be at the Goldsborough on Saturday. I'll be riding Pico...' There was a short pause. She looked up at him airily. 'He's a boy, by the way. So I trust that Pico won't put your horse off his stride. Unless, of course, Silverspoon is...' She hesitated with mocked modesty. '...gay... He's not, is he?' she added innocently.

Dominic was for a moment taken off his guard. 'Gay? Good God, no! He likes fillies with a bit of zip. Come to that...' He twitched his mouth. 'So do I!'

He glanced at Black Tulip who was nodding her head. Then turning back to Emily. 'I can see why he likes her. She's got a

115

lot of spirit.' His eyes twinkled. 'Yeah, I like a filly with a lot of spirit...'

She stood her ground. 'Well, this filly has got a lot of spirit!'

'Yeah,' he nodded. 'I know!' He smiled, leaning a little forward, and she could feel herself softening towards him.

There was a pause. 'You know...' He inched a little forward and dipped his head conspiratorily. '...I really am looking forward to a challenge on Saturday. We've ridden against Pico before. He's very good, jumps well, but he didn't quite make it, even with Louise on board. Then he smiled. There was another pause. Then he stepped back, flinging his arms in the air, and declared with great gusto, 'It will be a battle of the dapple-greys and...'

His father interrupted, making his way towards the gate. 'Come on, Dominic, I have more calls to make!'

'Sorry. Got to go.' He moved to follow his father, but turned at the gate, calling over his shoulder with a grin. 'See you at the Goldsborough. Best of luck!' The words hung in the air after he had shut the gate, then she heard the van drive away.

Emily stood for a moment, breathing heavily and looking at the closed gate. 'Challenge...' she growled under her breath. She'd give him challenge. Pico would give him a challenge he would not forget. They would once and for all beat that *conceited, cocky, arrogant pompous, conceited...* Words failed her. Just let that Dominic Hadley wait and see. Someone had to beat him one day, and take him down a peg or two, and it was going to be Pico, next Saturday!

'Nice-looking boy, isn't he?' remarked John, seeing the flush on her face.

'*Is he?*' she shrugged. '*I* didn't notice.' She spoke sharply and turned to stroke Tulip, her hand still shaking. John grinned at her back.

'Saddle up Pico, John.' It was a command. 'We have a bit of practice to put in. We have to win next Saturday!'

John grinned to himself.

Jenny could not think what Emily had to tell her, but it must be something special if Emily couldn't tell her over the phone. She couldn't wait to hear what it was. She got Henry into a

116

trot, then into a little canter. They could go almost half the way across the fields, then they had to cross onto the road and walk for about five minutes.

Twenty minutes later, she entered the yard at Rosemary Lodge. John called 'Hello,' and pointed towards where Miss Emily was, in the paddock. She rode over, watching Emily for a moment as Pico took a jump. Then she called out to her.

'Hi, Em. He's going well.'

Emily pulled Pico to almost a stop, turned him and trotted over to the gate, smiling.

'Hello, Jen. Yes, he seems OK.' They sat in their saddles either side of the gate.

Jenny was itching to know what she had to say. 'Well, come on Em, what have you got to tell me?'

'Wait a minute, you've only just arrived,' she said with a grin, letting Jenny in through the gate. 'Well, it's about that cocky Dominic Hadley. He was *here*.'

'Here! Why? He doesn't know about Major, does he?'

'No, of course not.'

'Didn't ask you out on a date, did he?'

'Oh! Good heavens, no! His father is the vet, Keith Hadley, from Packards Mill, and he came with his father today. I didn't make the connection. Anyway, apparently he's training to be a vet, so he comes out on calls with his father when he's home from college. And – you won't believe it – he said he can't wait to challenge me at the Goldsborough and that he never loses in a *fair* jump-off. And I would have to be prepared, if you please, to come second. Can you believe it?'

'Damned cheek! But at least he spoke to you. What did *you* say?'

'Well, I was pretty lost for words! I was really annoyed when he insinuated it wasn't a fair jump-off. But then, I suppose it wasn't really, was it?' she added with a grin.

'You don't suppose that he knew, do you?'

'No! He couldn't have. The conceited devil said his horse fancied Black Tulip, or some such nonsense, and that's why he went berserk. But I was laughing inwardly because, as you know, it was Major, who sent his horse wild, but I couldn't tell him that, could I? He is so full of himself he wouldn't have believed me. He is so damned smug. Thinks he can't be beaten, but

117

I'll show him. He was trying to make a pass at me in a snide sort of way. He probably thinks that he's Gods gift to women.'

Jenny smiled. 'Well, he *is* good looking, that's why he's so cocky. Doesn't need to talk to anyone, just relies on his looks. Anyway, you should be flattered, at least he has spoken to you. All the girls fancy him. That Maria Martinez is dying to get a date with him. Haven't you seen the way she flutters her eyes when he's at the shows, but he never looks at her, or anyone else for that matter! You never know what he is thinking.'

'Well, if he's thinking the Goldsborough's going to be easy, he's got another thing coming. Pico is petty good and we'll show him. We'll take that smug look off his face, won't we, Peeks?' She rubbed Pico's ears and patted his neck.

Jenny laughed. 'Come on, let's get this jumping-off to perfection, I'll time you and you can time me. Yes, you're right, Em; we'll show him. Won't we, Henry.' She leaned forward and pulled his ears. Then she added tentatively, as she urged Henry over a low jump, 'You don't fancy him do you, Em?'

'Fancy who? *Him?*' Emily looked surprised. 'Of course I don't fancy him! Whatever gave you that idea?' She frowned. 'Fancy him!' she muttered under her breath, then looked up and saw Jenny looking at her. They giggled shyly.

11

Dominic swung himself easily up into the saddle and walked Silverspoon out to the paddock. His younger brother, Graham, was already practising. His dapple-grey, Skybright, was a half-brother to Silverspoon, and they looked almost identical. Skybright took the jumps with ease as old Fred Mercer, the stable lad, a wiry, little man of seventy-three, lifted and raised the poles. There were two younger men who worked in the stable, Charlie Fenwick and Adrian Poole, but they were both busy with the mucking-out.

Old Fred had worked at Packards Mill for years. He even remembered it when it was a working mill, when the Coopers farmed the land, and wheat was ground into flour and delivered by horse and cart in sacks to the local bakery. Since then it had changed hands twice and the Hadleys had now been here for years, turning part of the stables into an animal hospital. The windmill sails still turned, but the mill itself was now used for storing the animal feed and hay. At the moment there were two horses and two ponies to be mucked out; they were patients. One poor pony had been there for two months. The gash on its head was now healing where it had been badly beaten. When it first arrived, it was so thin you could count its ribs, but it was doing fine now, and putting on weight and well on the road to recovery. Besides the hospitalized horses, there were also the two dapple-greys, which belonged personally to the boys, and were kept in a separate stable yard.

Keith Hadley had made room for at least eight horses but the stables were never that full. At the back of the stables there were kennels for dogs and cats, and he had two young veterinary nurses, Pam Western and Dorothy Gladbury, in attendance. But the horses in the hospital still had to be groomed, and that was a job for Fred, Charlie or Adrian – whoever was available at the time.

The two dapple-greys were kept in tiptop condition, and the boys entered every horse event, big or small. They practised hard and got good results; their eventual aim was to become professional showjumpers, but at the moment, they were both training to be vets, and when not at college Keith made them spend as much time as possible in the surgery. There was nothing like first-hand experience, he said. He took them, too, on his weekend rounds when they were home, saying that these clients would one day be their own clients and it was good to get known.

It was July and the big event of the Goldsborough Horse Show was on the following Saturday. Both the boys had entered different classes, as usual, but in one class they would be competing against each other. Dominic, convinced that Silverspoon couldn't be beaten, had bet his brother twenty pounds. They practised every minute that they had, challenging each other at every point, they were perfectionists. They were good pals, but in the ring, it was war.

And here they were again, Dominic about to start, Fred holding the stopwatch. No matter how quick their times it was never good enough, and both the brothers had fiery tempers. Fred thought if it came to the jump-off against the clock at the Goldsborough, he wouldn't like to take bets. And yet there was another side to them. They were both kind, they thought the world of their horses, and checked regularly on the animals in the hospital every day when they were home. They were dedicated to their studies, too, and ambitious. And for all their rivalry, they loved each other. Eventually their plan was to have a veterinary practice between them.

Fred was now adding height to the poles – one was up to six foot high and both Silverspoon and Skybright sailed over it with ease. They took the jump several times and then decided that it was enough for the time being. They needed a break and some coffee, and it was time that the horses had a rest. Fred took Skybright, and Adrian came and took charge of Silverspoon.

The boys went into the house taking off their boots at the kitchen door. Their mother would not tolerate mud all through the house, and Mrs Kimberly, the daily lady, had mopped the white tiled kitchen floor until it shone. The aroma of fresh coffee filled their nostrils, along with the scrumptious smell of just-baked scones. Their mother, Vivienne Hadley, was having a coffee morning.

'Oh scones!' exclaimed Graham.

'Don't you touch them scones,' Annie Kimberly growled sharply. 'Your mother wants them for the ladies.' She stood at the back of the table, a tablespoon in her hand, about to scoop cream out from a carton. She was in her mid-fifties, a round and dumpy little lady barely five feet tall, with grey permed curls and square rimless glasses. Her pale-blue eyes round as marbles had a look of 'don't you dare!'

Graham looked forlorn, his eyes sad like those of a small boy being scolded. 'Not just a little one, p-l-e-a-s-e, Kim?' He went to take one off the plate.

'No!' said Mrs Kimberly, giving his hand a friendly tap with the tablespoon.

Graham jumped away dancing about, saying 'Ouch! Ouch!' and holding his hand as if it had been chopped off. 'Not even a crumb? Please!' he begged, holding out his hand like Oliver Twist begging for more. She gave it another tap.

'Go on, give us one!' Dominic joined in. 'Mum won't know.'

'No!' said Mrs Kimberly. 'Go away and ride a horse or something. Your mother wants them for her coffee morning.' She turned away as the oven-timer tinged. Both Graham and Dominic grabbed a scone and walked out of the kitchen. She knew perfectly well that they had taken them, she could hear them going down the hall chuckling. She smiled to herself. She had been working for Mrs Hadley for ten years, and she had seen them growing up and was used to their mischievous ways. She had her hands full with a tray of hot scones when Dominic came back into the kitchen.

'They're good, Kim.' He had his mouth full, and he pinched two more, taking the tablespoon and quickly slapping jam and cream onto a plate, before he nipped back up the hall before she could put the hot tray down. 'Dominic!' she screamed at him in mock anger, then smiled and shook her head. 'You young devils.'

They sat in comfortable armchairs to eat their ill-gotten gains, and Graham switched on the television. There was nothing much to watch, and he flicked through the programmes. There

121

were at least ten or twelve ladies in the lounge, and when the door opened they heard voices and coffee cups rattling. Then seconds later the door to the TV room suddenly swung open, and a very smart lady with blonde hair wearing a blue suit and carrying a large black handbag dashed in and turned, almost closing the door behind her. She suddenly saw the boys. The surprise on her face was comical.

'Oh my goodness!' She put her hand to her lips. 'Oh! I am sorry, er ... excuse me, er!' she stuttered, frozen on the spot. 'I was looking for the loo ... I mean the ladies... The bathroom ... I'm sorry.' She was flushed and breathless and a little embarrassed as she turned to go out, half closing the door.

Dominic got up and caught it, smiling reassuringly. 'Follow me!' He showed her to the bathroom, which was the next door down the hall, and pushed open the door for her. 'Be my guest!'

The lady thanked him and nipped in quickly. She was just about to shut the door, when he said, 'That all right, Mrs Peters.'

The bathroom door was open just a crack. 'Oh! Do you know me? I'm sorry, I don't know you.'

'Dominic Hadley at your service, Mam,' he smiled, with a click of his heels, and then winced. He had forgotten that he had removed his boots.

She closed the door quickly, feeling quite silly. She remembered now where she had seen him before. It was at the Wickerbrook Show, but how did he know her name? Through Emily she supposed.

Dominic stood outside the door for a moment, smiling to himself, then stuck his hands in the small front pockets of his jodhpurs and walked back to the lounge with a jaunty air.

'That's Emily Peters's mother.'

Graham had his mouth full of the last bits of scone. 'Who's Emily Peters?'

'She's a girl.'

He looked up with surprised eyes, 'I should hope so with a name like Emily!' He licked the jam off his fingers and lifted his eyebrows. 'Do you fancy your chances then? What's she like?'

Dominic smiled. 'Blonde!'

'Oh yeah! That's a *very* good description.'

They were both looking at the screen, Graham flicked it over. There was a horse programme on.

Dominic eased back into an armchair. 'Emily Peters was the one who beat me at the Wickerbrook when Silverspoon was so disturbed.' He finished the last of the coffee. 'Mind you, she disturbs me too. But I don't think she likes *me*! I think I got off on the wrong foot with her the other day when I went on a visit with Dad. I was surprised to see her. But I think she was more surprised to see me. She owns Black Tulip, who used to belong to Louise Bartram. Nice mare, had a metal splinter in her hoof.' He grimaced. 'Bad, left fore, she can't ride her, the leg is very swollen. She's petite, pretty, got nice legs, I think.'

Graham glanced at him. 'Who, the horse or the girl?' He smiled. 'You *do* fancy her!' Dominic didn't answer, and they watched the programme through in silence.

Dominic called Emily with the excuse of asking after Black Tulip. He told his brother he was sure he would get a date with her.

'Bet you don't. I've seen her,' Graham said, 'and you'd be hard pressed to get her to even look to you, especially after what you told me last week. What did you say to her for God's sake?'

'Well, I sort of told her she couldn't beat me. And while I was around she would always have to be prepared to come in second place.'

'Well, that's a good start. She'll love you for that. Especially when you beat her at the Goldsborough on Saturday, too. Poor girl.' He scratched his ear. 'Why do you have to be so bloody cocky?'

Dominic lifted his head, a puzzled frown creasing his forehead. 'I'm not cocky.' But all the same knew he would beat her at the Goldsborough, of that he was in no doubt. There was no way she could win. There was no way he would let her win. Pico was a good horse, he would have no trouble keeping up with Silverspoon, and the girl was a very good horsewoman, but there was no way she could beat him, not again, oh no! It might be fun, though, telling her afterwards how well she had

123

done. Providing she came second, of course. He could see it now. They would be there together in the middle of the ring, he holding the trophy high above his head and she would be smiling as she received a golden cup, for what else could she do? Well, even if she came third, or wherever she came, he would still make a point of saying something to her, and perhaps suggest a cup of coffee or a drink ... or even dinner. He would probably need a drink first to give him courage. He was fine with horses; he had a lot of courage, a lot of spunk, he was daring in the ring, but with girls it was different, he became a little ... bashful? Shy? Reserved? Yes, reserved, and he quite often said the wrong things. He got tongue-tied with girls, and he had to admit he had been a bit cocky the other day in her yard. But that was the old bravado coming out again. He wished that he hadn't said such things, but now he had broken the ice, he could try apologizing. No damn it. The horse being sick was a good excuse to call, and maybe the first steps to getting a date.

Graham must have been reading his thoughts. 'Bet you don't get one!'

'One what?'

'A date.'

'You're on. Ten pounds!' They slapped hands, sealing the deal with smiles. He would get a date. He was not a guy to bet on anything if he thought there was any chance he was on to a loser.

Emily answered the phone, 'Who's speaking, please?'

'Dominic Hadley here. I'm just enquiring after Black Tulip. How is she getting on? I hope she's getting better.'

Emily was surprised. 'Oh! Yes. She's a lot better, thank you! But I'm surprised you care.'

'But I do!' He was sincere but could not help smiling into the receiver. 'I told you I was training to be a vet. I'm always concerned when Dad goes on a visit. That's why I come with him. I'd like to come and have a look at her, if I may?'

'I'd rather you left it to your father, thank you very much.'

'Oh, well, OK, but I think his opinion and mine would be the same. I'm going to make a very good vet eventually, and

124

you may need my services at some point. But I do have to get a little practice in sometimes.'

'Well, you're not practising on Black Tulip, that's for sure.'

'Oh well!' There was mock disappointment in his voice. 'I'll see you at the Goldsborough then. You are still going, aren't you? What time are you booked in with Pico?'

'I'm entered in the ten o'clock class, and at two o'clock.'

He already knew; he had checked up. He had qualified for the same classes himself.

'Oh great, me too! I'll look forward to the challenge. Hope you can stand the competition. I wish you luck!' His tongue was in his cheek, as he waited for her reaction.

Although she could not see his face, she knew he had that smug smile. She could hear it in his voice. She wanted to slam down the receiver, but something stopped her. 'Challenge! Competition! Do you think I am going there just to challenge you? If so, we'll give you a run for your money. I bet you'll get the shock of your life!'

'Oh so you like to bet, do you?' Are you going to take me on then? You had better be prepared for second place, I'm afraid. It's going to be a battle of the dapple-greys.' He almost sang out the words. 'See you at the Goldsborough, darling!' He rang off before she could answer.

Emily slammed down the phone. 'Blasted cheek. Second, indeed! Prepare to come second. And "darling"...!' She'd show him, the conceited pompous ass! Did he think he could break her down? Not on your life.' She stormed through the kitchen, passing her mother, who looked up in surprise.

12

Goldsborough House was a huge fortress surrounded by a moat, and standing in hundreds of acres of woodland, all of it belonging to the National Trust. Big functions were held there, catering for as many as three hundred people. Large pheasant- and grouse-shooting parties were held in the season, and salmon and trout fishing in the fast-running river. The hunt ball was held there at the end of October. Pride of place though, was given to the Goldsborough Horse and Pony Show. Horses had to qualify throughout the year to be accepted at the Goldsborough and only the cream of the horse world showed there. People travelled miles for a day out.

Emily was very proud to be taking part; it was the biggest event she had ever entered, and she just wished that Tulip had been fit. Together they would have won the Golden Horse Trophy, she was sure of it. Pico, she knew would do very well; he wouldn't let her down. At jumping he was good but not as fast as Black Tulip, who had speed and height.

It was a long drive, taking two hours from Rosemary Lodge. John drove the horse box, with Emily and Jenny sitting beside him, with Pico and Henry, in the back. His daughter Susan had stayed behind to take care of Black Tulip. They had left early to get a good parking spot. Half an hour later, Mike and Liz set off in the car, stopping to pick up John's wife Debbie, and then calling in at Mayberry Farm to pick up Carol and Joe Ellis. The sun was shining; it was going to be a good day.

When they arrived at the show ground it was already busy and buzzing. Their parents had already arrived before them, and Liz soon had the kettle on to make them all tea and coffee and toast. Then, leaving John with Henry and Pico, they all made their way to the main rings. As usual, there were hundreds of people and hundreds of horses. Sideshows, stalls selling equestrian wares, tea tents and beer tents, and the Tannoy

126

bellowing out instructions for a car to be removed, someone to come to the first-aid tent, and parents to come to the commentary box to pick up a four-year-old boy ... and finally a call for the competitors for the first big class of the day to go to the gate of ring number one.

Emily looked around for Dominic Hadley. She was saying to Jenny how determined he was to win, not just to win the class but to win over her. It really was to be a battle of the dapple-greys. It had really got to him being beaten by Black Tulip, and it seemed to her that he would do anything just to get his own back. He believed it was her fault that he had looked such a fool. He was arrogant and determined. But then, so was she.

Jenny smiled as she listened to Emily ranting on about Dominic Hadley. Everyone wanted to win. It was one of the biggest events of the year and it could lead them on to becoming professional. They both knew that beating Silverspoon was virtually impossible, but they were not going to give up trying.

Back in the horse box, they enjoyed a ham and cheese salad for lunch. Their parents had a glass of wine and raised their glasses, wishing them luck. John had his lunch on his knee, sitting on the doorstep, then he went off to get Henry and Pico ready, while the girls got changed. He looked at them with admiration. Both were immaculately dressed in new cream jodhpurs and black jackets which had been specially tailored for this occasion. Their hair was neatly tucked into hairnets, and just showed beneath their helmets. They were now mounted. Jenny adjusted her riding helmet to make the chinstrap more comfortable, and Emily stretched her fingers in her old leather gloves and took up the reins. They walked side by side to the entry gate of the main show ring. Their parents and Debbie followed, walking at a distance. John was left to close up and lock the horse box, then he went off to join them. There was a hubbub of people walking in all directions. The announcements through speakers were distorted. There was a burst of loud music from somewhere, but it died away into the distance.

As they approached the ring, Emily could see Dominic Hadley near the entry gate, head held high, as proud and as handsome as ever. She imagined his brown eyes twinkling under the peak of the helmet, and wondered why that kept crossing her mind.

Silverspoon stood quiet and composed, occasionally turning and swishing his silver tail gently. He was a magnificent animal. She had to admit that they made a handsome pair.

There were several riders waiting. Mary Clark was there with Coolie. She smiled and said hello to Emily and Jenny, and they all wished each other good luck. Each and everyone of them, if they would admit it, had butterflies in their stomachs. The Goldsborough was an exciting event, and the competitors had looked forward to it for a whole year.

Mary was talking to Jenny and Emily when Dominic Hadley smiled, dipping his head and touching the peak of his black riding helmet politely. His manners seemed impeccable, as he said, 'Good afternoon, ladies.'

It was such, an unusual occurrence that they all looked up in surprise. They smiled back, though Emily's smile was more of a smirk. They looked at each other curiously.

Mary eased in her saddle and remarked quietly, 'What's the matter with him?'

Emily thought it was just sarcasm. He wished them luck, and to her annoyance, she felt her face flush. She gave a quick grin, but it wasn't friendly.

Silverspoon did a U-turn, swishing his tail, and came back to sidle up to Pico. 'I hope you're looking forward to the battle of the dapple-greys, Emily.' It was almost a whisper, but he emphasized her name. And there was that twinkle in his dark eyes again. Emily caught her breath and felt her heart miss a beat. She lifted her chin and looked away, not knowing how to answer.

Pico was sensitive and felt Emily's unease. He became agitated. Was it something more? Emily's first thought was Major. She knew she was right when Henry sidled up to Pico, and their eyes became frightened and white. Suddenly the girls were fighting for control. Mary Clark took Coolie away, and the other horses spaced out; people moved quickly away for fear of being kicked.

Dominic was completely taken by surprise as he found himself high in the air, as Silverspoon suddenly reared and neighed loudly with fright. He came down and reared again, flaying his forelegs out in front of him, scattering spectators and horses, and catching Jenny on the shoulder, who went flying backwards off Henry's back. John just managed to grab at Henry's bridle as the huge hindquarters stepped back, only just missing Jenny, who was lying on the ground behind him. Her father, seeing the great white socks stomping backward, managed to lift her to safety, just in the nick of time. She was stunned and dizzy, and from somewhere two St John Ambulance men came running and between them they took Jenny off to the first-aid tent, her parents following anxiously.

Meanwhile Dominic Hadley was still struggling with Silverspoon, scattering the crowds as he moved back and back, with old Fred Mercer hanging on for grim death. Finally young Adrian Poole, jumped up onto Silverspoon's neck and brought him down.

Emily, struggling with Pico, managed to turn him and take him further away from the gate, knowing that Major would follow. Henry, who was the calmest of them all now, stood reasonably quietly with John, nodding his head. His eyes showed fright, but he had seen Major before and seemed to realize that there was really no danger to him.

Fred, holding the frenzied Silverspoon, managed to bring him to some sort of order, and Dominic jumped down off his back. He walked with determination over to where Emily was, just a little way from the crowd, and watched in amazement, as she seemed to be shouting and raving to herself as the horse went round and round in a circle.

'How dare you, Major! How dare you! Go away, go away! Leave me alone! Please, leave me alone!'

Dominic stood for a moment, his hands on his hips, breathing heavily. Was she mad?

'What the bloody hell are you raving on about? Can't you control that bloody animal?' He was looking up at her as the horse went round and round, tossing its head. 'What's the matter with you? Are you crazy, you stupid fool?' he shouted. 'This is the second bloody time you've almost scared my horse to death! Do you know you nearly got me bloody killed?'

Emily could hear him shouting at her but she was not paying attention. 'Please, Major, please go away.' Emily was shouting, and tears pricked her eyes, but she knew she must not let them go. She must fight on. She needed help: where was John? Pico was totally out of control. She tried to keep his head straight,

129

but he tossed and twisted and turned, nearly pulling her arms out of their sockets, while Dominic Hadley stood shouting up at her.

'I'm not bloody going away until I have sorted this out. And don't you shout at me, you stupid ... b...' He was going to say 'bitch', but he checked himself. He looked about him in utter despair. He was so infuriated. His handsome face was red and twisted with outrage. It was some time before he realized Emily's plight. White-faced with fear, she was close to exhaustion. He grabbed at the bridle just as Pico was about to rear, bringing the tossing frenzied head down. Adrian Poole grabbed the other side of the bridle, just as Pico began to rear again, and was hanging on for grim death. Dominic reached up, grabbing Emily out of the saddle, as Pico backed away and reared, flaying his forelegs and neighing and trying to pull away from Adrian. But Adrian was strong, and gradually he calmed him down.

Emily's parents had stood watching the scene in horror. Although they were used to having the horses in the yard, they were not riders and had never seen such a scuffle. Thank God that young Hadley had had the presence of mind to get her out of the saddle.

Emily clung to the lapels of Dominic Hadley's jacket, the peak of her helmet biting into his chest. She was shaking uncontrollably. Dominic drew his arms more tightly around her.

'Shush, shush,' he was saying gently. 'It's all right, it's all right it's over, it's over.'

Emily suddenly pulled away, breathlessly looking up into the handsome and concerned face.

'I'm so sorry. I'm all right, really I'm all right. Thank you!' She was sobbing. 'I'm sorry. He just won't go! I've told him to go away, but he won't go!' The tears started to flow more rapidly. 'I've told him. I've told him. What else can I do?'

Dominic felt a new surge of anger and irritation. 'What the hell is the matter with you? You told *who* to go away? You damn near killed me, and everyone else around, do you know that?' He was furious. Taking hold of her shoulders, he gave her a rough shake. The crowd gasped, thinking that he might hit her. But he had already calmed down again. He gently took off her helmet and held her close in his arms, stroking the net on her hair.

130

She burst into tears, clinging to him, mumbling into his chest. 'I'm sorry, I'm sorry.' Her black mascara marked the front of his shirt.

Her mother came and put her hand on her shoulder. 'Emily, Emily; it's all right, darling, it's all right now.' Liz fumbled in her pocket for a clean tissue, and Mike was patting his pockets, wondering which one had the handkerchief. But it was Dominic who pulled out a clean folded handkerchief and gave it to Emily.

She took it, putting it to her eyes, and holding it there. She sniffed. 'I'm sorry, but I just can't stop him, can I, Mum?' She looked back at Dominic, mascara running down her cheeks. 'I don't want him to go, but he must, he *must* go, he must!' Her voice fell to a breathless whisper. 'He keeps frightening the other horses.'

'Who does?' said Dominic with an annoyed and frustrated frown. What the hell was she talking about?

'Major, of course!' she sniffed, wiping the handkerchief down her cheek and smearing the black mascara even more.

'Major is a horse...' Liz explained apprehensively. 'He's ... still with us.' She was clenching her hands tightly at her sides, not knowing if she should have said anything. Better for Emily to explain later.

Mike, put a hand on his wife's shoulder and coaxed her gently away. 'Come on, Liz, she'll be all right.' Dominic seemed to be coping with the situation, and they were making a complete spectacle of themselves.

Dominic frowned again, not having the foggiest idea what any of them were talking about.

The crowd began to disperse. The next class had started. The announcement of 'Four faults, four faults' came over the Tannoy, and Mary Clark and Coolie were trotting round, waiting for the bell for the start.

Dominic asked Charlie Fenwick to go over and tell the commentary box to cancel both Silverspoon and Pico, as the horses and riders were unfit to participate in this class. As Charlie went off to deliver his message, Dominic called after him to tell them about Jenny Ellis, too. Charlie gave him the thumbs-up sign, as he pushed his way through the crowds.

Although Dominic was baffled, he nodded to Emily's parents, letting them know it was all right. With an arm round Emily's shoulders, he led her away.

'Come on, I'll buy you a cup of coffee!' This had been his intention in the first place, but he had not expected it to be quite this way. He wanted to get to the bottom of this anyway. He had no idea what she, or her mother were talking about. He knew that she used to ride a horse called Major, but it had been a long time since he had seen the horse at a show. He kept his arm round her shoulders as he guided her to the tea tent, finding a table. It was none too clean and full of dirty coffee cups, but he sat her down, saying, 'Wait there!'

While he was gone, Emily kept her head down. There were people standing all around her, drinking and talking, and she didn't want anyone to know that she had been crying. She looked up quickly and spied Louise Bartram in the crowd. She looked as if she was pushing her way through towards her, but she was hoping that she would not come over. Luckily someone stopped her. Emily did not want to talk to anyone about what had happened, and she wished Dominic Hadley would come back quickly. Her thoughts stopped in their tracks. What was she thinking about? What was she doing here with Dominic Hadley of all people?

The place was crowded, and he could not get close to the counter. But, being tall, he managed to catch the eye of the woman serving, and he came back in just a few minutes with two cups of black coffee, packets of sugar and powdered milk, and two small glasses of whisky on a tray.

Emily sniffed back her tears, feeling a little better now, and thanked him as he put the tray on the table. 'I'm sorry for all the trouble. Oh, I must look a mess!' She knew her eyes and her nose would be red.

His lips twisted with a smile. With streaks of mascara running down her cheeks, yes, she did look a mess.

'You look fine!' he lied. He took the handkerchief from her and wiped some of the mascara gently away. 'But you do owe me an explanation. You damn near killed me! It happened the last time. What exactly did you do? Here, drink this...' He proffered her the whisky. 'Is it some sort of magic, or witchcraft or something? Have you put a spell me...?' He was smiling,

132

knowing he was talking rubbish, but he did manage to get the slightest smile from her.

'I can't drink whisky.' She took the handkerchief, wiped her eyes and sniffed.

'Drink it! It will make you feel better!' He picked up the glass and offered it to her.

She took it and sipped it gingerly. He chuckled out loud as she pulled a face and then drank some coffee quickly. She sniffed again and wiped her eyes.

'Feel better?'

She nodded, with a slight smile, and then was serious again. 'I'm sorry, I can't stop him. I can't!' She shook her head. 'And I *really* am sorry. But he just won't go away.'

'You keep saying you're sorry, but *who* can't you stop?'

'Major.' Her voice was shaky.

'Wait a minute. Major is a horse? Right? I didn't see him. Is that the chestnut that you ride sometimes?'

She turned her blue eyes or him in surprise. 'I didn't think you ever noticed.'

'Oh, I noticed, but I wasn't paying much attention to the horse. All chestnuts look alike, until you know their character, of course. But he's not here today, is he?'

She shook her head. 'No. I mean, yes. I mean, well sort of. Look. I keep trying to explain to you.' She swallowed. 'You see, I know why Silverspoon plays up and is afraid. I know the danger Major puts you in. And everyone else for that matter, and I feel responsible, but what can I do?'

'Yeah...' He frowned. What was she talking about? He was puzzled. 'Why should you feel responsible?'

'Well,' she paused and sniffed. 'You see, we had an accident.'

'Who did?'

'Major and I.'

'Oh!'

'I was riding him through the woods near where I live, and he hit his head on a low bough, and he died! Right there in the woods! It was all my fault. I rode too hard. He tried to slow down but I urged him on, and now, well...' She splayed her hands. 'You are not going to believe this.' She paused again, then swallowed looking him straight in the eye. 'Major is a ghost! A ghost horse!'

133

'A *what?*' At his sudden loud exclamation people looked around. For a moment he was stunned, then a comical look appeared on his face. 'Oh, come on, don't give me that, you're joking!' He began to laugh loudly. Two men standing close by with beers in their hands grinned, and one said, 'I bet that was a dirty joke!'

'Don't laugh! I know it sounds stupid, but seriously, it's true.' She raised her voice, her head shaking. 'It's true! Just listen! And I will tell you everything.'

'OK, OK.' He put his hands up in defence and tried to calm down but he was still chuckling. 'I give in, I give in! OK. Come on then! Tell me, I'm listening.' He was finding it hard to contain himself.

She sniffed and wiped her nose with the handkerchief, and then started right from the beginning, when she first had the accident, how she had grieved, and how it had all started when she had bought Black Tulip. He listened attentively, politely, but disbelievingly.

'It's true,' she said at last. 'I am not spinning you a yarn. I loved Major, and I don't want to lose him, but he spooks the other horses. Black Tulip has got used to him now, but he still spooks her sometimes, and Pico was afraid today. He spooks Henry, too, but he is not quite so highly strung, although he did get spooked in the woods one day.' She told him about Henry getting stuck in the mire. '...And then there was the bucket swaying about in mid-air in the stable. My parents were there. They saw it happen!'

'In mid-air!' His voice rose, and the two beer-drinkers looked round at them again. He was looking at her in disbelief his mouth opened wide with sheer amazement.

'Yes,' she nodded, 'it's true! We all saw it, my parents saw it, and my mother almost had a heart attack. And John, that's my groom, got knocked over by bales of hay being flung out of the stable door that he had closed and locked, though I can't imagine why Major would be so violent.'

He listened to her in astonishment, finding it hard to believe, as anyone would, and yet knowing she wouldn't be just making up a story like this. He could see that she was truly distressed by it all.

'So you see, I'm so sorry, but what can I do?' She was close

134

to tears again. His strong hand closed over hers. It was soothing. She went on: 'When it happened to you the first time at Wickerbrook I felt awful, but I couldn't tell you that a ghost horse was in the ring with you, could I?'

'No! Not really!' An amused smile flicked across his mouth at the words 'ghost horse'. It sounded so ridiculous! 'No!' He squeezed her hand again. The smile widened. It seemed laughable. He felt mirth welling up inside of him, but he dare not laugh at her. He kept the smile under control and tried to put on a sympathetic look. Finally he asked simply, 'What are you going to do?'

'I don't know what I can do.' She was very serious, shaking her head in despair. 'He is there in the yard. Both John and I have heard his hooves on the cobblestones.' She shook her head again. 'He does obey me when I get really upset with him, but he won't go away ... I loved him, I still love him!' Tears welled in her eyes. 'And I don't really want to lose him, but he must go ... he *must*! I can't carry on like this. Can I? Someone is going to get badly hurt. Even when I ride out near my house, he comes. He is in the woods. I know he is there. I can feel him there. When Jenny and I ... Oh my God! Jenny! I must go and see how she is...' She stood up quickly.

I'll come with you. Wipe your face! It's all black streaks.'

She used his handkerchief and looked up at him. 'Has it gone?'

He smiled down on her. 'Yeah, you look fine!' Their eyes met again for a fleeting moment. The mischievous twinkle was still there and he was glad of the opportunity to get up. He felt he wanted to roar with laughter at the story of a horse lifting a bucket and throwing bales, but he didn't. Something he knew had certainly frightened Silverspoon, but could he really believe it was a ghost, a ghost horse?

Jenny was laying on a bed in the first-aid tent, her eyes closed, her face very pale. A St John Ambulance man was holding an icepack on the back of her head, while her parents who had been standing by for about half an hour looked on anxiously.

Emily and Dominic went in quietly.

Emily looked at Carol. 'How is she? Is she all right?'

Carol nodded. 'I think she'll be all right.'

'Yes, Em, I'm OK,' Jenny answered, still with her eyes closed. 'It's just a bump on the head, and my shoulder hurts a bit. Where's Henry?'

'Don't worry! John's got him.'

Jenny relaxed visibly. Joe Ellis took his wife by the arm and nodded for her to come outside, leaving the three riders alone.

'What about Major? Has he gone?' asked Jenny.

'I don't know. I think so. I hope so.'

A quick surprised flick crossed Dominic's brow. He looked from Jenny to Emily, realizing that the ghost business must be true.

Emily caught the look. 'Didn't you believe me?' Jenny opened one eye, surprised to see Dominic Hadley there, and then closed it again.

'Well, of course, yeah! Sort of ... yeah!'

She looked up at him earnestly. 'It *is* true, Dominic. I wasn't kidding you. And I *really* don't know what to do about it.' It was the first time that she had called him by name. He liked it.

'Well! We'll sort it out ... somehow.'

'*We?*' She looked up at him in surprise.

'Well. Yes. We are in this together now. You can't keep on frightening Silverspoon without me being involved. From now on, I'm going to hang around, just like this Major. That's if you don't mind, of course,' he grinned.

'What? Like a GHOST?' A smile curled the corners of her mouth.

He grinned. 'Well, not exactly. I do want to be seen.' He put on a charming smile, and his eyebrows rose. It was a quick comical gesture. He bit his lip. 'You see, I would never have got to talk to you if it wasn't for him.' He flung his hands out haphazardly. 'You see, well, I'm OK with the horses, but I'm a bit shy when it comes to people.'

'Shy!' Emily blurted out. Even Jenny opened her eyes. 'You shy!' said Emily again. What! With all that panache of yours! I don't believe a word of it.

Jenny struggled to get up. 'Am I interrupting something? Would you two like to be alone?' She smiled weakly. Just smiling sent sharp pains through her head.

'Alone? What a good idea!' Dominic guided Emily towards the door of the first-aid tent with a grin.

'See you later, Jen,' Emily smiled, concern vying with pleasure and embarrassment.

Emily smiled at Carol and Joe Ellis as she left. 'I'm glad she's all right, Mrs Ellis.'

'Yes, it's not that bad, thank goodness,' answered Joe Ellis. 'We'll be over at the box in a little while.' They went to fetch their daughter.

Emily and Dominic walked slowly across the grass, making their way back to Emily's horse box.

'It's a shame about the Goldsborough. We have both missed out.' Emily looked up at Dominic. 'I suppose I could qualify again for next year... It would be so wonderful to win the Golden Horse Trophy wouldn't it?'

He turned to face her, the slightest comical grin at the corners of his mouth. '*Win!* You surely didn't expect to win, did you?'

'Well, of course I did!' She looked at him equally astonished. She looked up at him indignantly 'Why not? You can't win everything. Someone has to beat you. Besides, Pico is every bit as good as Silverspoon.' She didn't add that he wasn't as fast as Tulip, and that, though he jumped high, his back legs let him down on occasions.

'Oh, so you thought you were going to get as far as the jump-off did you? You wouldn't have stood a chance.' There was that cocky arrogant attitude again.

She gasped. 'That's what *you* think... I have been schooling Tulip for a year.'

'Yeah, but you were not riding Tulip.'

'Well, Pico then. He's fast. But Black Tulip is faster, and next year we'll beat you, I'll bet you anything.'

'Anything? You really mean *anything*?'

She blushed. 'Well, almost anything.'

'Oh!' he sneered with mock disappointment.

Jenny and her parents had almost caught up with them. She was wincing with every step and still held a cold pad to her head.

'Are you two having a fight already? What are you arguing about?'

137

'Winning the Goldsborough!' said Emily. 'He doesn't think I can.'

'Henry will win it next year! I bet neither of you will stand a chance.'

'Oh, so you like a bet too, do you? You're on!' said Dominic with a smile. 'Next time we all ride together in the same class, wherever it is; a fiver.'

'Done!' said both the girls with a giggle. 'Providing I'm fit,' added Jenny.

'Oh no!' said Dominic. 'No excuses. If we are all in competition together, a fiver, OK?'

'OK!' the girls agreed. He put a gentle arm around both of their shoulders as they walked on, being careful not to squeeze Jenny.

They arrived back at the horse box. John was there with Henry and Pico. Carol and Joe and Mike were standing talking, and Liz had the kettle boiling as usual, ready to make coffee; she had seen them all coming across the grass, surprised to see Dominic Hadley with his arms around the girls. She thought of the coffee morning when she had talked to him at the loo door; she still felt a touch of embarrassment even now, but tried to put the thought quickly out of her mind, hoping that he had forgotten.

They all arrived at the horse box. 'Hello,' said Liz with a smile. 'I saw you all coming. I've made the coffee. How are you, Jenny?' She could see that she looked pale and in some pain.

Jenny smiled weakly and said, 'Not too bad, thanks, Mrs Peters.'

Dominic's handsome face broke into a wide grin. 'Hello! We meet again, Mrs Peters. We always seem to be standing in doorways, don't we?' She knew he had remembered, and the colour rose in her face.

Emily looked up at her mother who was standing in the doorway of the horse box. She was about to introduce Dominic, but she stopped. 'Oh! Do you know Dominic, Mum?'

There was a pause. Liz swallowed. 'Um, yes, we have met!' She tried a slight smile.

'I took your mother to the loo,' he teased, his eyes sparkling with amusement.

138

'It was at the coffee morning, Em.' Liz put in quickly. 'Er ... are you stopping for coffee?' she asked, hoping that he would say no.

He smiled, the twinkle still in his eye. 'Yes, please!'

Liz visibly winced.

After the coffee and cakes, Jenny came into the horse box to sit quietly. Her head ached, and she rested it back on the blue cushion and dosed off. Both Carol and Liz were there, and they glanced at each other with concern. There was a pull-out bed above the driver's cab, but when Liz asked Jenny if she would like to lie down, she refused. They sat quietly watching her, while the men, including John, went off for a beer.

Emily and Dominic walked around the showground. They watched Martine Milner, Derek's sister, on her bay mare Blue Ribbon, as she took each jump perfectly.

'She's beautiful.' Emily remarked, without turning round.

Dominic, was standing a little to the side, just behind her. 'Yeah, beautiful.' His gaze was on Emily. Her silvery blonde hair looked soft. He imagined it like silk running through his fingers. He lifted his hand to touch it, but then stopped. He knew it was too soon, and he could wait. He was on the way to earning ten pounds off his brother anyway. 'Yeah, beautiful,' he repeated in a hushed whisper.

She turned, looking up at him with a smile, but he turned quickly away to look at Blue Ribbon, as she took the last jump to perfection.

'Come on! Let's walk on.'

The touch of his hand on her arm felt strong, and she was thinking how masculine he was, how tall and handsome. Maria Martinez walked by and smiled, fluttering her eyelashes at him, and with an envious glance at Emily. They made their way through the crowds. He wasn't quite as arrogant as he had first appeared. In fact, he was quite charming. He just had that arrogant aloofness that made him seem offensive, but now, for the short time that she had known him, she found him to be polite and quietly spoken.

They crossed the bridge over the moat and went into Goldsborough House. They wandered around rooms full of antique furniture and threadbare tapestries. They walked up a sweeping stone staircase with its wide carved-ebony handrail. Each step dipped in the middle and was worn with age where hundreds of feet had trodden before. On the right-hand side, the wall was covered with paintings of grey-bearded faces, ancestors of the Kelly family, with eyes that followed them as they passed. One painting covered the whole of the wall at the bend of the staircase. Something about it made them stop. It was of Patrick Kelly the founder owner of Goldsborough House, sitting on a horse, also named Goldsborough. He was tall, with a dark, gypsy complexion, his face thin and angular, his mouth stern and his eyes blue and piercing. A mop of dark curls fell on his keen forehead. He was dressed in a black cloak with a purple lining and fur trimming, held by a large golden clasp of shamrock. The hilt of the sword at his side was figured in gold. He looked like a king.

They reached the top of the staircase and walked into a long oak-panelled gallery with a richly polished wooden floor. Ornate gilt furniture lined either side of the walls that were hung with more rich tapestries and works of art. Porcelain jars and vases stood on tables and in the alcoves. From the windows that were draped in heavy faded material, patterned in pink-and-red flowers, they could see the immaculate gardens, with well-trimmed box hedges and topiary trees. They went down and wandered around these exotic gardens. They were very beautiful but did not interest them. A notice pointed the way to the stables. There they found the actual stable where Goldsborough had lived. Apart from a fresh coat of black paint to preserve the wood, it had remained the same over the years. They also saw the well-preserved leather saddles and bridles and the old, rusty iron carriages with large wheels and thin spokes. The black leather on the seats had worn well over the years, but was now cracked and the horsehair padding was bursting out at the corners.

They had seen enough and wandered slowly back across the bridge through the crowds, making their way to Emily's horse box. There Dominic left her and walked across the field, feeling pleased with himself. In a way he felt he had won with Emily Peters. He had had his eye on her for some time, but for all his old bravado, he had not known really how to get around

140

to asking her out. Now he felt good, and he couldn't wait to tell Graham of his conquest.

He had a chuffed smile on his face as he approached Graham, who was brushing down Skybright.

Graham glanced up quickly. 'You looked pleased with yourself. What have you been up to? I wondered where you had gone. Adrian brought Silverspoon back.'

'Yep! I finally did it.' He stuck out his hand. 'And you owe me ten quid.'

'Do I! What for?' Graham stopped brushing.

Dominic grinned. 'Got a date with Emily Peters! I've even met her parents.'

'That was quick, wasn't it?'

Dominic told Graham about the ghost story. His brother listened with interest, then pulled a face. 'Sounds like a lot of old bull to me. Whoever heard of a "ghost horse" chasing round the ring at a jump-off. You didn't really believe her, did you?'

Dominic scratched at his eyebrow thoughtfully. 'Well, I must say I found it hard to believe, and I was a bit sceptical, until we went into the first-aid tent to see her friend Jenny. She's a nice girl by the way, good-looker too,' he added. 'She took a nasty bump during the excitement, but she seems OK now, although the shock probably hasn't set in yet. Anyway, when she asked Emily if Major was still there I began to wonder if it was true after all. She had her eyes closed when she spoke. She didn't even know that I was there, so it was no trick.'

'Oh, come on, Dom!' He turned back to his brushing of Skybright. 'Sad to lose a horse, but it sounds odd to me.'

'Yeah, I know, but...' Dominic clenched his fist and punched it into the palm of his left hand gently. 'You know, Gray, to make it more permanent with Emily Peters I may even have to give up riding.'

'Christ! That bad, is it?' Graham stopped in mid-brush, turning quickly to look at him.

'Oh, I don't mean give up riding altogether; I mean only when she is riding. It seems this ghost horse follows her around, and it doesn't only upset Silverspoon. It spooks all the other horses as well. But you wouldn't know about it, you are always in another class.'

141

'Well, she will just have to give up riding then, won't she? Not you. It was absolute chaos today, wasn't it? I was halfway through a class when it must have happened. I could hear the commotion, but at the time I didn't know you were involved. But do you really believe it? A ghost! A ghost horse! Oh come on, Dom, wake up! Get real. It sounds ridiculous.'

'I know it sounds strange, the way she explained it. Well, yes, I think it *is* true.'

Graham looked up from checking Skybright's hoof. 'You do sound serious.' There was a chuckle in his voice, his eyebrows lifting just like his brother's. 'Oh well,' he mused, 'I suppose girls will say anything to get a guy. And anyway, giving up horses for love won't hurt you for a while. You can always get back into the saddle again later.'

'Who said it was love?'

Graham smirked. 'Oh, come on! You've got that look, the look of *luuuuuve*.' He went on brushing Skybright with a big grin, pulling faces Dominic couldn't see.

Dominic stood staring at his back for a moment or two, then went up into the horse box, opened the door to the toilet, and scrutinized his face in the mirror over the basin, looking this way and that. What look was Graham talking about? It didn't show, did it?

13

Jenny recovered fairly quickly. The bump on her head soon went down, but she had a headache for a couple of days and the bruise on her shoulder still hurt. She had had an X-ray, but the doctor had said that there were no bones broken. He had given her some cream to bring out the bruising, and told her to rest her arm and put it in a sling for a few days. Emily went over to see her, and they wandered around the farm. Jenny was fed up because she couldn't ride Henry. With a bit of a struggle and help from Anita and an old chair, she managed to climb up onto Henry's back. Emily led him on a slow walk around the field, so that it didn't jar Jenny too much.

At the end of the week the shoulder was a little better. John collected Jenny and Henry in the horse box and brought them back to Rosemary Lodge. They just walked gently through the woods, where it was quiet and peaceful. They talked about Major. Jenny wondered what could anyone do about a ghost. And in any case, it didn't happen all the time, and horses had reared and bucked since time had begun, and it wasn't all because there were ghosts hanging about. They laughed it off, but Emily still looked at the tree, as they passed by, and now she wondered if Major was there and could hear what they were saying.

She told Jenny that she had a date with Dominic Hadley. He was taking her out to dinner.

'Told you he fancied you, didn't I?' Jenny's eyes went sideways, and she had a cheeky smile. 'But I thought you didn't like him.'

'I know, but he seems rather nice, not cocky or snooty when you talk to him, although it was the last thing I ever thought that I would be doing – going out on a date with *him*.'

'Where is he taking you?'

'The Garden House, Cambridge.'

'Oooh! Living it up. Sounds nice. I hope he can afford it.'

'Yes, I think he can. He seems to like nice things. After all I said about him, he's not really so arrogant. Well, is a bit but he seems sincere and genuine, and he's very polite. Not like most of the guys.'

Jenny lifted her eyebrows comically. 'Sounds as if you really like him.'

'I do.' They chuckled.

Emily was seeing Dominic Hadley a lot more often than she had imagined. He phoned her every day, asking about Black Tulip, even though he knew from his father that she was well on the road to recovery and that she was now riding her again. She knew it was just an excuse to phone, but she liked it. At weekends when he was home, they went out to dinner and to the coffee shop at lunchtimes, but they had never ridden their horses together. Although she enjoyed his company, he still had that arrogance which got under her skin. She was just becoming accustomed to his ways. He visited Rosemary Lodge, the first time on a veterinary visit, and then more often. Liz and Mike liked him, and their friends said that they made a handsome couple.

Jenny phoned Emily. 'Have you got this month's copy of the *Horse and Hound*? There is a picture of you and Dominic.'

Emily said that she hadn't received a copy yet, and Jenny laughed, saying, 'You wait.'

It was about an hour later when the postman put the mail into the box. Emily rushed to the door. The *Horse and Hound* was wrapped in a roll of plastic. She put the letters on the hall table and quickly unwrapped the magazine and thumbed through the pages. There it was, a picture of Dominic pulling her from Pico. She was almost upside-down, half in and half out of the saddle, with one leg straight up in the air, an ugly look of surprise on her face. She shuddered and thought that the photographer must have been quick to get such a shot. It had all happened so fast, but why, oh why, had they printed it? The caption read, 'Damsel in distress lands her man'. The story went on to describe how both dapple-grey horses had gone berserk, and how the girl, Emily Peters, had struggled to

144

control her horse, Pico, but had been rescued and pulled to safety by the gallant horseman, Dominic Hadley. It went on to say that they had both missed out on a chance of competing in the Goldsborough Show this year.

For his birthday, Graham booked a table at Macs Restaurant in Sudbury for ten people. Louise and her current boyfriend were invited; Derek Milner, who brought a girl named Lucy who no one had met before; Alex Freemore; and Jim O'Sullivan, a guy Graham knew at college. Dominic was driving, Graham beside him. They picked up Emily from Rosemary Lodge and then Jenny. There were a lot of laughs about the pictures in *Horse and Hound* as they sat drinking around the table. At first Emily had felt very embarrassed, but as they kept on and on about it, she began to laugh with them. Jim O'Sullivan was not into horses and didn't get the joke, but Mac, the restaurant owner, just happened to have copy, so when Jim saw it he was happy to join in with the taunting.

Jenny and Graham seemed to like each other. They got along well, and since that night, they had been out together a few times. Then one day the boys asked the girls to bring their horses over to their home at Packards Mill. John drove the girls and the horses over and waited for an hour or so chatting to Fred and Charlie and young Adrian, who showed him round the stables and the animal hospital. Dominic had warned Graham there might be some excitement if Major turned up, and Graham had said that he would have to see it to believe it. If Major was there, he didn't bother them.

On another occasion Jenny asked them all to Mayberry Farm to hack out and stay for lunch. They all agreed that her mother was a good cook. And the week afterwards they were all together again at Rosemary Lodge, and hacking out through the woods, which the boys agreed was a very pleasant ride. After they had had lunch, they played tennis and, of course, the cocky Hadley boys won again. It just seemed that they were both of the same mind; they just had to be winners.

They became a foursome and went out together at the weekends when the boys were home from college. They went to restaurants and ate good food and drank the best wine.

145

Both the boys were perfectionists at everything they did. They were always on time; they liked the best tables and tipped well, which got the best service. They had been to the cinema and had played several games of tennis at Rosemary Lodge. The bar at the Red Lion was fun, and they met new friends. There were party invitations and Young Farmers outings, mostly arranged by Louise Bartram. They visited farms and stables and horse shows and films. One Sunday, Louise also arranged a lunch and a jumping event at Wickerbrook Hall for twenty friends. They all arrived with their horse boxes, and there were jumps set up in the field, and mini-competitions and rosettes to be won, and a barbecue lunch. They went in the swimming pool. Then, after taking the horses home, they changed their clothes and all met back at the Red Lion for dinner.

Then there were the normal horse events that they had entered earlier in the year, and they found themselves competing against each other, the boys mostly picking up the cups and rosettes, and the girls winning their classes. This led them all to qualify for bigger events, and now they were all on the way to qualifying for the Goldsborough again.

Emily was happier than she had been for a long time and there had been no more trouble with Major. She felt at peace, though he was often in her thoughts. She had beaten Dominic once at Foxhead Hall. He had been a bit put out by it, but it had all been fair and square. As she said, you can't win them all, and he had soon got over it.

The names of Emily Peters and Dominic Hadley were well known, and although they weren't professional, people would come for miles just to see them compete against each other. There was a sense of drama and fun, and the spectators would clap at the looks and smiles they gave each other. When the big fences went up to seven feet and they still got clear rounds, there were roars of excitement. But quite often Dominic just got the edge, possibly winning by a second ahead of time. Emily accepted the situation with grace even when she came to be known as the One-Second-Less Girl, and she was quite flattered when asked for her autograph. Jenny and Graham had

146

done well, too, but the showmanship of both Dominic Hadley and Emily Peters, was the star event of any day.

They appeared in the horse magazines every week, and quite often on the sports pages of the daily newspapers. They qualified for bigger events, both hoping eventually that they would get to Wembley, the biggest horse event of the year in England. They also looked forward to competing in Ireland, France, Germany and Holland. They had dreamed of these days, and of becoming professional, and it seemed, the way they were going, that dream could soon be accomplished.

It had been all excitement, packing up Tulip and Henry and all their gear in the horse box and going on the ferry across to France. Of course, John was there to drive, and Anita and Jim Spencer also accompanied them, with Jim driving the car and following the horse box. In Ireland, all four of them had competed and it had rained the whole week, and there had been thick mud. But it didn't seem to worry the horses; they just splashed on over the jumps. Then Jenny caught a flu-like cold and was unable to compete, and came home. In France, the weather was sunny and bright, and Emily with her fair skin got a little sunburned, but they picked up money and prizes.

Holland was OK, but Graham had a bad run. Everything seemed to be against him. He had a fall and hurt his hand, and then at the end of the week Skybright pulled a tendon, and he gave up. Emily and Dominic stayed on in Holland, and then went off to Germany together, both doing well and giving their normal performance together.

It had been a lot of fun, meeting new people, with luncheons and dinner parties nearly every night, and large functions for charity. Emily enjoyed the dressing-up. She had bought four new outfits to cope with any function. And then there were the private cosy dinner evenings they enjoyed together. It was all so romantic – that is, until they had the big argument.

14

It was over a year now since Emily and Dominic had split up at one of the horse events in Germany. They had had a big argument in public; she called him conceited and arrogant, he called her stupid and careless, and almost accused her of cheating, and she stormed off, pushing through the crowd that had gathered around them; if they couldn't understand English, they could see by their faces that it was a heated argument. It was after a jump-off and she had beaten him, which didn't happen too often, and he couldn't bear to lose and being made to look a fool. And she had told him so in front of many spectators and even the press.

The next day it had been on the sports page in the papers, with pictures of the two of them and the horses. Big headlines in the *Horse and Hound* screamed 'HORSE LOVERS IN CONFLICT!' It went on to talk about their competing interests and the rivalry between them, and mentioned the love-hate relationship which had been going on for years. Emily was so annoyed she had mentioned something about never riding again, and the newspapers had picked up on it, reporting, 'Emily Peters quits the showjumping ring'.

Dominic and Graham Hadley still rode in events, but less and less frequently, now that they were well into their veterinary studies. The work was much more intense, and they could only practise at weekends, not really enough to compete in the major events. Jenny had got a job as a farm secretary, operating between three farms, working a few days a week in each. Sometimes she worked only in the mornings, which gave her time to ride Henry. Emily had taken a job in a travel agency and had been transferred to London. It was supposed to have been a temporary move, but she had been there now for almost a year. She phoned Jenny regularly. She missed her horses, but she was enjoying the London scene, and she tried to come home every other weekend, though it was not always possible. Jenny drove over to Rosemary Lodge about three times a week and rode out with John's daughter, Susan, to exercise Tulip and Pico. Susan was now working at Rosemary Lodge full-time, helping her father and exercising the horses.

The travel company, Lambington's Worldwide Travel, supplied living accommodation for some of their transferees and Emily had moved into a flat with a girl named Amanda Powers. The flat was pleasant and comfortable, although not very well furnished. It had two bedrooms and two bathrooms, a medium-size lounge and a small kitchen that looked out over chimney pots and small walled gardens. She had made friends through the girls that she worked with, and there were invites, too, to parties, and at one of them she had met a nice guy named Marcus DuBarry, who was a car salesman. They quickly found that they had something in common – horses. Marcus didn't own a horse of his own, but rented one in Hampton Court, a few miles' drive from London. He went down to ride about every two weeks. Close by was open countryside, and he loved to get away from the town. He invited her to go with him – he could arrange a horse for her – and she accepted. It wasn't bad for a first date.

It was a pleasant sunny Sunday morning when Marcus DuBarry, all dressed up in jodhpurs and checkered jacket, picked her up in his black shiny Jaguar at the flat. The London traffic was light as they left the town behind and got out into the suburbs, where the air was chill and fresh. After a forty-five-minute drive, they arrived at Barrington's Livery Stables and Riding School, just off a busy main road. The name was painted in big black letters round a large green wooden horseshoe that was fixed above the entrance to the stable block. They left the car at the entrance in the driveway, and she followed Marcus under a grey brick arch into the yard. He introduced her to Melissa Bayslock, owner of the stable, a thin, masculine woman with a drawn pale face and a dyed orange fringe that stuck out from under a blue-and-red paisley headscarf. She was about fifty, and wore a green T-shirt and grubby beige jodhpurs. She greeted them warmly, revealing a cultured voice that didn't match her appearance. Emily was reminded of Louise Bartram, although Louise was a lot better-looking and a great deal younger.

She asked Emily if she had ridden before. 'You will have to go out there in the traffic, but it is a very short walk, and my horses are bomb-proof! But, if you prefer, Anna will take you on a leading rein.'

Emily smiled inwardly. She hadn't realized she was being taken to a riding school. She answered innocently, 'No, I think I can manage on my own, thank you.'

The woman gave her a sceptical look. 'Now, you are sure, dear? Because I can't just let anyone take out a horse! Anyway, Anna will be with you, just in case. She will keep you both on a leading rein until you get across the road.' She nodded with a grin. 'Marcus always rides with Anna, don't you, dear? He feels safer that way.'

Emily held her breath, turning slowly to look at him, her eyes widening. The way he had spoken, she had thought he was master of the hunt and here he was being taken out on a leading rein. And so was she! It was beyond belief. Still, everyone had to learn.

Marcus smiled at Emily. 'I think it's wise to go with someone who knows what they are doing, don't you think? The road out there is a bit dodgy, but Anna will hang on to you.'

Emily nodded. 'Oh yes, very wise, but I *have* ridden before!'

Mrs Melissa Bayslock called out in a high-pitched voice, 'Anna, dear, saddle up Warrior for Mr DuBarry, will you, dear? And bring Fang round from the other stable for the young lady, dear.'

Anna, who was about sixteen years old, small and slim, almost childlike, came out of the end stable and dashed off to do what she was told. Fang sounded like a fiery steed, but looking at the riding school Emily was doubtful.

Warrior, black and about sixteen hands, lumbered slowly round the corner with his head drooping low. Anna was walking too fast for him. Emily thought he must have been woken out of a deep sleep, but he was brushed and clean, and there was a shine on his coat. He stood quietly snoozing while Anna saddled him up. The last thing poor old Warrior wanted was to go out for a walk. She was sure he would have been much happier out to grass. Anna went off to get the other horse, Fang...

Fang was a chestnut with a golden main and tail, similar to Major's colouring, but unlike Major he hung his head low and seemed uninterested. While Anna saddled him up, Emily went to him and ran her hand down his nose. She spoke quietly to him, and he lifted his long lashes and looked at her with big kindly brown eyes. She stroked his mane. Her hand felt greasy, and she thought if John had brushed it, it would have been like silk and shone like gleaming gold.

'How old is he?' she asked, turning to Melissa Bayslock.

'He's fourteen,' she answered. 'Nice old boy; he'll give you a gentle ride. You won't have any trouble with him.'

Shame, thought Emily, she would have liked a little bit of trouble. But he had most likely been hard ridden for a long, long time and now spent most of his time being hacked out around the same boring course with schoolchildren on his back learning to ride, pulling his mouth and kicking his sides. She patted him gently.

Anna saddled a bay for herself. His name was Mojo, and he looked a little sprightlier than the other two. Melissa said they were ready to mount, and led Warrior over to a mounting-block for Marcus. Emily almost burst out laughing, as the stocky Marcus struggled to get onto the horse's back. She even thought she heard Warrior groan under Marcus's weight. Anna held the bridle while Melissa made sure that his boots were set properly in the stirrups, that his hands were correctly positioned and that his fingers were entwined in the reins with the thumbs uppermost.

'Do you want a leg up?' asked Melissa, but Emily was already halfway into the saddle.

'No, I can manage, thanks!' She settled herself and took up the rein. Melissa came to check if she was holding it the right way, and Anna told her she should put her fingers this way, and your thumbs on the top. Emily thanked them with a smile, and waited while Anna climbed easily aboard Mojo. The three set off at a slow walking pace, Anna holding the leading reins.

151

Melissa was watching as Fang followed. The young lady sat well and she hoped she knew what she was about. Emily was thinking that by this time she would have been off and across the field, through the woods and back, and having coffee in the kitchen. She looked at her watch. They had already been there for nearly an hour. They walked through the yard under the old brick arch. Facing them was the busy main road, and traffic buzzing by at speed. They turned right and walked close into the kerb, following Anna, the traffic giving them a wide berth for a few yards, then they crossed in front of the traffic, which Anna held up with her hand. The horses and riders lumbered on slowly in front of the agitated drivers, who drummed their fingers on the steering wheel, impatient to race on. The horses turned in through the large gates of Bushy Park, and before them lay miles of green grassland and trees. They walked slowly along a pathway, Marcus following Anna and still held by the leading rein. Emily asked if she might be allowed to ride without it, and Anna let it go. They came to open grassland and Anna suggested a little trot. Emily came up alongside Marcus at a trot.

'Beautiful out here, isn't it?' he remarked shakily, as he bounced up and down, completely out of rhythm with the horse.

'Yes, gorgeous!' she smiled. 'I didn't know there was such a beautiful place to ride.'

They trotted on for a few minutes, then turned into a wide walkway with large oaks and elm trees on either side. The horses knew the path well; they had come this way for years. They slowed now to a walk, Warrior plodding on beside Fang, their heads nodding up and down in unison. Anna was a little way in front, still pulling on the leading rein as old Warrior plodded on, finding it hard work to keep up.

Emily thought that, after the hubbub of Central London, she could see why Marcus was hooked on riding; it was so quiet and peaceful here in this wide lane of bright-green tufty grass. It was another world, although you could still hear the buzz of the traffic, just beyond the trees and the hedgerows. Emily thought of home. She missed the trees and the woodland, the sun filtering through the leaves, and the birds twittering and calling to each other. She took a deep breath of the fresh cool

152

air, so clean after the dust and grime of the city, and it was all just forty-five minutes away.

Through the trees she saw four deer and pointed them out to Marcus and Anna. The deer looked up nervously, startled by their approach, stood stock-still, and then scampered away on long spindly legs into the undergrowth. Emily wished she could have chased after them, just to get a bit of excitement.

'Would you like to try a little trot again and then a canter?' said Anna, turning in her saddle. 'Will you be all right, Emily?'

She nodded and thought that Anna must have read her thoughts. 'Yes, I would like to try a little canter.' She could not stop a note of sarcasm creeping into her voice, but she had waited so long just to get moving. Fang, she thought, probably hadn't had a good canter for years, though he seemed content enough to just plod on beside Warrior.

Marcus nodded nervously. Emily saw him getting ready to quicken the pace. 'I have only done this once before,' he smiled at Emily. Anna told them to shorten the rein a little. Marcus grabbed at the black mane.

'How long have you been coming out here to ride?' asked Emily, as she came up trotting alongside Marcus. 'It really is a beautiful place.'

'Oh,' he said shakily, I have been quite a few times now, I found it through Tom Markham. He brings his kids here. He's a guy I work with. He rides and I came with him one week and liked it.' He was puffing and breathless as he bumped about in the saddle.

Mojo quickened the pace, and they all went into a slow canter. Marcus drew in a breath and wobbled a bit, holding the rein and the mane to steady himself. Emily could see he was struggling to keep his balance, and she put a hand out under his elbow to steady him and get him into the rhythm. They cantered on for a few yards. Suddenly, a bird flew out of the bushes, almost tipping the top of quiet old Warrior's nose. He shied, lifting his head with a frightened whinny and took off like a rocket. Anna screamed as he passed her and the leading rein was snatched from her grasp. It was then that Emily's dream came true. She got to gallop Fang as she went racing after Marcus, who was hanging on and shouting for the thing to stop. It was all he could do to hang on.

Anna chased after the two horses. Warrior, whom she thought so docile, was now racing full pelt for a five-barred gate beyond which cars were travelling at speed. Emily was surprised to find that Fang was really a good strong horse. He galloped like the wind. She could see the golden mane flying before her, and once again she was on Major. She came up fast along the left side of Warrior and leaned out and grabbed at the bridle. He was almost at the gate, but she managed to turn his head, bringing him round and slowly to a standstill, both horses and riders breathless and puffing. Anna who had been galloping close behind, slid Mojo to a shunting stop, breathlessly thanking Emily.

Marcus was also eternally grateful. He couldn't get his words out and was holding on tight and shakily to the black mane.

'Gosh, thanks, Emily!' He was panting for breath. 'I really thought he was going to jump that gate. Then, with sudden realization, he opened his eyes wide. 'How did you learn to ride like that? I know you said you could ride but...' He puffed. 'It was like cowboys at a rodeo show.' He shook his head and chuckled breathlessly. 'Thanks. Thanks, Emily.'

Emily and Anna were also breathless. 'You certainly do know how to ride,' Anna chuckled with admiration. 'And Melissa wasn't sure about you taking a horse out on your own!' I'm glad you were here because I don't think Mojo could have caught up with Warrior. I've never seen him gallop, and Fang surprised me, too. I suppose he's never had a good rider on him before. In fact, it's a miracle to see Warrior so active, cantering always seems such an effort for him. I knew he would not take the gate, but I was afraid he would throw you off Mr DuBarry. Are you all right?' He nodded and they all chuckled together, mostly with relief.

'What happened?'

'A bird flew out of the bushes,' said Marcus with a chuckle. 'And he just took off. I didn't know what to do.'

'Well, if it ever happens again,' said Emily, 'pull his head round; he can't go on if you turn his head.'

'Well, Fang amazed me as well,' Anna smiled.

'Perhaps no one has ever tried to gallop him before.' Emily furrowed her forehead. 'But I think that they all have it in them when they want to go.'

'Yes, I am sure you are right,' Anna smiled. She asked if

154

they wanted to go on or go back, and Marcus said yes, he would like to go on, now that he knew he was in good hands. He nodded at Emily.

'Not that I doubt your ability, Anna. I trust you,' he added quickly. 'I really am in *your* hands.' He smiled. 'Well, I'm now in the hands of two beautiful women, and I am beginning to like it more and more.' That caused another laugh, and they walked on without further incident. They were gone for an hour and then retraced their steps across the busy main road to the stable, where Anna couldn't wait to tell Melissa Bayslock what had happened.

Melissa was surprised that Warrior, of all horses, had taken off, and then she screwed up her thin face and looked at Emily. 'I thought I had seen you before; you've been in the *Horse and Hound*, haven't you? You rode at Olympia!'

Emily nodded with a smile.

'*Horse and Hound*! Olympia!' Marcus was astonished. 'Do you ride that much? What, gymkhanas and things like that?'

'Yes, something like that,' Emily chuckled. 'But Olympia can hardly be called a gymkhana.'

'Golly, you must have thought me a right twit asking you to come down here to a riding school.'

'You didn't say it was a riding school, Marcus; you asked me if I wanted to go *riding*.'

'Oh, did I really?' His eyes went sideways to look at her and he bit his fingernail. 'Sorry.' A little later, he added: 'I am going to book up for two weeks' time. I suppose you wouldn't come with me again, would you, Emily?'

She said she wouldn't mind. At least it gave her a chance to get out on a horse while in London. Melissa booked them in, for Sunday morning.

As soon as they were gone, Melissa went into the tack room, and rustled through the pile of old *Horse and Hound* magazines. Turning the pages, she showed Anna the picture of Emily and Black Tulip in mid-air jumping the poles. The caption read: 'Emily Peters and Black Tulip flying to victory'. Anna looked at Melissa open-mouthed.

'She's professional!'

* * *

155

Jenny phoned the office one day in the week, and Emily told her about Marcus and the riding experience, and they had a giggle.

'Well, he said he was into horses and went riding, but it was just a riding school, and a bit tatty. All the same, it was quite a good day out, and the old nag I was on went like the wind when he was asked. I think he was as exhilarated as I was; hadn't had a chance to stretch his legs for years.'

'Are you going out with this guy then? Jenny asked. 'What's he like?'

'No! It was the first time, and the last time! I'm not going again,' she chuckled. 'But he is nice enough, I suppose. Not my type, seems a bit of a mummy's boy, when it comes to horses. A bit portly, too, but well dressed, and not bad looking. Tries to be smooth. He's thirty-two but looks forty and is a car salesman.'

'Sounds a bit dodgy to me. The sort who can talk you in to buying anything.'

Emily chuckled. 'Well, he certainly convinced me about the horse-riding. Good job he wasn't selling me a car without an engine.'

Jenny laughed. 'Anyway, you don't sound very enthusiastic about him.'

'I'm not, but it's nice to have some company, and there is always a group of us. I have only been out with him once. We had a nice lunch, too, and we went to Hampton Court Palace. *He* had a riding lesson, and *I* had a history lesson. If you want to know anything about Henry VIII, I know it all.'

'Oh, I know all about Henry; he's out there now chomping on a bale of hay.' They giggled together. 'When are you coming home?

'Next weekend.'

'Thought you were supposed to be going riding?'

'I am. With you.'

'There is a show on at Carling Hall. I don't know much about it but I've entered Henry; he's going well. It's for injured jockeys.'

'I'll come with you. Carling Hall is quite a long way; do you want to borrow the horse box?'

'Could I? It's too late to enter Black Tulip now. If I had known you were coming, I could have got you a form.'

156

'Well, I didn't know I was coming. But I will come with you anyway. Have to go; the other phone is ringing. Phone John and make some arrangements. Must go, bye. She picked up the other line. It was Marcus DuBarry.

'Hello, Emily. I have booked a table for next Saturday night at Rochas Restaurant. I thought we might ask the Perrys if they wanted to go.'

'Sorry, Marcus, I can't. I'm going home next weekend. I have to go to a horse event.'

'Oh!' He was stumped for the moment. 'Well, what about the riding on Sunday?'

'No! Sorry I can't come.'

'Are you riding then?'

'No! Too late to enter. I am going with a friend.'

'Well, can't you put it off?'

'No!'

'Why not?'

'I don't want to.'

'Oh!' There was a long pause. 'Well, I'll come with you, then.' He sounded very persistent, and she didn't want him to come along, not with Jenny, anyway.

'Err... No! You can't.' She had to think quickly. 'I'm going ... with a man friend.' It went quiet.

'Oh!' She could hear the surprise and disappointment in his tone and imagined the thick pouting lips, like a small boy's who is told he can't have chocolate.

'Oh! All right then.' He finally conceded.

That weekend Emily went home. Her parents were pleased to see her, although she did not spend much time with them. She was off out riding with Tulip and Jenny and Henry most of the time.

Major was always there, watching, although he did not disturb Miss Emily. He found that when he did, Miss Emily scolded him and sent him away. Now he just watched in the woods and at horse shows, keeping his distance from the ring, as Black Tulip and Pico took everything in their stride. On quiet weekends at home, he stayed in the meadow, and when Miss Emily and Black Tulip, and Jenny and Henry, rode quietly out through the meadow and into the woods, he followed at a distance and stood there by the big tree, where he had met his untimely death, with his gleaming chestnut coat and his ginger silky mane and tail streaming out as if he was still in full gallop.

He would gallop on for ever, and in his heart he would always feel happy. And in Emily's memory he would always be the same, he would never age, and his big brown, kindly eyes would always be watchful, and Emily would never know, though sometimes she saw those brown and friendly eyes in her mind. But Tulip, Pico and Henry saw the shadow and they heard sounds beyond the human ear when they walked through the woods.

15

Carling Hall was the large stately home of the Warburton family. Jeremy Warburton was a good friend of Louise, and although Jenny and Emily had met him, they did not know him well. His father, Jonathan Warburton, bred racehorses – it had been a family tradition for centuries – and just occasionally they opened their fields for a charity horse event. This one was for the Injured Jockeys Association. Emily had come along as a groom for Jenny. It was a fairly big show, and there were the usual sideshows and equestrian wares to be had. Fifty to seventy horse boxes had already arrived, and as usual everyone was busy.

Dominic and Graham were there. Graham said he was going over to see Jenny. Dominic went with him, not knowing that Emily was there. Graham knew full well that she would be – Jenny had told him – and he knew that Dominic had been going through a rough time since the break-up. He loved Emily and wanted no one else; he had told him so several times. Both Graham and Jenny wanted them to get back together again, and this seemed a good opportunity for them to do so. Dominic was hopeless with women. He desperately wanted to apologize and didn't know how to do it.

As they approached the horse box, they could see John fixing the bridle on Henry. Jenny was standing on the step talking to him. Graham waved, and she waved back with a bright smile.

'Morning, John!' Both boys greeted him pleasantly as they usually did.

He looked up with a smile. 'Morning, lads!'

Graham patted Henry. 'He is looking good, John.' He gave Jenny a peck on the cheek.

Emily heard Graham's voice and came to the door of the horse box just as Jenny stepped out. She and Dominic came face to face, both very surprised.

The atmosphere was cold and strained as he managed a flat 'Morning'. A voice in his head was saying, 'Go on! Smile!' But his lips ignored it. Emily responded with a clipped, toneless 'Hello'. The blue eyes were hard. They no longer sparkled, and they avoided him. She tossed her head and went to Henry. Dominic, too, turned on his heel and stormed off back towards his horse box. She watched him go, longing to run after him, but her feet refused to move. Jenny and Graham glanced at each other. They both wondered whether they had done the right thing.

It was time for Jenny to enter the class, and Graham went back to his own horse box. He saw the strained look on his brother's face as the brown eyes flashed venomously at him. He waited for the full blast of his tongue. He didn't have to wait long.

'Why the hell didn't you stop me from going? You knew she would be there, didn't you? You and Jenny arranged the whole bloody thing. You asked me to go, over there with you, and you let me walk right into it!' He was fiddling with Silverspoon's bridle, and there was no need for it because Charlie had already done it. The horse's ears twitched at the sharp tone of his voice. 'I never felt so bloody awkward in my life. What are you trying to do to me? Make a bloody fool of me?' He was shaking with rage.

Graham grimaced, biting his lip. 'Well,' he said quietly, 'now that you have finally come face to face, why don't you make the first move? You love her, don't you?'

'Who says I love her?' Dominic scowled.

'You still do, or you wouldn't be making so much fuss. Go on! Make the first move.'

'What? Make what first move? It's up to her. I said "good morning", didn't I?'

'Big deal.'

Dominic clenched his fists tight, then opened and tightened them again. He was trying to control his anger. Fred glanced at Adrian, hoping he was ready to break up the fight should it come to that.

'What are you trying to do! Put me off winning this bloody class? Do you want to make a laughing stock of me, do you? Do you?' He swung himself up into the saddle, grabbed at the rein, and yanked Silverspoon's head sharply and rode off in a huff.

Charlie Fenwick looked at Fred, sniffed and rolled his eyes. They had seen these outbursts from Dominic many times. Graham took it all in his stride. He got a bit heated, himself, at times, but always soon regained his composure. Dominic, they knew, would stew for hours, sometimes days.

Graham sighed, hoping that Dominic would win his class; otherwise there would be more temper to contend with. His own class was not due to start yet, so he sauntered down to the ringside to watch Jenny, standing a few yards away from Emily, who also looked tight-lipped. She seemed determined not to look in his direction.

Although Emily watched Jenny, she did not really see her. Her mind was on Dominic in the next ring, but she did not dare to glance over in that direction. She could hear the crowd ooing and aahing and imagined Silverspoon doing his normal round. But then her mind snapped back and she was ready with a smile to congratulate Jenny on her finish as the old familiar voice over the Tannoy said, 'Clear round, clear round.' But although she smiled, her heart felt heavy. She watched as Graham reached up to take Jenny's hand, blowing her a kiss while walking along beside the prancing white socks of Henry. Then as Jenny jumped down, Graham was there to hold her in his arms, and give her a quick kiss. She wished Dominic was more like his brother, and that he had not been so pigheaded. If he had said 'good morning' pleasantly, she would have responded, but he was his normal arrogant self. She wanted to apologize and say that she was sorry, and I miss you, but the words would not come easily; they just went around and around in her head.

The speaker broke into her thoughts. 'Will Dominic Hadley and Alex Freemore please go into the centre of the ring to receive... She heard no more; he had won again! Did anyone else ever stand a chance? But he deserved to win, with all the practice he put in. He did work hard at it, she couldn't deny that. He was dedicated to riding and nothing short of winning came into it. Oh, but he was arrogant! Oh so arrogant!

Why wasn't Dominic like his brother. Why?

Graham had to go, and the girls walked back to the horse

box in silence. Henry was plodding slowly after them like a big faithful dog, with John a few steps behind holding on to his bridle.

They had not spoken, and they sat in the horse box. Emily made coffee. Jenny handed one to John, who was outside with Henry. John could feel the strained atmosphere between the girls. He could never remember them being like this before, and then he heard them mumbling.

'I'm sorry!' Jenny suddenly broke the ice.

Emily looked up. 'Sorry for what?' She was sharp. 'For trying to get us together again? You and Graham cooked that one up between you, didn't you? Anyway, he's not interested in me any more; in fact, he's not interested in anything except himself. His only interest is winning. I hate him! I just don't care any more.' She spat out the words. 'I'm glad I'm in London. And I don't ride much any more, or I would be bumping into him at every show. The arrogant pig!'

Jenny smiled inwardly. 'I know he still likes you. Graham told me. Why didn't you smile at him? It would have broken the ice.'

'Smile at him! After he publicly accused me of cheating! Did you *read* the papers? I don't want to break the ice! I want him out of my life! I live a completely different life now in London; I have a different set of friends; and I don't need any aggro from that ... that ... that conceited pig!' She spat out the words again and tossed her head away, then looked back at Jenny. 'And! If I want to, I can ride.'

'With Marcus DuBarry?' Jenny raised her eyebrows and put down the coffee cup very gently, a slight cynical smile beginning to play about her mouth.

Emily, for a moment, held her breath. She looked sideways at her friend. She could feel the laughter welling up inside her, then a smile creased her face. She guffawed, and suddenly Jenny burst; they fell about laughing.

John couldn't help overhearing Emily's angry outburst, but now he heard the girls laughing again, and he was relieved.

'Oh Jen. You should have seen this guy on a horse. Honestly, you would have died laughing, I know you would. You know, he was talking to me so confidently about riding. I thought he was good, but ... oh, Jen ... you should have seen him, especially

162

when the bird flew out of the bushes. Well, I've never seen such a big behind in a pair of jodhpurs. I didn't know that they made them that big. I really don't know what would have happened if I had not been there. I'm not bragging but I am glad I was. Because that Anna – mind you, she knows what she is doing – but by the time she realized what was happening he was halfway across the grass and it would have been impossible for her to have caught him. And this old nag that I was on could really go, but I don't think he had ever been asked!' she giggled. 'And the slow old Warrior with Marcus on board went like the clappers...' she chuckled. 'And he was all dressed up, too. New jodhpurs, tweed jacket, riding hat and crop, long black hunter boots with the brown tops, the lot, all polished to a high shine, in fact, brand new. He looked like the lord of the manor, and there was me in jeans and a sweater. I wished I had been properly dressed, but then when we arrived at a riding school, well!' The pair of them burst into fits of laughter so loud that John put his head in the doorway to see what was going on.

'Car salesman, did you say he was?' said John with a chuckle.

'Yeah,' Jenny nodded. 'Big talkers. They could sell coals to Newcastle.' They all laughed again.

Sunday morning Emily was in the yard with John. She had given a lot of thought to the situation yesterday and decided she was going to do her own thing. Why should she deprive herself of the thing she loved most, and if she came face to face with Dominic Hadley, she would totally ignore him.

'I have decided to come home at the weekends more often. I do miss my babies, John!' She was stroking Pico, as she and John were leaning over the paddock fence. 'I think I'll take Pico out for a spin. I'll just go and get my hat. Would you saddle him up for me, please?'

She went off into the kitchen and up to her bedroom where she had packed her hat away on the top shelf of the cupboard, not wanting to leave it in the tack room to get dusty while she was away in London. She had an old one in the tack room, too – the hat that she was wearing when she had had the accident with Major. She was just coming back down the stairs when the phone rang on the hall table. She picked it up.

'Hello, Rosemary Lodge,' she said cheerily.

'Hello, Emily.' It was Dominic. His voice was short and icy, but then he softened. 'Look, Em ... I'm sorry about yesterday at the show. I didn't know you were there, honestly, or I would not have come over to spoil your day.'

'Oh! It was all right!' She was equally sharp. She took a deep breath. 'You didn't spoil anything for me!'

'Well! If it's any consolation, it certainly spoiled my day. It upset Silverspoon, too; he knocked down a pole and we came second.'

'Hmm, I bet that upset you.'

'I keep thinking about you, Em... Don't you think it's time we buried the hatchet...? I didn't like the strained atmosphere yesterday. And if we are going to meet on rare occasions at shows, which will happen, I'm sure, at least we can be civilized about it. Can't we?' It went quiet again. 'Em? Emily?'

'Yes! I'm still here.'

'Well?'

'Well! Yes! I suppose so. OK.' Although they did not know it, they both relaxed either end of the phone. There was a long pause.

'How's London? How are you getting on?'

'Oh OK! It's fine!'

'Made some friends?' The way he said it she knew he meant 'boy friends'.

'Yes! There is a group of us that go out together.' It went quiet again.

'Oh! I suppose you are riding this afternoon with Jenny.'

'No!'

'I'm going over to look at a new horse.'

'You're going to buy it?' Her tone was uninterested.

'Don't know yet. Just going to look...

'Oh!'

'I'd value your opinion, if you'd come with me.' He was treading on eggshells, waiting for a blast down the line, telling him to get lost. He waited. It went quiet. He hoped that she was considering.

164

'Well! Why would you want *my* opinion?' She pushed her fringe back on her forehead.

'Well, I think you're a pretty good judge of horseflesh.'

Her eyebrows went up again. '*Me!* ... I'm sure you're quite able to judge for yourself! You know what to look for in a horse. And if you're going to buy it, it wouldn't matter what I thought! You'd do it anyway.'

'Oh! So you won't come?'

'Well!' She was hesitant. 'I'm not really doing anything...'

He waited with bated breath, hopefully, breathing in through clenched teeth.

'Yeah! All right then! If you like! I'll come! That's if you really need my opinion. What time?'

She didn't sound very enthusiastic, but his face beamed and he shook his hand in triumph at Graham sitting across the room, who, smiled, giving him the thumbs-up sign.

'Well, I was thinking about now, I could pick you up in about ten minutes.'

'Oh! No! I can't get ready that quick. Make it thirty and I might be ready!' She put the phone down, not even saying goodbye. He wasn't going to dictate to her the time. She would make *him* wait. She took a deep breath, putting her fingertips to her lips as if in prayer. Her heart leaping in her breast, she poked her head round the kitchen door. 'I won't be in for lunch, Mum; I'm going out.'

Her mother looked up in surprise. She was just checking the roast beef, pushing it quickly back into the oven and closing the door. Emily was about to dash up the stairs.

'Oh, all right! Where are you going, Em?' she called after her.

'Out with Dominic.'

'Who?' Had she heard that right? 'Dominic!'

Mike closed the newspaper he was reading and came out of the lounge into the kitchen.

'Where's the fire? What's all the excitement?' He had heard them shouting and Emily stomping up the stairs.

Liz looked surprised. 'I think she said she was going out with Dominic.'

'What? I though they weren't speaking.'

Liz smiled. 'Lovers' quarrel.'

Upstairs, Emily was changing quickly into blue jeans and new pink cashmere sweater. She brushed her long blonde hair, tying it up with a new matching pink bow. She renewed her make-up then struggling into her best short brown riding boots, the ones she kept polished especially for events. She checked her wallet for money in case there was another big row and she needed to get a taxi back. She was ready in eight minutes, and she wandered about the bedroom, nervously looking into the mirror, patting her hair, checking her make-up again. She sat on the bed, she picked up a magazine and flipped through the pages. She couldn't concentrate; the time was going slowly. She put it down, checked her hair again in the mirror and was running the brush through it when the door bell rang.

She grabbed her jeans jacket from the chair and her bag, and she came running down the stairs calling to her mother excitedly, 'I'm going,' then rushed to the front door breathless and smiling. She stopped short of the door trying to regulate her breathing, looking into the hall mirror, smoothing her hair, taking her time, then running her hands down the front of her sweater. Then taking a deep breath and letting the smile drain from her face, she opened the door slowly, lifting her chin with a severe look.

'Hello, Emily!' There was no smile on his face, but he stood there, tall and handsome, as clean and smart as ever, in blue jeans and a navy-blue sweatshirt. She wanted to leap into his arms. 'Ready?'

'Yes!' Her reply was short and sharp.

In the kitchen both Liz and Mike looked up as the front door slammed. Liz sighed tenderly. 'Yeah, remember when we had the terrible quarrel? I never thought I would see you again, but you came back and I forgave you, and we got married. Do you remember our wedding day?' She put on a simply girlish voice, her head on one side dreamily, a stupid smile on her face remembering her wedding that was thirty years ago.

'Yeah! I remember that day! It was the cup final, and all the guys in the office went, and I couldn't go.'

Liz looked astonished. 'Is that all you remember?'

'No!' He was going out of the kitchen door, but turned round. 'United won two nil.' He had almost closed the door

166

when he popped his head back round the door. 'But I'd do it all again!'

She smiled to herself, remembering the beautiful white dress she had worn. They had been happy all their married life, they had no regrets.

Then he opened the door again, popping his head round. 'But not on cup final day.' He closed the door quickly as she threw a tea towel at him. She could hear him chuckling as he went down the hall.

John opened the back door. 'I saddled Pico. Has Emily gone out?'

There was heavy tension between them. She hadn't said a word as Dominic drove through the country lanes. The day was pleasant and sunny, and she had no idea where they were going.

He glanced at her. 'Thanks for coming. Are you all right?'

'Yes!' She looked out of the window, turning her head away from him, as the car sped passed high hedges and green fields. 'Are you going to buy this horse?'

'Well, I am thinking about it, but I would like you to see it first.'

'Why me? Have you already been to look at it?'

'No! But I told you, I think you would be a pretty good judge of horseflesh.'

'Why didn't you ask Graham to come with you?'

It was the first time he had smiled. 'Because it's much more fun being with you. Anyway, he's gone over to Mayberry for lunch.'

'Oh! So he couldn't come, and you had nothing much to do, so you asked me?'

'Well, yeah! Something like that!' He looked a little sheepish. He pulled the car over to the side of the narrow country road, switched off the engine and turned to look at her. 'Aren't you flattered?' he said jokingly, but there was a touch of the old arrogance.

'Oh, very flattered, I'm sure. To be second choice. But why have we stopped here?' She looked out of the window onto a sea of rippling grass.

167

He put his arm along the back of her seat, just touching her shoulder and her hair. 'Em,' He said quietly, 'I've been so miserable without you. I've really missed you, Em.' Then he pouted like a small child. 'Even Silverspoon has his ears down, and he has not swished his tail for months. He really has missed Black Tulip; he hasn't looked at another filly, and I know he is in love with Black Tulip, and when I told him I was seeing you, he perked up and flicked his ears and swished his tail, and I am sure there was a smile on his face.'

She turned her head slowly round. His face was very close. Her face was stern. She looked into the brown smiling eyes, so very close. They were almost nose to nose, and then burst out laughing.

'Oh, Dominic! What utter rubbish! What will you think of next?' She felt tears of joy pricking her eyes. 'Oh, Dominic.' Her arms went around his neck. 'I've missed you, too.' She fell into his arms, and he hugged her so tight she thought she would break, and he was kissing her nose and her eyes, her mouth... It was like music. Yes, she was floating on music. Suddenly there was a bump against the car. The music became bleating, and, as they parted, they found that they were surrounded by a flock of sheep, being driven along the road by a grey-haired farmer. He ducked his head to window level and grinned with a black toothy grin, raising his cap knowingly.

Dominic waved a hand to him. They chuckled as a couple of black faces with innocent eyes surrounded by grey curls looked in on them. Dominic gave her a quick kiss again, and turned the key in the ignition. The engine roared into life. 'Emily, I love you. I am so glad that we are friends again.'

'Are we?' Her blue eyes shone with happiness.

'Oh, I do hope so, Em. I don't want to lose you again. And I can't tell you how happy I am that you came with me today.'

She smiled, touching his arm. 'Silverspoon will look much better with his ears up.'

They must have driven about twenty miles. The hedges grew thinner and opened out to reveal spacious green fields where cows and horses grazed in the late-morning sunlight. Beyond a wooded area of leafy trees, part of a slate roof was visible. Rising from a tall farmhouse chimney, a stream of grey smoke veered to the left on the strong breeze.

'I think this must be the place,' said Dominic. 'I haven't been here before.'

'How did you know that they have a horse for sale then?'

'A guy I know, Chris Clements, mentioned it. Said it should be a good buy. It's owned by a guy named Ben Mortimer, and it's a dapple-grey. That's why I am interested. He breeds dapple-greys. Usually these things get snapped up, but this guy apparently does not enter competitions, and is not known for riding. He judges, but I've never met him. Chris Clements said that the horse is in tiptop condition, and Ben Mortimer wants to sell it because he has just bought another dapple-grey. So I phoned him and made an appointment for today. And I'm so glad you came!' He reached out and squeezed her hand again.

She looked lovingly at him. 'You like dapple-greys, don't you?'

'Yes, they are my favourite. I had one called Silver Stream before I bought Silverspoon. They were related somewhere along the line. Skybright and Silverspoon are half-brothers, too.'

'I didn't know that.'

'You like dapple-greys too, don't you, Em?'

'Oh, yes. I love Pico, but I didn't choose him. Dad bought him as a surprise from Sir James Bartram, when Louise had a change. I love them both, but Black Tulip is my favourite. But jumping-wise they are both equally as good as one another, although, I think Tulip is the faster of the two.'

'I know!' He gave her a sideways glance. 'Can't beat Silverspoon, though,' he grinned.

She clicked her tongue. 'Oh, don't start that again.'

He leaned forward over the steering wheel, squinting at the name painted on the farm gate.

'Pennywake,' said Emily.

'No! That's not it.' He took a paper from the glove box, one eye on the road, and gave it to her to read. 'It's Land-something.'

She took the paper. 'Greenacres.'

'That's it.' He drove on a few miles.

'There's a house over there.' Emily pointed. 'And another one there on the right. Which side of the road is it on do, you know?'

'On the left, I think. Look, there it is. Look, painted on that post.' It was on the right: 'Greenacres Landing'. He turned off the road into a narrow farm track, and they bumped along slowly. It was just wide enough for one car, with a deep ditch at either side and high hedgerows.

They drove on. It was a long way. They came to a five-barred gate, with a painted sign that said 'Greenacres Landing'. It was closed. Emily got out and opened it, and Dominic drove through. She shut the gate again and got back into the car, and they drove on. Now the hedgerows had gone, and the land opened out flat for miles on either side of them.

'I can see why they called it Greenacres,' said Emily.

'I would have called it "Back of Beyond",' Dominic chuckled. 'There doesn't seem any ending to this drive, and I can't see a house anywhere.' It was dead straight, stretching out like a long narrow line in front of them. The house they thought they had seen from the road was nowhere in sight. They went over a humped bridge, and Emily pointed out some ducks on the water.

'Looks like we are getting nearer,' said Dominic.

They could see another five-barred gate and a house ahead. The gate was open, and they went through for a few yards on a crunchy gravel drive. The old farmhouse was on the left. Dominic stopped the car and switched off the engine.

'At last.'

He was just about to open the door when four Great Danes as big as ponies came bounding out with deep-throated barks. He closed the door again, and they sat in the car until a short old man came out wearing grubby grey trousers and a cherry-red sweater with holes at the elbows. His face was as red as his sweater, and his thin hair was mousy and balding on top. He looked as if he had just got out of bed.

'Down boys, down!' he shouted above the barking. He came round to Dominic's side of the car and the dogs followed him.

'It's OK, you can get out! They're all friendly, they just make a lot of noise.' He greeted them with a pleasant smile, showing broken yellow teeth. He had a twisted nose that had at some point been broken. He waved his hand down, and the dogs stopped, knowing that the visitors were welcome.

Dominic got out. 'You've got some good guards there.'

The man laughed. 'I don't know why! Even the burglars couldn't find us out here.'

As Emily got out, the dogs came round to greet her, their

170

heads reached higher than her waist. The man smiled across the roof of the car.

'Don't worry! They are very friendly. They love to be made a fuss of.'

She smiled, putting her hand out to touch each and every one on the head in turn, as they jostled each other to get near her.

'I'm George Mortimer. You'll be wanting my son, Ben.'

'Yes. I have come about a grey horse he has for sale. I phoned yesterday. I'm Dominic Hadley.' They shook hands.

'That's right, you phoned. He's expecting you. You found us all right then; not easy, is it?' He indicated for them to follow him. 'Ben is in the house. Come on in.'

They followed him through the front door. Two of the Great Danes followed. The farmhouse was large with grey flint stone walls on the outside. The dark-red front door was open and, inside, the hallway was long and narrow and carpeted in brown and pink flowers. Half the wall was woodwork, and painted dark brown. The rest of the wall was painted a shiny yellow cream that had darkened with age and reached up to a grey-white uneven ceiling. There was a smell of dampness and decay. They entered a spacious lounge, well furnished with antiques. The carpet was red, the walls a glowing pink, not very tasteful, and there was a smell of cooking, but Emily thought on cold winter nights, with the snow outside, she could imagine this room warm and cosy with a roaring fire in the grate. In front of it now stood a tapestry screen decorated with brightly coloured flowers.

George went off to tell his son.

'Hello! Ben Mortimer, how do you do?' He came into the room, hand outstretched to Dominic, and then shook hands with Emily. 'You found us then. A bit off the beaten track, aren't we?' He smiled. He was not unlike his father, of medium height, fairish hair, in his middle thirties, dressed in jodhpurs and long brown boots. A green sweatshirt, with a red-check collar showing at his neck. 'I've got the horse ready for you to look at. Jimmy Bennett phoned me, said you were interested in dapple-greys. I like them, too. Always reminds me of my childhood rocking horse. That's how I first got into horses, you know, jumping about on a rocking horse. Always swore I would

171

ride a real horse one day. I thought then that all horses were dapple-grey, so Dad bought me a dapple-grey pony, when I was five, and it has gone on from there. Come through!'

They followed him through to the spacious farmhouse kitchen, with a long pine table in the centre. Warmth came from a black Aga, which took up half the length of one wall, and there was a wonderful smell of stew that made Emily's mouth water. There was a woman standing at the sink peeling potatoes. She was plump, with grey hair pulled back tightly into a bun at the nape of her neck. She wore a navy-blue and white-spotted dress, and a full-length flowered pinafore. She gave them a severe look and then a shy smile, as Ben introduced her as his mother. She was obviously not used to visitors, but she wished them a quiet 'Good morning', keeping her head down and avoiding their eyes.

They crossed the yard into the covered stables with high arched beams. There were several stalls full of straw, wheelbarrows, shovels and buckets at each door, and four well-kept dapple-grey heads nodded to them from over the half stable doors, two on one side and two diagonally opposite. Dominic and Emily put out a hand to each of them as they passed.

'They're great,' said Dominic. 'How many hands?'

'These three are sixteen. Dusty, his full name is Silver Dust, but we call him Dustbin because he eats like a horse, if you can forgive the pun. But he never stops, can't even put him out to grass, but it is his own fault, isn't it?' He gave the horse a friendly pat. 'He is seventeen hands, ten years old. I bred him myself. This is the mother, Moon Dust.' He pointed to a mare looking over stable door opposite, a few stalls down.

'Is this the one we have come to see?' asked Emily stroking Dusty on the nose.

'No!' said Ben with a chuckle. 'He's outside.' They followed Ben out through the other end of the stable into a second open yard, where two girls in jodhpurs and green sweatshirts were busy mucking out. There were six stables here in all, and two were occupied, again by dapple-greys. Ben went to one, where a bright and sprightly-looking horse was wearing a head collar, and opened the door, and led out the seventeen-hands stallion. He pranced jauntily on long slender legs. He looked strong with huge powerful hindquarters swishing a silver tail

172

and a long silver mane that bounced on a sturdy curved neck. He looked fit and in peak condition and very much like Silverspoon, and so handsome he took their breath away. Emily had flashes of the first day that she had seen Black Tulip, and this seemed to be the same sort of situation.

Dominic patted the side of his neck and smoothed his hand down the cheek, talking quietly and saying 'good boy'. He rubbed gently down the long mottled nose, then looked up the nostrils to check they were clear. He looked into the big brown eyes; they were bright and friendly. The horse flicked his silver ears at his touch and sidled round a little nervously. The groom, Jessica, stood holding onto the head collar.

Dominic soothed him. 'Good boy, steady, steady!' He walked around him, running his hand under his belly and along his flank and up and over his grey-mottled hindquarters, and then down his long, slender legs. He had a vet's eye. There was a four-inch scar, halfway down the left leg, which had been healed for some time, but the hair had not grown back. The legs were much darker in colour as they neared the hoof. He inspected the hooves, which had been oiled and polished for the occasion, and he could see that he had recently been shod. He stood up and gave him a friendly slap on his hindquarters. Looking at Ben Mortimer, he nodded. 'He seems fine.'

'Would you like to ride him?' Ben asked.

'Yes, please! I would! That's if you don't mind.'

'Not at all.' Ben took hold of the collar. 'I must warn you, though, he's bit of a handful.' He turned to Jessica. 'Get a bridle and saddle up Stardust. And bring a helmet, please, Jess.'

'Oh, is that his name, Stardust?' Emily smiled. 'I like it.' She patted his neck and stroked his silver mane.

While the girl was saddling up, Dominic turned to Emily and asked quietly, 'What do you think?'

She nodded, looking up at the stallion, her blue eyes shining with delight. 'I think he looks nice, don't you?' She spoke equally quietly, but Ben overheard.

'Yes, he is nice.' He gave the horse a slap. 'Got a nice nature. I like him, but he's got a lot of spirit.'

'Then why are you selling him?' Emily looked surprised.

'Well, as you can see, I have six here already. A couple of

173

them are a bit old now, and I have four out there in the meadow. I expect you saw them as you came in, but I am about to buy another one...' He flicked his thumb over his shoulder. 'Stardust is a bit frisky. He's strong. He's a man's horse and my girls can't manage him. I am the only one here that can really ride him apart from one of the young lads, and I don't always get the time, and I need horses that we can all manage. You see, I have to go away on business sometimes. I judge at shows, and it takes me all over the country, and sometimes I am away for the weekend, sometimes longer. My girls here can manage very well. I leave Jessica in charge, and the place runs smoothly, but they can't always manage Stardust. He really needs a man's firm hand. So that is the only reason for me selling him. Mind you, I didn't expect anyone to come so soon. I only just mentioned it in passing to Jimmy Bennett, just the other day.'

Dominic rode Stardust for about ten minutes, then swaggered over to the gate. The horse was perfectly under his control. Stardust's nostrils flared like a fiery dragon's, and his large almond eyes seemed to sparkle with devilish merriment. He nodded his head up and down looking for praise, which he got from Dominic as he patted him on the neck.

'He is good! How is he at jumping? Have you any jumps I can try?'

'Sure!' Ben had a genuine smile. 'He can jump anything, and quite often does. That hedge, for instance! He can clear it like jumping over a matchstick.' They looked to where he was pointing; the hedge was high. 'He's got out on more than one occasion... We have a paddock over here. Bring him through.' He opened the gate, and Emily stood back as the great horse came trotting and prancing out of the gate, full of pent-up energy.

Dominic took each jump perfectly, and Ben suggested raising them, calling to Jessica, who was a big girl, to help him lift the poles at each jump. Dominic proceeded again. He went round and round, and each time they raised the poles. The last was now up to six feet, but Stardust flew over it like a bird. Dominic brought him to standstill, and over to the gate where Emily and Ben and Jessica were now all leaning.

He shed his stirrups and slid down out of the saddle, a big

grin on his face. 'He's great. You give him a try, Em!' He held out the reins for her.

'Me!' She looked at him in surprise.

Ben looked at him in astonishment. He knew the power of this horse. He needed a man's firm handling. 'Well, I…' He was about to protest.

'Go on, Em. Then I can see just how he looks.' Emily was thrilled to think that Dominic really did value her opinion *and* her ability to ride.

Ben was not so sure. He hesitated. 'I don't think it's a good idea; he's powerful.' But seeing that Emily looked confident and anxious to have a go, he said, 'Better lower the poles a bit, Jess!'

'No!' Dominic frowned. 'Don't worry! She can handle it.' He gave her a leg up.

Jessica gave him a fearful look. 'I hope so,' she muttered under her breath. 'I'll get you a hat,' she said out loud to Emily and dashed off into the covered yard, calling to the other girls. 'Hey quick, that girl is going to ride Stardust!' They all looked up, dropped what they were doing and walked towards the entrance where they could watch from a distance. Jessica came back and handed Emily a smaller helmet. 'Be careful,' she warned, and looked up at Dominic with fearful eyes, hoping he knew what he was doing.

He gave her one of his flashing smiles, and she almost melted at his feet. Never before had such a handsome man looked at her that way, and what a lucky girl this one was or was he trying to kill her off?! Dominic turned back to look at Emily, and, out of the corner of his eye, he saw Jessica still looking at him. He turned to look at her again and smiled to himself as she quickly looked away at the horse, her rounded plump face bright red with embarrassment.

Emily was in no doubt that she could ride this fabulous fiery steed, but praise from Dominic was praise indeed. She settled herself in the saddle, and he shortened the stirrups for her. Taking up the reins and turning Stardust's head, she walked him round and round for a few minutes, feeling the power in his lithe, silver body as he pranced jauntily up and down looking at the first jump. She trotted him round the perimeter of the paddock. He was lively and springy. She got the rhythm going,

175

then took him into a canter, and they cleared the first jump. She felt the power as his forelegs lifted off the ground and the boost from the back as they shot into the air and down the other side. She was lying flat against his neck; she felt as if her arms were being pulled from their sockets. He was strong, he was fast. They flew over the next fence… It felt great!

'She rides well.' Ben glanced at Dominic with surprised admiration, then looked back quickly, not wanting to miss a stride.

Dominic nodded, not taking his eyes off Emily. 'She certainly gives me a run for my money.' He was thinking how wonderful the horse went, and how beautifully Emily rode him. They looked as if they were used to each other and had done this many times before. There was not another woman to touch her.

She was racing towards the big six-foot fence. Ben Mortimer took a sharp intake of breath and gave Jessica a quick apprehensive glance. She looked back, her eyes round as marbles. The forelegs reared, and the great strength in his hindquarters boosted them up off the ground and took them through the air like a silver dart, his back legs almost straight out and missing the poles by a mile. He and Emily landed safely on the other side and cantered on round the paddock at speed, then she brought Stardust to a slow, controlled halt by the gate. Jessica started to clap, and all the stable girls watching joined in. Emily smiled and dipped her head as if taking a bow.

Ben let out his breath, relieved that the great horse had not thrown her off. He looked at Jessica in amazement, and Jessica clapped her hands together with joy. The horse snorted and dipped its head.

'He looks good, Em. Great to ride, isn't he?'

Emily was breathless, her blue eyes shining with excitement. 'Wonderful!'

Ben grabbed at the bridle and held the fiery steed still as Emily took her feet out of the stirrups, swung her right leg over and slid the long way down to the ground. 'But he is strong to handle, I must agree.'

'You did well, Em.' Dominic put his arm around her shoulders, giving her a friendly hug. 'Do you think Tulip could beat him?' he laughed.

She pulled a face. 'We'd give you a run for your money.'

He smiled. 'Yeah, I don't doubt that for one minute.' He looked at Ben. 'See what I mean. Didn't I just tell you.'

Ben grinned.

Emily looked up at Dominic. 'Tulip and I look forward to the challenge!'

Dominic laughed heartily and Ben, realizing it must be some private joke, turned and strode off leading the horse.

Dominic spoke to her quietly, knowing that Ben Mortimer was out of earshot. 'I like him, but I haven't negotiated a price yet.'

Ben handed the horse over to Jessica, who took him back into the yard to unsaddle him. The girls in the yard were all talking about Emily.

'Yeah, but she must be semi-professional,' said one.

'Nevertheless,' said another one, 'I wouldn't get on a strange horse like him, would you?'

'No, but she hasn't seen him take off like we have, has she?' They all nodded in agreement.

Ben and Dominic talked about a price. Dominic seemed pleased but said he would like to think about it and would let Ben know, probably tomorrow.

Back at home, Emily went up to her bedroom. She sat on the stool in front of the dressing-table mirror and ran a brush through her long blonde hair. She tied it back up with a ribbon into a ponytail. She got up and went to the window looking out across the green fields, now bathed in the dusk of the early evening. The nights were drawing in and it would be almost dark at five o'clock. The autumn sun that had shone today had gone, and the evening was cold. Soon the colder winter weather would be upon them, and there would be weekends when she would not be able to get home from London, weekends when she would not be able to ride. She was staring into space, and could see her own reflection in the darkening glass of the window... She wished that she did not have to go back to London. The city was exciting, her London friends fashionable and full of life, but she was a country girl at heart. She loved the countryside, the fresh clean air, the open fields, the smell of wet dewy grass in the mornings, and,

177

yes, the pungent smell of hay and manure from the yard! That was the life that suited her best, that was what she wanted to do with her life. She wanted to be around horses all the time; she missed Jenny, and their hacking out together, and the practice for the showjumping events. The idea of becoming a professional showjumper had flown out of the window; to do that she would need to give it her full attention and practise eight hours a day. And if she was truthful, she really had missed Dominic... Somewhere in the house the phone was ringing, and then it stopped.

Her mother was calling up the stairs. Emily blinked, bringing herself back to reality, and came down the stairs to answer the phone.

'Hello, Em.' Dominic had taken to calling her Em, as Jenny had always done. 'Have you got any plans for tonight? Do you want to go out to dinner?'

'I'd love to!'

'Good, pick you up at seven thirty. By the way, we are going to the hunt ball next Saturday.'

'Are we?'

'Why? Don't you want to go!?' The old arrogance was there again, just because she had not said yes first time.

'Well, yes! I'd love to go.'

'Well, you don't *have* to go. I'm not forcing you.'

'No! I would like to go, really!'

'Well, you don't sound very enthusiastic about it.'

'Well, you took me by surprise. Besides, I've nothing to wear.'

'Well, you knew I would ask you.'

'Well, I didn't know anything about it!'

'OK! OK!' he sighed irritably. See you at seven thirty.' He was gone.

She stood for a moment with the receiver still in her hand looking at it. 'Arrogant devil,' she muttered, slamming the phone down. 'Now what am I going to wear tonight?' She went back up stairs to her room and started to sort through the closet, making a mental note to buy a new evening dress, shoes and bag during the week in London, and she would have to make arrangements to come home again next Friday night and change places with one of the other girls, as it was her turn to work on Saturday this week.

* * *

She did not leave until after six on Monday, and the drive back to London had been hazardous. It was dark and had rained all the way. The road shone like glass, and the lights reflecting in it dazzled her eyes. The traffic was heavy, too, and it had taken her nearly three and a half hours to get home. She was tired when she let herself into the small flat; her room-mate, Amanda, was almost ready to go out to dinner.

'Do you want to come, Emily? I'm going out with the girls. I'll wait for you if you like.' She was not surprised when Emily said no; she could see that she looked tired and was ready for bed. Amanda left, saying she would try not to wake her when she came in.

Alone in the flat, she went to the kitchen and made some coffee. There was a tin of red salmon in the fridge. She opened it and made a sandwich, and sat down in front of the television. There was a film on, but it was already halfway though, and she was not very interested anyway. She took the empty coffee mug and plate back to the kitchen and rinsed them under the tap. The phone rang. She thought about not answering it – the last thing she wanted now was to stand chatting. It kept ringing.

'Hello.'

'Hello, Emily. Marcus here!'

She sighed and pulled a face. 'Oh, Hello.'

'Heard you were back. I've just seen Amanda. Do you want to come out for a drink?' His voice sounded high-pitched; he had probably had a few already.

'Oh no, thank you, Marcus. Not tonight, I am a bit tired.

'Oh come on, it will cheer you up a bit. It's a miserable night, still raining.'

'No, thank you. I've just spent three and a half hours driving through it.'

'Well, I'll come round and see you then, shall I?'

'No.' But he had already gone. She went into the bedroom, undid her weekend case, and took out her toothbrush, hair-brush, and make-up for the morning, and took it into the bathroom. She took a shower and was in bed within fifteen minutes. She dozed off quickly, physically exhausted, but was quickly awoken by the noise of a bell ringing. She lay with her eyes closed. She was in a dazed state, the bell still ringing. She put out her hand to turn off the alarm clock, then looked at the time – she had only dozed off for twenty minutes. Then she suddenly realized that the bell was still ringing – it was the front door bell. She got lazily out of bed, grabbing at her white towelling dressing-gown which she had laid across the bedroom chair, and went to open the door still tying up the belt. She opened the door an inch. Through the crack the plump face of Marcus DuBarry peered back smiling. He was raising a bottle of wine.

'Thought I would just pop round and cheer you up,' he smiled, almost poking his nose through the crack.

She opened the door with a reluctant sigh, and his portly figure swaggered in. He wore a smart grey suit and a white shirt and was holding the bottle high. She noticed that the knot on his red tie had slipped.

'Amanda said you had had a hell of a drive back from Suffolk. Traffic bad, was it?' His words were a little slurred. 'Hell of a night out there now, raining like cats and dogs. Just been to Rochas; good meal! If I'd known, I would have waited and taken you out for dinner.' He stopped. 'Did you see that boyfriend?' He wobbled a bit. She could see that he had been drinking.

She grimaced, closing the door quietly behind him. 'Look, Marcus! I told you, I'm tired...'

Ignoring her, he went into the small kitchen and got two glasses. What a cheek! He had not been to the flat before, and she would never have invited him up there.

'Thought we would have a little nightcap. What do you say?'

'I said NO, Marcus! I told you, I have had a long drive, and the last thing I want is a drink.'

'Just one for the road, eh!'

'I've been on the road, thanks.'

He poured the golden wine into the glasses on the coffee table with a slightly shaky hand, and offered her a glass. 'Cheers!' He wobbled back on his heels again, and then sat down heavily on the sofa.

'I've missed you this weekend, Emily. I went riding again on Sunday with Anna.' His head lolled. 'Of course, she kept me

180

on a leading rein.' He grinned. 'Didn't want any more incidents, did we?' He chuckled. 'She was very impressed with you the other week.' His head wobbled. 'Did you manage to get a ride, at the weekend? The weather wasn't bad, was it?' He mumbled on. 'But now it's raining cats and dogs, CATS AND DOGS,' he repeated, raising his shoulders to his ears then letting them slump heavily. 'Look! I'm all wet.' He splayed out his hands palms upward; they were wet from the wine bottle and the ice bucket, and his shoulders were just splattered from the rain. 'I expect you rode your horshees at the weekend.' He sat forward, looking her in the eye with a deep frown. He was trying to focus, but his head wobbled as if it was too heavy for him to control. 'I'll come down to Suffolk with you nexshed weekend,' he slurred, 'then we can ride out on your farm. What do you say, eh? Eh?'

Emily was bored and tired. She sighed. 'Marcus! Look! Why don't you go?'

'Oh no. No! Emily, not without you. I don't want to go to the farm without you, Emily. You know what! Emily? You know...' he said again, 'I would love to go down to your farm, Emily, but I want you to come. I don't want to go down on my own, do I? I don't want to ride on my own, do I? Shay a horsh runs off with me again...' He pouted like a child, and his head wobbled again. Then he perked up. 'What about next weekend, eh?'

'*Marcus!*' She was getting annoyed. 'I have *not* got a farm, and the last thing I want is you down there, riding horses. Why don't you go now?'

'Oh, I can't go now, dear, too late, too late. Can't ride in the dark, ha ha. Besides, it's raining.'

'You can't ride my horses anyway.'

'Why?' He looked surprised and sat up straight, pulling his shoulders back. He pouted, looking like a small boy that had just been scolded. He sipped at the wine, blowing bubbles into the glass. 'I can ride one of your horshees...' He corrected himself. '...Horses. I can ride one, can't I? It was just: unfotu-un-fortu-unfortunate that, that b-b-bird...' He stumbled again, with a drunken giggle. 'Hit old Warrior on the nose, and he took off. Now if I had been con-cen-trating, he would never have got the bester of me.'

181

'Marcus, look! I want to go to bed.'

'Oh, so do I, Emily!' he leaned towards her, leering at her. She drew away from him in surprise and stood up.

He stood up. 'Really, Emily?' He breathed, with a longing passionate look. He took her hands, as if he was about to sing an aria in an opera. 'I never thought you would get around to this! I never thought. That *you*! And I. Well, I didn't know you cared.'

'I don't, Marcus; I don't care much at all.' She was shaking her head and trying to pull her hands free. He swayed backwards; she was holding him up.

'Oh! But I am so glad that you do care, just a little bit, Emily!' He leered at her. 'I love you, Emily. Come on!' He was suddenly enthusiastic. His blue eyes widened and he giggled with eagerness, like a boy out on a prank. Letting her hands go, he started to put an arm around her shoulders. She wriggled away, and he took a step nearer, putting his arm around her again, and began to move her gently towards the bedroom. She untangled herself and turned round to face him, pushing him back, but he was too strong. He moved in on her, walking step for step forward as she walked backwards. So close was he that she had her hands up on his chest trying to hold him off. He was almost pushing her with his chest into the bedroom. The door was wide open; she wished it had been closed. She put her hand out to slam it shut between them, but it was too late. She was still stepping backwards when she lost her balance and fell onto her bed. He looked down on her with drunken desire, but as he bent forward she twisted sideways and sprang up onto her feet again. He lunged towards her a little unsteadily, saying 'Oh, Emily, Emily!' She punched him straight in the face, her arm stretched out at full length. He shot backwards out of the bedroom door and lay flat on his back in the lounge, his arms and his legs spread-eagled. He lay very still, blood trickling from his nose. She walked cautiously forward and stood over him, both hands covering her mouth. What had she done? Then, seeing that he was still breathing, and was just knocked out cold, she relaxed and grinned to herself. She went into the bedroom and shut the door, turning the key. She was thankful for her strong arms – an effect of riding – which had saved

182

her from a fate worse than death with Marcus DuBarry. She grinned with relief.

It was only a matter of a few minutes before she heard the front door open and close. She thought he had got up and gone out. She opened the door cautiously just an inch. He was still there and Amanda was on her knees, looking up at Emily in the open doorway.

'What happened?'

'I hit him.'

'Poor old Marcus,' she grinned. 'What did he do?'

'Nothing, thank God.'

'Then why did you hit him?'

'For what he nearly did. It was a case of life or desire.'

Amanda laughed. Between them they brought him round with icepacks on his nose. They gave him black coffee, Emily called a taxi, and they sent him off home in the pouring rain, groaning and holding his head.

16

Emily and Amanda were both in the flat. They had decided to cook a meal between them and have an early night. Outside, the October weather was drizzling and cold, but the central heating was on and the flat was cosy. They were both in towelling dressing-gowns and had both washed their hair. Emily had a towel wrapped around her head. The television was on, and they were both sitting at the table painting their nails. Emily looked up as the newsreader mentioned the Horse of the Year Show at Wembley Stadium.

'Oh, I didn't know that was on! I must get some tickets. Have you ever been to the Horse of the Year Show?'

'No, I'm not too keen on horses.' But they watched as the news showed snippets of past events. Emily said that she had seen it years ago with her parents. She felt more determined than ever to get better; she would love to ride at Wembley.

'I'll book tickets when you're in it. Just let me know when!' Amanda chuckled. 'I like to be in with the rich and famous.'

'Oh!' Emily huffed. 'You can't get rich with horses. They cost a fortune.' Then she smiled. 'But they give you an enormous amount of pleasure. She flicked her fingers. 'And you haven't much need for nail varnish either!'

The next morning in the office Emily phoned and got four tickets. Then she phoned Dominic to tell him. He arranged to pick her up at her flat, which he was anxious to see, and she said that she would have a bottle of champagne on ice ready and waiting. She phoned Jenny, and they made arrangements to meet at the stadium and have dinner afterwards.

Emily left the office an hour earlier. She had to shop for an evening-dress for the hunt ball the following Saturday. She went to Selfridges where she knew they had a big selection of designer makes. She tried on three black dresses and decided on one of them, a very slinky number with shoestring straps and a few diamante stones across one side of the bust line. It cost a fortune. There were the shoes, too. She chose stiletto heels in black satin, with diamante buckles. The assistant showed her a small handbag to match, and she bought that as well, the bag costing almost double the price of the shoes. But she had to look special for Dominic. He admired the way she looked; he had told her so many times.

Although she enjoyed her work in the travel agency, this week seemed to drag out. She couldn't wait to see Dominic and wear the lovely dress. And it would be wonderful again to ride Tulip and Pico; she and Dominic would ride out together. And just to smell the fresh country greenery again made her dreamy. London was exciting, with its bright lights and the hubbub of traffic and fast pace of living, but she missed the peace and quiet, and the fresh air. She decided there and then that she was going to go home every single week from now on, and if the office didn't like it, she would leave.

There had been excited talk amongst the girls in the office of transfers to Spain. Vicky said she would love to go, but Emily wasn't so sure; it would mean leaving her horses. So she decided that if she was asked to move on, she would definitely say no and give in her notice. She also did not want to lose Dominic, especially as they had only just made up again. She was so looking forward to seeing him and going to the hunt ball! She told Glenda and Vicky, the two girls she worked with, about the dress she had bought, and Vicky said she had never worn an evening-dress. Although she lived in London, she and her husband couldn't afford to go to fancy places, and Emily said that Suffolk was a great place for parties and she quite often had worn an evening-dress. Both Vicky and Glenda asked if she would have any photos to show them.

Graham, driving his Mercedes, stopped to pick up Jenny. He looked so handsome in his dinner jacket and back tie, and he whistled at Jenny as she came to greet him in a long black strapless evening dress, which showed off her creamy white shoulders. She had borrowed a pearl necklace from her sister-in-law because she had broken her own, and they matched her long drop pearl earrings. She had her dark hair pinned up at the back in curls, held in place with pearl hairslide. Graham kissed her on the cheek and said that he had never seen her look so beautiful. She got into his car, wrapping a pashmina tightly around her shoulders. They were to meet Emily and Dominic at Wickerbrook Hall.

It was crowded when they arrived. There was valet parking; Sir James Bartram thought of everything. Feeling very proud, Jenny took a glass of champagne from the tray offered by a waiter, and they soon mingled with their friends.

Emily opened the front door as Dominic rang the bell. She had seen him from the window coming up the drive. He stood open-mouthed as she stood before him framed in the doorway. The black silk clung to her slim figure; she looked as if she had been poured into the dress. Her blonde hair had been swept up at the back, like Jenny's, into a smooth chignon. Small diamond studs shone at her ears – her parents had bought them for her birthday – and round her neck was a thin row of diamante stones. His eyes ran over her from her head to the tip of her pink-painted toenails that peeped out from satin evening shoes under the hem of the dress. She carried a pale-pink pashmina over her arm. He said nothing.

'Well?' Her blue eyes questioned him as he stood there. She knew she had stunned him.

'Well, what?' The slightest smile touched the corners of his mouth. She looked so beautiful he was stupefied. His eyes had that merry twinkle.

'Well! Are we going to the hunt ball or not?' she said at last.

'Good God! You look stunning.' He had never seen her like this. Most of the time she was a young girl in jodhpurs or jeans, but now she stood before him a sensual woman. It was as if he were seeing her for the very first time...

'So do you.' She smiled. 'You look very handsome.' It was the first time she had ever seen him in a dress suit, and she felt proud that he had chosen her. All the girls fluttered their eyes at him, maybe it was because she had not fluttered her eyes that he liked her. 'I didn't even know that you owned a suit. Is it yours?' She looked him up and down with a dubious smile.

He looked surprised. 'Of course it is!'

He smiled as her mother came to the door. 'Well, are you two going or are you just going to let in all this cold night air. Gosh, you do look handsome, Dominic. Doesn't he Emily?'

He smiled. 'Not as beautiful as her, Mrs Peters!' He took the pink wrap from her and put it around her shoulders, then took her arm and guided her out to the car, calling goodnight to her mother.

It was a wonderful night, they met Graham and Jenny in the conservatory of Wickerbrook Hall, which for the evening had been turned into a bar. There must have been a hundred people milling about. The noise was horrendous, like one continuous babble, as people stood in groups, glasses in hand, talking. It was amazing that anyone could hear what anyone else was saying. After drinks and canapés, a smart red-coated master of ceremonies, who had been standing in the doorway, announced that dinner was served. There was a board with names and table numbers by the door. They found that they were on table twelve, and everyone slowly made their way into the marquee, where the tables were laid out for three hundred people, with glittering glass and silver on snow-white tablecloths, small vases of mixed flowers, and a number printed on a white card on a silver stand in the centre. At one end of the marquee, across a temporary wooden dance floor, a large orchestra played quietly. Dominic led the way, followed by Emily holding his hand, and Jenny and Graham, to table twelve, close to the dance floor, where they joined Mary Clark and John Carpenter, her boyfriend, whom none of them had met before. He said he was a lawyer in London, so he and Emily had something in common, though, of course, Emily knew nothing about law. And then it turned out that he knew nothing about horses. The farrier Tom Cunningham and his wife, Maggie, who was friendly with Louise, sat opposite Jenny and Graham. Also at the table were Louise and her current boyfriend, Sir Simeon Hatch, a tall, thin stick of a man with a weak chin and straight, thinning mousy hair. Emily thought him a bit foppish until she sat next to him and found that he was quite good company. He knew a lot about horses, although he rarely got to ride because he was a merchant banker in the City.

They had wined and dined, and everyone was ready for dancing. The orchestra played more loudly, and from then on they mixed partners, dancing with each other and drinking until late into the evening.

Emily was sitting with Maggie and Tom Cunningham. Everyone else was on the dance floor. She felt exhausted and her feet were killing her. Dominic had been dancing with Mary Clark, and she saw them talking to Alex Freemore, then they had come back to sit down and the band started to play a slow tune. As the lights were lowered, Dominic took Emily's hand and pulled her to her feet and onto the dance floor. He took her into his arms and they swayed to the soft rhythm. He held her close, breathing in the sweet perfume of her hair, his eyes closed and quite oblivious to everyone else on the floor. She nestled against his chest, feeling the strong warmth of his arms, as he turned her slowly round and round the floor. They were near the side opening of the marquee where it was cooler.

'Come on!' he suggested. 'Let's go outside for some air.'

They slipped out unnoticed into the chill night air, and walked across the open lawn, hand in hand. A pale moon shone down, and everything was bathed in silvery light. He put an arm around her as they walked over to a large oak tree and stood behind it, away from the chill breeze and hidden from view of the marquee.

He turned her to him, her back against the tree. She shivered, and he took off his jacket and put it around her shoulders. His shirt was a brilliant blue-white in the moonlight. He cupped her face in his strong hands, kissing her lips tenderly. Her arms went up around his neck, responding as she nestled into him. He was warm and comfortable, and the smell of his aftershave was now mixed with his sweat from dancing and had a masculine tang. He held her close in his arms, kissing her lips and then her cheeks, and whispering softly, 'I love you, my darling Emily'

She pulled away a little from him, her hands on his chest, and looked up into his face. It was in shadow. She could not see his eyes, but she knew they would be twinkling, and the outline of his jaw looked serious. Could he really mean that

188

he loved her? Could she believe it, or had he had too much to drink?

'I love you, Em,' he whispered softly, then leaned away and smiled down at her in the darkness and gave her a quick peck on the lips. 'I think I have loved you since that day at the Goldsborough.'

She smiled up at him. 'You were angry!'

'I know I was,' he grinned. 'But you looked so small and vulnerable up there on Pico, twisting about trying to control him, I wanted to grab you and take you into my arms.'

'Well, you did! Though you didn't whisk me away on your dapple-grey charger like a knight in shining armour, did you? You shouted at me.'

'Well, you were crying hysterically.'

'Well, all the more reason then! And so would you, if you knew that you had upset a very special day, and knew the problem but couldn't tell anyone, especially after all that hard practice, and losing the chance of winning the Goldsborough trophy...'

'Winning!' He straightened his shoulders with astonishment.

She shivered.

'You cold?'

'Yes.'

He kissed her cheek. 'Come on, let's go in.'

The magic of the moment had gone; she had said the wrong word.

Back in the marquee, the band had just played another fast pop song and the dancers were just leaving the floor, tired and hot after an enjoyable but exhausting evening. The band was packing up, and people were standing in groups chatting, and finishing their drinks. There were calls of goodnight.

They eventually got home at two o'clock in the morning. He dropped her off at Rosemary Lodge, kissing her goodnight in the car, then seeing her to the door. He waited until she went in, and then got back into the car and drove on home. The roads were quiet, thank goodness! He wasn't drunk but had he been pulled up by the police he would have been well over the limit.

Emily, in her room, ran the zip down the back of her dress dreamily and hung it on a hanger. Although she was tired, she

189

lay awake for hours, and eventually dropped off to sleep about five in the morning. She got up in time for lunch.

'Morning, darling.' Liz looked up at the clock on the wall. 'Oh, it's afternoon.' She smiled cheerfully, looking over her shoulder from the cooker. 'Did you have a nice time last night?'

Mike was sitting at the kitchen table. He looked over the top of his Sunday newspaper; he always read it from cover to cover. 'Did you have a good time? I didn't hear you come in.'

'I did!' said Liz. 'It was about two o'clock. By the way, Dominic phoned about an hour ago; he wants you to ring him back.'

'Oh, you didn't tell him I was still in bed, did you?'

'No! I just said you were not here at the moment. He probably thought that you were out in the yard.'

'Oh good...' She sat at the table, one hand under her chin. 'He is a good dancer.'

'Didn't he look handsome?' Liz smiled. 'I always think men look good in black tie, don't you? It seems to suit them all.'

'Bloody uncomfortable when it's hot,' murmured Mike from behind the newspaper.

'He certainly is a very handsome young lad. What's his brother like?'

'Graham's a nice guy. He looks very much like Dominic, but he's not so cocky, although the arrogance is there; it's in them both. He and Jenny are quite serious.'

'And you and Dominic?' Liz questioned, half turning for a quick moment, catching the expression on Emily's face, which seemed to say that they were not so serious. She frowned. 'I thought Dominic liked you?'

Emily smiled, looking thoughtful. 'Yes, I think he does.' She left the table to put her coffee cup on the draining-board. Liz was about to dish up the lunch, and she changed the conversation.

'Was Jenny's dress nice?'

'Yes, she looked lovely... It was black.'

'So did you. Didn't she, Mike?'

'Mmmmm. What! Umm!' He peered over the top of the paper, then, suddenly realizing, said: 'Oh, yes, dear, yes, er, what did you say? Oh yes, yes, the dress. Yes, you looked beautiful last night, darling. Did you have a good time?' He lifted the paper again and disappeared behind it.

After lunch Emily went out into the yard. She patted Black

Tulip and then went to pat Pico. She was talking to him when suddenly Tulip began to whinny and kick at the door, which started Pico off. She looked around her. She knew by the way they acted that Major was there, and she wondered why. It had been ages since she and John had heard a clip-cropping of his invisible hooves.

She was just getting Pico a bucket of water when John came into the yard. He didn't work on Sundays, but he nearly always popped in.

'Oh, hello, John! I think Major is around again.'

'Oh, is he?' John looked around him, knowing all the same that if there was anything there, he wouldn't see it.

'I have only just come out here, and they both got a bit agitated.' Just as she said it, the horses started to whinny again and Pico kicked hard at the stable door. His eyes were wild and white with fear. 'It's all right, it's all right,' Emily soothed him, rubbing his nose as he lifted it and nodded deeply. John was trying to soothe Black Tulip, and he had just gained her confidence when Major's stable door began to shudder. They both turned quickly, Emily's eyes wide with concern, as a grey shadow wafted across the yard and disappeared before their eyes.

'John?' It was a questioning whisper.

'That's 'im, Miss, but I wonder why?' He shook his head. 'Somethink 'as disturbed 'im agin.'

Emily went to Tulip, smoothing her nose, and patting the side of her face gently. She was quiet now that the misty grey shadow had gone, although her eyes still looked towards the paddock and, for a moment, she was a bit jumpy again.

'What is it, Tulip? What is it that makes Major come back every now and again?' Her thoughts drifted to Dominic, and his words rang in her ears. 'I love you, Em.' She was sure it was the drink. They were just very good friends. The odd kiss or two, but that was all. She was very fond of him, but whether it was love, she didn't know. She had never been in love, so how would she know?

'How would you know if you are in love, Tulip?' she asked in a tiny voice so that John couldn't hear. The horse slapped her lips. 'Do you know? How would I know?' She put her forehead against the long black nose and felt the warmth of

191

the soft velvety skin at the end. 'I love you, Tulip, I know that, but is it the same?' Dominic had felt warm last night. It had been a very comfortable feeling enclosed in his arms, but then maybe it was because she also had had a few glasses of wine. But why had she then, and why did she now, feel so mellow? She leaned away from Tulip looking up and stroking her nose again, feeling uneasy. Was this how a hangover felt? No, it couldn't be; she hadn't got a headache and she had not had that much to drink. But she couldn't settle. Was this love?

'You all right, Miss?' John called after her. She flushed. He must have been watching her.

'Yes I am fine, John, thanks. Late night. I'll be back.' She was walking towards the house.

He called after her again. 'Hunt Ball good, was it?'

She sighed. 'Wonderful, John. Wonderful!'

John nodded to himself and got on with what he was doing. Just before he was due to leave, he went to bring Tulip in from the paddock. She walked quietly beside him to the yard, and suddenly without warning she reared up and whinnied. Emily was just coming back out of the kitchen door and she saw it happen. She ran towards John, who was holding onto the head collar and for a split second was taken right off his feet.

'Major!' She growled out his name roughly, grabbing hold of the leading rein. 'Stop it! Where are you?' She looked around the yard, hoping to get a glimpse.

They were still hanging onto the leading rein, and Tulip was pulling back towards the paddock gate. Between them, they held her firmly, and as John seemed to have her under control, Emily let go of the red rope. John was still dragged back a few feet but he did not intend to let her go. He knew she would calm down, and he spoke sternly to her.

'Whoa, Tulip! Whoa, girl. Come on now!' She calmed, but her eyes still showed fright. 'That's a good girl.' He patted her cheek and smoothed her nose.

'Are you all right, John?' Emily was concerned as she came up behind him to pat Tulip.

'Yeah! I'm OK thanks, Miss! Are you?' he called over his shoulder. 'She just caught me off guard, but she is OK now.' He patted her and she walked calmly back with him into the

192

yard, and settled back into the clean stable, she went straight in and began to chomp on the hay net as if nothing had happened. John bolted the half door, then went to get Pico, who was chasing around like a mad thing. She and John stood by the gate calling to him but it was a few minutes before he slowed down, shaking his head, as if to rid himself of something. Then he saw them and came over to the gate huffing and puffing, and John was ready with the head collar. He was no trouble, Major must have gone.

The bit of excitement had not spurred Emily on, and she wandered aimlessly back to the kitchen, not knowing what to do with herself. She poured herself another mug of coffee from the percolator and she sat down dreamily at the table, warming her hands around the mug and staring into space.

Liz came into the kitchen. 'Hello, darling.' She looked at Emily, bending her head down so that she could see her face. 'Are you all right, darling?' she inquired with concern.

Emily had her elbows on the table, her hands resting on her cheeks. She lifted her eyes only. 'Major's back!'

'Oh! No!' Liz felt a pang of anxiety.

'Tulip took John right off his feet, and dragged him along, but he is OK; he managed to control her. I helped him and she is all right now. I don't know what to do about him. How can we stop him, Mum?'

'Well, I don't know, darling. I just don't know what to think. Are *you* all right?'

'Yes, why?' She took her arms off the table and looked up at her mother.'

'Well, you look a bit far away... You're sure you're all right?'

'Yes, of course. I'm fine.' She sipped at the hot coffee. She sighed. 'Why does he keep coming back, Mum?'

'Perhaps it's something in your mind, dear. Maybe you think of him and he comes back.'

'Me! I wasn't even out there, and I wasn't thinking about him! I was thinking about what Dominic said.'

Liz brought her coffee to the table and sat down. 'Oh, what did he say then? Have you had another row?'

Emily smiled shyly. 'Oh no, just the opposite!'

Liz moved her eyes only, looking at her sideways.

17

Emily was in the office. The phones had been ringing all morning. All three of them had been busy; she had just taken a phone call from a man wanting to book a ticket to Spain for two weeks in July. She looked out on the miserably cold drizzle of the October day, and thought that it would be a good idea to go somewhere warm. Perhaps she and Jenny could go out to Barbados. It would be lovely and warm there in November. But then could she suddenly go? No! Of course not! The office was busy; people were still booking for Christmas, and then there were the horses and still a few shows to go to. She had her elbows on the desk, her hands to her cheeks, studying the computer screen in front of her, but she was miles away, dreaming of golden sandy beaches, blue skies and hot sunshine seeping into her skin.

She was deep into her daydream, when the phone rang spoiling it all. She picked up the receiver. It was another customer wanting to book a two-week trip to Sardinia. She sighed. 'Yes, sir. When did you want to go?' She was pressing the keys on the computer. 'Oh yes, the first, and returning the fourteenth. Could you give me your credit-card number, Mr Johnston?' She was typing it all in as he gave her the details, then he rang off. She sat looking around the room, the walls filled with brightly coloured posters of golden sands, sun-drenched beaches, and girls in bikinis with bronzed bodies and smiling faces under large straw hats. She could almost feel the warmth of the sun! Perhaps she would ask Jenny after all. She could get flights and hotels at a cheaper rate and maybe they could go in January or February, when things were not so busy. Perhaps Dominic and Graham could come, too. She looked at a poster for sunglasses, in which a bronzed handsome guy with rippling muscles was posing on a sailboat. She wondered what it would be like to go on a luxury yacht or a cruise ship. She wondered if Dominic had a bronzed body, like the guy in the poster. She knew he had strong muscled arms; riding did that. Dominic's face and his hands were tanned from being in the open air every day. She pictured the look of self-importance that was always there, the way he moved his head and the softness of his voice: 'I love you, Emily.' It haunted her. She had spoken to him since, but he had never said it again, and she had told no one, not even Jenny. She came out of her daydream with a jerk as the phone rang again. It must have been the drink.

It was the night of the Horse of the Year Show. She had a shower, feeling excited as Dominic would be well on the way to London by now. Sitting in front of the dressing-table mirror in a dressing-gown, brushing her hair and leaving it loose. It reached well below her shoulders, framing her face like a spun silver veil. She sprayed it to keep it tidy. She had washed it and as usual couldn't do a thing with it. She sprayed another quick puff of perfume behind her ears and on her wrists. She went back into the bathroom again to check on her make-up. She was excited and nervous. He hadn't been to the flat before. She had straightened up the cushions and had got a bottle of champagne on ice and two glasses ready on a tray.

Amanda called from the kitchen. 'Do you want a cup of coffee, Emily?'

'No thanks, Mandy, I'm just getting dressed.'

She took a new black miniskirt from a hanger in the closet, stepped into it, and pulled it up over her slim hips, fiddling nervously with the zip as if she had not got minute to spare, as if it were a first date. She pulled the new pale-blue sweater over her head, and looked in the mirror, twisting this way and that. She was satisfied with the way she looked, but she would have to do her hair again. She looked at her watch. Time was getting on, but at last she was ready, slipping her stockinged feet into black high-heel leather boots. She came out of the bedroom breathless, as if she had been in a race.

'You look nice,' said Amanda with admiration. 'I like the sweater. Where did you buy that?'

195

'Harvey Nichols, yesterday. I bought it especially for tonight,' she smiled, twisting around to show Amanda the full outfit. 'Like it?'

She smiled. 'Nice. Do you want some coffee now?'

'No thanks. I feel too excited; Dominic will be here soon!' She plumped up the cushions on the sofa again, which did not need doing, and straightened the ashtray on the coffee table. 'He hasn't seen the flat yet.'

'I know, but it will be perfect. I'll stand in the kitchen and drink my coffee. Wouldn't want to mess up the cushions again.' She pulled a face.

'Oh, Amanda, I'm sorry.'

She smiled. 'It's all right. Sit down and relax for a minute. Anyone would think you were on a blind date.' She smiled, picking up her jacket and handbag. 'I'll skip the coffee and get out of your way. I'm off to the cinema with Betty. There's a James Bond film on. Have a lovely evening.'

'Yes, thanks, and you.'

Amanda opened the door and called over her shoulder. 'I hope this handsome Dominic will be here when I get back, I'd like to meet him. Give him a big kiss from me!' She closed the door and tripped lightly down the stairs in a warm coat and long leather boots.

Emily was sitting on the sofa. She got up and looked out of the window. She came back and sat on the sofa, then went into the bedroom to check on her hair again. She was just checking her lipstick for about the fourth time when the doorbell rang. She rushed out through the lounge and into the little hallway and flung open the door. The smile of excitement faded. Standing before her was the round plump face of Marcus DuBarry with two black eyes. He was wearing a loud brown-and-white chequered waistcoat under a sandy coloured jacket and a bright yellow-and-black spotted bow tie. He was holding a bunch of yellow roses to match.

'Hello, Emily.' He sounded sad. He walked in. 'You look lovely. Look, I just came by to apologize about the other night.' He gave her the roses. 'Peace offering,' he smiled. 'I really am sorry. I don't know what to say. I hope you will forgive me. And I think I lost my lighter when I fell over. I mean, when you knocked me out. God, you do pack a punch, don't you?'

196

He fingered his eyes, now turning a nice shade of green, purple and yellow.

She smiled. 'Sorry about that!'

'It was my own fault, although I have told everybody that I walked into a door. You won't tell anyone, will you?' He smiled. 'Can we just kiss and make up. I just wanted to make it up to you. I don't know what to say. I really am so sorry.'

She smiled as he gave her a friendly peck on the lips. 'Look, do you want to go out to dinner?'

'Sorry, Marcus, I am expecting someone and I am already going out, thanks.' She slipped into her jacket and threw her bag over her shoulder, as she ushered him to the door, which was still ajar.

'Well, perhaps we could go riding again next Sunday. Would you come?'

'No, I don't think so.'

'Well, think about it.'

He gave her another quick peck on the lips. 'If you want to come, I'll pick you up on Sunday.'

'You've got lipstick on your lips.'

Dominic stood in the doorway. He pushed the door with one finger, and it swung open. He had not heard all of the conversation, but he did hear 'pick you up on Sunday' and the lipstick bit. He just stood looking at the lipstick smear on the fat face. He also noticed the nicely shaded eyes before his fist connected with Marcus's chin, and he stormed off down the hall and down the stairs, not saying a word.

Emily not knowing what to do, looked at Marcus sitting on the floor dazed and holding his face, then dashed off after Dominic, shouting to him to come back. She rushed down the stairs and caught him just as he was opening the door to the street.

'Dominic! Dominic! It's not what you think, Dominic! Marcus is just a friend; he came to pick up his lighter.'

'Oh! So he comes here often, does he? Where did he leave it? In the bedroom?' He started to open the door, and she held onto his arm, tears welling in her eyes.

'Dominic! No.' It was a breathless whisper. 'It's not like that ... really it's not... It's not ... really!' She was shaking her head in despair. 'Please try to understand.'

197

They both looked up, as Marcus came to the top of the stairs. 'I found it, Emily!' He held up the lighter in his hand as he came down to join them. He looked at Dominic. 'Phew!' and he rubbed his chin. 'I'm sorry, old man!' he apologized. 'I didn't mean to cause any trouble.' He looked at Emily and nodded with a smile, waving the gold lighter in his hand. 'It was under the bed.' Once again he did not see Dominic's fist coming...

Emily chased after Dominic, who was striding with a vengeance down the street. She caught up with him and grabbed at his arm.

'Dominic, please let me explain. Please.'

He stopped dead and faced her. 'I think he explained it very well, don't you? Explain to him, why I hit him, when he picks you up on Sunday.' He shrugged his sleeve out of her grip, and marched off.

She chased after him again, grabbing at his sleeve again, and stopping him. 'Now you just listen to me, Dominic Hadley! Don't you go blackening my reputation, just because you got hold of the wrong end of the stick, and think your conceited cocky nose has been put out of joint. Yes, Marcus is a friend, and he *has* been to the flat, but only once, and Amanda was there.' She did not add that Marcus was drunk and that it was she who had given him the black eyes. Probably poor old Marcus might end up in the hospital with a broken nose, if he hadn't already got one.

They stood facing each other in the middle of the pavement, as Dominic clenched then unclenched his fists. 'Oh, Amanda was there, was she? I suppose he likes to make a night of it, does he?'

'Oh! Dominic! How could you? Yes, of course, Amanda was there! She lives there, for God's sake!'

She could see the muscles in his face beginning to relax as he took a deep, deep breath.

'Dominic?' She softened. 'Please try to understand! I live here in London, and I would be a poor soul if I didn't have any friends ... wouldn't I? And Marcus *is* just a friend, and the only time I have been anywhere with him is with a group of us, sometimes six or eight, if some of the girls bring a boy-friend.'

'Oh, so he partners you, does he? Was it one of the other guys that gave him the black eyes?'

'No! No! Not at all. He had an accident, and it's just a friendly thing. We go to a bar or to a nightclub or sometimes for dinner, but always in a group, and I come home alone. Amanda will tell you, and so does she. You can't afford to go messing about in this day and age. And besides, you have to understand that in London, I have to have friends. Everyone has friends, don't they?

'Mmmm,' he nodded. 'Mmmm, yeah, I suppose you are right, but where are you going with him on Sunday?'

'I'm not going anywhere with him on Sunday, or any other day for that matter. I am coming home with you!' She shook her head as she linked her arm through his and they walked to the corner. She put her arm up to hail a taxi. 'Come on, we don't want to be late for the show, do we?' She tried to explain it all to him in the taxi, but he didn't listen. He looked straight ahead and didn't say a word, ignoring her.

She wondered why she bothered with him, with his silly jealousy. He was like a child sulking over nothing. She felt like jumping out of the taxi and leaving him, but, as it was, she would have to sit with him for the rest of the evening while he sulked. She had wanted it to be such a lovely evening. She had waited so long for him to come to London to see the flat, and even now he hadn't even seen it. The taxi stopped. They got out, and Dominic paid the driver, almost flinging the fare at him, although it wasn't his fault. They mingled with the crowds and got into the long slow-moving queue. Finally they found their seats.

Jenny and Graham arrived, and they watched the events. Dominic hardly said two words to her, and Jenny remarked quietly to Graham about the tension between them.

Next day Jenny phoned to say they had enjoyed the evening and to ask about Dominic. What was the row about? Emily said that they were all right again now, but they had not said much in the car on the way home, and when Emily told her what had happened, they both had a good laugh, especially the bit where Dominic had knocked Marcus out.

'Poor devil,' Emily went on, 'he's already got two black eyes where I punched him, but I didn't tell Dom about that, and

199

then Dominic hit him again and knocked him out on the stairs. I haven't got the nerve to phone him and ask how he is. He must be feeling terrible. He must look as if he has been in a fight, and he didn't even throw a punch.' They were both still chuckling as they rang off.

Emily had now decided to come home most weekends despite the colder weather and the November mists. Sometimes she had to drive through fog, and it took her an hour longer, but she was determined to make it. She had not heard from Marcus DuBarry again, and Dominic soon got over his temper, and they rode out together. He had come over on Sunday and stayed for lunch, and she had been to Packards Mill.

The days and weeks went by, and the weekends seemed to come round fairly quickly. It was nearly Christmas. Emily and Amanda between them had decorated the flat with a Christmas tree and holly, and Amanda had suggested mistletoe over the door. Emily put her foot down. After all, Marcus might come back! They had laughed and decided against it.

Jenny came up to town one Friday afternoon on the train, and Emily met her from the station. That evening the two of them and Amanda went out to dinner and then on to a bar, where Jenny met a group of Emily's friends. They left at midnight, Jenny staying overnight in the flat, and the three of them went Christmas shopping after a toast-and-coffee breakfast.

It was Saturday. What a terrible day it was! Cold, miserable and thousands of people crowding into hot and stuffy shops. In the street a Salvation Army Band of drums, trumpets and tambourines sang its collective heart out above the noise of the busy traffic and trudging shoppers, while the women in their navy suits and bonnets with big dark-red bows tied under their chins shook tins, colleting money for the poor. Jenny wondered just how much her small contribution would go to help, for here she was in London, excited and raring to spend her money and some poor people would have nothing for Christmas.

Emily and Amanda took the excitement of London all in their stride. They saw it every day, but for Jenny it was wonderful, especially at Christmas, with the lights flashing and the shops

200

lit up. She could see why Emily liked London. There was a magic buzz about the city.

'What can I get for Graham?' Jenny was looking in a jeweller's window. 'I think it will have to be cufflinks.' They looked at each other and chuckled. Christmas seemed to revolve around slippers, perfume and cufflinks.

Amanda smiled. She didn't have a serious boyfriend or she would probably be looking at cufflinks too. Emily had already bought Dominic aftershave soap, cologne and deodorant in a beautiful presentation box. Then, after stopping for coffee, they wandered back to the jeweller's. Emily bought a stopwatch. Dominic and Graham were always timing each other over the jumps.

By now they were exhausted and they got a taxi back to the flat to pick up the car. Emily drove home, dropping Jenny off at Mayberry Farm. Liz, as usual, was in the kitchen when Emily bundled through the back door with her shopping bags.

'Hello, darling. Gosh, you look as if you've had a good day.'

'Oh, Mum, I'm exhausted.' She slumped down in the chair at the table. 'I'm dying for a cup of coffee.' She kicked off her boots, and Liz put a mug on the table in front of her.

She sipped at the coffee gratefully, and then, feeling a bit more rested, she changed her clothes and went out into the darkness, switching on the yard light to see to the horses. She told them both that she had ordered new rugs for them for Christmas, and Tulip nodded in appreciation, making Emily smile. She whispered, 'You're not supposed to know until Christmas Day, so don't tell John that I told you, will you?'

The yard was quiet, but Emily's ears were pricked for the slightest sound. She could feel Major's presence; she could not define the feeling or explain. It was a feeling like being watched. It had been years now since the accident, but no matter how long, she would never forget the fact that she had killed him, and was sure that he would not forget, either. It had been her fault; she would never stop blaming herself.

After half an hour out in the yard with her beloved horses, she went into the tack room, John had left the light on, which was unusual. She switched it off and come back, giving them each a last pat. Pico huffed as she turned off the yard light, as she called out, 'Goodnight, Pico.'

The night air was chill, and she shivered, looking cautiously into the gloom and hurrying as if she was being chased. Glad to get back into the house, she closed the back door behind her, shutting out the darkness and the creepy quiet. Maybe it was because she was now used to the continual drumming of the busy London traffic and the police sirens wailing in the night. At least there was the sense of people being around. She had never been afraid of the darkness in the yard until now...!

The kitchen smelled good. Warm and safe. Mum had a hot meal ready, and the three of them enjoyed it and then spent the rest of the evening watching TV. Emily went out into the hall and called Dominic, just for a chat. She told him that she and Jenny had enjoyed Christmas shopping, though she still had a few bits to get.

He said jokingly, 'Did you buy me anything nice?'

'No!' she lied with a smile. 'Didn't get *you* anything at all!'

'Now I'm disappointed. What I need is a new watch. My strap broke today and it fell on the floor and Silverspoon trod on it. Damn nuisance. Crushed to bits, it was. If you are writing to Santa Claus, put a word in for me, will you?'

'Oh, what a shame! Too bad. I've already posted the letter.'

She was smiling. Jenny must have mentioned it to Graham. 'Perhaps if you write a nice letter yourself, Santa Claus might just drop one down your chimney.'

He laughed. 'Well, that will be a ruddy lot of good. I've heard of waterproof watches; do they make fireproof ones, too?' They chuckled.

'What are you doing tomorrow?' he asked. 'Do you want to come over here and ride in the morning? We won't get too many more days. They're talking of snow. It's been damn chilly today hasn't it? And you can stay for lunch, or we can drive out somewhere and get lunch.'

'No, I can't come tomorrow. Dad has a business guy and his wife coming for Sunday lunch, and I think I ought to be here. They're bringing their teenage son, and I think I'm expected to entertain him. Why don't you come over here in the morning? You can bring Silverspoon or you can ride Pico, and stay *here* for lunch.'

'Not if you have got people.'

'Why not? Mum and Dad won't mind. They like you.'

'Well...' he considered. 'OK then, but if there's any problem let me know. I don't want to be in the way if your Dad is talking business.'

'There won't be any problems.' Emily phoned John and asked him to saddle both Black Tulip and Pico when he came up in the morning.

Sunday morning was cold. Dominic arrived early and, like Emily, he wore a rollneck sweater and a parka jacket. He carried a small brown leather bag with a change of clothes for lunch. John was there ready and waiting with both horses, and they rode out across the field and into the woods. A light sun filtered from a pale-grey sky through the bare branches of the tall trees, and the shushing sound of the golden-brown curled leaves and the snap and crackle of twigs broke the stillness as the horses' hooves trod them down. Droplets of water fell from bare twigs onto their helmets and shoulders, and the grassy path shimmered with a silvery hue before them, as the horses plodded on slowly over the green grass tinged with sugar-white icing. The breath coming from their nostrils encased their nodding heads in clouds of white steam that evaporated into the chill and crisp air. Soon the faces of their riders had turned to a rosy glow, their ears and noses tipped bright pink.

They came to the big oak tree. The low branch still hung there after all these years. Emily thought she detected a slight movement; she shivered. It was probably just the air settling into the woodland. Tulip had not noticed anything, but Pico suddenly shied and sidled as if going round something. Dominic quickly straightened him up, as he suddenly broke into a canter, Emily and Tulip following. They cantered out of the woods and across the fields, keeping to the side paths, then round another field, jumping the hedgerows, and then doubled back, retracing their steps back into the woods again. They slowed down to a trot, then to a walk, entering beneath the arch of bare branches again, both horses snorting and puffing with flared nostrils and pricked ears, their riders invigorated in the bracing air. They walked now through the narrow path, Pico leading the way home, and again passing the big oak tree.

203

'Stop, Dominic!' He pulled on the reins and Pico stopped, and he twisted around in the saddle, leaning back on the cantle to face her.

'What's up?'

'Nothing. I just wanted to stop here for a moment.' She shuddered, recalling the scene in her mind. She looked at the ground on which Tulip was now standing. He had lain right here!

Dominic saw her change. 'Don't, Em! It was an accident. Don't make yourself unhappy over it. Come on, let's go. Em! Come on!' It was a command. 'Come on, Pico.' He clicked his tongue and his heels, urging him forward as he turned to make sure Tulip was following.

As they came out of the wooded area, Tulip came up alongside Pico. Dominic smiled at her and reached out his hand and took hers. 'All right now?'

'Yes, that was good. It's a nice ride through there, isn't it?'

'Yes, it's great.' They rode hand in hand as they turned into the yard.

'Oh, John, you need not have waited for us!' Emily slid down from the saddle, as the groom took the bridle to steady Tulip for her.

'Oh, it's no trouble, Miss.'

Dominic slid down with ease, undoing the girth and taking off the saddle. It felt warm to his cold gloved hands and frozen fingers. He asked John for a rug to throw over Pico; clouds of steam rose from the backs of both horses. Then, leaving the horses to John, they went into the kitchen. It was warm and cosy. Dominic took off his gloves, rubbing his hands, and their feet and fingers tingled as they slowly thawed out. Emily poured out cups of hot steaming coffee, putting her hand round the pot to warm her fingers. They felt hungry, and the roast in the oven smelt good. Emily made toasted muffins oozing with butter to keep them going until lunch was ready. While they waited, they sat and watched TV, then Emily went to her room to get showered and changed, showing Dominic into the guest bedroom at the other end of the hall.

He was down first, dressed in grey trousers, white shirt and maroon V-necked pullover, and was having a drink before lunch with Mike. When the business guests arrived, he was introduced to Bill Stevens, his wife, Doreen, and their son, Neil, who was a tall skinny lad of about eighteen with a mop of sandy hair and a pale complexion.

Emily came down the stairs dressed in blue jeans and pale-blue sweater. Dominic was filled with joy at her beauty. She smiled shyly, shaking hands as she was introduced to the family. Liz joined them for a drink, then darted back to the kitchen and soon they were all sitting round the table. The conversation quickly got around to horses. Neil, although he didn't ride, was very interested to hear about showjumping and asked if he could see the horses. So after lunch they put on their warm clothes, and Emily and Dominic took him out into the yard. They showed him the tack room, and he admired Emily's rosettes and cups and remarked on the smell of the leather and the polish, a strong, pungent smell she, herself, never noticed. He said he had never been on a horse, but it must be exciting to ride.

'Well, would you like to have a try?' suggested Dominic.

Neil hesitated, looking up at Tulip. 'Well,' he chuckled apprehensively. 'I don't know. I am into computers; I'm not the outdoor type.'

'Oh, go on!' Emily encouraged. 'Tulip is quite safe, and we will look after you.' He agreed reluctantly to have a go. 'I'll get you a warm anorak.' He was wearing an expensive leather jacket, and went into the tack room with her to change. She gave him John's old jacket, while Dominic saddled up Black Tulip. They helped Neil into the saddle. He was really nervous, and held on tightly to the black mane. Dominic, holding the bridle, started her at a gentle walk around the paddock, while Neil hung on for grim death, slumping forward over her neck, shouting 'WHOO-AAAH!' His voice came out in nervous gasps. After a while, though, they had him walking slowly round the paddock on his own, and he was doing well. Until, that is, Tulip decided to quicken the pace and started a little trot. Neil shouted out, as if the horse had bolted, but Dominic, now on Pico, was quickly at his side. Emily, standing watching, smiled, remembering Marcus DuBarry.

They told him that the Wickerbrook Show was in March and he should make a point of coming. They told him to look out for their horse boxes and to come and have lunch with them.

He thanked them, now glad to be back on solid ground after Tulip's great height. He patted her, and stamped his feet, trying to warm them, wrapping John's old jacket more closely around him.

'Gosh, this is a cold job in the wintertime, isn't it?' he commented, as he watched Emily and Dominic coming back with a bucket of fresh water for the horses.

'Yes,' Dominic answered. 'But you get used to it when you have animals. They can't fend for themselves, so you just have to do everything for them, and if you do the job properly you get good results at the shows. Practice and keeping them fit and well is all part of the job.'

Neil and his parents left about four thirty. They had about an hour's drive, and it was already dark and damp with a slight frost on the ground. Liz shivered at the door as they said goodbye and waved them off. Emily and Dominic donned their parkas and gloves again, and went out into the yard. The horses whinnied as Emily switched on the light, but at the sound of her voice, they both nodded a greeting over the half stable doors. A little later when Emily was talking quietly to Black Tulip, Dominic walked up behind her and put his arms around her, kissing her cheek. She half-turned her head towards him with a smile, leaning her head back onto his chest. He felt the softness of her silky hair on his chin and breathed in her light perfume. He turned her to face him, and she put her arms up around his neck, and he pulled her close, bending his head. His lips brushed hers gently. He held her tightly, kissing her long and passionately. They clung together for a few minutes, and then Tulip behind her started to whinny and kick at the door. Pico, two stables up, was clearly agitated. Dominic looked up, gripping Emily tighter, looking around him, alarmed and ready to protect her.

'What is it? What's the matter with them?'

Emily pulled away from him. 'It's OK, it's Major, he's here again.'

'Who? Major? Where?' His eyes were wide and alert. He looked around him scanning the yard. The light formed shadows in dark corners, and he could see nothing.

'You can't see him,' Emily smiled. 'But the horses can, that's why they're so upset.'

206

'How do you know?'

'I know the signs. It hasn't happened for some time now, but he is back again, I don't know why.'

Tulip stopped kicking at the door, and the yard seemed quiet again. Dominic was still looking into space, alarmed and ready for anything that came at them.

Tulip whinnied again. Dominic turned his eyes to her and then at Pico. Then he looked at Emily. She seemed unworried as the sound of clip-clopping echoed through the yard.

Dominic felt the hairs stand up on the back of his neck and a cold shiver ran through his body. They both jumped as Major's stable door suddenly flew open and a bale of straw flew across the yard. Then the water bucket came through the air and clattered onto the cobblestones. It rolled for a minute and then stood upright, the handle standing up in the holding position. It stopped in front of Pico's stable, and he went into a frenzy, neighing and kicking hard at the door.

Dominic couldn't believe his eyes, as the bucket suddenly lifted by the handle, stood a few inches off the ground and then came slowly towards them. Emily reached out to take it, but it clattered to the ground at their feet. They stood stock-still, watching as a shadow moved before them. They cringed back, Dominic pushing Emily behind him, but the shadow stopped in front of Tulip's stable and the mare whinnied, stepping backwards into the stable and knocking down the hay net. Dominic pushed Emily further from the stable and into a corner of the yard for safety as Tulip came crashing forward bumping her chest into the door. It shuddered violently, but the bolt was secure.

From the corner of the yard, Emily stepped from behind Dominic, shouting at Major to stop. Suddenly there was silence, and Tulip relaxed. Pico stood calmly at the stable door, nodding his head as if nothing at all had happened. For a fleeting moment a slight mist lingered around the light bulb on the wall and then wafted away in the still air.

Emily and Dominic exchanged glances, and he slowly took hold of her hand. He seemed afraid to move. They were both tense, their ears strained to the limit, listening for the slightest sound or movement, but there was nothing but the rushing sound of silence.

207

Emily freed her hand from Dominic's grasp. 'It's all right,' she whispered, creeping forward cautiously. He was close behind her as she neared Major's stable, and he put a hand on her shoulder ready to grab her out of the way of any danger.

She reached the half stable door and peered in. It was stacked full of bales of hay.

'Major?' she whispered. 'Major!' Her voice was stronger and louder. 'Major! Are you there?' Dominic seemed to hear a clop of a hoof, but he wasn't sure. He looked round quickly to see if either of the horses had got free, but they stood calmly, nodding their heads. There was a sudden draught, as something intangible came between them. They stood now, a few feet apart, facing each other either side of the open stable door. 'Major? Major!' They listened, but there was only the sharp ringing sound of her voice as it echoed off the walls. Emily moved her eyes only. 'I think he's gone!' She relaxed.

Dominic, still tense, his eyes circling round the whole yard cautiously, whispered, 'How do you know?'

'I can feel it! Can't you? When he's here, there's an atmosphere. Can you feel the difference now?'

'Atmosphere! You can certainly say that again! And that sudden draught ... was that him leaving? It felt as if something pushed between us.' He was still looking cautiously around the yard. He shook his head in disbelief. 'And look at this bale of straw! I can't believe it.' He was shaking his head. 'I have never experienced anything like that before in my life. I remember you telling me about the bucket! But ... but...' He was lost for words. 'Well, now I've seen it all.'

Her eyes opened wide. 'You mean you didn't believe it? What? After all this time? And after all I've told you, you didn't believe it? Well! I'll be damned! I wasn't spinning you a line. But he doesn't usually throw things about. He's only ever done this once before, when a bale caught John in the chest and almost knocked him out, but usually we just hear his hooves clopping around. You can usually tell if he's here, even when you don't hear anything. You just have to look at Tulip and Pico; they know before we do.'

'You've *seen* him though, haven't you?'

'Yes, twice. It only lasts for a second, but it seems longer. But it has been a long time now since he was last here. Maybe he's jealous of you and me together. Or, maybe he is jealous of Tulip and Pico, and he thinks I love them more. Maybe it's my attention he is seeking.'

He came close and took her into his arms. '*I'm* seeking attention; I hope you love *me* more!' She smiled up at him and hugged him fondly and they stood cheek to cheek. 'I'm glad he was there that day at the Goldsborough,' he whispered in her ear. 'He brought us together. I love you, Em!'

He felt her shiver as a light breeze went through the yard and tightened his arms around her, and he felt an uneasy tingle go right through his body. 'Don't be afraid, Em. It's eerie, but don't let it get to you.'

'Do you think he is watching us now?' Emily whispered.

Dominic looked cautiously around the yard. 'No! He brought us together; he wouldn't be jealous of me, would he?' He drew her close again and kissed her forehead. She was on tiptoe, looking up at him again, and their lips met. She felt that her feet had wings, as she melted in his arms, and she thought she could hear music... Then she thought, get with it, Emily Peters, you are in the yard, and there is no orchestra out here. But there was music playing; it was pop. They both turned quickly – the radio was playing in the tack room. She looked up at him in alarm.

'There is someone in the tack room,' she whispered. 'John always turns the radio off and takes the plug out in case of fire.'

'Come on.' He took her hand anxiously and they slowly tiptoed hand in hand across the yard. She felt for the key, which was hidden in a gap between the wall and the wooden post; it wasn't there! Dominic quietly picked up the shovel that was near the wheelbarrow and was ready for the attack, as Emily slowly and silently turned the door handle. He edged her out of the way, gripped the door handle and flung it open quickly, the shovel in his right hand at the ready. Nothing happened. They froze, looking into the darkness, the only light the green digits on the radio, as the music played on and then stopped suddenly! Emily felt around for the light switch and snapped it on. The room was empty. The radio stood on the high shelf as it always did, the plug hanging on the wire in mid-air, not connected. They stood together, rigid, cold shivers

209

running down their spines. They looked at each other wide-eyed and then back at the radio.

'Oh, Dominic!'

He was dumbfounded. There was nowhere to hide. He began to relax and was about to put down the shovel, when Snowball suddenly jumped from the roof onto the gate and scampered away. It made them both jump, and they stood holding their breath.

'Come on!' Putting his arm around her shoulders, he guided her away, closing the tack-room door. 'Where's the key?' 'It wasn't there!' She put her hand into the gap, and there it was, back in the hiding place! She gave it to him, 'Oh, Dom, it wasn't there, I'm sure, and the door was unlocked, wasn't it? And it never is; John always locks the door.'

He nodded. 'Maybe he made a mistake.' They walked across the yard, both glancing behind them nervously. They stood in the darkness by the paddock gate, away from the yard light. There was nothing but the dense quietness of the night, and the darkness turning to grey as a pale new moon came from behind a cloud. He held her tightly against him, their hearts beating fast; she was glad of the warmth of his arms.

He felt her shiver. 'It's all right, it's all right.' He gave her a little friendly shake and put his cheek against hers, and hugged her close, whispering in her ear. 'It's all right, my darling, it's all right. Don't worry.'

She pulled away, looking up at him. 'Oh Dominic, I *do* worry. I'm scared. What am I to do?'

He spoke quietly. 'I don't know. But you have to stop worrying about it. It's uncanny, I know, but, but...' He was lost for words. 'Come on, let's forget it.' He tried to change the subject. 'We can sort it out between us, can't we? I love you, my darling. I have never felt like this in my life. I am happier being with you than with anyone. I love you, my darling Emily, and I have never said that to anyone before. Ever. And we're not going to let a horse come between us, are we?' He was smiling down at her. 'He's not going to spoil our life, is he?'

He was serious. It was the third time he had said he loved her, and this time he was perfectly sober.

She smiled. 'No, certainly not. Not a ghost horse.'

He grinned at the words 'ghost horse'. 'Emily!' He hugged

210

her and kissed her cheek. 'Emily!' he whispered softly in her hair, 'I love you, I could spend my life with you. Could you spend the rest of your life with me?'

She looked up shyly into his handsome face, and whispered, 'Dominic, I like you, I like you a lot, but I don't know if it's love. I don't know how love feels. I know I like to be with you. I like to be with you all the time. I think about you a lot. I wish sometimes that you were here and not away at college. I love to be near you, is that love?'

'Could you spend the rest of your life with me, Em? Me alone?' He was looking at her intently, but her face was in shadow. 'Could you?' His brow rose and crinkled expectantly.

She bit her bottom lip. 'Are you asking me to marry you, Dominic? I don't know ... we have a lot in common. Horses, I mean.' There was a pause. 'We like the same things. I love being with you, but...'

'Then tell me that you don't love me!'

'I can't.'

'Then you do love me?' he said hopefully.

She hesitated, 'Well...'

'You couldn't spend a lifetime with me, is that it?' He clicked his tongue and looked away. The arrogance was there, as if he was God's gift to women and he could not be refused. But there was sadness, too.

She sighed, 'I don't know.' She felt his shoulders stiffen and his chest expand as he took a deep breath and pulled himself up to his full height with annoyance, leaning away from her. She knew she had hurt him. She could feel the arrogance about him. Could she live with that self-assured cockiness? And they did have the occasional tiff! She wondered if it would always be like this, arguing over some minor thing, making her frustrated and miserable. In all her twenty-two years, she could not remember her parents having so much as a cross word. She looked up at him. She liked him more than she could say. She liked him more than anyone else she had ever met, but could she bring herself to say, 'I love you, Dominic!' The answer was no... She didn't think she could. 'I don't know, Dominic, I just don't know. I don't think I'm ready for marriage yet...'

There was a pause, and those eyes that had worried her

211

from the very first moment, she knew, would have lost their sparkle, and from the set of his jaw he was bitterly disappointed.

'Will you let me know?' he spoke softly, but his tone was cold. It was more a command.

'Know what?'

He tutted and sighed, turning away from her in despair. '... If you can spend the rest of your life with me? Or have you forgotten the question already?' His voice rose; there was anger there. 'All you have to say is "I love you, Dominic", and I will know.' The words hung heavily between them.

Looking up at him, she said nothing, her lips tight together. She nodded slowly, lowering her eyes.

Smiling down at her, relaxing from the heat of the moment, no longer angry but warm and passionate, he lifted her chin, looking lovingly into the deep-blue eyes. He brushed her lips with his. 'I can wait, Emily!' His voice was husky. 'I can wait.' He kissed her lightly on the lips. 'I can wait, Em. Take your time. I'll always love you, no matter what you decide and I will always be here. Waiting.' He sighed deeply. 'I had better be going.'

They walked hand in hand across the yard and back into the kitchen. Liz and Mike were in the lounge watching the television. He thanked them for lunch and for a nice day, and Emily went to the front door with him. He gave her a quick kiss and called goodbye as he drove the silver Mercedes away. She was disappointed that he didn't look back and wave as usual.

18

Monday morning was chilly and misty. It was seven o'clock and barely daylight. John had arrived and had saddled up Black Tulip, and Emily rode her out across the field and towards the woodland. She did not go far.

John had been surprised to see the bale of straw out in the yard and had muttered away to himself. He guessed what had happened as soon as he came into the yard. He pushed the bale to one side with his foot. He would ask Patrick to come and stack it back, but he would not mention that it was Major. It would be too much to explain. Patrick would probably never believe it anyway.

Emily came back after just thirty minutes. They had had a good canter across the fields, she slid down and handed Tulip over to John, who threw a rug over her and walked her around for a while before turning her out into the paddock. Emily took Pico for a quick canter and, again, was back in no time.

She gave Pico a pat, telling him he was a good boy, then handed him to John, saying goodbye. She was off to London, though she might see him next weekend but wasn't sure yet. He told her that he would take care of everything as usual and to drive carefully. She gave Tulip a stroke down the nose and went off into the kitchen for a quick cup of coffee and piece of toast, then went up to shower. She came down dressed in a dark-blue suit, fine black tights and black high-heel shoes and matching bag. Her hair was tied neatly into the usual ponytail with a red ribbon.

She reached the travel office two hours later. The drive hadn't been too bad, and the mist had cleared by the time she left the Suffolk border. Dad had always said it was better to travel earlier, while the traffic was light. In London it was bright and sunny but certainly not warm.

Vicky Eastern was in the office when she got there and had

already taken a couple of holiday bookings and was talking on the phone. They exchanged smiles, Vicky raising her hand as the phone rang on Emily's desk just as she sat down. Glenda Williams came dashing in to answer it, thinking that Emily wasn't there. Monday morning was already busy.

Emily, looking at her computer screen, was talking to man on the phone who wanted a flight to Italy in July. It was almost nine months to July, but on that particular day, club class was already full. He decided to go the week before, and she managed to book him in; there were only two seats left. She sat gazing at the poster on the wall of sunny Spain, with the blue sea and the golden beaches. Another call came in, someone wanting a booking to Spain, and then another, a man wanting to go tomorrow business class to Berlin. Boring and freezing cold, she thought, but business was business, she supposed, and had to be done.

It was about ten thirty when her boss, Ed Lambington, called her into his office. He sat behind his desk waiting and leaning back in a leather swivel-chair. He was of medium height and stocky build and balding, with a ring of dark hair. He was business-like and no-nonsense; the most the girls ever got out of him was just a plain, sharp 'morning', not even 'good morning, girls', but his smile was always pleasant.

She tapped on the glass door and went in. He looked up and smiled. 'Sit down, Miss Peters...!' He looked at the paper before him. 'Emily!' She sat in a hard dark-brown leather chair facing him. He put his elbows on the desk, his hands together and his fingertips resting against his lips as if praying, then quickly folded his arms in front of him, leaning on the desk.

'Well, Miss Peters, you no doubt know that there has been talk about transferring some of our personnel. Well...!' He leaned back in the swivel-chair, clasping his hands across his chest. '...There's a place in Palma de Mallorca.' He saw her swallow hard. There was a pause. He was watching her reaction. 'We need someone there.'

'Sorry, I can't go.' She shook her head with a slight smile.

He went on: 'We need someone who can run the complete office. I have to make a choice. And I am sure that you would do a good job. What do you say? The opportunity is there!'

'I can't go.' She shook her head again. 'Majorca! Why me?'

He sighed, leaning forward, elbows on the desk again, interlocking his fingers. 'Because you are the best choice. Why? Don't you want to go?' He raised his eyebrows in surprise. He thought that she would have jumped at the chance.

'Well, I'm flattered, of course, but...'

'You have commitments? A boyfriend perhaps. Well, of course you must have, a pretty girl like you... But surely he would understand?'

Emily sighed. 'Well, yes, I do have a boyfriend.' She thought, I *had* a boyfriend. 'But I also have horses, which I can't just go away and leave.'

'Well, something could be arranged. We could get a groom to look after them for you.'

'Oh, I have a groom,' Emily said quickly. 'And I have no worries about him looking after them, but my horses are my life. I showjump, and I have to keep in practice and they have to be exercised every day. Besides, I am committed to showing events throughout the year.'

'You have horses in London?' he queried with a frown.

'No, in Suffolk.'

'Who exercises them during the week?'

'My groom and his daughter. But I have to practise hard for shows. When would you want me to go?'

'After Christmas, January; it's not very warm then, but the summer will be super.'

'Summer!' Emily looked aghast. 'How long would I be there?'

'Well...' he grimaced, pursing his lips. '...I would say about nine months, maybe a year.'

'Oh, no! I can't do that, I'm sorry.' She stood up, shaking her head. 'It's definitely impossible.'

'Think about it for forty-eight hours and then let me know.' She shook her head.

'Sorry!' and she opened the door. 'Oh Emily!' She turned, looking back over her shoulder. 'The pay is three times what you make here!' He nodded with a smile. 'Think about it!'

She did think about it, for the rest of the day and that evening. She discussed it with her parents over the phone, and her father encouraged her to go.

'Think of the opportunity, Emily,' said Mike. 'It will get you away from the village, away from London, broaden your outlook

215

on life. You'll meet new and interesting people. Have a go at it. I'm sure it's the right thing to do.'

'Well, what about Tulip and Pico, and the events? I just can't go away for a year.'

'John will look after them, you know that. Go, darling, it's a great opportunity. Go and see how the other half live.'

She came off the phone in deep thought, then phoned John at his home. She knew he would do his best and she really had no worries there. He had told her everything would be OK. Then she spoke to Jenny, who was thrilled for her to have the opportunity to go to Majorca and wished she could go with her, but Emily explained that it was not going to be a holiday, and the weather wasn't good there in the winter months.

'Well, it's a good time to go. The shows don't start until March, and you haven't got much to do ... the weather's not good at the moment for practice anyway, is it? And I'll go over every day and exercise both Black Tulip and Pico to keep them fit, and I can ride out with Susan. I will get on the phone and cancel all your showing events. But I'll miss you, Em.'

'I haven't gone yet, Jen.'

'No, but you will.'

Emily had put a lot of hard work into her riding, and, if she went, she knew she would have to start all over again next year. But then the shows didn't pay the bills, and the job was more important. But Majorca! It was a long way away; at times even London seemed too far. She put the phone down after talking to Jenny and sat staring at the wall. She was in two minds whether to say she would take the job, but in the end she supposed she would have to go. The only one she hadn't told was Dominic. Could she leave him? Could she really disappoint him again? Would he think she was leaving just because he had asked her to marry him? Would he think she was running away? Of course he would, and all because she did not want to face him, because she could not give him an answer. Dominic, whom she'd said she didn't love, was really her biggest problem.

The London office had closed two days before Christmas until after the holiday. Emily was in Suffolk and she and Dominic, with Jenny and Graham, had been to a party and on Christmas Eve, the four of them had gone out to dinner, at the Midsummer House Restaurant in Cambridge. They had exchanged presents during the evening because on Christmas Day they would all be with their own families.

Dominic had given her perfume and a gold bracelet engraved with the words, 'Emily, with all my love, Dominic'. She loved it and said she would wear it always. He was very pleased with the stopwatch and the aftershave, too.

Jenny tried on the gold earrings that Graham gave her, and they looked lovely; and he was happy with the Gucci cufflinks. The four of them had a lot of laughs, and the evening was great. They left the restaurant and went back for a last drink at the Red Lion, where they met a whole group of friends. They got home late, after kissing everyone else and saying 'Merry Christmas' a dozen or so times. Then Dominic drove her back to Rosemary Lodge.

They were alone now in the tack room. He was kissing her.

'Merry Christmas, my darling.' He hugged her close and whispered in her ear. I'll miss you tomorrow. I wish we could spend Christmas Day together.'

'So do I, Dominic.' She smiled up at him, feeling cosy and comfortable in his arms.

She told him about the transfer to Majorca. There was a long pause. He gently let her go, biting the inside of his lip thoughtfully, his mouth twisting. He was lost for words. They sat on the old tack-room table, swinging their legs and holding hands in silence.

'Is it because of me?'

She shook her head.

'Please don't go! Do you have to? How long will you be gone?'

'Well...' it was her turn to bite her lip. '...At least nine months or a year.'

'A year!' He jumped off the table and marched to the door, then turned around to face her. Then he said just what she thought he would say. 'You're running away because you don't want to marry me, is that it?' He was angry and disappointed. 'Oh, I know you don't love me. And I know you're not ready for marriage yet! But I can wait, Em. I can wait, as long as it takes, there will never be anyone but you for me. So whenever you are ready, I'll still be waiting, I promise.' His voice softened; he was close to tears. 'But I'm sure we could be happy, Em!' He took her by the shoulders. 'We could have a good life, Em.' He shook his head again and sighed. 'Is it the money that worries you? If so, Em, I can afford it. We could rent a little flat for the time being, and when I've finished studying I'll have my own practice and I know I can make it. I know I can, Em, I just know it. I won't let you down, and I could give you a good life. Please, Em! Don't run away from me! Please! I love you.'

She leaned away from him. 'It's not that, Dom. I'm not running away. And I know you'll be a great surgeon.'

'Well, then. Tell me you love me then. Why can't you tell me?'

'Oh, Dominic,' she sighed. It was a tearful sob. 'It just seems as if it's all happened at the same time. And well, I don't really want to go to Majorca, but my boss said they need someone, and I am the only one capable of running the whole office, or so he thinks. There was a pause. 'And I suppose it will be an experience, and yet I don't really want to go.' She sighed. I'll have to give up riding, and we are booked into lots of events in the spring, aren't we? And I wanted to get the practice in, and I can't now, can I?' He sat on the corner of the table again, quietly listening to her. 'And I'll miss you!' She squeezed his hand and looked up into his eyes, but in the darkness she knew their sparkle was gone. She turned away, tears welling in her eyes. She jumped down off the tack-room table and walked to the door.

He followed her, standing behind her, putting his hands on her shoulders. He turned her to him, and she wept, her head resting against his chest. 'I should be happy and I'm not,' she mumbled.

'Come on, don't cry! You'll spoil your make-up.'

'I've changed to waterproof.'

He looked down at her with amusement. 'I hope so. My mum never could get it out of the other shirt!' The twinkle was back in his eyes and they chuckled amiably together.

'It's silly, isn't it? I should be happy to get promotion and go abroad, but I've never been away completely on my own and it scares me a bit. I should be flattered to think that they think that I'm good enough, but I'm not.' She shook her head. 'I don't really know what I want. What I really want is to be a showjumper; and maybe get another horse, maybe turn professional one day.'

'Well, say that you will go, give it a month, and then, if you don't like it, jack it in and come back! You know I'll miss you, and I'll be counting the days...' He kissed her forehead and lifted her chin with his hand. 'And you know I will still be here waiting when you come back, no matter how long it takes. What about Tulip and Pico?'

'Well, John will look after them, of course, and Jenny said she would come over and exercise them.'

'*Jenny!* You've told her already! Why didn't you ask *me* to exercise your horses?' He was getting irate again, flinging his arms about as usual. She was quite taken aback.

I'm sorry!' She was on the brink of tears again. 'I just thought you were so busy with your studies, and what with riding and events and things, you wouldn't have the time. Besides, Jenny is close and can be here in five minutes in the car and she could come every day...'

'Yeah!' He bit his lip again. 'Oh, Em, I'm sorry. Yeah, you're right.' He hugged her to him. 'Come on, I don't want to argue. For God's sake, we are supposed to be enjoying ourselves, it's Christmas!' He took the tissue from her hand and dabbed at her eyes. 'Friends?'

She smiled up at him and agreed, 'Friends. I must look a mess!' She wiped a finger across her eye.

He bent to give her a quick peck on the lips and kissed her wet eyes. 'You look gorgeous,' he said, then added: 'Well, in the dark, anyway.' He grinned, and she slapped him playfully on the shoulder.

Dad and Uncle Ross were enjoying a cigar, and the aroma filled the house. They had had a lovely Christmas lunch, and Mum and Aunt Pam had cleared the table and cleaned the kitchen, and were now both cutting up Christmas cake and making tea. Emily had been out in the yard with her cousins. She wandered into the kitchen and found Gavin sampling the cake.

'Did I hear the phone ringing, Emily?' Liz looked up. 'Who was it?'

'Dominic. He's coming over here tomorrow. We're going riding.'

'Oh, aren't you riding out with the hunt at Wickerbrook?' asked Gavin, a bit surprised.

'No! I never gave it a thought.'

'We are!' said Heather, coming into the kitchen. 'Why don't you come?'

'It's too late now,' said Emily.

'No, it's not.' Gavin was crunching through some icing. 'Give Louise a ring. You know what she's like, the more the merrier. She'd be pleased to see you there.'

Emily thought about it. It sounded fun, and she went off to ring Dominic again.

Boxing Day proved to be good. The weather was bright, dry and sunny, although there was a chill wind. The boys were already there. Charley Fenwick was just unloading Skybright, and Dominic had just finished saddling Silverspoon. Swinging himself up into the saddle he rode over to Emily and Jenny.

Gavin and Heather were already mounted, and Gavin introduced them to Dawn Davis, a girl he had got friendly with some months ago. She lived in Ipswich, but she and her family were spending Christmas with her grandmother and he had asked her to join him in the hunt. She had ridden with the Suffolk Hunt on several occasions, and had a chestnut mare named Honey Bee, whom she stabled at a local farm as they lived in town.

Everyone met on the front lawn at Wickerbrook Hall at eleven o'clock. A small group of spectators stood around, dressed in warm clothing, to watch the well-groomed horses twisting and turning quietly while forty-nine Beagle Harriers mingled amongst them, their brown-and-white tails wagging gaily. The riders looked smart in black jackets and cream jodhpurs. Sir James Bartram, Master of the Hunt, mounted on a great stallion named Basil, looked immaculate, as did the other huntsmen in snow-white jodhpurs and bright-red jackets. The colour, for some reason, was referred to as 'hunting pink'. The rest of the

220

party wore black jackets and cream jodhpurs. It was a colourful spectacle on this dull and cold morning. The green grass hard and dry under hoof, and the bare branches of the trees hung with droplets of ice like diamonds. Three maids from the Hall came round to the riders with trays, offering mulled wine and mince-pies, an English tradition at the Boxing Day meet for hundreds of years.

The hunting horn sounded and the dogs began to bark excitedly. The thirty-strong hunt prepared to move off, the whipper-in lingering to make sure no stray hounds were left behind. The spectators waved them goodbye, some following for a short distance on foot.

Once they were out of the drive and into the open fields, they trotted and cantered, Emily, Dominic, Graham and Jenny keeping mostly to the back, trying to keep together. After a time came sound of the horn – a fox had been sighted and the chase was on. Over the hedgerows, over fences, through fields and farmland... The horses followed the sniffing noses of the hounds, but at the end of the day there was nothing but hungry, exhausted huntsmen and women, tired horses and panting, flaked-out hounds with their tongues hanging out, gasping for water.

John and Charlie Fenwick had taken the horse boxes home after the hunt had left in the morning, and now they were on their way back. Graham had called them both from his mobile phone to come and pick them up. So when the hunt was over, they were back at Wickerbrook Hall to take charge. Sir James had arranged a buffet dinner for all the hunting party and their wives or husbands, and there was food laid out in the covered yard for all the grooms. Emily, Dominic, Jenny and Graham enjoyed the meal and drinks, and stayed talking to Louise and Simeon Hatch until nine o'clock, when they left, as most of the party did, tired and exhausted.

Emily was in the Cambridge Office. Ed Lambington had transferred her back just for the last week after Christmas so that she could be near her family before she left for Majorca on New Year's Day, and now the days were creeping up fast. She was busy staring at the computer screen, when a voice suddenly said, 'Excuse me! Can I book a flight to Palma de Mallorca?'

The girls, Jane, Marion and Pat, sat spellbound, looking at the tall and handsome customer.

'Yes, sir!' She looked up. 'You're not serious?' She smiled, and the girls exchanged glances. They couldn't believe she would speak to a customer like that.

'No! Just kidding. I was in town. What are you doing for lunch? Can you get away?'

'Yes, but not until one o'clock.'

'Good. I'll go for a walk round and pick you up in an hour. OK?' He blew her a silent kiss, and walked to the door. He flashed a smile. 'Hi, girls!' They all said 'Hi' together. All eyes watched until he had disappeared from view. There was a collective sigh.

'Cor! What a hunk!' Jane smiled. 'Nobody ever comes up to my desk like that.'

'Eyes off! He's mine. That's Dominic.'

'What! That's Dominic?' She was astounded. 'Fancy you going off to Majorca and leaving him behind! Do you want me to look after him for you while you're gone?'

Pat was looking on, a big grin on her face. She raised her eyes to the ceiling.

'Some people get all the luck,' said Jane with a smile, leaning her elbows on the desk and looking back at the computer screen. 'Just hope my next customer is half as handsome.'

'You'll be lucky!' Pat was straightening the paper she was about to jot down a note on, when the door opened and a short, stubby man with a red, shaggy beard and balding rosy head came in and stood at Jane's desk.

'Good morning!' He had a pleasant voice. 'I should like to book flight to Majorca, next June.'

Jane didn't know how to contain herself. Out of the corner of her eye she could see both Emily and Pat, and she knew Marion was rolling about in fits of silent laughter behind him, making faces at the other two. The red-bearded man sat down on the chair in front of Jane. She could now see Marion but she kept her eyes on the screen, not daring to look up, her stomach bubbling inside. She was even afraid to smile at him or she would have burst into laughter. The few moments he

222

was there seemed to take a lifetime. He was leaving, politely thanking her with a small bow. He turned acknowledging the other girls, who all smiled sweetly, and as he shut the door they all burst into fits of laughter. Emily saw him glance back through the glass door, and she felt a bit embarrassed.

Dominic and Emily had a hamburger for lunch. He had bought her some flowers, and a small gold necklace.

'Oh thank you, it's lovely, but Christmas is over.'

'Not for me, it's Christmas every day when I'm with you.' He smiled and took her hand across the table. But my Christmasses are quickly coming to an end.' He looked dreamily at her. 'I'll miss you, Em. Only two more days.'

She nodded sadly. 'Yeah, I know.'

The New Year's Eve party given by Sir James Bartram at Wickerbrook Hall was fabulous. There were two hundred people, and Louise had invited seventy of her friends.

Several rooms had been set out with tables. The food was delicious and the wine flowed. The Grand Ballroom was decorated with flowers, ribbons and balloons, and a seven-piece orchestra played. Jenny and Emily had brought new evening dresses. This time, Jenny had chosen gold with sequins, and Emily, pale-blue chiffon, which brought out the colour of her eyes. Her skirt swirled around her as Dominic led her around the dance floor.

Louise was flapping around in a strapless silver-sequin dress. Someone remarked unkindly that she looked like a fish. Her jolly hockey-sticks voice could be heard above the music: 'Oh, darling, how extraordinary, darling!' and 'Deborah! How wonderful to see you, darling! Harry, have you got a drink?' She went round checking that her guests were all right, and that everyone was happy. 'Emily! Off in the morning. How we will all miss you, darling, but you must keep in touch. We will miss her, won't we, Dominic?' But before he could even nod she had moved on to someone else. Lifting her glass of champagne high, so as not to spill it, she squeezed her small, slim body through the crowd. 'Alex, darling, have you got a drink?' She took one from the waiter holding the tray and handed Alex Freemore a glass. 'Mary, I love your dress; pink suits you so.' The evening went well. They enjoyed delicious food and wine and they danced until they dropped.

At midnight, hundreds of red and green balloons and confetti were released from nets in the ceiling and cascaded down. Streamers were thrown, and there was excitement as everyone was kissing everyone else and wishing them a happy new year.

Dominic kissed Emily passionately, oblivious to the cheering and shouting, and the balloons bouncing on their heads. It was as if time stood still and they were the only two in the room.

'Happy New Year, my darling!' he whispered in her ear. 'I love you, Em.' He squeezed her. 'I love you so much, and we only have hours to go.'

She looked up at him, tears of happiness in her eyes. 'Oh Dominic, Happy New Year!' She clung to him, but she could not bring herself to say 'I love you, Dominic!', although he must know what was in her heart. She did love him, but it was the hardest thing for her to say, the words just didn't come easy to her; she didn't know why.

The band played on. Everyone was dancing; popping balloons getting entangled with streamers. The atmosphere was vivid with excitement. Tomorrow with the dawn would come the start of a whole new year, and, for Emily, a whole new way of life.

19

The morning was bright and crisp, and there was the touch of a fairy-like frost on the fence and the hedgerows and the bare branches of the trees. Luckily, after such a late and exciting night, Emily got up without a hangover. She had a light breakfast. There was a feeling of excitement and sadness. She wasn't hungry. She had been outside with the horses for half an hour, but she had not ridden. She had talked to them both, and hugged and kissed them on the nose, telling them not to forget her and that Jenny and Susan would ride them and John would look after them. She said goodbye with a heavy heart. She walked away and wanted to go back again but finally went back into the house. It was time to leave for the airport. She slipped into her soft black leather coat as Dominic arrived and began loading her bags into his car.

On the doorstep she turned to give her mother and father a hug. 'Oh, Mum, it will be months before I see you again.'

'Oh, you'll be all right, darling,' Liz said encouragingly. 'Maybe we'll come out to Majorca for a holiday, won't we, Mike? We've discussed it. Give us a ring when you get there.' She tried to smile, holding back tears of anxiety.

It was the first time she had been away from home alone. Before, it had been just a weekend or four days, and then with the horses, and with other riders. She had Tulip to look after, and Jenny, Dominic and Graham had been there, and Mary Clarke and Alex and Derek. It had been like being at home with friends all around. But this was to be a whole new experience.

It would take them at least two hours to get to Heathrow. The traffic was heavy, and she hoped that she would not miss the flight. She sat quietly beside Dominic. They both had so much to say and yet neither of them spoke. She was thinking: was she doing the right thing? He was thinking: what on earth

225

was he going to do without her? And he still didn't really know how she felt about him! Out of the corner of his eye he saw her shiver.

'Cold?' He reached out and touched her hand, then turned up the heater.

'Yes! It's nerves! I hope it will be all right. I am worried about it, and I really don't want to go. I am a bit scared of being there on my own. I should have been more firm and said that it was impossible for me to go. Besides, I don't want to go and leave Mum and Dad and Tulip and Pico.'

He glance at her. 'And me?'

'Oh, Dominic, I don't want to leave you, either. You know I don't. She paused. 'Dominic, you will write to me, won't you?'

'Of course! And I'll phone you every day. I promise.'

They approached the airport, her stomach churning. It was like the feeling you get in the dentist chair; her mind was in a whirl. She wished it *was* the dentist; it would only last about half an hour and she would be home again. The sound of a heavy jumbo jet went over their heads. 'Please God, keep me safe on this flight! Please God help me to find my way at the other end.'

Dominic waved at a porter to take her bags, and she followed him into the terminal, while Dominic left her to go and park the car. Already she felt alone, even amongst these hundreds of people. They were all leaving the country to go somewhere, and she wondered how many of them felt as she did. She was waiting for him near the ticket desk when he got back. They were early and went for breakfast. They talked really about nothing. She said she felt scared of flying on her own, and he held her hand saying, 'Think of the hot sunshine.'

'It won't be hot sunshine.'

'No, but it will be in the summer. At least there won't be snow.' He was trying to cheer her up, but he did not feel cheerful himself. In his heart, he was saying, please don't go, but he hoped that she would be happy in Majorca. A year wasn't so very long after all; maybe he could manage a long weekend, but it was doubtful, although he said that he might be able to, just to encourage her. She in her own heart knew that he could not come, what with his studies and horse events it was virtually impossible. Then they were calling the flight.

At this moment both their hearts were heavy. He walked with her to passport control.

He kissed her goodbye. This would be the last time he would hold her for a whole year. He kissed her again and hugged her so long and so tight that she thought he would never let her go. Then another quick kiss, before she went through, turning to give him a last wave and an anxious smile. It felt so final.

He stood for a minute or two after she had gone from his sight, staring through the doorway at the backs of other passengers as they passed through passport control to disappear as she had done. A feeling of despair and loneliness came over him, and she had only been gone a moment. He felt so small and alone in the vast terminal. He waited, anxiously hoping that she would suddenly come rushing back, saying she had changed her mind. For him the emptiness and loneliness started here. She had gone out of his life, but he hoped it would not be for ever.

Emily found her seat by the window. A plump and motherly woman came to sit beside her. The woman said she was visiting her grandson. His wife had just had a baby girl; she was just two weeks old. She was staying in Majorca for a month. It was the first time she had been there in the winter, but she had been on holiday there every summer in July, when the weather was very hot. Her grandson had been living there for six years.

Emily said she was going out there to work for a year. The woman thought it was marvellous.

'If only I had had the opportunity when I was young. What a lucky girl you are!'

'I'm not so sure. I didn't want to leave my home. I have a boyfriend and horses. And we showjump.'

'Oh, make the best of it, my dear. See the world while you're young, travel everywhere, you won't regret it. You probably won't get the opportunity when you are older. I travelled everywhere with my husband on business, sometimes not wanting to go, but then found it very enjoyable meeting new people, seeing new places, and I wished I had done it when I was younger. Now, of course, I'm a widow, and I don't get to travel at all, but I do have my memories.' She smiled kindly. 'And like you, I have had to leave my dogs behind, but only for a month. I don't like leaving them, but I know that they are well cared for, and they give me such a greeting when I go back!' She leaned her head back on the seat and closed her eyes, and Emily took out her book, and tried to read but she could not concentrate. She closed her eyes and dozed. Time flew by, and they were landing.

She was glad of the woman's help in finding a trolley, and her luggage. They said goodbye, and the woman wished her luck. She found a cab waiting outside the terminal. The driver spoke very little English, so she showed him a paper with the address on it, and she was on her way. The air was cold, like England, and she was glad of her leather coat. It was not a bit as she had imagined, not like the sunny posters on the wall that she had looked at every day. The car sped away, passing fields, and then, approaching the town of Palma, she saw the beautiful cathedral, with its turrets and figurines. They passed bars and shops, and on her left the mass of sailing vessels with tall masts in the harbour. Then they were on the busy motorway. On one side there were hills, and on the other, open fields of grassland, where bony cows grazed. Beyond was the sea. It was not like home, but she was here now and would have to make the best of it. The car turned right, driving up a winding mountain road, through the village of Calvia, and then into the village of Capdella, then up another steep, narrow lane. Finally it stopped. The sign said 'Nido de Agullas' – Nest of Eagles. This was her new home for the next year.

20

Emily had been gone for a whole two weeks. It was Saturday, and Jenny had been round every day to exercise both Tulip and Pico, and each day she had phoned John first to say she was on her way. But this morning the phone was engaged, so she just drove over. She guessed he would be expecting her.

She got out of the car. 'Morning, John,' she called, with a wave of her hand. She could see him in the paddock, and as she turned into the yard, he waved back to her.

'Oh!' She stopped. 'Hello, Dominic. I didn't expect to see you here. I didn't see your car outside.'

'Oh, hello, Jen. No, I parked round the side. I just came in to check on Tulip. I still check on her leg from time to time, and I've checked Pico, part of a vet's job.' He chuckled. 'Dad keeps us on our toes. Graham has gone off to Foxhead, and I am off to Wickerbrook Hall to see Louise. Mystic Nights has got a cough. Damned cold, isn't it? I suppose you have come to exercise them?' He could see that John had already saddled Tulip.

'Yes,' Jenny nodded. 'With Susan, if she's here. If not, I'll have to come back for Pico.'

'Mind if I come with you? I'm not in a hurry.'

No, not at all.' She was delighted. 'I'd be glad of the company. I'm missing riding with Emily already.'

John was just coming into the yard. 'Morning, Jenny. It's a chilly one, isn't it?' He rubbed his gloved hands. 'Did I hear you say you were riding, Dominic? Do you want me to saddle Pico for you?'

'Oh, no John, it's all right, I can do it.'

'No, I'll do it.' He was already walking into the tack room, and coming back with the bridle and the saddle. He soon had Pico ready, and Jenny and Dominic rode out across the fields and into the woods, both horses knowing the routine. They had walked this way so many times.

229

The woodland was bare of its green beauty, and now pencil-thin strips of white frost coated the overhead arch of thin branches. The chilly air of the early January morning nipped at their noses and their cheeks, giving them a rosy glow. It numbed their gloved hands, and seeped into their thick warm anoraks. They talked about Emily, both feeling that it was not the same without her. Dominic said she had phoned and seemed to be getting on fine. Jenny had phoned her, too.

Dominic shivered and clicked his tongue and his heels. 'Come on, let's get warmed up.' He got Pico into a slow canter, and Jenny clicked her heels and Black Tulip followed. They were soon cantering at a steady pace, clouds of white steam coming from the mouths of both horses and riders as they ploughed among the bare branches, coming out into the open fields under the cold grey sky. Hooves crashed through the crisp white grass and the ice-covered puddles, which crackled like the thin toffee on toffee apples. They rode for an hour and came back into the woodland at a walking pace, Tulip following Pico through the narrow pathway. It was quiet, and the birds called to each other; they had nowhere to hide in the high bare branches. The only other sound was the crunching of leather from the saddles and stirrups and the puffing of the horses, breathing out fiery steam from their flared nostrils into the bracing air.

'Well, that's warmed us up!' smiled Dominic, looking at the red glow on Jenny's face.

'Yes, I bet Em wishes she was here. I told her last night that I was coming over.'

'Yes, I bet she is missing them,' Dominic smiled. 'I expect she told you that there are three other girls working in the office, well, two, and an older woman, who speaks a little English but not enough to hold a conversation or take phone calls. She has been very busy. She said she was in a nice apartment, with an English girl named Christine. She apparently works in Palma in another branch of the same travel agency.'

'Yes, she told me, but the weather was not very warm, but it certainly can't be freezing like it is here, and at least she knows it is going to get really hot in the summer.'

'Yes, that's more than we can say, but I guess anything is better than this.' He looked up at the grey sky tinged with pink as they came out of the woods and started across the last field. 'I think it's even too cold for snow.'

They turned into the yard, and John came out of the tack room rubbing his hands and putting on his gloves. He tucked his thick woollen scarf tighter round his neck.

'Gawd! It's a raw one the smornin' ain't it? 'Ad a good ride 'ave yer?' He took hold of Tulip's bridle with numb hands.

Dominic led Pico to the stable, where he would be warm and snug, then taking the saddle with him, he went to get a rug to throw over the steaming dapple-grey body. John, meanwhile, was doing the same for Black Tulip, whose sweating coat was shining like black satin. Although both horses were fit, they had now grown a thick winter coat, and they looked shaggy and scruffy, although John still brushed them and tried to keep them looking in the peak of condition. The thick rugs that Emily had bought at Christmas were an added bonus in this freezing weather.

Dominic went to pat Tulip, and Jenny overheard him whispering: 'I bet you miss her as much as I do, Tulip.' He smoothed her nose and patted her neck. Jenny smiled to herself, and felt a little sad for Dominic. She, too, missed her friend's company, but being close to the horse brought Emily closer.

Liz came into the yard, wrapped in a big jacket, jeans and boots, carrying a tray with mugs of steaming coffee for John, Al and Patrick, who were somewhere around the garden. 'What on earth they could do in this weather, she did not know. 'Hello, Jenny. Oh, hello, Dominic!' She was surprised, then looking at Jenny, she said, 'I didn't hear you come back, and I didn't know you were here, Dominic.'

Jenny smiled. 'Dominic was here first, and we have been riding together.'

'Oh, that was nice. Do you want a cup of coffee?'

'Not for me, thanks.' Dominic shook his head. 'I have to be getting on with my rounds. Off to Wickerbrook now. Got to see Louise.'

Liz smiled. 'Dad got you on the go again?'

He nodded with a smile. 'Yeah, I'm off to see Mystic Nights. He has a cough. They're afraid all the others will get it, too.'

Liz grimaced. 'I'm not surprised in this weather.'

Dominic nodded and rubbed his gloved hands against the

231

cold. 'Got to be going. Bye. See you!' He smiled at Jenny and waved a hand.

Jenny followed Liz into the kitchen. It was warm and smelt of fresh coffee. 'I don't know how you young people managed to hold onto the reins out there in the woods. It's freezing.'

'Neither do I!' said Mrs Porter, with a duster in one hand and a tin of polish in the other. 'It's cold enough to freeze brass doorknobs.' She closed the door to the hallway and was gone.

Jenny and Liz grinned at each other. 'Sit down, Jenny.' She poured her a mug of coffee and put it on the table in front of her.

'Thank you, Mrs Peters.' Jenny slipped off her gloves and clasped the mug, warming her hands around it. 'Emily phoned me last night. She seems OK.'

'Yes, she's all right. It will take a few weeks for her to get used to a new way of life, but she sounded quite happy.'

'Oh, yes, I know. We had a good chat, but of course she's missing the horses. I know how she must be feeling. I would miss Henry terribly. He's my best friend, except for Emily, of course!' she smiled. 'And although it's cold out there, it's still a pleasure to ride; I think its super.'

Emily woke to the sun streaming in through the window. Although the days were pleasant, it really was on the chilly side. They had the central heating on in the apartment, and she was glad she had packed some warm clothing. She showered, did her make-up and her hair, dressed, and came out of the bedroom into the fairly spacious lounge of the two-bedroom apartment. It was comfortably furnished as a summer holiday rental with white cane chairs and green-and-pink flowered cushions. On the glass-topped coffee table was a glass ashtray, and a small bird ornament, there was a television in the corner, which was of not much use as everything was in Spanish. On the other side of the room near the window was a polished wooden dining-table with four chairs, and in the middle a bowl of fresh flowers that Maria, the daily maid, had put there the day before. The window looked out over the branches of thin and gnarled almond trees, now bare and desolate in the winter sunshine. In the summer they would be ablaze with pink blossoms.

The kitchen, next to Christine Anderson's bedroom, was small. She could hear her shower running as she made a pot of coffee for them both, and while the coffee was brewing, she walked out onto the small verandah. The fresh morning air was chilly, being so high up, and she shivered, rubbing her arms over her sweater and folding them tight in front of her. She breathed deeply. The apartment was built into the mountainside, high above the town of Paguera and about thirty-five minutes from the capital, Palma. From the patio, she could see the gnarled almond trees growing at odd angles out of the tufty, straw-coloured grass and hard red soil that sloped steeply down to the lower plains. There was a distant view of the sea. The landscape reminded her of Western films where Indians chased cowboys across barren land. This made her think of horses, and she wondered what it was like at home and wished she could just ride Tulip again. How they would love to gallop across this infertile landscape. It crossed her mind that in such a bare place poor Major would not have knocked his head or lost his life.

Looking into the distance, she could see a yacht sailing on dark-blue water. The sails looked like triangles the size of a handkerchief. She wondered who would want to sail out there in the wintertime. Far below, although she could not see it, was the town of Paguera, not too busy now, but, in the summer, she supposed, the place would be swarming with tourists. In summer, too, the yacht club in Palma she had seen from the taxi would be bustling and alive, with craft sailing in and out of the harbour. The sun would be blazing down on the beautiful people. She was reminded of the wall posters in the office and of the guy with the bronzed, muscled body and sunglasses. She had visions of Dominic.

Looking straight down below her, over the verandah, the green leaves of the bougainvillaea climbed the white walls from the steep depths of the garden. By the thickness of the dry grey branches it had been there for many years. Christine had told her that it only bloomed in full sunlight, and in the summer it was bright pink. She thought of those hot sunny days to come, turning her skin to golden brown.

People were on the move in the small village of Capdella. She could hear a car slowly winding its way up the mountainous country road to her left, and then she spied it as it passed a gap in the trees. The office where she worked was in Paguera, and it was a long and winding drive down, but worse coming up. The coffee smelled good. She went in and poured a cup, then took it out and sat in one of the low white cane chairs on the verandah. It was quiet and peaceful, and the air coming from the distant sea smelt tangy, clear and mountain fresh. Christine came to join her, cup of coffee in hand. They sat together for twenty minutes, then Christine had to leave. It was a good thirty-five minutes' drive to the centre of Palma, with a lot of traffic, and she wanted to pick up her cleaning before going into the office.

Emily went into the kitchen for a refill and put some toast into the toaster, waited for it to pop up, buttered it and then took it outside on to the verandah again. The sound of a heavy engine was coming up the winding road. She had learned from Christine that the water trucks came up three or four times a day to fill up the tanks. They were lucky to be able to just turn on the tap. Down in the village, which was five minutes' walk down the steep narrow lane that was just wide enough for one car to drive on, the village people still drew water from a central well in the middle of the street. In some modern-day age, about the nineteen thirties, the well had been fitted with an iron pump and the villagers came several times a day to fill their buckets.

The village was old. The houses, sun-drenched for most of the year, badly needed a coat of white paint. There was not much in the little village: a small general store where they could buy groceries; a small shop that sold a few cotton dresses and displayed shoes in a window no bigger than a postage stamp. And another that sold hand-embroidered tablecloths and napkins. Majorca was famous for beautifully embroidered cottons and linens.

The doors to the shops had beaded curtains in a variety of colours, which let the air flow in and kept the flies and insects out. On the corner, a large white-painted house had a solid brown wooden front door with 'BANCO' written on a polished brass plate. Inside, to Emily's surprise, it was fitted out like any normal modern bank. The man at the desk spoke good English; the name on a plate in front of him said: 'Mario Borzello'.

Christine had been in Majorca for nearly two years, and could speak Spanish. Emily, though, had found it difficult at first when she went down to the village shop for bread, milk and eggs, making signs and pointing things out to the Señora in charge. Trying to buy a tin of ham seemed impossible until a very small boy came into the shop and said *'jambon'*. Señora Maria had thrown her hands in the air and clasped her cheeks with the sheer joy of understanding. From then on, each time she went shopping for food, Emily took a cookery book with her, and pointed to pictures of tomatoes and potatoes, bread and eggs, etc. and she found by doing this that people were friendly.

Not knowing the language meant that so far she had not made any friends. She sighed and wondered what Dominic was doing, probably going for a ride before he and Graham set off for the veterinary college in Cambridge. It was going to take them five years to qualify. She thought of Jenny riding out in the mornings, and then stabling Henry, probably even managing a ride at lunchtime. A dog was barking somewhere, reminding her of the first time she and John had gone to Mayberry Farm with the horse box – how Emma, Paddy and Jan, the Golden Retrievers, had barked with excitement. And then her thoughts went back to Dominic and his family's two black Labradors, Bob and Bernie. Oh, how she had made a fuss of them! She could almost feel the softness of their heads as they nuzzled into her.

'Gosh, it's so quiet here; I miss you, Dominic!' she whispered, sighing with her eyes closed. She took the plate and the cup into the kitchen and rinsed them under the tap – they would be covered in ants if she left them. Maria, who came to do the cleaning every morning after they left, would put them away. Christine had employed her. She hadn't had time for cleaning, and she was glad that Emily could now share the expense. She closed the verandah doors, picked up her leather jacket and bag, and went down the stairs and out to the small company car. She drove carefully down the steep winding mountain road, hoping she would not meet another water truck coming up. She was only just getting used to driving on the right-hand side of the road, and the local roads were very narrow! At the end of the long drive down, she reached the main coast road through the town of Paguera. It was now busy with early-morning traffic. The shops were just beginning to open, people were already sitting outside the cafés, enjoying a cup of coffee, despite the chill of the morning. Paguera had always been very Spanish, but now it had a big German community, and most of the boards outside restaurants advertised beer, bratwurst and sauerkraut. In the season, it would be hard to get a table anywhere. She drove on, then parked the car, her thoughts on checking on some accommodation from a booking she had taken in the week; the new people would be arriving tomorrow.

Señora Maria Sanchez smiled and nodded, a telephone receiver to her ear, as Emily came into the spacious office, with its four desks, computer screens and grey metal filing cabinets. Marquita, who was sitting at her desk, wished her 'Buenos días, Senorita Peters.' Emily nodded with smile, saying 'Good morning, Marquita,' then added, 'Buenos días!', as she nodded to Rosina, who was just switching on her computer. She sat at her desk and checked on the pile of English mail that the girls had left for her to sort out. There were a couple written in Spanish which she passed back to Maria, who was the older of the three. Maria would telephone head office, which would arrange for them to be translated into English and faxed over for Emily to read.

The day had been busy. She finished at 5 o'clock, and drove back up the winding mountain road to the apartment. The afternoon had warmed a little and she took a cold drink from the fridge out onto the little verandah. She looked out again over the parched, rugged landscape to the distant sea.

Dominic was like a fish out of water, so Graham told Jenny.

'He's finding it hard to concentrate, but he is burying himself in his studies, or trying to, and then he says he is not getting anywhere, and there is no way I can help him.'

'Well, can't we take him out for a meal or something? Let's

236

all go for a pizza tonight,' Jenny suggested. 'Maybe it will cheer him up a bit.'

When Graham mentioned it to Dominic, he said that he didn't want to go for a pizza; he had too much studying to do and didn't fancy pizza, anyway. Graham suggested a drink at the Red Lion, instead.

'No thanks, Gray. I don't want to go on my own.' He shook his head. 'I miss Emily. Oh, I know we have our differences, and she makes me mad at times and we argue, but I miss her. I love her, Gray! We didn't see each other every day, but I miss her every day now. The whole place seems empty without her.' He sat down heavily in the armchair. They were at home in the lounge. He leaned forward, his elbows on his knees, rubbing his hand through his dark hair. 'I love her! What am I going to do for a whole year?' There was a sob of despair in his voice. 'I asked her to marry me, did you know?'

Graham just lifted his eyebrows. He said nothing, but walked to the window and looked out. 'What did she say?' He had his back to his brother. 'Is that why she went away?'

'No! Oh, you know!' He shook his head. 'I don't really know. She sort of said that she was not ready for marriage, and then this job came up. I begged her not to go. She said her boss had said there was no one else. I believe her, but if it had been impossible for her to go, they would have had to find someone else, wouldn't they? I'm so fed up!' He jumped quickly out of the armchair and stormed out of the lounge. Graham heard his feet stomping up the stairs and his bedroom door slam.

Vivienne came into the lounge. 'What's the matter with Dominic?'

'Oh, you know, Mum; girl trouble! He's fed up about Emily going away.'

Vivienne raised her eyebrows. 'Oh, yes, I know, but he'll have to get over it. He will have to learn that he can't have everything his own way, and people have to live their own lives. He has been difficult since she left; he's not eating properly and he's not studying. I think Dad will have to have a word with him.'

Graham and Jenny went for the pizza. They sat at a cream plastic-topped table in the corner, facing each other. It was not a bit romantic. The lights were bright and there were people standing at the counter waiting for a take-away.

'I wish Dominic had come with us,' said Jenny. 'It would have made a break for him. Emily is fed up, too. I got an e-mail from her just before we came out. She says she is spending most evenings in the flat. The girl she shares with often stays in Palma after work and does not get in until quite late or stays the night; she has a boyfriend. She sometimes asks Emily to go out for a snack when she is there, but it isn't often. She say the girls in the office seem nice, but she can't have a conversation. That's what's worrying her. It's all sign language and the odd word.'

It was at the end of the fourth week, Emily was in the office early and alone. Maria, who was usually there first, was sick and had not been in for a couple of days. It was all so awkward and frustrating. The phone rang continuously and the voices rattled off in Spanish, and she had to keep referring to Marquita.

Emily was reading off the computer screen when the phone rang. She picked it up, saying, 'Hola!', one of the few Spanish words she knew.

'Hola! Oh, hello, Señorita Peters.' A man's voice in broken English came down the line. 'Eduardo Costello, from Palma. Maria, she's not in office?'

'No, not this morning, but can I help you?'

'Please, Señorita.' He told her that Señor Carlos Calmanetti and family would be arriving Sunday afternoon at the Casa Puerto Vista in Porto de Andriax and that he couldn't go to inspect the house because his daughter was getting married.

'Just one moment!' Emily shuffled through her paperwork and found the document she wanted, and then checked the computer screen. 'Hello! Yes, I have it here: Calmanetti, Carlos. Family of five ... wife Sophia ... Ricardo, Julius and Maria.' Another Maria, she thought; they all seemed to be Marias! 'Yes, they arrive on Sunday afternoon.'

'*Si si!* That is so. You will please to take-a my place. My daughter Maria' – he pronounced it 'Mah-ha-ria – 'she marry!'

Emily smiled into the receiver. She could hear the joy in his voice. She congratulated him and said that she would go out to check on the villa and greet the Italian family on Sunday.

Emily sat for a moment, her elbows on the desk, looking down at the brochure of the luxurious Casa Puerto Vista. It was a house with arched terraces and bright-pink, bougainvillaea cascading down over the roof of a lower terrace. The ornamental gardens were laid out to perfection. In the immaculate gardens was an Olympic-size swimming pool, a red paved tennis court, and in the open space at the far end of the garden, a large cross, painted in white on the grass, for a helicopter to land. She turned the page. The interior was of polished wooden floors and dark antique furnishing; drapes of dark-red velvet, and a wide staircase and ornate wrought-iron banister with a polished wooden handrail. The ten bedrooms were luxuriously appointed in cream, pink, blue and pale-green silks, each with its own dressing room, white marble bathroom, and verandah. Emily turned the page and got the address. She would go out there on Saturday and check that all was in order for the family's arrival, but she had better brush up on her Italian, which was about as good as her Spanish, or worse.

21

On Saturday morning, Dominic and Graham took Silverspoon and Skybright out into the paddock. They had old Fred out there putting up the jumps for them. The day was cold and crisp, making their hands and feet tingle. Fred was frozen, even in his warm jacket with a big scarf slung around his neck. His nose and cheeks were bright red and his ears bright pink, and great clouds of steam rose from his mouth as he bent and stretched, lifting the poles. But now a watery sun shone down warming and softening the dark earth.

One no better than the other, they each took the six-foot jump. Old Fred put it up yet another notch. The Wickerbrook Show was coming up again in March, and Louise was busy recruiting again. She had phoned Dominic and, in her sharp and businesslike manner, had asked about Emily. 'We will miss her this year, Dominic,' she had said. 'Great competitor, great competitor! Who is taking care of Black Tulip and Pico? I expect she has left them well provided for, what, eh! Got to keep them working. Got to keep them fit, eh!'

Dominic grinned. To hear her voice on the phone you could imagine a buxom woman in her middle forties, instead of a mid-twenties waif of about seven stone.

'Well, Emily left Jenny Ellis in charge of the exercising. She goes round every day, and I go a couple of times a week, mostly at weekends. Graham sometimes comes, too, and Jenny sometimes brings Henry and we all go together.'

'Oh, that's good. That's good! Well! Have to go, old chap, work to be done, work to be done. Ha ha ha! There is a meeting at the Farmers' Club on Tuesday. You will be there, won't you?' She changed the subject completely. 'What about the Goldsborough in July? Do you think Emily will make that?'

'Oh yes, I'm sure she will,' said Dominic, crossing his fingers. 'I'm sure that she's already entered Black Tulip.'

'Do you remember the last disaster at the Goldsborough? Dear me! What a time that was.'

All he said was 'Yes.' How could he forget! It was that disaster, as she had called it, that had brought him and Emily together.

'Yes, yes. Very bad do, that! I didn't actually see it, but everyone was talking about it, my dear, just about everyone. Disastrous day for you, darling, what!' There was a pause; he waited. 'Anyway,' she said, brightening, 'better luck next time, old chap. Sorry, I must go. Nice talking to you. Bye!'

Before he could say another word she was gone. He smiled to himself. That was Louise, always in a hurry and possibly dialling another number already. Flashes of the Goldsborough came into his mind. And thoughts of Emily. He looked at the book on his desk and he started to dial her office number.

A Spanish girl answered: 'No English. Señorita Peeeters? No!'

He got the idea that she was not available. He suddenly realized that it was Saturday, and she only worked alternate Saturday mornings. He thanked her and put the phone down, and went to his room feeling depressed. He had just wanted a short chat. He just wanted to hear her voice. He sat at his desk, picked up a book and began to study. He read for about ten minutes, then put the book down. His mind was not on it, and what he had just read he had no idea. He kept getting flashbacks of the day he really first noticed Emily Peters – she had been riding Major then – in one of the smaller events. He had thought even then that she was a good horsewoman, though no match for Silverspoon! He went into a daydream, imagining he could feel the silkiness of her blonde hair. He stopped, taking a long breath and shook his head. He got up from the desk and went to the window. He caught glimpses of Fred and Adrian Poole working in the stable yard, their breath puffing out in white clouds of steam. He wondered if it was warm in Majorca; he wondered what Emily was doing. He sighed. There was an ache in his heart. Oh, why was love so frustrating? He never thought it would be like this. He had never felt like this before. He could not live without her. He knew that she was fond of him, but why could she not bring herself to say that she loved him? Perhaps it was the way he treated her. He did lose his temper quite often, he knew that...
Perhaps he should let her win the next time they rode in the

241

same event, but then it was going to be over a year before that happened. He frowned, twisting his mouth up sideways. No! As much as he loved her, he could not lose at a show; he could not spoil his image! And in any case it would be cheating, and she would never stand for it. No! A job was a job, and he had to go on and win. Silverspoon would never forgive him if he allowed himself to be defeated on purpose. He gazed at her photograph, and sighed deeply, 'Oh, Emily, Emily!'

Emily spread out the road-map on the dining-room table. She was turning it this way and that. Oh, she was hopeless with maps. After thirty minutes she decided to call a taxi.

The Casa Puerto Vista was above Porto de Andraix, and according to the brochure, overlooked the harbour. The taxi approached Porto de Andraix. There were shops and restaurants to the left, and to the right the harbour packed with yachts at anchor. The mid-morning sunlight caught the windows of the numerous villas set into the grey rocky hillside amid splashes of bright-pink bougainvillaea. Through the open window she heard the metallic clinking sound of the rigging as the tall masts swayed gently on the swell. On the deck of one yacht, two men were preparing to sail. There were few people about, but in the season, she imagined, the port would be a hive of activity.

They were up on the hillside road now, and Puerto Vista came into view. She knew from the brochure that it was two hundred years old, and as they approached she saw the name painted on blue tiles on the wall. The taxi drove through the open wrought-iron gates. The villa's once-pale walls had aged to a deep golden yellow, contrasting with the red roof tiles. Perched on the roof was a four-arched bell-tower, above this a weather-vane of a black galloping horse. Her first thought was of Black Tulip.

The taxi stopped at the front of the house. She made signs asking him to wait for her, and he nodded. She walked up the wide steps to the large black front door and rang the bell. She waited and rang again. There should have been someone there – a maid at the very least – but obviously no one was at home. Putting the large heavy key into the keyhole, she pushed open the door and found herself in a spacious, cool stone hallway. She stood for a moment looking at the high ceiling and the curved red-carpeted staircase. A large round table stood in the middle of the hall, and on it stood a clock with four faces: it was eleven thirty. She felt as if she was intruding, as if she was being watched. Somewhere there were fourteen staff, some of whom lived in, but no one came. She looked around to get her bearings. To the right, a low ornate table with twisted legs stood against the wall with a large vase of flowers on it. To the side of this, behind double glass doors, was the dining room. To the left across the terracotta-flagged hall was the lounge, and straight ahead the long sweeping staircase led up to a hallway above. From where she stood, facing the staircase, the hall narrowed and continued, seemingly to infinity on either side, with doors along the walls. She decided to look at the dining room first. Opening the double glass-panelled doors, she looked into a luxurious room with a long polished table. Around the table there were cream cushioned chairs for twelve guests. The walls were covered in a cream-and-red silk Regency stripes. The only other furniture in the room was an antique sideboard, on which stood a silver candelabrum, with five long white candles, and a cut-glass decanter surrounded by six glasses. At the far end, facing her, more long glass double doors looked out onto a paved patio surrounded by a low stone wall and steps down onto the well-cut lawn. She walked out onto the patio, and round to the lounge, which also had high glass panelled doors, looking over the harbour and the toy-like sailing boats below. She tried the lounge doors and they were open. She went into a well-furnished room with yellow flowered sofas and deep comfortable armchairs set on a creamy coloured marble floor with rich cream-and-rose-pink rugs at either end and a glass-topped coffee table. There were fresh flowers in the enormous marble fireplace, above which an oil painting showed a beautiful dark-haired woman in a black dress. Everything looked well cared for. Suddenly she heard footsteps behind her. In the doorway stood a middle-aged lady dressed in black. A Spanish woman.

'Signorina Peters?' She spoke reasonable English. She came forward, her hand outstretched. 'I am Signora Vincentti. We were expecting you. Signore Costello, he telefono...' She pointed a finger to her ear and made a round movement, '...to a-say that he could not come and that you were to take his place. I am very please to meet you Signorina, but I did not see you arrive. I look...' She pointed to her eye. '...And I see a taxi. We live at the gatehouse. My husband, Alberto, is the butler. Normally Juan is there at the gate, but I sent him off on an errand.'

Emily smiled and shook her hand, 'How do you do, Señora Vincentti. I did phone and leave a message.'

'Si, si Signorina! I did get your message, but I let the staff go off for a few hours. The laundry girls are downstairs. The place is not completely empty, and we are ready for the Calmanetti *familia*.'

'I will come to introduce myself to Señor Calmanetti early tomorrow evening, if that is all right. The house is beautiful, Señora, and the view is magnificent from here, isn't it?' They stood together taking in the view of the harbour.

'Have you been here long, Señora?'

'Twelve anni, Signorina. My husband, we come from Roma when Signore Calmanetti take this villa.'

'Oh, so you are Italian.' Emily raised her eyebrows. 'And Señor Calmanetti owns the villa! I wasn't aware of that. I thought it was just another rental. I thought they were renting for a month.'

'Si Signorina, the Signore, he telefono, he say that he come for one month. And not Signore Calmanetti, he not own the villa, but he father, father.' She moved her hands round and round in front of her. He build it, Signore Carlos!' She was nodding her head and still rolling her hands in a circle.

Emily smiled. 'Oh you mean, Mr, I mean Signore Calmanetti's grandfather owns the house.'

'*Si, Si.*' She circled her hands again. 'Grande, Grande.' She nodded and pointed to the painting of the woman over the fireplace. 'He wife.'

Emily smiled. 'Oh, I see, great-grandfather!' Signora Vincentti nodded. Emily looked at the paperwork. 'But if they own the house, why do they book through the agency?'

'They have to book, Signorina. This villa is rented many times!' The hands circled again. 'They have to book when they needed to *vacanza!*'

244

'Oh, I see.' Emily nodded. The word *vacanza* she guessed must mean 'holiday' or 'vacation'. They walked around the rest of the rooms together, and she was introduced to some of the staff. At the front door she shook hands with Signora Vincentti, and, from the taxi window, waved goodbye. The house was majestic.

Christine was watching the television. The programme was a Spanish lesson. She said she could understand some of it, but not all, but it helped her to learn the language a bit. She was surprised when Emily suddenly said she was going out; she had to see a client.

'What! On a Sunday?'

'Yes, I offered to go. I went yesterday. The family who own Puerto Vista are coming this afternoon, and Señor Costello from your office can't go to meet them.'

'Oh yes, I know. His daughter is getting married. He is so excited, he has told everyone. 'Oh, so you have seen the place. What's it like? I have seen the brochure; it looks lovely!'

'It's fantastic,' said Emily.

Half an hour later, at five fifteen, Emily drew up in front of the house. She rang the bell, and Alberto Vincentti opened the door. She introduced herself, saying that she had met his wife, yesterday. He spoke good English and said that he was expecting her, showing her into the comfortable lounge. He would inform Signore Calmanetti that she was here. She waited, looking out of the window, hoping that his English was good.

In a few minutes the door opened, and she turned as Signore Calmanetti came in. He was tall, well over six feet, and well built with wide shoulders and a dark, tanned, angular face, which showed he spent a lot of time outdoors. His thick steel-grey hair, brushed back high from his forehead, curled thick to his collar. He was, she guessed, in his mid-sixties, though it was hard to tell. He was a handsome man with brown eyes and a friendly smile. He offered a large bronzed hand for her to shake.

'Evening, Miss Peters, glad to know yer!' To her relief he was American.

245

'Oh! Good evening...' She hesitated, not knowing how to address him. '...Mr Calmanetti.'

'Oh, just call me Rick. The name's Enricho, but everybody calls me Rick.'

'Oh, excuse me.' She looked at her clipboard. 'I thought the name was Carlos. I hope you didn't mind me calling. I just wanted to see if everything is all right. It's our policy to call on all rentals before they arrive, just to see that the staff have cleaned, and so on. I called yesterday, and met Senora Vincentti. I wasn't aware until then that you were the owner of this villa, so I thought I would just call and say hello.'

'Oh! Sure, sure, everything is just dandy, thanks. The staff look after the old place well. It looks just the same and so peaceful after New York City, and I am *glad* that you dropped by. The house is in my father's name, Carlos, but he died six years ago. I didn't change the name, even though I now pay the bills!'

'Oh, you live in New York. I thought it might be Rome; the name you understand, and I am glad that you speak English. I was expecting to struggle with Italian. I have only been here in Majorca for a few weeks and I'm finding Spanish very hard to understand.'

'Yeah,' he chuckled, 'the name is confusing, but I was actually born in Texas. My father was Italian, and the Spanish confuses me, too.' He chuckled heartily. 'I have a house in Texas, but I live half the year in New York City.

'And where are you from, Miss Peters?'

'England, near Cambridge.' Everybody had heard of Cambridge.

'Oh! I have been there! I was stationed at Lakenheath; there is an American airbase there. I bought me a little house down there in a quaint little village called Lavenham.' He pronounced every syllable.

She beamed. 'Oh! That's almost where I live, about fifteen minutes away. Long Melford, Sudbury.'

'Oh great, yeah I know it. Then we have something in common. Can I offer you coffee or tea?'

She hesitated for a moment. 'Er ... yes please. Coffee would be nice.'

'Come through!' He waved his arm with a flamboyant gesture as if he was forwarding a cattle drive. She had seen it many times on the television. Head 'em up and move 'em out!' She smiled to herself and followed him through the hall past the stairs and into the large, spacious kitchen that yesterday had been so quiet and clean. Today it was bustling, the chef at one end chopping food and maids walking back and forth carrying boxes, plates or bottles or washing dishes or cleaning tabletops. There must have been at least seven people working. Rick explained that he had brought his own chef and some staff with him from New York, in addition to the fourteen staff that normally worked at the villa.

They passed through to the breakfast room, where she was introduced to the rest of the family, who were sitting round the table having afternoon tea and cakes. Rick said that this was the favourite room in the house where everyone seemed to gather. He grinned, nodding his head sideways. 'Next to the kitchen, handy for making coffee, and nearer to the fridge for drinks from the outside verandah...'

Rick introduced her. 'This is Miss Peters ... Emily!' He gave her a friendly smile. 'This is my wife, Sophia.' She smiled and held out a delicate hand. Emily recognized her as the lady in the painting over the fireplace in the lounge. 'Our daughter, Maria.' Maria nodded with a smile. She was dark like her mother and aged about eighteen. 'And our sons, Riccardo and Julius.' They both stood up. Both were handsome and tanned with thick dark hair that curled into the collar of their white shirts. Riccardo, who was about thirty-five, was the older and the taller of the two. He shook her hand and smiled with Italian charm. Julius gripped her hand enthusiastically. 'Hi there! They call me Jay!'

Rick pulled out a chair for her and a maid placed a cup and saucer in front of her, asking if she wanted her coffee black or white.

'You are English, Miss Peters?' Sophia inquired. 'How long have you been in Majorca?' Slim and petite, she was very expensively dressed in a pure-silk flowered dress. Emily noticed the gold chains around her neck, the gold watch, and the diamond and ruby rings on her fingers, as she waved her hands.

'Oh, not long, barely a few months.'

'And do you like it here?'

'Well, yes.' Emily nodded. 'I like it but I find Spanish hard

247

to understand, and I do miss home, but I have to stay until the end of the year.' She explained about leaving her horses. They were all interested. As far as she could gather they had a huge horse farm in South Carolina, and racehorses in Texas.

Rick said that he had one entered for the Budweiser Million and had great hopes of it coming in the first three. 'Look out for it, and back it each way. It's called Variegated, and it's a grey.'

Emily told them about Pico, Silverspoon and Skybright.

Riccardo said, 'I ride nearly every day.'

'In New York?' She was surprised.

No,' he smiled. 'I live in South Carolina. I run the horse farm for my Dad. We breed 'em, break 'em, train 'em, ride 'em. You name it, we do it. Got quite a few at stud.' He grinned.

'Sounds great. How many horses have you got? I have never been to America.'

'Well, there you have it.' He slapped his hands together. 'You gotta come! We'll give yer some of that old Southern hospitality.' He spoke jokingly in a Southern drawl. And they all laughed, making her feel very much at ease. 'There are two hundred and fifty in the South that I take care of, and one seventy-eight in Texas. Is that right, Pa? Jay manages them.'

'That's a lot of horses.' Emily looked amazed. 'Are they all yours?'

'Mostly. Some we got at livery, but most of them Dad has bought over the years, and we breed, of course.'

'Yeah! We stand a chance of winning a few races,' Rick chuckled.

'I got a few in Spain, too,' said Ricardo. 'But they are not all for racing.'

Changing the subject, she asked Sophia if everything was all right with the house and was there anything that she could do for them. But they all seemed perfectly happy. She finished her coffee, put away the clipboard in her large handbag, and stood up saying that she must go. She thanked them, and they thanked her. Riccardo walked her out to the car and politely opened the door for her. She got in and turned the key and the engine roared into life. With a dashing smile he waved her goodbye.

That evening, back in the apartment, she phoned Dominic. The phone rang for a long time before Graham answered. They exchanged pleasantries, and he called Dominic.

He was pleased to hear her voice. 'How is it going, Em? Gosh, I miss you, darling!'

'Yes, I know. I miss you too.' She went on to explain about the American family, and how she was so pleased to have had a conversation in English, about South Carolina and Texas and the horses.

'Sounds great! Maybe we could go to America and visit them one day. What do you say?'

'Oh, I'd love that, Dom.' He could hear the excitement.

'I wonder why they come to the house in Majorca in the wintertime; you would think they would be there in the summer, wouldn't you?'

'I don't know, it is strange, but I suppose Texas and Carolina are mostly sunny, aren't they? I don't know much about it. Perhaps they come away for a break, or perhaps it's that they are not so busy at this time of the year. They have hundreds of horses. The house is really fabulous. I think the way Riccardo spoke that they just wanted to get away, and have a family get-together, and Rick, I think, was glad to be in the peace and quiet after New York.'

'Who is Rick and who is Riccardo?'

'Rick is the father and Riccardo is his son. There are two of them, the other one is called Jay. And they have a daughter, Maria. Everyone is Maria out here.'

'How old are the sons?'

'Gosh, I don't know, about twenty-five to thirty-five. Why?'

'Just wondered. Good-looking?'

'Well, yes, both dark-skinned like their father, Italian-American. You know the type.'

'Yeah!'

'What's the matter?'

'Nothing?' It went quiet. 'Just that you seem to be on good terms with Rick and Riccardo, and what's the other one? Jay.'

'Oh well, I spent a very pleasant couple of hours with them, had coffee. They made me very welcome.'

'Oh! Did they?'

'What's the matter with you?' She could hear the coldness in

249

his tone. 'I'm not seeing them again, if that's what you are thinking. They're clients, it's business.' Her voice rose with annoyance. 'I only met them this evening for the very first time!'

'Oh, all right, all right.' He sounded annoyed. 'I was just asking that's all. How long do you think it will take before one of them asks you out on a date?'

'Oh, Dominic! Don't be so stupid. I'm on business.'

'Hmmm! So are they.'

'Oh, don't be so stupid!' She changed the subject. 'I have been talking to Jenny. She says there is to be another Wickerbrook show in March.' It went quiet. 'Dominic? Dominic!'

'Yes, I'm still here!' It went quiet again. 'I've entered.' She could hear his disgruntled tone.

'It's no good you getting upset, Dominic. I'm working, and I do have to talk to people.'

'Yeah! Yeah! I know!' It went quiet again. 'I miss you, Em, I can't wait to see you, and it's going to be months yet.'

'Yes, I know,' she sighed. 'I know, I miss you too, and I miss my home and my horses, and I miss my normal routine, and I am fed up. I'm sitting here now on my own. Christine is rarely here. I work all day, talk business and make sign language. I phoned Ed Lambington yesterday and asked if he had a replacement. He said he was looking into it.'

'Well, can't you just quit?'

'No, Dominic. Not yet. I have got to give it a chance, and the office was in a bit of a muddle when I first started, but I have got it back into shape now. I wish I could understand the language though!'

'I have been over to Rosemary Lodge with Jenny, and I rode out through the woods. She took Tulip and I took Pico.'

'Oh, that was nice. Thanks! How are they going, I miss them.'

'I hope you miss me as much.'

Oh, I do, I do. Really. You know I do.'

'Do I?' There was a pause. He sighed. 'Well, I just happened to be there doing my monthly check on Tulip, and Jenny arrived so I went with her. And tomorrow she can't go. She's doing something for her dad, so Graham is coming with me. I saw your mum and dad. They said you had phoned. They're missing you, not as much as I am though.'

'Yes, I miss you, too!' She bit her lip. There was an awkward pause. 'Well, I suppose I will have to go! She gave a deep sigh. 'I'll talk to you again in a couple of days, OK?'

'Yeah! Goodnight, Em. I love you. Bye!'

She put the phone down slowly and thoughtfully. He was jealous! All she'd said was Riccardo was dark and had curly hair. But then maybe she shouldn't have said that. Well, that's how you would describe anyone; you would describe a girl as blonde or dark. He was just jealous, that was all. But then she had nothing to hide. If she had, then she wouldn't have told him. She sighed. Maybe he really did love her; maybe it wasn't just a figure of speech; he had sounded very sincere. If she did stay with him, would he be watching every other man that she spoke to? Life couldn't go on like that; she couldn't live like that. She turned it over and over in her mind. Marriage! She imagined herself in a white wedding dress, floating down the aisle towards him, and those eyes watching her, admiring her, as she neared the altar. Every girl's dream was to wear a white dress, but... She sighed heavily, and flopped down in an armchair. 'Oh Dominic, I don't know!' she said out loud. 'What am I to do? I just don't know,' she whispered, shaking her head. 'I just don't know, you frustrate me at times with your arrogance.'

Dominic and Graham were riding out. It was cold and too icy for jumping. They got Silverspoon and Skybright into a slow, gentle trot and went around the fields. The exercise warmed them up, and kept the horses in trim. That evening Louise Bartram was having a get-together, as she called it, at Wickerbrook Hall, which meant a few drinks and canapés.

'I don't want to go!' said Dominic. 'Not on my own.'

'You won't be on your own. Jenny and I are going, and you will know everyone there anyway.' Graham couldn't understand him. Before he met Emily Peters, Dominic had never refused a party or a night out anywhere; but now he was a stay-at-home. He had no go. He rode Silverspoon without any enthusiasm. Riding was now a chore; Silverspoon had to be exercised so he exercised him. There was no fun in him any more. He was distant, a man lost and alone in his own world. Even Louise

Bartram had asked Graham if Dominic was all right the last time they were at a Young Farmers Meeting. He was usually the one that asked the questions. 'Why don't we do this?' Or, 'Why don't we do that?' He was the one that kept the club on its toes. But now...?

'He's in love,' said Jenny with a smile. She and Graham had just come out of Peggities Restaurant. It had rained hard while they were in there, and the red neon sign shone on the wet tarmac in the carpark, as they walked hand in hand towards the car.

'Well, I'm not like that, am I?'

'I don't know.' She raised her eyebrows.' Are *you* in love?'

Graham nodded very seriously, turning to her. 'Yes, Jen, I am. I love you with all my heart.' He smiled at her and drew her to him and kissed her gently.

'Oh! Graham!' she whispered, putting her arms around his neck and standing on tiptoes. He kissed her, passionately. He had kissed her many times, but never like this. She had never felt like this before.

He whispered in her ear, 'I love you, Jen. Will you marry me?'

She stood for a minute, holding her breath, her arms slipping from his neck. 'Aaah! Wait a minute. You must give me time to think...' She put her hand to her head. Barely a second passed. 'Right!' She looked up. 'I have given it great thought, and the answer is ... definitely yes.' She giggled as he grabbed her and hugged her. Then she pulled away, looking up at him.

'But I will need plenty of time to organize everything! I want all the trimmings: white dress, roses, bells, and ... oh, I don't know. I'm too excited. Oh! But please, please, ask me again, it sounds so romantic.' She beamed with delight, putting her arms up around his neck as he lifted her and twisted her round and round. He kissed her again. A heavy shower made them run quickly for the car, both giggling with the magic of the moment.

Dominic was driving. They were on their way to Rosemary Lodge to exercise the horses. He hadn't said very much.

'How is Emily?' Graham asked. 'Has she phoned?' He felt he was treading on eggshells. He knew there was something wrong

252

by the way his brother was acting. He, Graham, was bubbling inside and wanted to tell him that he and Jenny were engaged, but he had promised not to say anything.

'She phoned last night. She's OK. But I'm not!' His voice was sharp and clipped. 'I wish she would give up this bloody job.' His voice rose angrily. 'She doesn't want to be in bloody Majorca anyway. She told me so. Why the hell doesn't she tell this Ed what's-his-name, her boss, that she's quitting the job? She says she's missing me and the horses, though I think she misses the bloody horses more.' He put his foot down, and they sped round the corners of the winding country lanes. 'Now she tells me that she has met this bloody cowboy. Apparently he has a horse farm in bloody South Carolina of all places, and it sounds as if she is having a bloody good time.'

'Oh, come on, Dom. She's working.'

'Working! Yeah! Sounds like it!'

'She told Jenny she was fed up, always on her own, and can't speak the lingo.'

'Why the hell doesn't she jack it in then?' He spat out the words. 'This bloody cowboy speaks the lingo!' He eased his foot on the accelerator, as they turned into the lane leading to Rosemary Lodge. He was red in the face with anger. 'I asked her to marry me, and she turned me down. I think that's why she went away.' He put his foot hard on the brake and jolted them forward.

All Graham said was 'Oh.' He couldn't tell him his secret now. He would phone Jenny and tell her not to mention it to Emily, and they wouldn't buy a ring yet. He was sure she would agree.

They turned into the drive, and the car came to a sharp stop, shooting them forward against their seat belts.

'I am thinking of giving up college and going out to Majorca. For the next few months, anyway.'

'You can't!' Graham was aghast. 'Dad will go mad, after you have come this far. Don't be so bloody stupid! Emily would never forgive you. She loves you; ask Jenny!'

'Then why the bloody hell doesn't she tell me that! Not Jenny!'

Graham sat for a moment looking at his brother.

'Come on, Dom. Cheer up; she'll give you the right answer

one of these days, you'll see! I am sure that she loves you. Perhaps she is just not ready yet.' He thought back to last night. Jenny had said she needed time; perhaps it was the same with Emily.

They got out of the car and walked into the yard. John was there with both horses already saddled. They were on time. Dominic was never late. This morning he was so annoyed with himself that he hardly said good morning to John. He swung himself up on to Black Tulip, turned her head and rode out.

Graham raised his eyes to John, apologizing. 'Good morning, John! He's had a bad night.' Then he swung himself up onto Pico and followed his brother out of the yard.

John shook his head. 'Young people!' he muttered. He was standing with his hands on his hips still looking after them, but by now they were out of his sight. He turned to go into the tack room, when the quietness of the yard was disturbed by the clip-clopping of invisible hooves.

'Major!' John's voice was firm and strong. 'Major!' The stable door rattled vigorously, but then there was silence again as he watched the door, but there was just the wind rustling the leaves on the trees. John rubbed his hands against the chill of the morning and went into the tack room, shaking his head.

Emily came out of the office into the bright sunshine. The days were getting a little warmer. 'Comida' she had said to Marquita tapping her watch and snapping her teeth together.

Marquita had nodded and smiled. 'Si bien.'

Emily stopped on the way to buy a red leather handbag, which she had seen days ago, and then an English magazine, which was on a rack outside a shop, and dog-eared and dusty from the traffic as well as out of date by two months. She reached the bistro where she had lunch nearly every day, and sat at the same table on the verandah, overlooking the busy main road. The manager spoke a little English, and they exchanged a few words as he handed her the menu with a smile. She chose a chicken salad, and thanked the waiter as he put a cup of hot black coffee in front of her. Two men came and sat at a nearby table, and had a laugh with the waiter, then ordered their meal in Spanish. She took out the magazine

254

and began to thumb through the pages. The waiter brought the chicken salad.

'Good afternoon, Miss Peters. All alone? May we join you?' She looked up into the smiling faces of Riccardo and Jay Calmanetti.

Jay ordered a bottle of wine and three glasses, and both men ordered fish.

'Is the travel business busy?' asked Riccardo. Emily said that phone calls came in every minute of the day; mostly English people wanting apartment accommodation. In the season the place would be jumping... He asked what she did at weekends.

'Oh, I sometimes stay with friends,' she lied. She didn't want them to know that she had been there for two months and had not yet made a friend.

'Are you busy this Sunday?' asked Riccardo. 'Would you like to come up to the villa for lunch?'

She hesitated. This is what she had dreaded. 'Well, No! I ... well ... I'm not doing anything special. Yes, I think perhaps it would be nice, thank you!' She smiled, wishing she had said 'no' firmly.

'Bring a swimsuit! If the weather's like this, it will be warm enough to sit round the pool, though I doubt if it will be warm enough to swim. Soon conversation turned to horses, and soon they were laughing and joking together. The wine had gone slightly to her head. She suddenly looked at her watch, and told them she had to get back to the office.

She had only been back in the office about thirty minutes, still feeling elated from the wine, when the phone rang.

'Hi, it's Riccardo. Say, would you like to come out for a drink this evening? Nothing starts here until about ten, but we can go to a bar for a few drinks, maybe dinner and then go on to a nightclub.'

Once again she dithered. 'OK, dinner perhaps, but no nightclub. I have to be in the office in the morning.'

'OK! What's your address? I'll come and pick you up for dinner, then we can have a few drinks before turning in for the night.'

'What?' she exclaimed.

'Oh! Sorry!' She could hear him chuckling on the other end of the line. 'I didn't mean it like that. I didn't phrase that very well, did I?' What I meant was, I won't keep you up too late.'

She felt relieved but still a bit apprehensive. There was a pause.

'Hello, hello.'

'Yes, all right. I'll come, but tell me the place, and I'll meet you there.'

They arranged to meet at ten o'clock at the little bar near Cordoba's Restaurant, where they had had their lunch.

She arrived back from the office and put her feet up for an hour. Then she showered, fixed her make-up and hair, and puffed perfume behind her ears and on her wrists. She put on a matching black dress and jacket, took the new red bag, and put on a pair of red shoes almost the same colour. She was ready. It would take her at least fifteen minutes to drive down the winding mountain road. Although it was dark, the sky was clear and starry and the weather a lot warmer than it had been. She came tripping down the stairs to where her car was parked in the very small driveway, and there was someone standing there in the darkness. She froze as he came forward into the light.

'Oh! Hello!'

She put her hand to her throat. 'You gave me a fright! How did you know where I lived?'

Riccardo smiled. 'Sorry! Hi! I thought I would come and pick you up. I phoned the office and the girl told me.' He ushered her into his car.

'Oh! Do you speak Spanish?'

'Fluently.' Almost before she had recovered her breath, he drove off down the winding mountain road, and they were soon out onto the highway.

'Where are we going?' she asked.

'I thought we might take in a nightclub in Palma after dinner. OK?'

'I told you, I don't want to be late. I have work in the morning.'

He grinned. 'We won't be too late.' He drove for about thirty-five minutes before parking the car in a dark street. They walked a few minutes to the small restaurant and had a cosy dinner by candlelight in a secluded corner. There were several other couples, although it wasn't crowded. It was a bit out of the way, and she wondered how on earth did people – Riccardo for instance, who didn't even live in Palma – find these places! It was a good evening. They wined and dined until after midnight, and then they left, taking a short walk back in the direction of the car. Suddenly he led her to a door in the wall. She was a little apprehensive, as he rang the bell and they waited. It opened an inch. Riccardo said 'Calmanetti', and they went in and the door quickly closed behind them.

Walking up the dimly lit and narrow staircase, her heels sank deep into carpet. She could hear music playing. An usher opened the door for them, and the music became deafening. In the centre of the room coloured spotlights shone down in solid beams from a glass mosaic ceiling, blue cigarette smoke curling in the light. The black glass floor that was lit from beneath reflected coloured lights onto a hundred dancing feet, and at the edges people sat at low tables in comfortable soft black leather armchairs, their faces blocked out by shadows.

Waiters rushed about with trays held high serving drinks, though how they ever found anyone in the shadows it was hard to tell. They were shown to a table, and Riccardo ordered a bottle of champagne. The room was cool and air-conditioned, and she was glad that she had brought a jacket.

'OK?' he shouted at her above the rhythmic drumming of the music. She nodded back with a smile, relieved to think she was in a busy place. From the street, it had looked like an ordinary house, eerie and forbidding in the darkness.

'Come on, let's dance!' He jumped up taking her hand and guided her like a blind person to the floor to join the throng of bobbing heads. They pushed their way through and found themselves a space in the centre. It was so crowded they couldn't move their arms, but it was fun.

When they got back to the table, desperate for a drink, the champagne was in the ice bucket with the glasses. A waiter came from out of the darkness. Emily could not see his face. 'Good evening, Señor Calmanetti! Good evening, señorita!'

'Good evening, Carlos.'

The waiter poured the amber liquid, they clinked glasses. She wondered how many other girls he had brought here, it certainly wasn't a place to sit alone. They talked as much as

257

they could in the noise and laughed together. Riccardo ordered another bottle of champagne, then lit a cigarette. A curl of blue smoke travelled up past his handsome forehead and disappeared above his thick black hair. He was certainly the most handsome man in the room.

They danced again. He held her close, swaying cheek to cheek to a slow rhythm, breathing in the perfume of her hair. She closed her eyes enjoying the moment, but feeling uneasy. This wasn't her scene; she felt embarrassed; she hardly knew the man. When they sat down again he held her hand in the darkness, oblivious of people around them.

It was very late when he dropped her off at the apartment – three o'clock in the morning. She crept in, closing the door quietly behind her. She was surprised when Christine opened her bedroom door. She was still dressed. 'Had a good time?' she smiled. 'I have only just come in. Do you want a cup of coffee? I have just made one.'

They sat out on the little verandah, under the stars, each wrapped in a blanket, each telling the other about her evening. Christine told her about her new boyfriend. His name was Claudio. He was rich. His father had vineyards, and he ran the wine business. She was excited about seeing him again tomorrow evening; they were going to the Blue Angel night-club.

Emily laughed. She had been at the Blue Angel in Palma that night, dancing and drinking champagne. It had been the best night she had had since she arrived in Majorca, in fact, the best night she had had in years. They sat chatting until early dawn, then they each went to their room. Both had to be in the office in the morning.

She had only been in the office ten minutes, when the phone rang. It was Riccardo.

'Hi, how about dinner tonight?'

'Oh! Um! I can't!' She hesitated.

'Why? Got a date?'

'No ... yes. With a friend.'

'Boyfriend?' He left the word hanging in the air.

'No! Girlfriend,' she lied.

258

'Put her off. I'll pick you up at seven thirty.' The line went dead.

'Riccardo!' But it was too late. She couldn't go out, she really needed a night in. She dialled the number of Casa Puerto Vista. The butler, Vincentti, answered. He told her that Signore Riccardo had gone out early and had not yet returned. He obviously hadn't phoned from the villa. She thanked him, leaving a message for Mr Calmanetti to phone her.

She was tired after the late night and being in the office all day. It was an effort to get showered and dressed for dinner, and she did not feel a bit hungry. She had tried to contact Riccardo all day, to say that she didn't want to go out tonight, but he seemed to be incommunicado. She had better be ready when he came, she didn't want to let him down.

At seven thirty sharp he rang the doorbell. When she opened it, he marched straight in, armed with a bouquet of flowers and a bottle of champagne, a big smile on his face.

'Hi yer!'

She looked startled, as he pushed passed her. She almost laughed. Americans had no qualms. An Englishman would have waited or asked politely if he could come in.

He handed her the bouquet, which was beautiful. She found a blue jug and went to the kitchen to fill it with water.

'Nice place you have here.' Didn't all American's say that? She had heard it so many times in films. He looked around the lounge, and then walked off into Christine's bedroom. She had left the door wide open, then he came out and ambled into the kitchen, opening the door onto the verandah. He stepped out to look at the view, which was dotted with twinkling lights, then came back into the kitchen and looked in the fridge.

'Gotta bucket and some glasses? This has been on ice all day. He saw the ice bucket on top of the fridge and filled it, and put the bottle in. 'Gotta keep it cold!' He was already in the cupboard, looking for glasses.

She stood there speechless. She had only known him for two days and already he was invading her privacy.

'What's the celebration?' she asked tight-lipped, standing there with her arms folded, watching while he popped the cork and poured the cold champagne into the only two fluted glasses they had. He handed her a glass of amber bubbles, they clinked glasses, and she sipped the ice-cold fizz. 'What are we celebrating?'

He grinned, his even white teeth flashing. 'I had a big win at the races today. He went past the post like a dream.' He looked at the ceiling, flinging his arms out in typical Italian style.

'Races?' she enquired. 'Where?'

'Florida.'

'You went to Florida to the races?'

'No! Watched it on the TV. But I had a big bet. We bred Diamond Clip. I was in no doubt that he would win from the day he was born, so that is what I am celebrating, a big win. And I thought I would celebrate it with you! Gotta pocket full of cash.' He grinned, slapping his side as if he wasn't used to money.

He poured more champagne into her glass and they moved out onto the verandah and sat in the cane chairs. The night seemed chilly after the low warmth of the central heating, but the air was fresh and she breathed in deeply, pulling her pashmina closer around her shoulders. They sat under a clear starry sky.

They drove into Parguera. He had booked a table at a restaurant. It was cosy. They sat at a small table in the corner. Under the flickering candlelight, they discussed their favourite subject – horses. He told her about South Carolina and about his ranch and how it worked, and how they broke in horses, and she in return told him about Black Tulip, and how beautiful she was, and showed him pictures of Tulip and Pico, which she always carried in her wallet.

'They look great!' He smiled, handing them back to her. He liked her smart riding outfit, and said how nice the English looked when they were all dressed up. In America it was too casual – jeans and checked shirts, no different from any other day. But the English knew how to dress for the occasion, and he admired that, especially the hard helmets, which were sensible. He had to admit he had never worn a hard hat, and he had taken many a fall over the years.

She told him how much she missed riding. She missed her home life and her parents. But she never ventured into the story of Major. Her life wasn't glamorous, but it was all she

260

longed for. She was going back to England as soon as possible. Suddenly she became aware that he was looking at her intently, and she gave him an inquiring look. He suddenly leaned back in the chair.

'Say. How would you like to go riding at the weekend?'

Her mouth dropped. 'Do you mean it? I would love to go.'

'OK, I'll arrange it.'

Her blue eyes shone with joy.

After dinner, he drove her back to the flat. They got out of the car, and he walked with her to the outer door at the bottom of the stairs. She was standing with her back to the door, and he put out his arms leaning his hands on either side of her, trapping her in between.

He looked down at her. 'I enjoyed tonight. Thank you for coming.'

She looked up at him. 'Thank *you*! I enjoyed it, too.'

He bent his head. He was close, and his lips brushed her cheek and then her lips, and he felt her pull slightly away. 'Sorry,' he said.

She swallowed hard, feeling embarrassed. 'It's all right,' she whispered, moving as if to open the door.

He leaned away from her, putting his arms to his sides. 'Well, I had better be going. I'll call you in the week. OK?'

'OK!' It was a hushed whisper, and a slight smile touched her lips. He called goodnight as he reached the car, and she called back and went in closing the door behind her and ran up the stairs to the flat, opening the door. She closed the door and leaned back on it breathlessly. She didn't know if it was from running up the stairs or the touch of his kiss or the situation she thought she was getting into. He was handsome and American, with the sun-bronzed Latin look of the guy in the poster on the office wall. She was attracted to him, she had to admit, but that was all. But then any girl would be attracted to him. He was every girl's dream, except hers. He wasn't Dominic. She felt strangely uncomfortable. She thought she might have offended him by not responding to his attempted kiss. After all, they had drunk champagne, and he had taken her out and given her a good evening. It was the least she could do to thank him. After all, what was in a kiss...?

Throwing her bag onto the sofa, she walked into the kitchen, switched on the light, and made some coffee. She felt uneasy. Had she done the right thing or the wrong thing? No, it was the *right* thing. She sat on the sofa with the coffee, had a few sips, left half, and went to bed. She lay awake for ages, still with the uneasy feeling that she might have offended him. But it was too late now. She switched off the light and snuggled down.

22

Emily couldn't wait. Saturday morning at twelve thirty, she left the office and dashed out to buy herself a pair of short ankle boots suitable for riding. Tonight she would go to bed early, and be ready when he called for her in the morning. The thought of riding again was wonderful. She had seen some horses in the local riding school not far from the apartment, and she wondered whether Riccardo had something like this in mind. She wouldn't have thought so, but she wondered where he *would* take her. Being in the business, he probably had sorted something reasonable out for the day. Just to get a ride would be something.

She checked her hair in the dressing-table mirror for about the fourth time, retying the red ribbon, then retucked her white T-shirt into the waistband of her blue jeans, poking a lipstick, a tissue and some pesetas into the tight front pocket. She was ready to go. Her new boots felt comfortable, and she eased around the bedroom, trying them out. She felt excited and yet nervous, but why she did not know. All she was going to do was ride a horse, which she had not done for months. She just hoped that it would not be some old nag.

She looked at her watch for the umpteenth time. It was ten past six, and she hoped he would not let her down. She looked out of the bedroom window over the sparse treetops. Way down below she could see the sea and a tanker that looked like a toy from this distance. She walked out through the kitchen onto the verandah. The morning was mild. She came back in, locking the door. He would be here in a few minutes, she went back into the bedroom for a sweatshirt. She looked in the dressing table mirror again, touching her hair and again checking her lipstick. The doorbell rang at six fifteen, and she jumped

263

as if in surprise. She ran quickly and excitedly to open it. Riccardo was wearing blue jeans and a white T-shirt that made his dark skin look more tanned. The short sleeves with a navy-blue band on them clung tightly to his bronzed and muscled hairy arms.

'Ready?' he beamed, looking with admiration at the neat figure before him.

'Nice morning,' she smiled, coming out of the door and locking it behind her, and he followed her down the stairs and out to his car.

They had been driving for about fifteen minutes along roads of red dry earth, roads she did not know.

'How far is it?' she asked.

'Couple of hours.' He took his eyes off the road for a second, giving her a quick grin.

'A couple of hours!' Alarm bells rang in her head. Where were they going? She sat quietly, as they drove past trees, scrubby and skinny cows grazing on patches of parched grass no bigger than an open newspaper. Shrubs and gorse, brown and dry, grew in rare patches, blown by the breeze that blew across the open plains. There were plantations of bare trees. They were almond plantations, he told her, and in the summer they would be clouds of pink blossom. It was a wonderful sight in the autumn, too: the farmers and their wives and families in large straw hats knocking off the almonds with long sticks into green nets spread on the ground beneath the trees. There was the odd house, built in the middle of nowhere. She wondered how the people lived out here. Where did they shop? They passed a man driving a donkey cart on which there were two large plastic bins. Water slopped out of the bins with the jogging movement of the cart. He had obviously been to a well. He would only have half of the water by the time he got to where he was going, surely?

A few miles on, Riccardo turned the car. Ahead of them were some large galvanized sheds. Emily thought that the stables looked poor; but what else was she really expecting? She just hoped that the horses were reasonable. Riccardo drove around them, and there Emily saw a private aeroplane. A man came to greet them as the car stopped.

'Morning, Mr Calmanetti!' The man was American. Riccardo

264

got out and went to shake hands with him, and then he opened the door for Emily to get out. She did so, looking around at the barren land, feeling a little bewildered and now a little apprehensive. There wasn't a horse in sight, but what she had thought were stables was an aircraft hangar with two aircraft inside.

'This is Miss Peters!' Riccardo introduced her to Captain Nick Winegold, a tall man in black trousers and a white short-sleeved shirt with gold epaulettes on the shoulders. They shook hands. 'And this is Roberto Gonzales.' Obviously Spanish, Emily noted. He smiled and said 'Hola', apologizing in sign language that he couldn't shake hands. His hands were smeared with oil. He wiped them on a filthy cloth.

'We are all ready for you, sir,' Captain Winegold smiled, and Riccardo took Emily by the elbow, and guided her to the aircraft. As she got in, the co-pilot, Barry Heslop, turned and said, 'Good morning, Mam. Nice day for it.'

She smiled, acknowledging him. As she sat, seat belt in hand, she finally said, 'Riccardo, where are we going?'

'Riding!' He gave a quick grin.

'Horse riding?'

'Yes, of course.'

'Where?'

'Valencia.'

'Valencia!' She sat up, in complete astonishment. She looked around her at the thick padded cream seats and the brown carpet and the polished wood and brass fittings. Her mouth dropped even lower when an American stewardess in a smart navy-blue uniform asked her if she was comfortable and would she like a cushion.

'But, Riccardo, I thought we were going somewhere close by!'

'Well...' He smiled, sitting down opposite her. 'Fasten your seat belt. It is close ... by air!' He grinned again. 'I have some horses there on a small ranch, and I want to check up on them.'

'But I thought you said your horses were in South Carolina?'

'They are, most of them, but I have a small place in Valencia. That's why I came here with my parents. They were coming on vacation so I thought it would be a good idea to come

265

here for a week or two and I could check up on the horses. I phone from home twice a week, but I haven't been here in over a year, and when you said you wanted to go riding, what better opportunity? I can kill two birds with one stone.'

The engine roared into life, the twin propellers spinning fast as the aeroplane taxied down the bumpy, primitive runway. Emily sat in amazed silence, gripping the arms of the seat. It was the first time she had ever been in a private plane. She gulped. There were dozens of questions she wanted to ask but words failed her. The aircraft soared high into the sky, and they were looking down on the red island below, at sparse trees and rooftops, and then out over the open sea, where boats sailed the green waves and white peaks showed the water was choppy.

The stewardess offered them coffee from a flask.

'Riccardo, if we are going to Valencia, why didn't we book at the airport?'

'There wasn't a flight. Besides, this is much better, and we can come back tonight. Why? Don't you like it?'

'Oh yes!' She hadn't thought about coming back. 'But how did you find a private plane in such a remote airfield.'

'It's ours! We charter it out when we are not here. Nick is our captain. Dad also has a GV, Gumman Golf Stream. We arrived from New York in it, and Nick is staying in Palma for a few weeks while we're here. The Beech Craft is always ready if we need it; Nick is on call anytime.'

Emily's eyes were nearly popping out of her head. All she knew was that she was in a private aircraft, travelling in luxury and being literally swept off her feet by a handsome American who wanted to ride a horse. She didn't want the dream to end, but sometime she would wake up.

Patricia, the stewardess, said that breakfast was ready, and they moved to the rear of the plane to where a small table was laid. She served fruit, yoghurt, toast, smoked salmon and coffee. After breakfast they returned to their seats. Emily looked down onto the sea; she still couldn't believe this was happening.

They landed at another small private airport, but this time it was more established. There were several private aircraft parked, three standing in a line. Mechanics were working on one, and there was one just taxiing out to the runway. The

266

large hangar doors were open, and she could see planes inside and several people walking about.

The sun was hot and fierce when they stepped down. A sleek black limousine was waiting for them, with a uniformed driver, who introduced himself as Fernando. He shook Riccardo by the hand, greeting him in Spanish. It was about twenty minutes' drive to the stables. The car turned into the long tree-lined gravel drive, and a large white villa loomed up in front of them, with bright-pink bougainvillaea growing up the walls. The wheels crunched as they passed in front of a stone fountain, with five winged horses rearing, and on their backs five angels pouring water from pitchers. They moved on around to the back of the villa to a stable block and stopped.

They both got out and a Spanish man, short with a deep tan and a drooping black moustache, came out from the stables to shake hands, he greeted Riccardo warmly, and Riccardo introduced him as Miguel Rojas, the ranch manager. He bowed and took Emily's hand graciously. In broken English he offered them coffee, but Riccardo said that he just wanted to check on his horses. They wanted to ride as soon as possible and make as much as they could of the one day. Riccardo mentioned Sam Jorrino, and Miguel apologized, saying that he was exercising a horse but would be back shortly. They followed him into the stables, an enormous place with a high raftered roof. Riccardo told her the place was fifteenth century, typically Spanish with arched stable doors. There were many horses looking out over them, one big bay was being led out. There were about twenty men working, lifting bales of hay, pushing wheelbarrows, some sweeping hay into piles. It had a romantic Old World feel, and the men's modern-day dress of jeans and T-shirts looked totally out of place. Emily was mesmerized. She stood inside the stable door, taking it all in, the smell of the horses and the hay making her feel homesick, her thoughts racing back to her own small yard.

When Riccardo had looked around, asked a few questions and inspected every one of the horses, he gave a few orders and seemed satisfied with what he saw. He asked Emily if she was ready to ride, and two horses were brought out, both seventeen-hand fiery chestnuts in peak condition. Their coats shone like mirrors as they pranced nervously on slender legs,

267

swishing their tails and nodding their heads. While the grooms saddled them, they fidgeted, anxious to be off.

Riccardo watched Emily's blue eyes light up. 'They're a bit frisky. Are you sure you'll be able to manage, would you like one of the boys to come with us, to take you on a leading rein?'

She looked at him and frowned. For a moment she thought he was joking, and then realized that he was serious. She looked back at the horses. They *were* frisky, but she would challenge any horse to get the better of *her*! She smiled to herself. 'Challenge', that was a word Dominic always used, and if he could only see her now, he wouldn't ask her; he would say, 'Come on, Em! Have a go!'

'No,' she said innocently. 'I'll try without the leading rein. I think I will be able to manage.' The innocent look she gave him was turning to a bubbling excitement inside her. She couldn't wait to mount this fiery steed, and she hoped he would go charging off with the wind under his tail.

Riccardo was looking doubtful, wondering if he had done the right thing in bringing her here. The horses were ready, and the grooms held them steady. Riccardo mounted, taking the reins, his horse twisting and sidling. He turned him round and was ready in case he needed to dash after Emily, should the horse prove too flighty. He watched as Miguel gave her a leg up and adjusted the stirrups.

'Are you OK?' He looked anxious. Although a groom was holding the bridle, he reached out to take the other side to steady the horse as it bumped the rear of his own horse and sidled away nervously, trying to pull away. She grinned at him, sorting the rein in her hands. The horse sidled and twisted away from Riccardo, lifted his forelegs a little off the ground, pulling back again and whinnying.

'You can't handle him, he's too strong!' His own horse trotted impatiently on the spot, but he had him under full control.

'He's OK! I can manage, don't worry. I'm ready let him go.' The grooms stood back, afraid of being kicked or trampled, while Emily sorted him out, straightening his head and calming him by patting his neck and talking to him, and then, with the slightest squeeze of her knees, he went forward, trotting out of the stable yard into the brilliant sunshine, eager and

268

lively and raring to go. Emily held him back. She knew how a jockey must feel before a big race.

Riccardo, following the swishing red-gold tail, admired the way Emily sat on him, and the way she handled him. He came up alongside of her.

'You, OK? Is he too strong for you? Would you like to try something else? Or would you rather not go?'

'No!' she sang out with a smile. 'He's fine. I'm all right, really. It's OK. It's just taking us a minute or two to get used to each other.

They trotted on for a while, out into the open countryside, along pathways at the side of fields, and then they were out into open countryside where there were miles of grassland.

'Shall we try a little canter?' suggested Riccardo. 'Will you be OK?' He knew the horse was strong. They were bred for racing, really *too* strong for a slip of a girl to handle, but she seemed to be managing.

Emily nodded with a smile, confident that she could handle this beautiful seventeen-hands chestnut stallion. The ginger silky mane bobbed in front of her hands, as they got into a slow rhythmic canter. He went faster, and the mane was flying back in front of her and she was on Major again. She clicked her heels and said, 'Race you!' then shot forward, into a full gallop. She heard Riccardo shout behind her and she smiled, and turned her head, she could see him chasing after her. He obviously thought she was in trouble, but she rode on and on, the wind in her face and her hair. The great horse was striding out and she could feel the power under her and she felt exhilarated. Finally she slowed and came to a stop on the top of a hill under a large spreading tree. Riccardo was close on her tail.

He was breathless and asking anxiously, 'Are you all right? Are you OK?'

She smiled at him, her breath coming in short bursts. 'Yes, of course I am. He's wonderful!' She patted the horse on the neck as he brayed and puffed and snorted. She reached out to touch his ears. 'He's lovely. What's his name?'

'Major.' He saw the look of shock on her face. 'Are you sure you're all right?'

'Yes. Tears pricked her eyes, and she closed them. There was

269

a sadness and yet happiness in her voice. 'Yes, I am now.' It was a sigh of perfect contentment, and she patted Major's neck again. The touch under her hand was warm and moist. She whispered, 'I feel you have come back to me!' and the tears rolled down her cheeks.

'You sure you're OK?' Riccardo jumped down from the saddle, throwing the rein over a low branch and came round to her. She slipped her boots out of the stirrups and slid the long way down. He was holding the bridle, and then took the rein and threw it over the same branch.

He turned her to him. 'Are you crying? Why? Is it the shock? You handled him so well. I didn't know you could ride like that.'

'I get a lot of practice!' She tried to smile as the tears welled quietly, and she sniffed them back.

'What's the matter?' He took her into his arms and held her tight. It was not Dominic. He lifted her chin and looked searchingly into her blue eyes. Then bent to kiss her lips, softly at first and then fiercely, and then he let her go abruptly.

'I'm sorry!'

'Oh!' she smiled shyly. 'It's all right. You did fly me here and it's all so overwhelming.' Then wiping the tears with the back of her hand. 'I'm sorry, too! It's just the horse's name, Major. I had a horse called Major, too, a chestnut and very like this one. I lost him; he died.' There was a pause. She went on to tell him about what had happened on that fateful day in the woods, but she did not say anything about Major's ghostly activity. She didn't want him to laugh.

He said how sorry he was and could understand just how she felt. He had had to have horses put down, and he regretted it. He was never that close to any horse – he had so many – although he did have his favourites.

'It's lovely out here, isn't it?' She looked down into the wooded valley below. Riccardo pointed out a small village, its red rooftops mostly hidden among the trees. 'That's where we are going for lunch. We're only thirty minutes out of the capital.' They sat under the shade of the tree, and talked for a while until they felt rested, and then cantered back to the stable by a different route.

After the grooms had taken the horses, and they had thanked

Señor Rojas, they went into the hacienda to freshen up, and Maria, the housekeeper, brought them an ice-cold fresh lemonade in tall glasses out on to the verandah. Sam Jorrino, the head groom, came and shook hands with Riccardo, and he introduced him to Emily. He and Riccardo had a short discussion, and then the driver took them to the small town that they had seen from the top of the hill, and they found a little restaurant for a late lunch. They drank red wine, and Emily felt quite mellow. Then after an hour or so, the driver took them back to the small airport. It was evening and Captain Winegold was waiting. They had a dreamy flight back to Majorca, dozing most of the way.

Emily said that she had had a wonderful day, but as she got into Riccardo's car, he said, 'It's not over yet.' They stopped at a bar for drinks, and then went on to dinner, and he finally brought her back to the apartment at midnight. He kissed her goodnight gently in the car. This time she did not pull away. He thanked her, saying it had made his day.

Riccardo turned the car round and drove the half-an-hour journey back to Andraitx with a feeling of contentment. He had enjoyed her company. He liked this little English girl. He liked the way she had handled a horse. He liked her voice. He had never seen eyes so blue or shining with sheer delight and exhilaration, and when the sadness had taken over, he felt he wanted to take her in his arms and make love to her right there under the tree. But he was glad that he had contained himself. He wanted to see her again, and they would eventually get close. He didn't want to come on too strong and spoil what they had so far. The day had been great; he might even suggest doing it again. He knew she would not refuse. He admired the way she rode: she looked so delicate, yet could handle a horse as well as anyone he had ever met, and certainly as well or better than any man!

23

Emily, still feeling excited from the day before, was in the office. It was busy, as was usual on Mondays. She planned to phone Dominic when she got home, but made a mental note not to tell him about Valencia.

She had not been in more than ten minutes, and the aroma of the percolating coffee already filled the apartment. She kicked off her shoes and slipped out of her suit, and put on a blue towelling dressing-gown. She went back to the kitchen and poured herself a cup of coffee and was about to go out onto the verandah when the phone rang.

She snatched at it. 'Oh! Hello, Dominic!' He must have heard the surprise in her voice. 'I was just about to call you!' She was so pleased to hear his voice, and they chatted away until she accidentally mentioned in her excitement the small matter of Valencia and the horse named Major! It was too late; she was in too deep.

'How did you get there?'

She hesitated, 'By plane!'

'What! In a day?'

She bit her lip. 'It was a private plane.'

'Oh! Who with?'

She hesitated again. 'With Riccardo...' She screwed up her face, in anticipation of what was to come.

Of course, it had all ended in a big row, and she had slammed the phone down on him in exasperation. Why couldn't he understand! Stupid fool! She was fuming. The coffee had gone cold. She stormed into the kitchen and threw it down the sink, and poured another, then left it on the table and decided to have a gin and tonic instead to calm her nerves. She sipped at it, but it did no good. She could hear her own voice in her head asking questions and answering them, getting more and more annoyed as she went on. Why couldn't he understand?

Didn't he trust her? If she had anything to hide she wouldn't have told him! And she didn't really want to keep it from him anyway. But she knew how he would react and of course she had let it slip out by mistake, and it had all ended in a big quarrel.

She went to the kitchen. She was still fuming inside, and about to have a second gin and tonic, when Christine came in, slamming the door, equally fuming.

'I have had a terrific row with Claudio. It has all finished! I never want to see him again!' She flung her bag down on to the coffee table and stormed into the bedroom, then came back dressed in a red towelling dressing-gown, and slumped down on the sofa, her arms folded, her chest heaving.

'Here!' Emily came out of the kitchen and handed her a gin and tonic. 'Looks like we both have the same problem.'

Christine took the glass, took a few sips and said '*Men!*'

'That's the problem!' Emily mused with a slight smile. She was glad that she was not alone. '*Men!* I am sure we can do without them.'

They sat there sipping gin and tonic and relating their stories to each other. Christine was intrigued to hear about the trip to Valencia. After a few more gin and tonics they ended up laughing and having a good time, forgetting all about 'men'.

The week went on. Christine now came home every evening and they went on girlie nights out or cooked a meal together and sat out on the verandah, talking into the early hours of the morning. At the weekend they went to the beach. The weather was now a lot warmer, and they walked for miles, and then sat on the sand and chatted by the sea, which looked black and uninviting and was surely cold. They stopped at a little bar for a soft drink and had ice cream. One Saturday afternoon, Emily had driven into Palma to meet Christine and they had gone shopping. It was the first time that Emily had been into Palma in the daytime. The shops were great, and she planned to do it more often. She bought a beautiful white ostrich-skin bag and shoes to match, and presents for Mum and Dad, and a soft leather wallet for Dominic. Although she had sworn not to speak to him again, she knew that sometime she would. In her heart she was hoping that he would ring, and if he didn't, she would swallow her pride and give him a call. He was never out of her thoughts, and she knew that she could not live without him. She bought a soft black leather bag for Jenny and presents for John and Susan. She thought of posting these off, but maybe it would be better to keep them until she went back home. It would be nice to see all their faces when she gave them their presents.

The days went on, and Riccardo hadn't phoned and she hadn't phoned him. She felt tired when she came in from the office, and was quite happy to sit and read. She could hear Christine in the kitchen; it was her turn to cook a light meal. She picked up her book again, reading the same line over and over again, then put it down on the sofa beside her. She wondered why Riccardo hadn't called. She hoped that she had not upset him again. He had kissed her, and she had responded. Or maybe she had ridden the horse too well? That was it! She had had no qualms, no fear or uneasiness. After all, the men like to be the macho ones, Dominic for one. Perhaps she should have played it a little nervously and been a little coy, asking for Riccardo's help. Like a damsel in distress. But why should she? She wasn't a dizzy blonde! She was all churned up again, muttering to herself, still fuming inside … *men*!

Then there was Dominic! Shouting at her down the phone, and so angry! And all over nothing! What would it be like if they were married. She would be afraid to talk to a shopkeeper! He was jealous! That was it! It was jealousy, that's all! Didn't he think she could look after herself? There was that macho thing again. Arrogant devil! He would never change! *Men*!

Christine came into the lounge, coffee in both hands.

'Do you want a cup of coffee?'

'NO!'

'I'm sorry I asked. I heard you talking to yourself.'

'I wasn't talking out loud, was I?'

She put the cup and saucer down on the coffee table in front of Emily, and sat down on the sofa beside her.

'What's the matter?'

'Men!' Her blue eyes flashed.

'Oh!' she smirked. 'Don't talk to me about men! I have had it up to here with them!' She put her finger across her throat

274

as if to cut it. 'I've decided, I'm giving up on men, I'm not going out with another one, and that's final! I think we both need a drink.' She went back into the kitchen, opened a bottle of wine, and they sat out on the verandah chatting about men. About their faults and their stupid attitudes and angry outbursts. The wine softened them and, when they had finished the bottle, they decided to go to a little restaurant for dinner to cheer themselves up. The cold chicken and pasta salad that Christine had prepared in the kitchen was stuffed back into the fridge for tomorrow.

They sat at the bar before dinner and got chatted up by a couple of German tourists. They told them to get lost. Their English was not very good but they soon got the message. The waiter showed them to a table in the corner, and they talked over the candlelight for hours. Emily mellowed with the wine and had to confess that, although she and Dominic had their differences, she still liked him. She missed him terribly and she hoped that he would phone her again, and she was sure that he would, and if he didn't, she would ring him in the morning, and try to explain that there was nothing going on between her and Riccardo.

Christine listened. 'Are you sure that there is nothing between you and this Riccardo? Guys don't take you on private plane trips just for the fun of it. What is going on?'

'Nothing,' Emily was surprised. 'You're sounding like Dominic! ... I've never encouraged him in any way. I didn't *know* we were flying to Valencia; he just asked me if I wanted to go riding. I thought it would be just down the road somewhere.' She smiled to herself, remembering Marcus DuBarry, this was the second surprise she had had with riding. She told Christine about that experience and made her laugh.

'Are you telling me that you don't *like* this guy Riccardo, who's loaded with money?' Christine sat with her mouth open. 'Emily, what's the matter with you? Can't you see he fancies you. Think of the life you could have.'

'I'm not interested in how much money he has. He's a very nice guy. I like him, and sure, everyone needs money, but happiness is more important to me. I'm happier at home with my horses. I miss them, and I miss Dominic. I love him!' She shook her head and started to giggle. The waiter poured more wine. 'You know, Chris, I can't believe I said that!' She was laughing with tears in her eyes. 'I love him, Christine, I love him. And I don't want to lose him.' The tears welled again, and she reached into her handbag for a tissue and dabbed at her eyes, feeling embarrassed as a couple on the next table looked across. 'I love him,' she choked, 'and he doesn't know that I do!'

'Then ring the guy in the morning and tell him. Ring him *tonight*! Make his day, and put him out of his misery. Then he can sleep in peace, or maybe if you phoned him tonight, he wouldn't sleep at all.' They laughed.

Dominic and Graham had just come into the lounge. Graham switched on the TV and Dominic slumped down on the sofa, his brown eyes darting from side to side. Angry thoughts were still going through his head. Graham knew that he was still stewing over the argument he had had with Emily. He had told him a bit about it, said she was going out with an American cowboy, as he called him. Graham couldn't believe it, that wasn't Emily's style, and his brother always got irate very quickly anyway. 'Why don't you phone her? Swallow your pride, go on, do it!'

He glanced at Graham, thought about it, and breathed in heavily. He got out his wallet and looked up the number she had given him, then moving to the end of the sofa he picked up the receiver and dialled. He waited, tapping his finger on his knee. She answered.

He was all apologies and so sorry for getting upset and making her unhappy. He did understand that she had to have some time to herself and go out and about, and that she had to have friends, and would she ever forgive him?

She was so pleased to hear his voice and the way he was trying to make up with her. It brought tears to her eyes.

'Oh, Dominic, it's all right. I forgive you, and I know how it must sound on the phone. You must be feeling awful but, really, I have nothing to hide. I love you, Dominic! I love you! Only you! Surely you must know that!'

'*What!*' he boomed down the phone. 'Say that again. Do you? *You do! Really?*' He almost jumped up off the sofa. 'Do you mean it? Say that again, Em!'

'I love you, I love you,' she whispered in a sob, smiling with tears in her eyes, longing to be there with him, to be in his arms. 'Oh Dominic, I miss you! So much!'

Graham wondered what was going on, seeing his brother dancing and bouncing around on the sofa with the phone to his ear. He hoped that Emily hadn't dumped him for the cowboy. Then he turned round and shouted, 'She loves me' and then went back to talk to Emily. She smiled at his exuberance. And Graham gave him the thumbs-up sign and left the room with a smile, to give him some privacy.

Emily came off the phone, her heart light. Marquita looked across and smiled. 'Domineeek?' Emily's blue eyes shone. Marquita raised her eyes knowingly: '*Amor!*'

Emily was already dialling the number of head office in London, asking to speak to Ed Lambington.

'Mr Lambington, this is Emily Peters. Look! I am quitting! I have to leave here as a soon as possible. I must come back to England.' He begged her not to leave, offering her much more money. She refused, saying that it was not the money but her life. She had to get back to her normal life, and she was going back to Suffolk, not London. He said that he had no one else to take over. Emily mentioned Christine, saying that she loved Majorca, and that she could easily take over the Paguera office; she spoke a little Spanish, enough to answer the phone, and make herself understood. Ed considered this. He could probably get another girl to take over Christine's job, and promote her to manager in the Paguera office, now that Emily had sorted it all out and got it back on its feet again. He said he might be able to arrange it, but to leave it with him for the time being. She told him not to take too long.

Dominic was like a dog with two tails. He got on with his studies. He rode Silverspoon until his legs almost dropped off. He went over the jumps whooping and shouting. Old Fred and Charlie and Adrian stood watching with stupid smiles on their faces, thinking that he had won the lottery. He was happy, smiling, joking, and making fun and dancing round the kitchen

277

with Annie Kimberly, who really didn't know what had hit her, so Graham told Jenny.

'What has happened to him then?' asked Jenny with surprise.

'Emily told him she loved him.' They laughed.

At the end of three weeks, Emily had a call from Ed Lambington, saying that he had arranged everything, and that Christine could take over the office the first of the month. Emily was so pleased. She booked herself a flight, and started packing that evening. She phoned her parents and said that she would be home on Saturday. They were pleased, but she told them not to tell Dominic as she wanted to surprise him. She phoned Jenny. They had a long chat, both excited to be seeing each other again, and they arranged that Jenny would ask Dominic to go over on Sunday morning to exercise Black Tulip and Pico. She was to ask Graham to make an excuse not to go with him, and Emily would be there! It would be such a surprise.

'Oh, Em, he'll be so excited. He hasn't been the same since you told him you loved him. I hope you meant it. You did, didn't you? Graham and I can't do a thing with him, and neither can his parents, and Annie Kimberly runs when she sees him coming because he keeps dancing her round the kitchen. But she doesn't mind really.'

When Christine came into the apartment that evening, all smiles and excitement, Emily was ready with a bottle of champagne.

'What do you think, Emily? I've been promoted.'

'Yes, I know!' she handed her a glass.

'You know?'

She took the glass. 'Champagne? What are we celebrating?'

'Your promotion and my leaving.'

Christine looked aghast. 'Emily! You haven't lost your job?'

'No! I quit. I'm going home.' Her blue eyes shone with excitement.

'Are they transferring you back to London?'

'No! I am finished! *Completo, finito*!' She laughed. 'And I'm going back to Suffolk on Saturday, and I can't wait.' She told her about the surprise she was going to give Dominic just in case he phoned on Saturday after she had left. Christine was to say she was out.

Emily topped up the glasses.

'Where did you get the champers?' Christine was a bit bewildered. 'And how did you know that I had been promoted?'

'Well, I sort of suggested it. Lambington phoned me. And I bought two bottles on the way home.' She chuckled with excitement. 'And I can't wait to see Dominic. I just can't wait to see his face when I turn up in the yard.' They clinked glasses.

'And I have made it up with Claudio! He took me out for lunch today.' They had big smiles, clinking glasses again enthusiastically, almost smashing them and spilling the bubbly liquid.

'Here's to love,' giggled Christine. The radio was on, and they were playing flamenco music, and they began to dance, stamping their feet and clapping their hands, shouting, '*Viva, viva! Olé, Olé!*' Until the man downstairs banged on the ceiling. They giggled, not realizing how noisy they were, and Emily popped the cork on the second bottle, and they flopped down into the chairs on the verandah. The night was warm and the stars seemed, to Emily, brighter than they had ever been in the black velvet sky.

It was the third time in the week that Emily had phoned the Casa Puerto Vista to tell Riccardo that she was leaving. Each time she had phoned Alberto had said that Señor Calmanetti was not at home. Emily was in the office. It was Friday morning, her very last day. She thought she must ring Riccardo. She couldn't just leave even if she had upset him in some way. She just had to find out!

'Hello, I would like to speak to Riccardo Calmanetti, please.' It was a woman who answered. The voice was very pleasant and sounded like Sophia's. She said that he was not available at the moment.

'Is that you, Sophia? Hello! Emily Peters here. I haven't heard from Riccardo for a couple of weeks. Can I leave a message?'

'Yes, of course. But this is his daughter, Lucia. Just a moment, you can have a word with my mother.'

Before Emily could get her breath back, a voice said, 'Hello, this is Maria Calmanetti. My husband isn't here at the moment. Can I help you?'

'Oh! ... er!' Emily swallowed hard, stumped, struggling for words, the smile already drained from her face. The woman must have noticed the pause. 'Oh! Mrs Calmanetti...' She had to think quickly. 'Oh ... Would you please tell Mr Calmanetti that Miss Peters from the Paguera Agency is leaving! For England! Thank you!' Then she added quickly: 'I ... had a word with him when I came to check on the house a week or two ago. If you would tell him please... Thank you!'

There was a smile in Maria Calmanetti's voice. 'Yes, of course! I'll give him the message.'

Emily slammed the receiver down, letting go of it as if it was hot. She held her breath, her whole body tensing. 'His *wife*!' It was her own voice shouting in her head. 'So that's why he hadn't phoned. "*His wife!*" Another blessed Maria! And his daughter! How old was she? How old was she?' The voice had sounded quite mature.' She wrung her hands hard together, then sighed quietly. 'Aaah, *men*!

Marquita looked across. She thought Emily was praying.

24

The bags were by the door. At a smile from Emily, the cab driver took them down the stairs, and she gave a last-minute look around the flat before closing the door, and locking it. Then following the driver down the stairs, she got into the back of the cab. 'The *aeropuerto, gracias.*' She turned to have a last look as they drove away. There was something about leaving... She felt a bit sad as the taxi turned the corner and the apartment was lost to her sight. Halfway down the mountain road, she looked back as they passed the gap in the trees. It was the last and briefest glimpse of the villa that had been her home for best part of the year. But now she was really going home. There was nothing she wanted more, but there was still something sad about leaving.

The flight was good. Her father was waiting at the airport to meet her. They hugged and kissed and he remarked on her golden suntan. They chatted all the way home in the car, about Majorca, the weather, about Christine and Riccardo. She asked about Black Tulip and Pico. And Dominic! She could not wait to see Dominic again. And what they had talked about she related again to her mother when she arrived, after more hugs and kisses, and within ten minutes of arriving home she was out in the stable yard, kissing Black Tulip on the nose and Pico, and patting him, and rubbing his ears, breathing in the atmosphere. She had missed the smell of the yard, the horseflesh and the hay, the tack room with the smell of polish and saddle soap. Nothing had changed. And there was John coming into the yard pushing a wheelbarrow, pleased to see her back home again to brighten his days.

She asked him about Tulip and Pico. They had missed her, he said, and so had he and Susan. 'They have both been well, although Pico had a bit of colic a month ago, but he got over it. Mr 'Adly came out, not Mr Dominic, you understand.

And I 'ave just 'ad 'em both shod, and Miss Jenny and Mr Dominic and 'is brother 'ave been over regular, like, and of course Susan has ridden 'em so they 'ave 'ad plenty of exercise!' He asked her if she had been riding while she was away, and she said, 'Only once,' remembering Valencia, though she did not elaborate.

Emily didn't answer the phone all the rest of the day, for fear it might just be Dominic.' After the celebration dinner that Liz had cooked for the three of them, Jenny popped over later in the evening. There were hugs and kisses and they had a lot to chat about. Emily gave them the presents and showed them photographs and they talked, and she wished that she had taken her camera the day of the flight to Valencia. Jenny drove home around nine thirty, and they settled down to a nice cosy evening in front of the TV, a pleasure that she had long looked forward to.

She nipped out into the yard later in the evening. It was so nice to be back in familiar surroundings, doing the things she loved best, talking to her horses. The night had a chill, and there were no stars. There was nothing romantic about the yard, but, to her, it was the best place in the world.

Jenny had said that Dominic would be there in the morning at seven o'clock. John had promised to be there earlier to saddle up the horses, though when he saw Dominic coming up the drive he would disappear.

She kissed and stroked both Tulip and Pico and then said goodnight. She went up to her room with a happy feeling, looking at the old familiar things that she had left behind. These were the things she had not realized she had missed, her old teddy bear with only one ear and the faded yellow ribbon still tied around his neck, the pictures on the wall of Jenny, Henry and herself on Major; trinkets on the dressing table, the hair ribbons and hairpins still in the pink china pot where she had left them... It felt so cosy in her own room, and nice to have the old familiar things about her. She picked up a photograph of Dominic in a silver frame. She wondered how he would look now, after being away for nearly a year. Would he have changed? She decided to phone him. She went down into the hall and dialled the number. It was ringing, and then he answered.

'Oh, Emily, it's great to speak to you!' He sounded so pleased. 'What have you been doing today?'

'Oh,' she mused, 'just travelling around. What have you been doing?'

'Oh, riding, the usual thing, I took Silverspoon out. Graham and I came home last night, did the usual rounds for Dad this morning, and I am going over to Rosemary Lodge in the morning to ride both Tulip and Pico. Jenny can't make it, and Dad's got Graham working.'

'Oh, thank you!' she said innocently. 'How are Tulip and Pico?'

'Oh, they're both OK. I went over last week when I was home...' and so the conversation went on. He didn't know she was just half an hour away, but he went to bed feeling happy for speaking to her.

She went back to her room, still holding the photograph. She smiled at him, whispering, 'I'll surprise you in the morning, my darling!' She pulled the blue curtains, shutting out the cloudy night sky, then went to her cupboard and took out a clean nightdress, and slept peacefully in her own bed.

The Sunday morning was reasonably warm but it was drizzling. Emily and John were in the yard. The car was coming up the drive. John nipped out through the paddock, and Emily darted into the tack room.

Dominic switched off the engine and got out, slamming the door. Mike, Liz and John watched him go past the kitchen window.

From the tack room, Emily heard the powerful tread of his boots coming into the yard. She was bubbling with excitement as she peeped through the crack of the half-open door. Both Tulip and Pico were saddled and tethered in the yard. He thought that unusual, but then perhaps John was a bit pushed for time, or maybe Jenny had changed her mind. He would have to take them one at a time, unless Susan was here, which she was sometimes; he had ridden out with her on a few occasions.

'Morning, John!' he called out loudly, his voice hollow in the empty yard. He looked towards the tack room. There was no answer. John wouldn't be far away. He went first to Tulip and gave her a pat. 'Hello, old girl!' He checked the girth and lowered the stirrups, and then checked the bridle, then turned to Pico, rubbing his nose in a friendly way. 'I'll come back and take you later, old boy,' giving him a friendly slap on the neck. 'Morning, John!' he called again. He listened. It seemed strange that John didn't answer. He walked to the end of the yard and looked out across the paddock. John wasn't there. He came back to Tulip, grabbed at the reins and put his foot in the stirrup.

'John's not here!' Emily suddenly came out of the tack room. 'I'm in charge this morning!' Her blue eyes were shining with amusement. Dominic stopped dead, the hairs on the back of his neck prickled. He took his foot out of the stirrup, glancing over Tulip's back, uncertain of what he had heard. He gasped as Emily swaggered towards him. His mouth dropped, his eyes popped, and a huge smile appeared on his handsome face. No, he hadn't changed! They ran to each other with arms wide open. 'Emily!' It was a gasp. 'Emily, darling.' He hugged her tightly, lifted her and twisted her round, he kissed her and hugged her again. It started raining hard, but neither of them noticed. 'Darling, why didn't you tell me you were coming?' The old familiar twinkle was there in his eyes. 'I would have picked you up at the airport. When did you get home?'

'Late yesterday afternoon, but I wanted to get settled in again.' She leaned away from him, still held tight in his arms. 'And I wanted to surprise you!' Her blue eyes were glassy with tears of happiness.

'Surprise me! Well, you certainly did that. But you phoned me last night? You were *here*?' He hugged her again. 'Oh, Em, darling, I've missed you so. Oh, how I have missed you. Why didn't you phone and let me know?' He held her away from him. 'Look at you, you haven't changed a bit. You look great, you've got a nice tan. How did you know that I would be here this morning?'

'Jenny and I arranged it.'

He clapped his hands together. Stupid question! 'Of course. I wondered why Dad sent Graham off to Foxhead and didn't ask me to do the rounds this morning. I suppose Graham knows you're here as well. She nodded. 'And nobody said a word to me. How long have they all known?'

'Two weeks.' She smiled up at him. 'I've really missed you, too, darling. You don't know how happy I am. I have dreamed of this moment from the day I left.' Pico huffed. Emily looked round. 'Yes, it's true, Pico. I've missed you, too. I've missed you all.' They laughed and hugged.

'How long are you here?' His eyes were wide and anxious. 'You're not going back, are you?'

'No!' She shook her head with a wide smile. 'No! I've quit!'

'Oh, thank God for that.' He hugged her to him with relief, then held her away, looking at her in earnest. 'Well, what are you going to do now?' She smiled up at him. 'I don't know, get a job here in Sudbury or Newmarket, somewhere close, I might even try Lambington's again at the Cambridge branch, although he never mentioned a vacancy. But in any case, I'm not going very far this time, and certainly not to London, I promise you.' Tulip was fidgeting her feet and nodding her head; she was fed up with waiting.

'Come on!' said Dominic. 'We'd better give these animals an outing. Have you ridden yet? Did you ride last night?'

'No, and I can't wait. I was too tired yesterday after travelling.' He gave her a leg up onto Black Tulip, and then was about to mount Pico.

'Oh, I haven't got my hat. It's in the tack room.' He went to get it and handed up her old hat. It was almost bare of its black velvet. Then he mounted Pico.

'Looks as if you could do with a new hat.'

'No,' she smiled, 'I like this one for riding out; it reminds me of Major.'

He smiled at her lovingly, 'Where's John?'

'I sent him in for a coffee, he will be here when we get back.'

They went on the normal route, out across the fields, and soon they were into the woodland. The shower had stopped, but the raindrops continued to drip from leaves and branches onto their helmets and their shoulders, but they did not notice. Emily filled her nostrils with the pungent fragrance of damp earth and greenery, something she had imagined so many times and had missed and longed for. This was her home. This is

285

where she wanted to be, and this is where she would stay with Dominic, and spend the rest of her life with him.

They rode for and hour, trotting and cantering across the fields, jumping the occasional hedge, and then walking side by side. The drizzling rain had started again. There was so much to talk about, and so much to tell. They were laughing happily when they came back into the yard where John was waiting for them. They slid down, and Dominic loosened the girth on Pico and took off the saddle. 'Good morning, John!'

'Oh, I'm not so sure, son. Is it?' he said, holding his palm upwards, and looking up at the grey drizzle as he took Tulip's bridle.

Dominic smiled. 'It's wonderful, John! It's the most beautiful day of my life. It's not raining on me.'

John unsaddled Black Tulip and hung the saddle over Major's stable door, the overhang of the roof protecting it from the rain. He changed the bridle for a head collar, laying the bridle across the saddle. Dominic had already changed Pico, and he led both horses out to the paddock. He was almost finished for the day. He went back to take Tulip's saddle and bridle into the tack room, but the saddle and bridle had gone. Dominic must have moved it. He was about to poke his nose into the tack room to say he was going, when he saw them kissing. He came away quickly, a smile on his face. He glanced down at Major's stable: the saddle and bridle were there where he had put them. He stood for a moment, puzzled, his hand to his mouth. Was he seeing things? He was sure it hadn't been there a moment ago. As he turned, the bridle suddenly lifted and went slowly across the yard in front of him and dropped to the cobblestones by Tulip's stable. His heart was thumping. He looked to his left and to his right. 'Major!' he scowled quietly. Then taking the saddle carefully off the door into his arms, and looking around him warily, he took it over to Tulip's door.

Suddenly he turned in alarm as, across the yard, Major's stable door shuddered violently and flew open. John stood stock-still, too stunned to even shout, as a large grey shadow hovered a few inches above the ground and then moved towards the paddock. He heard both Tulip and Pico whinny, then suddenly the yard went extremely quiet. He could hear the rain pattering on the roof, the trees whispering and the birds

286

twittering amongst the rain-soaked leaves. He walked quickly out of the yard, locking the gate behind him.

Emily and Dominic had a last kiss and a hug in the tack room, then came out. Dominic took Tulip's saddle and bridle back into the tack room, and they went into the kitchen where Liz had made them coffee. She asked Dominic if he was staying for lunch, which, of course, he was, and he and Emily spent the rest of the day together. As the drizzle cleared, they walked hand in hand across the meadow. They had so much to say, and yet they were quiet, just happy to be together once more. They stood leaning on the fence, just watching Tulip and Pico grazing. He left in the early evening, after helping her to bring the horses in and shut them up for the night. He would phone her in the morning, before he and Graham left for another week at college. It saddened her to think that he would be away again, but still it had to be, and it wouldn't last for ever.

Emily pottered around the yard for a few days, helping John with buckets of water and cleaning tack, then exercising both the horses. In the early evening, she drove over to Mayberry Farm and rode with Jenny on Tammy. They had a lot to chat about. Jenny was now working at four farms, and on occasions she went over to Foxhead Hall when their farm secretary, Fiona Bradshaw, was away on holiday, and now the two of them had a day off in the week, taking over each other's jobs. Jenny said it was working well. Emily told Jenny that she was going to find a job. She didn't know where, but she was going to go to Cambridge to look round.

It was Wednesday lunchtime at college, and the boys were sitting together with a plate of fish and chips in front of them. They decided they would have a party to celebrate Emily's homecoming. They arranged to have it in the back room of the Red Lion. They bought invitation cards and sent them out, suggesting the dress code as cocktail dress and lounge suits. They had decided on asking ten couples each, and thought it would be nice to include their parents, Emily's parents, and Jenny's parents, making it a family party. Dominic organized the food, a buffet meal, with George Roberts at the pub, and Graham had got a disco. They had arranged it for two weeks' time, and the thank-you cards came back quickly. Everything was set.

Within those two weeks, Emily got a new job in Newmarket. She was shopping with Jenny for a new dress for the forthcoming party and, to her surprise, she saw that Lambington's Travel Agency had just opened a new branch and were advertising in the window for an assistant manager. She went in. The manager wasn't available, but a young guy scribbled her details on a piece of paper, and said he would get the manager to get in touch with her.

The following evening, Emily was surprised to get a call from Ed Lambington. He said that he hadn't realized that she wanted a job or he would have transferred her, to which she replied that he hadn't told her a new office was opening in Newmarket, 'almost on my doorstep'. She started in the Newmarket office on the following Monday, and was soon in the swing of things. Although she was busy, it was not as busy as it had been in Spain, and at least everyone spoke the same language and could take phone calls and read the paperwork.

She rode out, mostly early mornings, before going to the office. The evenings were drawing in. It was dark at four thirty, and the winter would soon be upon them. But at the moment the autumn weather was pleasantly cool and Emily was happy to be back to her normal routine. She was booked into local shows. Jenny had kept up her bookings in case she should suddenly come home. She was booked into three in the next month, at the weekends. It wasn't difficult to get booked for a class, but much easier to cancel. She had to get in plenty of practice. Next July it would be the Goldsborough again, and she needed a lot of practice to qualify.

Susan was in the yard. She had come up to help John, having given up her job at the grocery store and having nothing much else to do. John gave her some money for her help, which she jokingly said kept her in CDs and lipstick. This morning she was busy mucking out the stables; both Tulip and Pico were in the paddock. Hearing the sound of galloping hooves on the cobblestones, she turned quickly and came to the stable door. She thought one of the horses had escaped from the paddock, but there was nothing there. The sound continued. It must be the radio, her father had it on in the tack room. She turned to go back to her job, just as the door to the stable opposite shuddered violently and flew open. She felt a rushing of wind, as something raced through the yard past her.

John flung down the hosepipe – he had been filling the water trough in the paddock – when he heard her anxious cries and came running. He could see the alarm on her white and frightened face as she leaned over the half door of Tulip's stable, and he came to her with comforting arms. For a moment they stood either side of Tulip's door, and he told her there was nothing to worry about. He proceeded to tell her about Major, something he had hitherto kept secret from his girls. He didn't think there was any harm in Major; indeed, he had not been there for some time. It seemed funny, though, that he had come back now that Emily had arrived back home. 'He obviously just likes to be near her.'

He looked cautiously into the stable. Susan was now just a little behind him. There was nothing in there. She felt nervous as her father called to Major, and they waited in silence, but there was no response.

Susan was uneasy as she went back to her job of mucking out Tulip's stable, and she kept looking over at Major's old stable. She and John both looked up in alarm as they heard the clip-clopping of hooves again, and the door of Major's stable that was now closed rattled as if it had been shaken hard.

Liz came out into the yard with two mugs of coffee on a tray. She saw them both standing like statues. John told her what had happened.

'Oh gosh, John, it's been quiet for months. I hope we don't have to go through all that again.'

'Me too, Mrs Peters; all that ghostly business ain't for me.'

'Why don't you put a Bible in the stable?' Susan suddenly suggested.

They looked at her in amazement. 'A Bible!' said John. 'Why?'

'Well, I remember a girl at school saying that they had a problem in one of their rooms in the house, and her mother put a Bible in there, and whatever it was went away.'

John and Liz exchanged glances. Liz thought at least they could try. She went back into the house and came back a few minutes later, a Bible in hand.

John looked up. 'Are you really going to try it, Mrs Peters?' She nodded, opening the stable door and placing the Bible on a bale of hay. She came out quickly, closing the half door, and the three of them waited in anticipation, not knowing what to expect. They were ready to run. Long minutes went by. Nothing happened.

John relaxed. 'There's nothing there now. He must have gone.' They watched the door for a few more minutes.

'Yes, I think you're right.' Liz turned to go back out of the yard. She had got to the corner when suddenly the door flew open and the Bible flew across the yard with such a force that it hit the wall and fell into the water barrel. John was the nearest and fished it out quickly before it sank. All three were shocked. Susan was scared and dashed into Pico's stable, closing the half door and looking out over the top. She couldn't believe her eyes.

'Dad, what is it? Is it really a ghost?' she whispered, her breast heaving with fear.

John shook the water out of the Bible and wiped it down the side of his trousers. He nodded. 'Yes, Susie! He has been here for a few years now, hasn't he, Mrs Peters?' He nodded to Liz. 'I never told you about it because I didn't want to worry you.'

'It's true, Susan. But don't worry; he's really quite harmless. He's not usually violent, is he, John? And he was such a lovely animal. We all loved him.'

'Well, I wish you'd told me, Dad. Does Mum know?'

'Yes, I told her ages ago, but Mrs Peters is right; he really is quite harmless.' He still kept his eyes on the door. 'It may be that he's trying to tell us something.'

'But what?'

'I don't know, Susan, I really don't know.'

25

It was Saturday evening and the cars were arriving. The Red
Lion carpark was almost full. Dominic had picked up Emily.
Her father had said they would drive themselves, as they would
probably want to come away earlier than the younger set, who,
he was sure, would party on until the early hours of the
morning!

When they arrived, a small stage had been erected for the
disco, and the music was playing quite loudly. Tables were laid
with snow-white tablecloths and pink carnations, glittering glass
and silver, and at one end of the room, a buffet table was
laden with delicious food. Emily was pleased to see all her
friends gathered together, and they all welcomed her back.
Dominic took two glasses of champagne off the tray that the
waiter offered and handed one to Emily. He admired the new
black silk cocktail dress with shoestring straps, the tight straight
skirt hugging her slim hips. There were two small frills just at
the knee, from where her slim suntanned legs went down into
strappy black silk sandals. With a click of his tongue and a
wink, he smiled his approval and kissed her just as the
photographer snapped them.

Everyone gathered around them, asking Emily questions about
Spain. Dominic, they said, was a changed guy since she was
back.

'We thought he was dying of a broken heart,' said one girl
in a red dress.

'Yeah, he even went off the drink,' said Derek Milner. 'And
that's saying something!' There was a ripple of laughter.

'Well, I'm going to make up for it tonight!' Dominic chuckled,
lifting the glass of champagne high. 'Now! Has everyone got a
drink?

Cheers!

The group dispersed, but they were soon caught up in another, until some of them started to dance. The evening was getting off to a good and noisy start. At nine o'clock, the food was served, and a long queue was formed. The chefs carved turkey, ham and beef, and the guests helped themselves to the rest of the delicious fare displayed before them. They sat at the tables, which were laid for six or eight places. Dominic and Emily, Graham and Jenny, sat with Louise and her current boyfriend, Brian Sherman. Louise chopped and changed her men like she changed her horses, they never knew whom to expect next. Mary Clark and John Carpenter were there; they, at least, were still going strong.

The parents all sat on the same table, enjoying the food and the wine. After they had all eaten Dominic got up onto the small stage, and there were yells and shouts of 'Speech! Speech!' The noise was deafening, until he put up his hands for silence, when it died out to a few whoops and fists banging on the table. Finally he was allowed to say a few words, thanking them all for coming and thanking the caterers, to which they all clapped their appreciation, and again for Martin Sayers for providing the disco music. He went on to say nice things about Emily and that they were all glad to see her back home again, to which they all clapped in agreement, and he went on to say that he hoped that she had not lost her touch with riding, as he himself wanted a bit of competition and he did not want to keep winning all the time, which got a laugh and jeers from most of the men. He mentioned Jenny Ellis as Emily's best friend, and then asked both the girls if they would come up onto the stage, which they did, leaving their table to much applause, giving each other a puzzled frown. They stepped up beside Dominic, and Graham joined them.

Dominic put his hands up for quiet again. 'Both Graham and I have a little presentation to make...' Graham turned the girls to stand back to back. They were smiling, not knowing what to expect. Graham made a comment about seeing which one was the tallest. He had his hand above their heads measuring, and the guests laughed as he tried to push Jenny down. 'And now to the special announcement.'

Graham faced Jenny, and Dominic faced Emily.

Dominic said, Girls, we would like you to accept these bouquets...' Graham had hidden them at the back of the stage

292

earlier in the evening. The girls each took a bouquet and gave their man a kiss to applause and shouts from their friends.

Then, with both girls still standing back to back with big smiles and arms full of flowers, Dominic and Graham both went down on one knee, offering an open ring box and saying together, 'Will you marry me?'

The guests went wild, standing, clapping, whooping, cheering, whistling, banging on the tables and Cliff Richard singing, 'Congratulations'. No one ever did hear the girls' response, but it must have been yes, as both couples were locked in each other's arms and kissing, quite oblivious of the shouts and screams and whoops of joy. And the clapping guests got into the rhythm of the music, and soon everyone was dancing and singing, and congratulating the happy couples, and admiring the rings; Jenny's two diamonds and a sapphire, and Emily's large diamond solitaire...

The parents all looked at each other with bewildered smiles as they stood and clapped with the rest, but asking each other, 'Did you know about this?' They were all surprised and pleased. And even more surprised when they were all called up onto the stage, and Dominic and Graham presented Liz, Carol and Vivienne each with a large bouquet of flowers, both the boys giving their mother a kiss and saying sorry for having kept it a secret. Keith hugged both his sons, giving them friendly slaps on the back, and both Mike and Joe shook their hands heartily offering congratulations. The partying went on into the early hours, and the parents stayed to the end. There would be a lot of hangovers the next morning.

On Sunday morning, the smile was still there when Emily looked into the bathroom mirror. She showered and dressed and was in the yard by six thirty showing the beautiful diamond ring to both Tulip and Pico, who seemed to nod their approval.

John came into the yard, as he did every Sunday morning to refresh the water buckets, and do a quick muck-out. This morning Susan was with him. Emily turned away from Tulip to greet them.

'How did the party go last night?' asked John.

'Oh, very well,' smiled Emily. 'It was an engagement party.'

293

'Oh!' John raised his eyebrows. 'Who got engaged?'

'I did. And so did Jenny.'

She waited for it to sink in. His eyes nearly popped out of his head. 'You did!'

She beamed. 'Yes!' and wiggled her finger at him. The sun caught the diamond, and it sparkled, shooting red and blue sparks.

'Oh!' exclaimed Susan, looking at the ring closely. 'It's beautiful. Congratulations, Emily!'

'Yes, congratulations, Miss!' John admired the ring with a smile. 'That's a surprise; you kept a good secret.'

She smiled. 'I didn't know, John. It was a surprise to me, too.' She went on to tell them about the party.

'Are you thinking of having a double wedding now then?' asked John.

'Oh, I don't know about that. We haven't even talked about a wedding yet. To be honest I'm as surprised as you, John. I haven't got over the shock myself yet. Although I did find out last night that Jenny and Graham were already unofficially engaged. But even she was stunned when they had us up on the stage. You can imagine the excitement, can't you? We were both surprised, and we had a wonderful night.'

Susan went about her job happily humming, and John went into the tack room.

'Which one do you want to ride first, Miss?'

'Oh, John, I'm so excited this morning, I don't know. I could ride them both at once.' They laughed.

'I'll take Tulip. Do you want to come with me, Susan? You can take Pico if you like.'

Susan gasped excitedly. 'Oh, yes please!' She had ridden both Pico and Tulip while Emily had been away, but she had never ridden with Miss Emily, and she considered it quite and honour to be asked.

They rode quietly for a while, Pico following Tulip, trotting across the fields until they entered the woods. Then Emily turned in the saddle, leaning back on the cantle, 'You ride him well, Susan. Did you ride out much while I was away?'

'Yes, mostly with Miss Jenny, and I have been with Mr Dominic, I mean Mr Hadley, once.' She sounded so proud of the fact. 'And I love Pico!' She leaned forward and caressed his ears. 'It

294

must have been exciting last night, getting engaged. Fancy you not knowing.'

'Yes, it was a great surprise. Have *you* got a boyfriend Susan?'

'No, but I go out with Tim Roberts. He's a farmhand at Foxhead Hall. I met him at the village fête last summer. We occasionally go out, but I wouldn't call him a boyfriend. Usually there is a group of us that go out together, but I have been to the cinema with Tim on my own. But that's all; we are just friends.

'Do you like him? I mean, *really* like him?'

'Yes,' she nodded, lifting her eyebrows with a shy smile.

'Oh look, there's a woodpecker!' Susan's eyes lit up as Emily pointed to a green woodpecker tapping away on a tree. The bird flew away as he saw the horses approaching.

'I have never actually seen one pecking on a tree, have you?' said Susan.

'Must be a lucky omen!' said Emily with a smile.

They were all there for the show at Foxhead Hall early on Saturday morning. John had driven them in the horse box, and Emily was feeling a bit apprehensive; she hadn't been to a show for over a year, and she hadn't had a lot of practice, well, not as much as she would have liked. She hoped that Black Tulip had not forgotten how to jump in the last months, although Dominic, Graham and Jenny had given her some schooling.

Both the mums had gone with them, with Susan left in charge of Pico back at Rosemary Lodge.

Jenny and Emily were not in the same class, and Jenny was on first. Emily walked down to the starting gate with her, and waited until it was her turn. There were four in front of her: a guy named Trevor Benson, who had a good round but knocked down the last post, and then two sisters, Patricia and Elizabeth Colbert and then there was Graham. She really didn't stand a chance against Skybright, but she was going out there to beat him.

Graham smiled and wished her luck with the same cocky arrogance as Dominic. She pulled a face at him.

'You can't win them all,' she mused, as she went into the

ring. She did well and got a clear round, then it came to the jump-off between Henry and Skybright. Jenny rode around the ring, taking her time, muttering 'Steady, Henry, steady,' as he tried to quicken his pace. He was a powerful horse but he listened, and for the moment she held him back, then got into a canter. When the bell went she let him have his head, and he leaped high over the first fence and then the second and on and on to the last, and flew over it like a bird.

It was Graham's turn. He, too, got a clear round and so it went on, with the fence now up to six feet six inches high. Henry took it all in his stride. The spectators clapped, as Henry cleared the jumps with Jenny crouching low on his back as they flew through the air. And then Skybright cleared every jump, too; the last fence now up at six feet eight inches.

Jenny trotted Henry round, whispering to him, encouraging him. They went into a canter now, as the bell rang for the start. Over the first jump they went, and then the next... There were only four to go now, and the only sound was the huffing of Henry's breath and the scrunching of leather as Jenny bounced up and down in the saddle. She drove him on, and the big six-feet-eight brush fence loomed up in front of them. Jenny couldn't see the other side. Henry lifted his forelegs, and his huge brown and powerful haunches, rippling with muscle, took off, his belly clearing the top of the brush fence and his right hoof barely touching it. The pole wobbled.

There was a huge 'Aaaaaah' from the crowd, as his front legs hit the ground and they galloped on at speed, the fence wobbling behind them. Jenny pulled him up, leaning forward to pat his neck, as they walked serenely out of the ring, Graham blowing her a kiss.

'Nearly, Jen!' Emily commiserated.

Jenny gave her a disappointed grin. 'Well, we were lucky to get this far. I don't think we would have made the next round; it's asking too much. But I think something put him off...' She grimaced at Emily. '...He seemed to be going so well, and suddenly...' She flicked her hands. '...It's probably the height!'

She slid down, and John took the bridle.

'Bad luck. Shame, darling,' said her mother.

'Yes, a shame,' said Liz. 'But never mind, you did so well, Jenny.

Emily and Jenny stood at the fence watching Graham, as he entered the ring. He rode confidently, back straight, head held high and proud. He trotted round the perimeter and then cantered. Graham quickened the pace, as the bell went for the start. The first jump they cleared with ease, and then the next, and so on until the big imposing brush fence stood in front of them. Graham had time just to straighten Skybright up before his front hooves reared into the air, his back almost straight, and his huge hindquarters leaped into the air clearing the brush ... they landed safely on the other side to a roar and clapping from the crowd.

He was still in full gallop when suddenly Skybright's eyes rolled and became wild. He pulled up short, lifting his head in fright, and baulked almost to an instant standstill as if he had run into an invisible wall. He crashed into the barrier fence, splintering the wood and scattering the watching spectators as the fence snapped with a loud crack. The splitting wood formed a sharp knife-like shaft, catching Skybright on the upper part of his foreleg. Blood spurted out, and Graham, taken unaware, was completely out of control...

Adrian Poole was standing at the gate next to Jenny and Emily. He rushed into the ring and grabbed at the bridle, just as Skybright reared, taking him completely off his feet. Adrian fell in front of him, and the horse crashed down on his shoulder and then jumped over him. There was a loud shout from Adrian and screams from the watching spectators, as the horse and rider went charging around the ring and over the jumps again, until he came to the six-foot-eight fence. His eyes were wild and rolling and showing white. Neighing hysterically, he crashed through the middle of the fence, bringing it down. Graham was hanging over his neck and losing a stirrup, but, quickly slipping back into the saddle and turning Skybright's head, he slowed down until he regained complete control. He watched helplessly as the St John's Ambulance team of three men and a woman came running, pushing through the onlookers and lifting poor Adrian Poole onto a stretcher, and took him to the first-aid tent. It was then that Dominic came racing onto the scene. He had just dismounted outside the next ring and had heard someone mention Skybright going berserk. He was in the ring, taking hold of Skybright's bridle, and leading him from the ring, Emily and Jenny walking alongside. Graham dismounted, and they led the horse back to the horse box, where Fred took over. Charlie Fenwick had gone off with Adrian.

Fred had tethered Silverspoon and came forward anxiously to take the bridle off Skybright. He examined the gash at the top of the leg; the blood was running down to the knee.

Graham, who had been shaken but was now quite composed, said that he didn't know what happened. 'He took the last jump with ease and then he just suddenly shied away ... well, you know the rest. He was truly afraid of something. How is Adrian? Does anyone know?'

Fred, with a bucket of cold water and a sponge, was trying to stop the bleeding on Skybright's leg, as Keith Hadley arrived on the scene and took over, first making sure that Graham was all right.

'They took Adrian to the first-aid tent on a stretcher,' said Emily. 'He was trying to get up, so I don't think he was hurt too seriously. I think it was his shoulder, but they took him on a stretcher anyway. But I'll go over and find out for you.'

'I'll come with you,' said Jenny. As the girls walked away, they heard Dominic say, 'Come on, Gray, you need a drink.'

The girls walked across the grass towards the St John's Ambulance tent. Emily looked at Jenny. 'Are you thinking what I'm thinking?'

Jenny nodded. 'I think it could be him. Henry was unsteady.'

She nodded. 'I am sure of it. I've seen it happen so many times before. There is no other explanation. Oh, Jenny, I feel so awful, what can I do?'

'Well, it's not your fault, Em. You can't help it. What can you do?'

They reached the first-aid tent and went in quietly. Adrian was sitting on the bed with his arm in a sling. Charlie Fenwick was there with him. The St John's man said he thought it was fractured, and he had called an ambulance to take him to the hospital for an X-ray. It arrived just at that moment. Emily said she would go with him, but Adrian told her to stay or she would miss out on her class and he made a joke, wishing he could be there to see her win over Dominic! They laughed, but she said she was going all out to try. And Charlie got into the ambulance and went with him.

As expected, of course, Emily came second. Dominic was the champion of the day yet again, and rode out of the ring flinging his arms into the air, the crowd clapping. Then, when they were in the middle of the ring to collect their prizes, he leaned from his saddle over to Emily and gave her a kiss, and the crowd roared and clapped. These two really had become celebrities on the show-jumping circuit!

In the evening after the show, the four of them had arranged to go out for dinner but first they went to visit Adrian Poole in hospital. They had heard he was being kept in overnight as the X-rays had shown that he had a crushed shoulder, and the left side of his breastbone was damaged. It was going to take months to heal, and the doctors feared he might lose the use of his left arm altogether. Graham said he felt terrible about Adrian, although it wasn't his fault that Skybright spooked.

Polly's Kitchen was a small restaurant just fifteen minutes' drive away, tucked away in the countryside. The four of them sat talking, mostly of the day's events, and then got round to the Goldsborough. They would all have to practise as the show was coming up fast. In the meantime there would be a lot of smaller shows to compete in. Luckily the Goldsborough Show was in July, when both Dominic and Graham were on holiday from college.

Dominic said he thought Adrian Poole looked pale and shocked. If he were going to be laid up for months they would have to get someone else to help old Fred and Charlie Fenwick in the stables.

'I feel terrible about Adrian getting hurt,' said Graham again. 'But there was nothing I could do. Skybright just reared; it was as much as I could do to control him. I wondered what was happening; something must have frightened him.'

Jenny glanced at Emily. 'Em and I think it was Major.'

'Major!' both Graham and Dominic exclaimed at once.

'Well, I don't know, but I suspect it was, and if it was, then I feel responsible about Adrian. But what can I do about him? Major, I mean.' She looked sad. 'The only solution I can think of is not to go to horse events.'

They all looked shocked. 'Oh no, Emily!' Jenny exclaimed with horror.

'Oh no, darling, you can't give up riding!' Dominic was aghast. 'There has to be another solution.'

'Like what?'

He sighed, biting his lip, and looking at his brother and Jenny. 'Well, I don't know what, but there has to be another solution.'

'It's the only way!' she said. 'I'm afraid someone is going to get killed. He just won't go away, and the other horses are terrified.' There was a pause. 'That's it!' She banged her hand on the table. 'I'm backing out of the Goldsborough.'

'Oh no!'

'Oh, you can't do that, darling. Not now!' Dominic was shaking his head.

'No, of course you can't!' Jenny looked at her steadily.

'Yes, I have made up my mind. I will just keep to riding around the fields and the woods. I am not going to enter any more horse shows.'

Dominic had no answer. He sighed and turned his head away, then turned back. 'She's right, though. Someone *is* going to get killed...' There was a pause. They all looked at each other, and then looked away. It was an utterly devastating situation. Emily had been riding all her life, and now she was prepared to give it up because of a ghost. There had to be something they could do. But *what*? That was the question.

'I think we all need another drink.' Dominic called the waiter.

For days after, John arrived in the mornings to find Emily gazing into Major's old stable. There was nothing to look at except straw, but she stood there meditating. He thought back to the old days when she had first lost Major, how she had stood in front of the stable blaming herself.

'Do you want me to saddle up Tulip or Pico first, Miss?'

She looked startled at the sound of his voice. 'Oh! I don't mind, John,' It was a whisper, as if she had no energy and did not want to disturb what was on her mind. Then she turned back to the stable and stared again.

John looked at her curiously, turning away, and in a few minutes he said Tulip was ready. She mounted quietly and walked slowly out of the yard as if in a dream. John stared after her, knowing there was something wrong. He didn't like to ask what, but guessed that it was something to do with Major and the incident with Adrian Poole.

Emily just sat there as Tulip plodded on through the woods. The birds twittered and the trees whispered as the gentle breeze rustled their leaves. 'What am I going to do, Tulip? What is the answer? Major is a problem!' Tulip's ears twitched at the sound of her muttering. She leaned forward and patted her neck. They walked for half an hour then turned back through the woods and were now entering the yard. John had just saddled Pico. He was surprised to see them back so soon. They had walked all the way without any effort. As Emily slid down, she seemed to be in a kind of trance, John thought. She mounted Pico without a word.

It was the weekend and Dominic was due home. She was glad. She wanted someone to talk to. He called her before lunch, when he had just arrived, and she drove over to meet him at Packards Mill. They spent an hour or so in the stables, chatting to Fred. She patted Silverspoon and Skybright, and they walked around the stable block, looking at the sick animals. She felt so sorry for them all, especially a ginger cat that had a huge bandage on its paw. Dominic said that the paw had been chopped off by farm machinery, but luckily it had been rushed into the surgery and Keith had sewn it back on. It would heal eventually, although the cat would probably have a limp.

Graham had taken Jenny out for lunch; Emily was to have lunch with Dominic and his parents. After, he suggested that they go for a ride in the car; he wanted to see another horse.

'What happened about Ben Mortimer, and that horse we looked at, Stardust?'

She was sitting next to him in the car. He smiled at her, taking his eyes off the road for a moment. 'Decided it was too expensive, couldn't afford it. Had other things to spend some of my money on.' He grabbed at her hand, and she realized that he had spent the money on an engagement ring.

'Oh, Dom. You shouldn't have. You wanted that horse so badly.' She looked at him with sad eyes. 'We'll save up, I'll help you.'

He smiled. 'Nope!' He shook her hand lovingly. 'The next thing I am aiming for is a house, and we can get married. OK?'

'OK!' she nodded, with a smile. They sat quietly for a while, as he drove along the country lanes.

'Well, why are we going to look at another horse today?'

'Well, it's for sale, but it's also been sick and Dad has asked me to vet it. I'm not thinking of buying. But, anyway, we'll have a look.'

They arrived at Ludrook Farm, and she stood aside while Dominic examined the horse. He assured the owner, Trevor Pennybroke, that the wound on the leg had healed and the horse could be ridden again. He suggested a nourishing diet. It was a bay, sixteen hands and not pretty. Its coat was dull, and it stood with its head down, looking dejected. She wished she could take it and give it a good home and a brush to make its coat shine. It looked as if it needed a good meal, but then perhaps the person who bought it would do just that. She thought the name Trevor Pennybroke suited him. He looked as if he could not afford to look after himself, let alone a horse. Maybe that was why the horse was for sale. He only had the one horse, and the name was Champion. Emily thought that perhaps at one time he had been. She was reminded of old Warrior, who had appeared to have no life in him but had dashed off like the wind, but she really didn't think that Champion could muster up the strength.

She said to Dominic on the way back in the car that the horse didn't look cared for, and he had to agree and said there were many horses like that. He had seen them when he had gone on visits with his father, and he and Graham had talked about it for hours, but what could they do? As Dominic said, 'You can only advise them on how to look after their animals, but some of them can ill afford to look after and feed a horse. I suppose they keep them because they love them.'

She nodded. He was right. She supposed that as long as they were loved that was everything.

He dropped her off at Rosemary Lodge and said that he would pick her up again at seven thirty, and they would go out to Polly's Kitchen, the little restaurant they loved.

* * *

They were sitting on a table for two near the window. They clinked glasses, sipped red wine, and ate Polly's famous steak-and-kidney pie and apple pie and cream to finish. There were four people on the next table enjoying the same meal, and they could hear people in the other room laughing.

'How is Adrian Poole?' Emily sipped at the wine.

He pulled a face. 'Not doing so well. He has to attend the hospital three times a week. Dad has kept him on doing a few light jobs, like feeding the smaller animals in the hospital. At the moment we have three sick cats. Dad won't let him feed the dogs – we've got six there now – in case they get a bit boisterous. One of them is a devil. As soon as you open the cage door he bursts out. He got run over and has a broken hip joint, but you wouldn't think so the way he runs!' He had a little chuckle at the thought. 'Adrian's a sort of general help to Dad's nurses, Pam and Dorothy and Jim Brown.'

'I feel terrible!' Emily grimaced. 'Suppose he loses the use of his arm? He's only about twenty-one, isn't he? How awful that would be!'

'Twenty-two.' He took her hand across the table. 'Don't feel bad about it, darling, it's one of those things that happen. It's not your fault, nor Graham's, though he's feeling terrible, too. Anyway, Adrian is quite happy to be doing the small jobs. He was only joking about it yesterday. He was giving Skybright a carrot and he slapped him gently, and I heard him telling him not to feel bad about what happened; when he got back into action, he was going to give him the ride of his life. Skybright nodded in agreement.' He gave her hand a friendly squeeze.

'Could he handle a horse with one arm?' Emily looked concerned.

'I don't know. I've never seen a horse with one arm, have you?'

She looked at him for a second, then started to laugh. They clinked glasses again.

'That's better. I like it when you laugh.' He squeezed her hand across the table again. 'It makes your blue eyes twinkle.'

She looked at him lovingly. 'Your eyes twinkle all the time.'

'Do they? I hadn't noticed.'

'Well, you can't see them, can you?'

'No!' They laughed again.

Then more seriously she said, 'Dominic, I really am not going to the Goldsborough.'

He was about to protest.

'No, Dom! I have made up my mind. Every time I go to an event, Major is there, and I am afraid of what he will do. It's worrying me, so I think it best if I keep away.'

'But, Em, you can't give up riding just like that! It's silly, darling. Put it out of your mind.' He took her hand again. 'If it is Adrian Poole that is worrying you, don't let it. Graham was quite capable of controlling Skybright. If Adrian hadn't run out to grab at the bridle, it would never have happened. It was just unfortunate that the horse reared at that moment. No one is blaming you, or Graham, least of all Adrian.'

'Oh, Dom, I don't want to give up riding. I'll still ride out at home every day, but I just feel I must stay away from the shows. Even if I just went to watch, he might be there. I was talking to Mum about it last night. She said I should go to the Goldsborough, but I feel so responsible for what happens. You told me yourself that I almost got you killed.'

'Oh that was just a figure of speech; I was uptight.'

'But admit it, it's true. Isn't it?'

'No.'

'It *is* Dominic. You know that Silverspoon is normally well behaved, and he went absolutely crazy, just like Skybright did. And Major is the problem, and it is only because of me. Black Tulip flinches a bit, but Pico is still very scared, and Major also worries Henry, but he is not so highly strung.'

'Look, Em, you can't give up the Goldsborough. You can't just give up riding because of a ghost!' The four on the next table looked across. Dominic smiled, and they went back to their dinners.

'It's bloody ridiculous. Besides, he's not always there, is he?'

'But I shall never be free of him, and I don't know what to do about it. I worry about it all the time.'

They argued back and forth, getting nowhere, and Emily said she was not going to the Goldsborough and that was final. 'Look what happened the last time!' she said finally.

He wrinkled his nose, lifting his glass. 'That was the last time. Best thing that ever happened to us. Cheers.' They clinked glasses, she smiled and the tension eased.

*　*　*

Emily and Jenny practised had every day, now that the time
was coming up for the Goldsborough. Jenny kept her on her
toes. She was sure that she would change her mind. And Tulip
and Pico had to have regular exercise anyway, and so far Emily
had not yet cancelled her entry. She was still in two minds
whether to go or not. She wanted to go, but felt she shouldn't.
But this year she felt she had a chance, especially as she had
made sure that she was not in the same class as Dominic.
Jenny was in a different class from Graham, too. When they
were all together, they laughed about it. They could all be
winners, but only one could win the Golden Horse Trophy.

They had by now convinced Emily to go, and she couldn't
resist. In her heart she truly wanted to go, but she said she
would come as a spectator.

'You'll never do that,' said Jenny. 'You'll be itching to ride.
Gosh, you have practised hard enough. Anyway, he might be
there even if you didn't ride. Come on, forget Major! Tell him
to stay at home.'

Emily thought about this, and although it seemed stupid, she
thought she might do just that. That evening, when she was
out in the stables after John had gone, she went to Major's
stable and called to him. Of course there was no reply, but
she started to talk.

'Major! Now you must stop this nonsense, do you hear me?'
She listened. There was nothing. 'You mustn't come to the
Goldsborough Show, do you hear? Or any other show. You're
frightening the other horses, Major! Are you listening?' She
thought she heard a huff, but it could have been either Tulip
or Pico, she wasn't sure. And she knew that she was talking
nonsense, anyway, but at east it made her feel a bit better, and
maybe it would do some good. Who knew?

June came. The weather was cold to start with and then got
warm, and stayed that way until almost the end of the month.
The boys had broken up from college, and the four of them
spent a lot of time with the horses. As Dominic said, practice
makes perfect.

305

Jenny suggested they take a day off and go down to London to see a show. Emily managed to get four tickets, and so they left early on Saturday morning to make a full day of it. Dominic was driving. The motorway was very busy even though it was early. It took them three hours to get there, and then trying to find somewhere to park was a nightmare. They dropped into the Four Seasons Hotel for breakfast and got the doorman to take the car away. That was the first problem solved. Next they got a taxi to take them to Knightsbridge to shop in Harrods and Harvey Nichols, then they went their separate ways to shop, arranging to meet in the bar at the Four Seasons Hotel for afternoon tea. They relaxed for two hours, resting their feet and having a drink, before ordering a taxi to take them to the theatre. In the meantime, the boys got a porter to take the shopping down to the car.

They sat in deep, comfortable armchairs, enjoying a glass of wine, when suddenly a raised voice said, 'Emily!' She looked up into the round, plump face of Marcus DuBarry.

'Well, hello, Marcus!' She stood up in surprise. He took her hand and gave her a friendly kiss on both cheeks. He was looking very smart in a grey suit, white shirt and red bow tie.

'Fancy seeing you here in town.'

She smiled. 'Oh, we're only here for the day.' She introduced him. 'This is my fiancé, Dominic.' She noticed Marcus flinch, as his hand automatically fingered his chin.

Dominic stood up, towering over him and grinning. 'We've met before,' he said, squeezing his hand tightly. Emily laughed inwardly as Marcus winced.

'And this is my friend Jenny, and this Graham, Dominic's brother.' Graham stood to shake hands, but Marcus, still feeling the tingle in his fingers, just nodded politely. There was a pause.

'Well, fancy seeing you, Emily. It has been a long time.'

Dominic asked him if he would like a drink, but he refused politely saying that he had just come to pick up a friend. They were going out for drinks and then dinner.

Emily thought, poor girl, hope he doesn't have too much to drink. But she said instead, 'Have you been riding lately, Marcus?'

'Oh yes, yes!' He was enthusiastic. 'I've been going down now every Sunday, still with Anna, you know, trotting.' He

306

mouthed the word and sort of gave her a half wink, knowing that she would understand. 'We are really into it now!' He nodded with a slight smile. She knew that he was feeling uncomfortable. There was a pause. He stood with a fixed smile on his face. Emily didn't know what to say.

Suddenly looking over her head across the room, he said, 'Oh, must go! There's my date!' He wished them all a pleasant evening and dashed away, glad to get out of an awkward situation with Emily.

Emily turned to see him greeting a middle-aged woman in a black dress and jacket. Her white-blonde hair was piled high upon her head, and her bright-red lips formed only the semblance of a smile. She had obviously been out with him before. That liaison would not last long.

They sat down again, and immediately Jenny said, 'So that was Marcus DuBarry.' She pulled a face at Emily. 'So he's still riding then.' She smirked, looking round. 'I shouldn't think he takes *her* riding.'

Emily grinned and began to tell them about Marcus and his riding. She had told them all before, but she had them laughing all over again.

'Poor old Marcus,' she concluded. 'He'll never in a million years make a horseman. He hasn't got a clue. I wonder if he takes his new woman riding.'

Dominic looked at her. 'His *new* woman? Why? Were you his *old* woman?'

Emily looked surprised. 'Gosh, no, Dom! Good heavens above, look at him. Give me a break. I was only with him when there was a group of us. It was only on this one Sunday that he asked me to go riding. He's quite a nice guy really. But not my type.' She reached out to take Dominic's hand, squeezing it to reassure him. Graham ordered more drinks all round, just as the waiter came up to clear the glasses.

'One more drink and we must get a taxi. We don't want to miss the show, do we?'

It was Monday morning, and Emily was in the office. It was reasonably busy, people still wanting to book last-minute holidays. It was July, and just two weeks remained to the Goldsborough show. She had put in a lot of practice with both Pico and Black Tulip. She had them both booked into different classes. Emily was still having second thoughts about going, and she still had two weeks in which to change her mind. She really didn't know what she wanted to do.

The phone rang on the desk and she answered it. It was someone booking for Majorca, wanting to go to Port Andraitx. She booked them into Hotel Italia and sat with her elbows on the desk, wondering if Riccardo was there. Should she ring the villa? Perhaps not. She also wondered about Christine. She dialled the office number and waited, hoping that Marquita wouldn't answer. She was in luck. Eduardo Costello picked up the receiver and said, 'Hola!'

'Hello, Eduardo. It's Emily Peters.'

'Emily! How nice to speak to you!' He asked her how she was, and they spent a few minutes talking about Majorca and the English weather. She asked if she could speak to Christine, and he said, 'Un momento!' There was a pause and then Christine picked up the receiver.

'Hello, Emily. How are you?' She sounded pleased.

'Hello, Christine.' They began to chat away. 'I was surprised to hear Eduardo.'

'Yes, he doesn't come here often, but he just came into the office as the phone rang. How are you? How is it going there?'

'Fine.' Emily told her she was much happier now that she was back in England, and she told her that she had a job in the travel agency's Newmarket branch.

Christine told her that the Calmanetti family had been out again, but had gone back now to South Carolina or Texas or wherever. 'They seemed to have places everywhere.'

'Yes, I know. I think they only meet up about once or twice a year in Majorca. Have you seen anything of Riccardo? He never phoned again.'

'No, I haven't seen anyone. Eduardo went up to the villa, but I don't think there was anyone there. But that was some months ago.'

'He was married, did you know? And had a daughter.'

'Really? How old? But then I am not surprised.'

'I don't know, but she sounded quite mature on the phone.'

'You spoke to her?'

308

'Yes, I spoke to his wife, too,' she laughed, 'but I soon put the phone down.'

Christine laughed and then asked if she was still riding, and Emily said yes and told her about the Goldsborough that was coming up in just a week or two. Christine told her she had found another new man. His name was Carlos, a guitar player in a hotel nightclub in Paguera. Emily laughed, and they chatted away happily for several minutes more. Emily came off the phone, a smile on her face. It had been good to catch up on old times. She went back to her computer, as a couple came in with a small boy. Soon they were sitting in front of Pam Miller's desk, and she was looking up the flight times on the computer for them. The boy, who was about four years old, was running around the office, touching papers and books, but they did not correct him when he pulled a pile of brochures off the deck and knocked over a stand, spilling travel books right across the floor. Neither of them seemed to turn a hair. They were more concerned with querying the air fare for the child.

Janet was picking up the brochures and Emily stacking the books back. If it was up to her, she'd have made them pay double for the little monster. Italy wasn't far enough for them.

26

Saturday came, the day of the Goldsborough, and it was a beautiful sunny day, with a light breeze. Emily and her mother had been out in the yard since five in the morning with John and his daughter, Susan. They were packing up the horse box with the food that Liz had prepared the night before. John had polished all the tack, and he and Susan were busy stowing the last-minute things on board, before putting in both Black Tulip and Henry, who had spent the night at Rosemary Lodge. John had taken Pico over to Mayberry farm the night before so that he would be looked after for the day. Emily had entered Pico, but had cancelled his class, although now she wished she hadn't.

They were ready to leave. The three girls were to go in the front seat of the horse box with John. It was a bit of a squash, but they managed. Mike and Liz were to leave an hour later, picking up Carol and Jo Ellis from the farm and John's wife, Debbie, from Ridgeway Lane. It was a long drive and would take them about three hours.

A few miles down the road, Dominic and Graham were also setting off with Fred and Charlie Fenwick and Adrian Poole, who had asked if he could come along although he still couldn't work. Dominic and Graham sat with Charlie, who was driving, and Fred and Adrian sat in the small living area of the horse box. Behind them, beyond the small bathroom, Silverspoon and Skybright stood calmly and comfortably side by side, both used to travelling. It was a smooth ride but Adrian, although comfortable, felt every bump in the road.

The two parties arrived at the Goldsborough grounds within ten minutes of each other. John was just letting down the back ramp, when he heard Dominic shout 'Hello!' as they passed and parked a few yards further on.

The day was going to be exciting. They all felt it. The weather was on their side; it couldn't have been better. Standing at the door of the horse box, Emily looked across the field taking in the scenery. This was the life she loved! A perfect English day with warm sunshine, the grass and the trees so green, the sky above so blue, with a few white fluffy clouds. She breathed in the pungent aroma of horseflesh and the smells of grass and hay. Already there were hundreds of people milling around, and the horseboxes were coming in one after the other. The carpark was full and the bowler-hatted ushers were directing traffic into the next field. Crowds of people were walking from there into the show ground. There were families with children, some in buggies, dogs on leads just out for the afternoon's entertainment, some groomed and ready for the dog show later on in the afternoon. The small tents were set up and selling equestrian wares and they were already busy with shoppers. There was a hubbub of human voices, and the drumming of engines as the boxes rolled in, and the music coming from the speakers blared out. There was a military band tuning up on a bandstand, looking very smart in their red jackets, the gold buttons and the brass instruments sparkled, reflecting the sunlight. Flags wavered from tall poles in the light breeze, and banners in an array of bright colours advertised everything under the sun. Above all the noise and hubbub, horses neighed, with fright or excitement, catching the atmosphere of the day. Some were being brushed; some were saddled and ready for an early class; some walked around carrying their riders, still dressed in jeans and T-shirts; some being led by a leading rein to stretch their legs; and some being warmed up in the practice ring... There were Tannoy announcements echoing out, but the information they gave was totally distorted.

It was time for the riders to get ready. Dominic and Graham both gave their girls a kiss and wished them good luck.

Time was getting on. Graham went into the box to change his clothes. He mounted as the announcement came calling for the horses and riders in his class. Dominic walked with him beside Skybright down to the starting gate. The contestants were eighteen in all. The first girl to ride was Lily Martinez. She rode well, her horse, Fedora, jumping high, and they got a clear round, much to her surprise. She was not concentrating on jumping; her mind was on Dominic Hadley, on

311

whom she had a crush. She never gave up hope; she still kept trying.

Then there was John Hopkins, who unfortunately knocked down the last pole. 'Four faults, four faults' said the Tannoy as he came out of the ring with a look of disappointment, grimacing as the girl groom took the bridle and led his horse, Mandolin, away from the gate.

Keith and Vivien came to join Dominic at the gate just before Graham was due to go into the ring. They all wished him luck as he squeezed his knees and Skybright moved slowly forward. They trotted around the ring, looking at each jump. Graham was in no doubt that Skybright could take them all easily. It was no surprise when the announcement came over the speaker 'Clear round, clear round'.

'He went well, Gray!' Dominic said as Graham nonchalantly came out of the gate.

The whole group stood aside as the next rider, Derek Milner, with Kerry, entered the ring. They waited until the last of the riders had had their turn. Five had got clear rounds, and these five had to jump again, and so it whittled down to three: Lily Martinez and Fedora; Kerry with Derek Milner on board; and Graham Hadley and Skybright. It was jumping against the clock.

The spectators were quiet, as they watched and waited anxiously as Fedora cantered round. A great 'Aaah' went through the crowd as she knocked down the second set of poles, but went on to finish the course. Then it was Skybright. The Hadley group standing at the fence, tensed up, as Graham came out of the trot and into the canter, taking the first jump and the next and the next, and finishing with a clear round, and a good time. Derrick Milner, next on Kerry, also had a clear round, the time exactly the same as Skybright. It was a tie; they had to jump again.

The tension was electric. Not only did they have to jump again but the jumps were raised by two inches. Again it was Graham's turn, and he got a clear round, then it was Derek's, who also jumped clear. The last poles were put up for the fourth time; the last jump was now six feet six inches high.

Skybright circled the perimeter of the ring. Graham keeping him at a steady canter elbows tucked well in, the leather scrunching with every stride. There was the huffing of the horse's breath and the thud of his hooves as the bell went for the start. They went round again, eyes focused on the first jump. They took it. They took the next, and the next, until after a sharp turn to the right, there before them was the big six-foot-six-high brush fence. Graham steadied Skybright, centring him and guiding him into position holding him back and then letting him have his head into a gallop... An intake of breath went through the crowd as the great horse leaped into the air and seemed to sail across the sky, clearing the brush with a foot to spare and landing safely on the other side. Graham, with a big smile, brought him to an almost skidding standstill, then trotted out through the gate to clapping and cheering from the crowd. The announcement coming over the speaker, 'Clear round, clear round', was hard to hear. Dominic, beaming, lifted his hand for Graham to slap.

The crowd was now quiet again as Derek Milner and the big bay, Kerry, were announced and walked serenely into the ring, first trotting round and then going into a canter and taking the first jump with ease, cantering on to the next, just tipping the red-and-white painted pole. Milner looked behind him and was thankful it had not fallen. He raced onto the next, turning a sharp right and facing the last big fence. He raced at it, not giving the horse time to recover from the turn, jumping high and at an angle ... and a hushed 'Aaaaaah' went through the crowd as Kerry's front legs clipped the brush and the whole fence fell to the ground with a crash before them. Dominic was clapping and jumping for joy, and both Keith and Vivien called, 'Well done, Graham!' The crowd clapped and again the announcement of 'Four faults, four faults' was lost in the hubbub of noise.

Derrick Milner came out of the gate, punching his fist into the air with a gesture of 'Oh damn it', clicking his tongue with annoyance. He patted Kerry on the neck, nonetheless, and leaned out of the saddle to shake hands with Graham. They smiled at each other, waiting around now for the prize-giving, which would take them into the class for the Golden Horse Trophy. Graham got a large silver tray and Skybright was presented with a red rosette in his bridle. Derek Milner received a small cup, and Kerry shook his head as a rosette was stuck into his bridle, lifting his nose and nearly knocking the judge off his feet.

Emily, Jenny and Dominic were equally successful, and now it was the last class and the big event of the whole day – the competition for the Golden Horse Trophy, and there was to be a jump-off against the clock, between Dominic, Graham, Jenny, Emily and Alex Freemore and Mary Clarke.

Hundreds had crowded around the ring to watch as they had each had their chance to challenge Silverspoon and Dominic Hadley, and each one of them had either knocked down a pole or lost on time, and now it had whittled down to just two; it was now up to Alex Freemore. The crowd around the ringside waited anxiously.

Dominic rode into the ring, proud as ever, tall in the saddle, the peak of his black velvet helmet low over his eyes, immaculately dressed in cream jodhpurs and spotless black jacket. He moved with that calculated, conceited aloofness that Emily, had come to know so well. She remembered the first time she had seen him; she had disliked the very sight of him then, but now she had come to understand him so that she could almost read his mind. She was praying under her breath that he would win this big trophy!

They were all waiting now with baited breath, the whole crowd of spectators as silent as the grave. The jump-off against the clock was about to begin and Dominic Hadley and Alex Freemore were about to go into battle.

Dominic was to go first. Silverspoon calm and collected, as usual, cantered steadily, so very used to every move that the man on his back made. The jumps were now whittled down to three. After the bell, Silverspoon took the first two in his stride and then turned to the last big fence, standing now at six feet ten inches high. Silverspoon leaped into the air and landed safely on the other side, and the crowd roared, as the big horse cantered towards the gate, slowing, then walking calmly. Dominic had that confident smug smile on his face that he always had after a successful jump, as if Silverspoon was mechanical and could be switched on and off at will. The time was announced, but couldn't be heard for the cheering.

Then it was Alex Freemore on Red Streak, a big seventeen-hands chestnut. He also took the six-foot brush with ease. The

314

announcement came over the speaker: 'Clear round, clear round'. Again the time was inaudible. Then there was mumbling and chattering and the noise rose, while the last fence was lifted to seven feet. Hush descended once again as Dominic came into the ring, trotting round in the silence, with just the squeaking of the leathers and the huffing of the horse's breath, getting Silverspoon into a rhythmic and calculated canter, as they took the two smaller jumps, then veered sharply to the right... Now the big seven-foot fence was in front of them. Straightening him and steadying him, he clicked his tongue and his heels, and heard the gasp from the crowd as Silverspoon burst into full gallop and the roar went up again as they jumped high and clear, flying through the air like some strange gigantic bird.

They all settled again and watched as Red Streak cantered steadily, Alex Freemore doing much the same as Dominic, and the roar went up as he cleared the last fence and the loudspeaker rang out, 'Clear round, clear round'. Alex gave Dominic a satisfied grin as he came out of the gate, and again they waited while the fence went up to seven feet two.

There was so much tension and mumbling excitement amongst the crowd now and the speaker called 'QUIET PLEASE!' Then there was a sudden hush as Silverspoon came into the ring, his long, slender legs prancing, his head held as high and as proud as his master's. Dominic had a presence like no other, a stately bearing commanding attention; no one dared to take their eyes off him. Emily clenched her fists. She was praying that Silverspoon would not make a mistake, and hoped that Major was not there. She was desperately trying to keep him out of her mind as the great horse with its silver mane and regal head like a giant rocking horse's passed by with his tail swishing. Like his master he was determined to be a success. They trotted to the start, the bell breaking the complete silence. They trotted round again and then cantered on to the first jump, and then on to the next, the tension so great that Emily was biting the inside of her mouth. He turned sharply to the right, the clock ticking away, Dominic positioning Silverspoon now at a full gallop and heading, straight for the centre of the big seven-foot-two brush fence. Neither horse nor rider could see the other side. Silverspoon reared his forelegs high in the air and the great horse for a split second seemed to be

315

standing completely still, then, like a silver space rocket, launched his great powerful haunches off the ground, leaping into the air. They flew across the top of the brush like Pegasus in the Greek fable, with inches to spare, and a great roar went through the crowd before they touched the ground. Emily relaxed, her body exhausted with tension.

'Clear round, clear round' came the announcement that no one could hear for the clapping and the cheering that went through the spectators. Emily smiled up at Dominic and patted Silverspoon. He grabbed at her hand affectionately.

'Quiet please, quiet please!' The hollow sound of the Tannoy rang out. 'Next Alex Freemore and Red Streak.' Dominic had jumped down and was now standing by the fence with Emily, giving Silverspoon a rest from the weight on his back. He squeezed Emily's hand, and she looked up at him with a nervous smile, knowing that he would have to jump again.

Alex Freemore rode confidently into the ring and proudly eased Red Streak into a trot. The great seventeen-hands chestnut nodded his proud head, as his rider leisurely got him into a rhythmic slow canter until the bell for the start broke the silence once again. They went right round the perimeter of the ring again, the tension so great now it could be cut with a knife. Over the first jump, and on to the next. To the soft huffing of Red Streak's breath and the crunching of the well-polished leather, then, as they turned into the big seven-foot-two fence at a gallop, Red Streak suddenly refused and shied away, almost running into the barrier but swerving away just in time, Alex losing a stirrup but managing to keep his balance. Red Streak lifted his head, his eyes white with fear. He neighed piteously for help, kicking out his back legs, as if to get rid of whatever was there behind him and trying to throw his rider as he backed into the pole of the previous jump.

Emily quickly turned to Dominic, her eyes wide. He glanced down at her. He knew what she was thinking. Jenny and Graham came up beside them, and Jenny touched her friend's arm. They glanced at each other and then back at Red Streak. They did not have to say anything; the look on their faces was enough.

They watched as Alex Freemore straightened Red Streak up, untangling his legs from the red-and-white poles, backing and baulking, and then they had another rush at the seven-foot fence and the great chestnut leaped into the air and cleared it with ease, but it was too late.

Emily held her breath, and squeezed Dominic's hand tightly. He had won the Golden Horse Trophy, but she did not feel excited. The crowd ooed and aahed as the brush fence fell slowly, slowly to the ground. Alex tried to calm the wild-eyed Red Streak, bringing him to a stop, patting his neck to soothe him. Suddenly the horse reared and neighed loudly, flaying his forelegs in the air, and then came down onto the ground. His groom grabbed at the bridle as Alex held him back. Harris Freemore was there to help, holding Red Streak's head down putting his arm across his nose. The horse calmed down quickly. Alex sat on his back, a bewildered look on his face.

'Eight faults, eight faults', came the Tannoy announcement. 'The winner of this year's golden horse trophy: Dominic Hadley and Silverspoon.' The voice was lost as a great cheer went up from the crowd, and the announcement went on, 'Will the riders of Silverspoon and Red Streak and Skybright, please go into the centre of the ring to receive their prizes. Thank you.'

Emily gave Dominic a hug and a kiss, before he mounted Silverspoon. He was smiling, his stomach bubbling with excitement as the whole team – Fred, Charlie, Adrian, Graham and Keith – all patted each other on the back. Emily and Jenny clasped hands. Suddenly Silverspoon sidled and tossed his head, and they all stood back, but Dominic managed to keep him calm as he rode forward into the ring, followed by Red Streak and the still bewildered Alex Freemore, Graham bringing up the rear. Red Streak had now settled and the trio stood side by side and shook hands with friendly smiles. Alex said, 'Well done, Dominic! No hard feelings.'

They each received a handshake and congratulations from Mr Norman Andrews, chairman for the Goldsborough Annual Event. He handed Dominic the large Golden Horse Trophy, and the photographers flashed their cameras. He held it high above his head with both hands – it was a dream come true; he had never felt so proud in all his life! The spectators were clapping, and there were hoorays and whistles. Alex and Graham leaned over, patting him on the back. Then Red Streak received a blue rosette and Alex Freemore a gold tray, and Graham

317

received a small gold cup. Graham and Alex filed out of the ring, acknowledging the shouts and whoops of delight from the crowd, and Dominic did a lap of honour, slowly cantering and holding the Golden Horse Trophy high above his head to clapping from the crowd.

27

Emily went into the yard to ask John to nail the red rosette up over Back Tulip's stable.

'What a good day we 'ad yesterday, Miss. All of you winners! And Mr Dominic copping the lot, and that Mr 'Adley sporting the champagne, and right into the night, too. Cor, that was good, wasn't it?'

Emily smiled as she watched John hammering the nail in over the stable door. It was not often that John drank champagne. For him, it had been a real treat, so he had said, over and over again.

'And Debbie said she 'ad never 'ad a day like it in her life! Weather was good, wasn't it, Miss? Couldn't 'ave bin better. There!' He stood back admiring the red rosette. 'Good girl, Tulip!' He patted her on the nose. 'Now, I s'pose I'd better get off and go and collect Pico from Mayberry. 'E'll be sorry that 'e missed out.'

'I've just phoned Jenny. She said she is coming over, so if she's ready, you can bring her and Henry back in the box.'

John went off nodding happily, leaving Emily alone in the yard. She got Tulip out of the stable and saddled her up, and took her out into the paddock to practice a few jumps, not that she needed any practice after winning a cup at the Goldsborough. She really deserved a good rest after all the practice that they had, but it had paid off.

She was quietly jumping the poles which John had set up when Tulip suddenly shied away. The first thing that she did was growl, 'Major!' It was just at this point that Dominic and Graham came up in their horse box just outside the yard. They could see Emily in the paddock, and saw Black Tulip shy away from a jump. They were about to get out of the cab, when, alongside Emily, they saw a chestnut with a mane and tail flying in the wind. He appeared to be galloping at speed, and he

319

was taking the jump beside her. Black Tulip took the next jump and the chestnut took it, too, and Tulip suddenly twisted around and reared, Emily hanging on as the mare dropped onto her forelegs and bolted straight out across the paddock and over the fence with Emily hanging on her neck. As she charged away across the field, Emily managed to get back into the saddle. They were going like the wind.

It all happened so fast. Dominic and Graham were frozen in their seats, then, as one, they both jumped quickly out of the cab and ran to the fence. But there was nothing they could do but watch as Emily finally managed to take control, turning Black Tulip's head, and came racing back towards them, gradually slowing down in the middle of the field. The horse lifted its head in a frenzy, shaking and neighing, its feet prancing in the long grass trying to rear. Emily held the mare's head down, turning her again.

Dominic was the first over the fence, running towards her. He grabbed at the bridle, as Tulip raised her head, about to rear again. Emily was fighting and shouting, 'Tulip, Tulip!' trying to make her quiet, as she tossed her head from side to side. As the horse cooled a little, she slumped in the saddle.

'You all right, darling?' he called up to her anxiously, trying to keep Tulip from rearing again.

She nodded breathlessly, dishevelled and shaking, her hair in disarray. She was half dismounted, with only one foot in the stirrup. Graham was at her side, lifting her down. She leaned heavily against him, her legs feeling like jelly, while the horse sidled and tried to pull away from Dominic with snorting, grunting noises.

Jenny and John saw them all across the field, as John drove around to the paddock and parked behind the Hadley box. They wasted no time climbing the fence and running towards them, although Tulip was a lot quieter now. John grabbed the other side of the bridle, and between him and Dominic they calmed Black Tulip, who now stood huffing and puffing, nodding and stamping her feet.

Dominic left the mare to John and went to Emily, taking her into his arms, as Graham grabbed at the bridle to help John. Black Tulip nodded, pulling her head up and stepping sideways.

'What happened?' asked Jenny anxiously.

320

Graham was about to say that another horse came from nowhere and looked around to see where it had gone. But Emily blurted out breathlessly, 'It was Major. He was in the paddock!' She sounded alarmed but managed a breathless half-smile. 'And Tulip just took off across the field, and I had a hard job holding her.'

Dominic nodded over Emily's head, as he held her shaking body. 'We saw it all, this horse just came from nowhere.'

Emily looked up at him amazed. 'You saw him?' Her voice raised to a high-pitched surprise. 'I just wasn't ready for it. Tulip just suddenly took off. I thought that she had got a bit more used to him by now, but he obviously scared the wits out of her. But you actually saw him? I don't believe it. I never saw anything.'

'Yes, we were just arriving in the horse box...' Graham said over his shoulder, still hanging onto his side of the bridle. 'And we saw this horse jumping the fences beside you. It just suddenly appeared, didn't it, Dom?'

There was a pause. Emily looked at both the boys. 'Well, what are you doing here anyway?'

'Well,' said Dominic. 'We were going for a ride. Jenny phoned Graham and said she was coming here, so we thought we would turn up and surprise you!'

'Yeah,' chuckled Graham, 'but it was you who surprised *us!*'

Tulip was a bit calmer now, and John started to lead her away back to the yard. They began slowly to follow.

'I can't believe that you actually *saw him.*'

Dominic nodded. 'Yes, if he's a strong chestnut with a ginger mane and tail, then we saw him. Just as Tulip was taking the fence, suddenly he was beside you, taking the fence at the same time. He seemed to be at a gallop much faster than you, but not passing you.'

'Well, I told you he was a chestnut.'

'Yes, but he seemed to be going like the wind!' said Graham. 'At first I thought someone had fallen off and he had come across the fields because he was saddled. In fact, I didn't really see him go, but he followed you over the paddock fence, didn't he, Dom?' He looked across the field. 'He can't have gone far.'

Dominic looked at his brother. 'Graham, it was a ghost!'

Graham looked at his brother, wide-eyed. 'You mean we

321

actually saw a … a… But it looked so real. I always thought that ghosts were transparent. But it wasn't. It was real. It was solid. Are you sure?' He glanced across the field.

Emily smiled. 'It's true. I didn't actually see him, but I knew he was there from the way Tulip was acting. And I wished that I had seem him, too.' A sad look came into her eyes.

Jenny put her hand on Emily's arm. 'Don't, Em. You don't want to see him again. You've got Tulip and Pico. He's dangerous.'

'Maybe he's trying to take me with him. I think he is dangerous, too.'

They walked back through the field and climbed the fence into the paddock of Rosemary Lodge. John had left Black Tulip in the paddock, and she was in the far corner. They made their way around to the yard.

John had let Henry and Pico out and tethered them in the yard, and was just opening up the ramp to let out Silverspoon and Skybright. He asked the boys if they would like him to saddle up for them. Dominic said, 'No, we're not riding now.'

But Emily said, 'Yes, John. We will ride, but we are going in for some coffee first. You can saddle both Pico and Henry, please.'

'I wouldn't have thought that you would want to ride now.' Dominic looked at her with a frown.

'Why not?' She gave him a questioning look. 'Oh! You don't think I would let a little thing like that put me off, do you?'

'A *little thing*? You could have been thrown off and killed! I thought you said you wouldn't ride while he was around. You said he frightened the other horses.'

'But I was on my own here.'

Dominic looked at Graham and scratched his head. 'Well, what about us all riding out together then? What if he comes back, and one of us takes off.'

'Or what if all of us take off,' added Graham.

She shrugged. '*If* he comes back again and I don't think he will, not yet anyway… But if he does, and there is any trouble, then you'll all know how to handle it, won't you?'

They all looked at her with stunned astonishment.

'Oh, Em!' Jenny gasped with a smile.

Dominic sighed, opened his mouth to say something, looked

322

at Graham, and changed his mind. Graham just grinned, raising his eyebrows. What could they say?

Liz was at the oven. Mike was sitting at the table deep into the Sunday paper. Liz was surprised to see them all, and Mike, at the sound of their voices, put down the paper and stood up to shake hands. Emily told her parents what had happened out in the paddock.

'It was so real!' Graham was shaking his head. 'I really thought it was a riderless horse. He just suddenly appeared taking the jumps, then disappeared. It was that quick, and so real, and yet unbelievable!'

'Yeah, you can say that again!' said Dominic. 'But it happened, just as Graham said. I mean, it wasn't even *ghostly...*'

'I know.' Emily looked concerned. 'It makes me wonder what would happen if he materialized at a show. Jenny and I saw him in the woods, didn't we?'

'How do we know that he doesn't materialize at a show,' said Jenny. 'We haven't seen him, but somebody might have done. After all, Em, you didn't see him just now.'

'Did any one give a thought as to why Red Streak shied yesterday?' asked Emily. They all looked at her.

'You don't think that Major was there then, do you?' Dominic looked aghast.

Emily glanced at Jenny, who nodded. 'I know he was. Both Emily and I thought so, didn't we? When a horse shies and hits the fence like that, it's not normal, is it? We all know that.'

'You mean that I didn't win the trophy fair and square then?'

'I'm in no doubt that Silverspoon could have cleared that fence at seven foot four if it had gone up again!' said Graham.

'Neither am I!' said Dominic. 'But I would like to think that I had done it fairly.'

'So what are you going to do?' said Emily with a wry smile. 'Phone Alex Freemore and say, "Sorry you lost, Alex, but there was a ghost horse chasing you around the ring."'

'Don't be so stupid, Em! Who would believe that?'

She smiled. 'Well, now you know how I felt when I beat you.'

'Well...' Dominic wanted to retort, but what could he say?

'Well, you won, Dom,' Graham said, 'and you would have

323

beaten him anyway. Silverspoon can clear up to seven foot four easily. You know he can; he has done it so many times in our paddock, and he's fast and quick on the turn!'

'Yeah, I know.' He shook his head in despair, 'But it doesn't make me feel good.'

It was on Tuesday that Dominic called Emily with some sad news. Adrian Poole had been admitted to hospital on Sunday afternoon, the day after the Goldsborough, and that morning he had died at five o'clock. His parents had left the hospital Monday evening. They said he was in good spirits. It was the last time they saw him.

'Died!' Emily was shocked. 'What happened?'

'Well, according to his father, he felt unwell after being out all day at the Goldsborough. He should never have come, I told him not to do anything and to go and lie down if he was tired; but he didn't and, apparently, he was exhausted. Sunday morning he collapsed at home in the garden. His father rushed him to the hospital and they found that he had not only crushed his shoulder, but the impact of the horse jumping down on him had also damaged a valve in his heart. I don't know, but I guess the day out at the Goldsborough was just too much for him.'

'Oh my God!' exclaimed Emily, slumping down into the, armchair that stood beside the table in the hall. 'How awful! How awful! I just don't believe it. I don't know what to say. Oh, Dominic...' She looked up and saw her anguished reflection in the mirror. 'He wasn't very old, was he?'

'Twenty-two. His birthday was last Thursday.' He was choked; it was almost a whisper. 'It's unbelievable, isn't it? But I thought he looked tired at the Goldsborough, and I told him to lie down in the box, but he said he was OK! It's just so unbelievable, isn't it? I can't get over it.'

Emily felt sick in her stomach. 'But didn't they find this damage to the heart when they X-rayed him?'

'Apparently not. Maybe he should have rested. Anyway, it's too late now.' He was breaking down. 'I'll talk to you later.'

* * *

324

It was the typical day for a funeral: drizzling with rain, the atmosphere stuffy with not a breath of air, warm and overcast with heavy grey clouds. The rain brought out the perfume from the assembled wreaths, the flowers the only bright thing on this dull and miserable July Saturday afternoon.

The large group of mourners gathered at the graveside under black umbrellas. Keith and Vivienne, Dominic and Emily, and Graham and Jenny stood together hand in hand. Alongside were Fred and Charlie, in dark suits and ties – they had never looked so smart – and Annie Kimberly, who had worked in the Hadley kitchen and who now wept uncontrollably into a white handkerchief. Beside her, with an arm around her, was Jim Brown, and with him the veterinary nurses. Adrian had been such a lively lad, keeping them all going with his jokes and his whistling. He didn't deserve to die, this young man who had spent the last few weeks looking after the sick animals that he loved.

Adrian's large family stood across the graveside from Emily and Dominic, his father and eldest brother either side of his mother.

Emily did not know the family but she could see the utter devastation on all the drawn faces. Mrs Poole seemed near to collapsing as her husband and son held on to her arms, protecting her from the drizzling rain with large black umbrellas.

There were sobs as the coffin was lowered, as the Reverend Sullivan said, 'Ashes to ashes, dust to dust...' Emily held on tighter to Dominic's arm. She could feel the tears beginning to flow, and Dominic handed her a handkerchief, and she saw him pinch his eyes with his forefinger and his thumb, trying to contain his feelings. It was hard for anyone not to be emotional.

Some of the mourners began to move away from the graveside, walking back to their cars, and leaving the Poole family to stay a little longer with their own grief. They had all been asked back to the house for tea, and now they stood in the dining room in groups, chatting quietly. The atmosphere was not as strained as it might have been. No one had ever mentioned it, but Graham felt fingers pointing at him because it was his horse that had killed Adrian. And Emily could not get the thought of Major out of her mind. She felt every bit as guilty as Graham, although it was neither of their faults. Major was the original cause, and she wondered how many more people would suffer because of him.

28

Months went by, and there was to be a surprise birthday party for Louise at Wickerbrook Hall. Everybody was invited. It was to be evening-dress, with dinner and dancing.

Louise had come down from her bedroom, dressed in bright shimmering red. The skirt clung to her slim figure as if it had been sprayed on, the back open to her tiny waist. Her dark hair was swept up and dotted with tiny red rosebuds. She was feminine and ladylike. In short, she was almost unrecognizable as her normal self, dressed in jodhpurs, boots and green roll-necked sweater.

She told Emily and Jenny afterwards that she had come into the lounge, where her parents greeted her and her father offered her a glass of champagne. He introduced her to some business acquaintances – three couples in their late fifties or sixties – and then he suggested they go into the dining room. 'Lead the way, Louise!' he had commanded, which she did, opening the double doors to the dining room. A blast of clapping and 'Happy Birthday to You', rang out from fifty guests. The long table was laden with silver and glittering glass and red flowers to match her dress.

Louise was so taken aback. She put her hands to the sides of her cheeks with a huge beaming smile and tears misting her green eyes. It was the first time that anyone had ever really thought that Louise Bartram could be so touched. In the daytime she was always so brusque and masculine. Louise was seated at the head of the table next to her dear friend Sir Simeon Hatch, who looked very smart in black tie, despite his thin and weedy appearance. Emily had met him before at the Hunt Ball, when she had found him quite charming and entertaining. To Louise's right sat Dominic and then Emily in a darker-red strapless silk, which enhanced her pale golden skin and hugged her slim figure. To the left of Sir Simeon sat Jenny in a halter-neck black dress, with a gold necklace and large golden earrings, and then Graham. Their respective parents were placed in the middle of the long table, and at the far end sat Sir James and Lady Cynthia, who looked stunning in a shade of midnight-blue raw silk, which gave a blue hue to her stylish silver-grey hair.

The evening was a great success, the food and wine superb. After dinner they were asked to take their seats in the conservatory, where a string quartet played Mozart, while the guests drank champagne or liqueurs and the men smoked cigars. Later in the evening there was disco music in the ballroom, which had also been decorated, much to Louise's surprise. They danced until two in the morning, and when the disco finished they sat around finishing their drinks. It was two forty-five when Emily finally said goodnight to Dominic.

Mike drove carefully through the quiet country lanes, Liz beside him, Emily in the back. It had been a wonderful evening. She knew she had enjoyed it because her head was swimming and her feet ached from dancing in high-heel shoes. The night was dark and still. There were no stars and her eyes felt prickly and tired. She looked out on tall, shadowed trees and black hedgerows as the car sped on passing through the country lanes. Her head nodded. She dozed for a few minutes and then woke up as the car went over a bump. Out of the window, the night had changed everything to dark blue, grey and black; in the morning it would all change back to green and brown again and the air would be fresh with the dew! Now that the nights were beginning to draw in, the autumn leaves were already turning to gold and would soon fall thick to cover the ground. Her eyes closed again and she imagined riding through the woods, with the golden-brown dry leaves rustling and crackling under Black Tulip's or Pico's hooves... She was awakened by her father's voice.

'What's that orange glow in the sky? Looks like a fire!

Emily blinked her eyes. She could see the glow across the fields through the trees. The car sped through a village with small cottages on either side of the road, dimly lit by a few street lamps, then there were open fields.

They turned into their village, the smell of burning seeping into the car. Rosemary Lodge was alive with policemen and firemen. Both Liz and Emily screamed. Emily was the first out of the car, running and lifting the long skirt of her evening-dress up over her knees. She dashed into a stable yard that was no longer there.

'Where are my horses? The horses, where are they?' she was screaming, turning this way and that, to policemen and firemen alike.

The police sergeant, George Bains, came over. She had seen him in the village but they had never spoken.

'It's all right, Miss! Everything's under control. The horses, two of them, are out there in the paddock, none the worse for wear as far as I can see. When the firemen got here, they were already in the paddock. But I'm afraid they couldn't save your stables.

Emily didn't even answer him, but rushed straight out to the paddock. She could see two dark shapes on the other side. She called to Tulip and Pico, and they lumbered slowly over to her. She patted them both at once, close to tears with relief and an arm around both of their necks. The smoke was choking and the acrid smell of burnt wood and hay was strong in the air. They must have inhaled a lot of smoke. She wondered how they had got out here into the paddock. Maybe they had run in fright and jumped the fence, but they would have to stay together tonight unless she could find a head collar to move Pico out into the next paddock.

Mike and Liz were with the sergeant and the chief fire officer when she returned to what was left of the yard – just half of the gate and the cobblestones. The lights from the fire engine still illuminated the devastated scene, and grey smoke was still rising into what was left of the night. The occasional flame reared up, but the firemen doused it with water.

'Well, we can't do anything tonight, sir,' the sergeant was saying, 'but I will be round in the morning, and we will try to sort out the cause.'

'You didn't leave any electric fires or anything burning, did you?' asked the fire office. 'Do you smoke?'

Mike said 'No. We have radiators in the stables and the tack room, but we only use them in mid-winter.'

'What about your groom, John Carter?' asked the sergeant. 'I don't know him, but I know he works here.'

'Oh, no,' said Emily. 'John doesn't smoke.'

'Is he reliable?'

'Oh! Yes! Very reliable,' replied Emily, surprised that anyone could possibly fault John.

'Hmmm, I'll be round in the morning!' concluded the sergeant.

'So will I,' said the fire officer. 'Anyway it's all right now, you're safe, and your horses are safe, young lady. It was lucky that a driver was passing and saw the glow, and called us on the mobile before it got too bad. But the wood is old and dry, and I'm afraid we couldn't save it. You are lucky,' he said to Mike and Liz, 'that it wasn't windy or the house might have been damaged, too. But everything is OK now. I'll see you in the morning. Goodnight for now.'

When they had all gone, Mike, Liz and Emily stood in the darkness, both Liz and Emily holding their long evening-dresses up from the wet ground, the cobblestones still warm through their thin silk evening shoes. They breathed in the acrid smell of burning, and, for a moment, they watched the grey curling wood smoke and the smouldering black bales. Emily felt a draining sadness. The yard could be rebuilt, but it would never be the same. The yard had been there for over seventy years, and the atmosphere could never be the same. How had the horses got out? It was too late now to phone Keith Hadley, and they seemed all right as far as she could tell in the darkness, but she would phone Dominic first thing in the morning and ask him to take a look at them. They must have inhaled a lot of smoke. Mike told her to turn on the water as he held the garden hose over the almost empty watering-trough. The horses drank thirstily.

Mike sighed and slumped his shoulders. 'It's sad, but thank goodness the horses were out in the paddock.'

'They weren't out there when we left. I can't think how they got there.' Emily looked towards the paddock. 'They must have got out...' she shivered. '...But I don't know how. The gate to the paddock is always closed, and it is now.'

'Perhaps they jumped the fence in fright,' said Liz.

'Yes, probably. But how would they have got out of the stables? Not unless John has been up and put them out, but I don't know why he would. And he would never have put them both in together. They must have been terrified. And if John

330

had been here, he would have phoned Wickerbrook Hall to tell us about the fire. He wouldn't have left either, he would still be here now.'

Mike nodded. 'Well, there's nothing more we can do tonight. Come on, let's go in.' He put his arm around both of their shoulders and guided them in, unlocking the front door.

Liz went straight to the kitchen, switched on the light and put on the kettle for tea. They sat at the kitchen table, sad and down-hearted, with the strong aroma of smoke filling every room.

'I wonder how it started?' Liz kicked off her shoes and took off her jacket.

Mike thought it might have been a loose wire 'Perhaps I should have had it checked. It's been a long time.'

Then Emily suddenly sat up. 'You don't think Major...?'

'No!' said Mike. 'That's impossible. How could he start a fire.'

'Well, he switched the radio on in the tack room, and it wasn't even plugged in.'

Her parents looked at her open-mouthed.

'What!' Mike gasped. She told them about what happened when she and Dominic were out in the yard. They couldn't believe it. 'You must be mistaken.'

'No, it wasn't plugged in. Ask Dominic!'

They fell silent and sat for a few more moments finishing their drinks. They went to bed for what was left of the night, but Emily could not sleep, pictures of Major kept coming into her mind. How on earth could he have started a fire? She tossed and turned and sleep would not come. She wished she had phoned Dominic when they had come home, but then what could he do? He would be as shocked as they all were. She got out of bed and went to the window. A grey dawn and drizzling rain greeted her. She opened the window, and the air smelt of smoke and burning. Looking to her left, she could see Tulip in the paddock, but not Pico. Her first thought was that he might have collapsed, then she wondered if the gate was open and he had got out. She quickly jumped into a pair of jeans and a sweater, and ran quickly and quietly down the stairs, out of the kitchen door, and across to the paddock. To her relief, Pico was standing in the far corner, which she could not see from her bedroom window. She called them to her, and they plodded slowly, nodding their heads, and she patted them both and talked to them gently, asking them what had happened and how had they got out into the paddock. They did not seem any the worse for what must have been a very frightening experience.

She left them and walked across to where the cobblestones of the yard were now barely visible under the heaps of damp smouldering wood. She suddenly remembered the tack room and walked to where it had once been. The smell of charred wood was nauseating, and slight whiffs of smoke still rose gently into the quiet morning air. She couldn't see anything that had been saved: the saddles and bridles, rugs and brushes, everything had gone. She was still out there when John arrived around six thirty.

'Cor! Bloody hell! What's 'appened 'ere?' he gasped, and before Emily could say anything, he rushed forward. 'Where's the 'orses?'

'In the paddock, John. They're all right, but I don't know how they got there. You didn't come up again last night and turn them out, did you?' She knew it was a silly question. He would never have put them in together.

John shook his head. 'No, Miss, they were stabled when I left, like always. When did all this 'appen?'

Mike came out of the kitchen door and went back for his jacket. It was raining hard. He was putting the hood up as he came into what was once the yard. 'Morning, John. Mess, isn't it? I'm waiting for the police.'

'Well, when did it 'appen, Mr Peters?' John sounded bewildered. 'We didn't 'ear nothin'. Although Debbie did mention this morning that she heard cars going through the village in the night, and said she could smell burning. I got up and looked out of the window, because I had lit a bonfire earlier in the evening and it was still glowing, so I naturally thought that was what it was... I never thought...'

'Well, we came in around three,' said Mike, 'and the firemen had just about finished putting it out, so I don't know how or when it happened. But luckily the horses are all right, and they caught it before it took hold of the house.'

'Christ! What a bloody mess!' John was shaking his head. 'Did they manage to salvage anythink?'

'No!' Mike rubbed his hand across the back of his neck. 'I don't think so. We seemed to have lost the tack and the lot, everything!'

The police arrived at eight and soon after the chief fire officer, with two firemen. After discussing with Mike Peters what they were going to do, the firemen set about going very carefully through the wreckage.

After hours of searching, the chief fire officer said that he thought that it had started with a cigarette.

'But no one 'ere smokes!' said John.

'What did you have in your tack room?' asked Sergeant Bains, who was standing by listening.

'The usual things,' said Emily, 'saddles and bridles.'

'Yeah and rugs and brushes and the like,' said John.

'What time did you leave?' asked Sergeant Bains.

'Well, like I always do, about six. I see's that the 'orses is all right stabled and got water and such. I locked the side gate, like I always do, and went 'ome.'

'Yes, John always goes about six,' said Emily, 'and he's always careful.'

Another fireman came to join them, and spoke quietly for a minute to the fire officer. Finally, Nigel Sewell, the officer, said, 'Apparently, we can't find any trace of saddles or bridles in the tack room.'

Emily, John and Mike looked astonished.

'I thought so!' Nigel Sewell nodded. 'I think I can tell you what happened here. You had a break in, and they stole all your tack.'

Emily gasped. 'No! How do you know?'

'Well, there's nothing in the tack room at all. They have cleaned you out. And I would imagine that a cigarette was probably thrown away carelessly and caught the straw.'

'But the horses?' said Mike. 'They were in the paddock with the gate closed. How did they get in there?'

'Well,' Sergeant Bains joined in, 'the thieves most likely put them out into the paddock. We had a case like this in Cambridge

333

around Christmas last year, where thieves stole tack from a farm and put six horses out to grass so that they didn't kick up a fuss and wake the household.'

''Ow do you know there was no tack in our tack room?'

Nigel Sewell smiled. 'Because if there had been anything in there, the saddles would have charred and still looked intact and the metal bits and rings from the bridles, stirrups, buckles, etc, would have been there. They would not have burned and there's nothing over there at all, come and have a look.'

'I suppose you are well insured?' asked Nigel Sewell.

Mike nodded.

'Yes,' Emily nodded, 'but the money won't bring back memories, will it? It will never be the same again, will it?' She looked at John.

Nigel Sewell sympathized, nodding his head gently. 'No! I know what you mean. You can rebuild, but it will never be the same!'

They turned as Keith Hadley's car came up the drive. Dominic and Graham were with him. Emily had phoned Dominic earlier in the morning, she had also phoned Jenny. They were shocked at the devastation. Dominic put his arm around Emily and gave her a comforting hug.

Liz came out into the yard, her eyes wide with alarm. 'Mike! The horse box has gone!'

Sergeant Bains looked at her. 'Where was the horse box?'

'I always parked it over there at the side of the meadow,' said John. 'I only bring it in 'ere when we're loading to go out to a show.'

'Show me,' said George Bains, starting to walk away, followed by his constable, and John walking beside him. The others followed, while the chief fire officer went back to chat with his two firemen, asking if they had found anything.

Liz had missed seeing the horse box from the kitchen window when she realized she was looking at a view she hadn't seen for ages. When she rushed out into what remained of the yard, she was hoping that John would say that he had parked it somewhere else, which, of course, he seldom did.

The sergeant and the constable seemed to check every blade of grass where the horsebox had stood. Sergeant Bains grimaced, as he stood up from a squatting position. 'They seem to have been very thorough. Can't see anything, can you, Forster?'

'I don't know, Sarge.' He stood up with a frown. 'What's that?' He was pointing and standing a little way from George Bains, who moved closer to him and then squatted down. Then the two of them probed carefully in the long grass with plastic pens to reveal the smallest piece of torn green card.

Sergeant Bains produced a small plastic bag from his pocket and, carefully put the piece of card into it. Looking at it, he saw part of a name printed in gold letters: 'Jaz–'.

'What do you think, Jim? Jazz Club? Do you know of one?' He turned it over. There were two numbers written on the back: 5 and 2. 'Probably part of a telephone number, do you think? Look into it, will you?'

It was Dominic who answered him. 'No, I think it might be Don's Café. It's in Newmarket. It's not a Jazz Club. It's a small place, where they play jazz once a month. I think it's a piece of the menu. I have got one at home. I will let you have it. I haven't been there for a long time; it gets too crowded, mostly with stable lads.'

'Stable lads!' The sergeant raised his eyebrows.

'I'm not sure, mind, but it looks like the same piece of card from the menu. It's green just like that.'

As they walked away, Emily and Dominic went to the paddock where Keith was examining both Tulip and Pico. He announced that they were fine. Perhaps they had inhaled a little too much smoke, but other than that he thought they were fine. 'Give them plenty of water!' was his advice.

After the police and the firemen had gone, John started to sweep up a bit of the yard. Mike told him to leave it. He would get someone in to remove all the rubble, or what little there was left. They came in that same afternoon; three men with shovels and a fork-lift truck.

John and Emily stood near the charred side gate, watching as the rubble was lifted onto a lorry. Suddenly Emily ran forward.

'Just a minute, just a minute!' she shouted over the noise. The man, surprised, switched off the engine, as Emily stepped in front of the fork-lift and picked up a bucket. 'It's just an old bucket, but it has sentimental value for me. Thanks!' She

335

smiled, holding the bucket as if it was precious. She wondered if Major was still here. She was standing in what had been the middle of his stable, surrounded by the strong smell of soggy and charred straw. She tried to conjure up a presence, but she could feel nothing. She moved to the side. 'You can carry on now, thank you!'

Still standing with the bucket in her hand, she wondered if Major, in some mysterious way, had started the fire. She wondered if the fire had finally sent him to his rest, and she wondered where his spirit would go now that his stable was no longer there! In her mind's eye she could see the large brown eyes looking at her, and her nose tingled as tears pricked her eyes. She must not let them fall. This was no time for sentimentality. The noise of the fork-lift truck brought her back to reality. She still had Tulip and Pico, thank goodness, and they were safe. Dad would have to build new stables now. He was well insured, but it was going to cost a fortune and take months to rebuild. But for the time being, Tulip and Pico could stay in the paddock – the weather was warm – but in a few months' time, they would need to be stabled; she would have to make arrangements for them to be looked after.

It was decided that Pico and Tulip would be best stabled at Mayberry Farm.

John went there every day, and he got on well with Anita, helping her and Jim Spencer with Henry and the other horses. Emily did not always go over to ride early in the morning, but she and Jenny rode out after work nearly every day, and at the weekend they rode with the boys either at Mayberry Farm or Packards Mill.

It was on Friday night following the fire that Dominic and Graham went for a drink at Don's Café in Newmarket. It was crowded as usual, and the same jazz band was playing. Dominic had already dropped the green menu card at the police station for the sergeant to compare with the small fragment they had found in the grass. The club was packed with stable lads drinking beer. He wondered how they fared the next morning when the horses had to be got ready for the day's racing; the yards opened up at around four o'clock in the morning.

They ordered a beer and stood leaning on the corner of the bar, trying to listen in on conversations, in case someone should drop a hint about breaking into yards that they could relate back to Sergeant Bains. After four beers, and asking a few questions, they eventually left without any information whatsoever.

Dominic phoned the police station to ask if the cards had been compared. The sergeant said that they had been analyzed and it was the same card. He had a man down there in the bar last night, and it turned out that he and Graham had been questioning the undercover policeman! Sergeant Bains suggested, very politely, that they should leave the detection to the police. His undercover man had discovered something, but he was unable to disclose the information yet.

29

After the insurance claim was settled, which took the best part of a year, Mike had the contractors in working There were six new stables and a tack room, all built around the old cobblestone yard. There were new taps for the hoses, and a sink in the yard, and the tack room was fitted with shelves and cupboards, and special stands had been fitted to take Tulip's and Pico's saddles. There were polished mahogany hooks for riding jackets, waterproofs and riding helmets, and smaller hooks at the side for riding crops. The new brightly coloured rugs of blue and red were stored in wire baskets on the shelf, and below them all the new brushes and lotions and polishes were set out. At one end there was a small kitchen, and below the sink there were special places for the water buckets. To the side of this was a large walk-in cupboard for storing brushes and brooms. On the kitchen table stood an electric kettle, above which was a cupboard with mugs and plates. There was even a small fridge so that John could leave his lunch or get a cold drink or milk for his coffee if the family or Mrs Porter were not available. Outside in the yard, two new wheelbarrows stood beside a large dustbin. There was a toilet and a basin, something they had never had before. Everything was new and fresh.

The new silver horse box with a smart green stripe along the side had been made specially to Emily's specifications; the old one had never been found. Emily had chosen the colour scheme of pale green and light wood for the interior. It was very chic and was bigger than the old one. It had a spacious bathroom with a shower and sleeping quarters, and it could take four horses.

Emily decided to christen the new stable with a champagne party. Bales of hay had been put around for the thirty guests to sit on, but mostly they stood and wandered around with glasses of wine or champagne. Liz had done all the food with Carol's and Mrs Porter's help, and they had laid it all on the pine table in the tack room. Mike had hired a waiter to serve at a small table where a bar had been set up. Everyone was there: Louise and Sir Simeon, Mary Clark and John Carpenter, Alex Freemore and his girlfriend, Patsy, Derek Milner, and Tom the farrier and his wife, Maggie, Anita and Jim Brown, Fred and Charlie Fenwick, even Lily Martinez, who was thrilled when Dominic offered her a drink and asked how she was. She was so tongue-tied she just smiled and fluttered her eyes.

Music played while the guests wandered around the yard, looking into the stables and admiring the new mangers and light fittings and door handles. It was all so modern.

Sir James, drink in hand, was walking round with Mike. 'You've done a marvellous job here, old man. Tragic business, but now it all seems for the best! Don't want to buy another horse, do you? Louise is talking of selling Mystic Nights, if you're interested.'

Mike twisted his lips, with the slightest shake of his head. 'I will have to think about that, James; I'll have a word with Emily. If we did get any more horses we would have to employ someone to give John a hand.'

Louise marvelled at the new tack room, wandering around with Simeon, sipping her drink and talking.

'Gosh! This *is* lovely, Emily. You could live out here, old thing; it's smashing, what! Jolly nice, isn't it, Sim?' She didn't really give poor Simeon a chance to answer.

'I'm thinking of selling Mystic Nights, if you're interested, Emily,' she went on. 'Got my beady eye on another mare!'

Emily pulled a face, a bit uncertain. 'I don't think so, Louise. I'm really not sure yet. I really have enough to do with Tulip and Pico, but thank you anyway!'

'Well, think about it, dear just think about it!' She waved her hand. 'Aah, Mr Cunningham! Just the man...' She took hold of Simeon's hand, and he followed behind her like a faithful dog.

The evening went on until midnight. It was getting too cold, and the guests gradually dispersed, leaving Liz, Emily and Debbie to clear up the left-over food, and the barman to

339

wash the last of the glasses. It had been a very successful evening.

It was in the January that Keith Hadley lost his mother at the age of ninety-seven. Although the boys saw her from time to time, they had not visited her very often. Emily had met her once with Dominic. She had seemed very frail, a tall woman in a long black dress. Emily remembered taking her hand. It had been thin skin and bone with deep-blue veins and heavily spotted with brown age spots. Her face was thin and wrinkled, and surrounded by a halo of frizzy thinning white hair, but there was still a trace of the beauty that had once been there. She had greeted them warmly with a delicate smile, leaning heavily on an ebony walking stick. Her pale-blue watery eyes peered from behind silver-rimmed spectacles, filled with tears of joy at seeing her grandson. She had lived in Norfolk, in a large house called April Manor, all her married life, and liked nothing better than to walk and sit out in the beautiful gardens. Even then, when Emily had met her, she loved to sit on a bench under the big oak tree, as long as she was wrapped up warm, and the nurse, Wendy Newman, saw to that! Grandma always said that there was nothing like fresh air to keep one going, and she intended to live forever! Her husband had passed away seven years before, and from then on Grandmother Hadley, who had always been quite spry, had gone down hill rapidly.

It was a very cold day when the boys met the girls at April Manor, a large red-brick Victorian house set in acres of land, hidden from view behind tall pine trees and almost opposite the small church of St Mary's, which Rebecca Hadley had attended all her married life.

The funeral was sad as all funerals are. There were only a few mourners, mostly village friends, and Wendy Newman, who shed uncontrollable tears and was comforted by the gardener's son, Stephen. Emily shed a tear even though she had not known the old lady well. The nurse told them that Grandmother had been sitting under the oak tree just a week ago, and she, Wendy, had been just a yard away, picking her a sprig of holly with bright-red berries. Grandmother had said it was the brightest shrub in the garden at this time of the year, and she had laughed when Wendy Newman replied that the holly was almost as old as she was. Grandmother had hoped she had never been as prickly, and the nurse had assured her that she had always been kind and gentle.

They sat now in silence, the small group of family, villagers, and friends of the church, who had known Rebecca Hadley. The coldness of the church walls seemed to seep into their bodies, as the organ played quietly in the background and the Reverend Riley began to speak. For a fleeting moment the sun came in through the stained-glass window near the altar, and shone across the head of the coffin. It was as if God was welcoming another daughter.

There had been just a light flurry of snow. It had whipped across the graveyard and hung, now, on the feathery leaves of the pines under a heavy grey sky. How the gravediggers had managed in the hard and frozen soil was a mystery. But the wreaths of flowers were beautiful, and helped to brighten the sad, dull day. Then afterwards they had returned to April Manor, where Millie Bernshaw, the cook, had a hot meal waiting for them.

Three months on, the March winds came again. Louise had recruited hundreds of people for the Wickerbrook Show, which was to be at the end of the month, a little later than last year. They were hoping for a better day.

Graham and Jenny's house plans were well on the way. Keith had lent them the money, and the builders had been there for months. They talked of nothing else but their wedding, although they had not actually named the date, though it would be near Christmas.

Saturday morning, Dominic phoned. Emily could hear the excitement in his voice. He had something to tell her. He came over in the horse box and brought Silverspoon, and soon they were riding side by side in the woods near Rosemary Lodge. He told her that he and Graham had had the surprise of their lives yesterday, when they had been to the reading of Grandmother Hadley's will. They had come into money. Big money! His handsome face beamed with delight. 'I never gave it a thought, although I knew she had a few bob. She left a big chunk to Dad, and the rest to us boys. We're her only family.

'Graham is going ahead with the building of the house, and can afford to finish the job now. He is going to talk to Jenny about naming the day, and we're going to build a surgery down near the gate so that we can set up a veterinary practice between us next year, providing we qualify, of course!'

Emily congratulated him. 'And what about us, Dom? Are we going to get married?'

'Whenever you're ready, my darling. Just say the word. And we'll build the biggest house you ever saw. What would you fancy?'

She smiled shyly. 'Well, I've always wanted a large old farmhouse with lots of stables and a dozen horses, but my real dream would be Wickerbrook Hall.'

Dominic smiled. 'Would it really?'

'Yes,' she sighed. 'Have you ever seen their stable block, and all those wonderful horses. If it were mine, I would turn it into a riding school and coach people in top-class showing and jumping. I would only turn out the very best riders, and I would have only the very best horses.' She went off in a dream.

'Penny for your thoughts!'

She smiled. 'Oh, it was nothing, just dreams.'

'Shall we look for a house, then, like Wickerbrook?'

'I'd love to just look! But anyway, let Jenny and Graham have their day first. They've been talking about it for some time and we don't want to spoil it for them by planning *our* wedding.'

'Yes, I agree. By the way, Graham has invited us over to look at the house. It's almost finished now.'

'Yes, I was with Jenny when she chose the curtain materials. I'd love to have a look at the house, wouldn't you?'

They trotted on passing the tree where Major had had the accident. Emily never failed to look. It still saddened her, but there was nothing to see. There had been no more trouble with him since the stable had burnt down.

Dominic came up alongside. 'I'm thinking of going out to see Ben Mortimer tomorrow morning. Will you come with me?'

'Yes, I'd love to. Why? Are you thinking of buying Stardust?'

'Well, I don't know yet, although, now I can afford it, I

342

thought I would have another look. Ben also has another one. No harm in taking a look. I phoned him this morning, and I will call him back and say that we are coming, shall I?'

The next morning, Ben Mortimer greeted them warmly, and took them out into the stable.

'The mare I spoke to you about is in the yard.' He called to Jessica, who was pleased to see them again.

'I've still got Stardust here, if you're interested, but, of course, you want to see the other one. Dominic nodded, and they walked through towards the yard. 'Had a couple of potential buyers for Stardust since I saw you last,' Ben was saying over his shoulder, 'but he proved to be a bit too much to handle, as you know. Although I remember you two didn't seem to have any trouble with him!' He smiled at Emily. Ben was still talking as they walked out into the yard, the wind nearly knocking them over.

'This is Silver Lady.' He slapped her on her grey hindquarters as she lumbered out of the stables. 'Got plenty of zip in her, but she is a lady and quite gentle. She'll go well today with this wind under her tail!' he mused. Jessica was holding her bridle, while Dominic looked her over and ran his hands down her back, over her flank and under her belly, and down her long slender silver legs that got darker below the knee towards the hoof.

'She's quite sound. I have the vet to see my horses regularly. Chris Clements said that you were a vet?'

Dominic looked up. 'Yeah, that's right.' He nodded and stood up, away from the legs, and gave her a gentle pat on the neck. He moved round to her head and looked into the eyes. 'Almost finished my training, another year to go.' The eyes were brown, clear and bright. He looked up each nostril – they were clean – and looked in her mouth at her teeth.

'Want to ride her?'

'Yeah,' Dominic nodded. 'Yeah, I'd like to!'

Ben took hold of the bridle and told Jessica to get her saddled up. But it was another girl, Margaret, who appeared, almost hidden behind the large saddle which she carried, and flung it up high onto the back of Silver Lady. The horse seemed quite placid as Margaret stepped aside. Ben checked the girth and lowered the stirrups, and held onto the bridle while Dominic

343

mounted her. They went out into the paddock, Emily and Jessica walking behind.

Emily stood by the fence with Ben and Jessica, while Dominic put the horse though its paces. George, Ben's father, joined them.

'She's magnificent-looking, isn't she?' he said to Emily. 'Best-looking filly I ever did see. She's a super ride; I rode her myself yesterday.'

'Oh, I didn't know that you rode, Mr Mortimer!' She turned away from Dominic and the horse to look at the podgy figure of George Mortimer. He looked older than he was, his face heavily weathered from being out in the open most of the time, but, still, she could not imagine him riding a horse like this, or even wanting to.

'Rode all my life,' said George.

'Dad used to be a jockey!' said Ben. 'Have you never heard of George Mortimer?'

Emily smiled. 'No. I'm sorry, I haven't!'

'She's too young,' smiled George. They turned to look as Dominic took the last jump for about the fourth time and then rode over to where they were all standing by the fence.

'Can we put the last jump up?' Dominic asked, and Jessica went in to higher it.

Silver Lady took it at six foot, and then again at six foot two, and then at six foot six.

He wiped his hand across his forehead, lifting the peak of the helmet a little. 'She's great!' He was a little breathless. 'Jumps well; I like her.' He nodded an smiled at Emily. 'Come and have a go.'

Emily was pleased to mount the beautiful mare, and Dominic handed her his helmet. They laughed when it came right down over her eyes, and Ben sent Jessica to fetch a smaller one. She came back quickly with two, brushing the velvet of one across the crown and handing it up to Emily.

'It's a bit dusty, I'm afraid.'

'That's OK, as long as it fits!' She put it on, clipping the strap under her chin; it fitted perfectly! She gently pulled the rein to the right, and Silver Lady turned her regal head, and they trotted round the ring. Then she tightened the rein, then loosened it, just as they took the first jump which was quite

344

low, and then the next and the next. They did this three or four times more, and then did it again and also jumped the big six foot six fence and Silver Lady flew over it like a bird. Dominic clapped softly, smiling to himself. Emily certainly knew how to handle a horse!

'What about Stardust? Do you mind if I ride him while I'm here? Then I might decide.'

Jessica brought him out to the paddock already saddled. The big dapple-grey pranced excitedly on the spot, his silver mane bouncing gently on his neck, his hooves thudding softly in the grass. He twisted and sidled, but Jessica straightened him up, pulling back on the bridle with all her strength. His head nodded over her shoulder as he tried to surge forward, wanting to get ahead of her too fast.

As they came near, Ben Mortimer took charge and thanked Jessica. He held him steady while Dominic swung himself up into the saddle. Jessica unlatched the gate, letting Emily and Silver Lady out and Dominic and Stardust in, and took Silver Lady back to the yard. Stardust trotted fast round the paddock, almost at a canter, with the wind strong in his face, but Dominic held him back, then they cantered around and around the edge of the paddock, both getting the feel of each other. He was such a beautiful animal, but fiery, not composed and calm like Silverspoon. Emily wondered how, if Dominic decided to buy him, he would fare at events, but seeing him now take the six-foot-six fence, she knew that Dominic would master him!

Dominic finished his ride, came out of the paddock and jumped down. Jessica took hold of the bridle, Ben and Dominic walking shoulder to shoulder as they went back into the yard.

Emily and Jessica walked behind, holding onto Stardust. He still walked at a fast pace even though he had been jumping for at least thirty minutes. He pranced and sidled and seemed to have endless energy, especially when the wind blew his mane. Like most horses he jumped a bit when the wind blew up his tail. Emily thought Ben's horses certainly were in tiptop condition, bright and alert, and she wondered just how many events he had judged. She had never seen him at any of the horse shows.

Dominic was saying that he would be in touch. They waved goodbye once again to Ben and George, who had come to see them off.

They drove back into Cambridge. It was almost lunchtime, and they parked the car and walked to the small café that they had visited many times before. He would have liked to take her somewhere special, but they were not dressed for smart places, coming from the stables in jeans, boots and sweaters.

They ordered their food, and Dominic ordered a bottle of champagne.

'Champagne!' She was surprised. 'At lunchtime! What are we celebrating?'

'My good fortune!' he smiled. 'To us, my darling, to our future!' They clinked glasses and sipped the ice-cold bubbles.

'To us!' she said, smiling into his mischievous eyes. 'Well now, have you decided about Stardust? Are you going to buy him? Is that why we are celebrating?'

'I might,' he said flippantly. 'Who knows? Now I'm rich I might find something even better.' He smiled, and they clinked glasses again as the food they had ordered was put in front of them.

'Well, what about our wedding then?' he said suddenly.

'Dominic! I told you if Jenny and Graham are planning a wedding soon, let them do it. It wouldn't be fair, to steal their thunder!'

'Well, we could make it a double wedding.'

'Oh! No! I want my own special day, and I know that Jenny will want hers. We'll wait.' She put out a hand and took his. 'You really don't mind, do you, darling? Then if you buy Stardust, which I know you do want to, then we can save up again, and get married next year. I would like a June wedding.'

'*Save up!*' he laughed. '*Save up!*' He looked at her in astonishment. 'Em, my darling, you'll never have to save up in your lifetime again. We have got millions!' He shouted out the word, throwing his hands in the air, and several people looked round, and he and Emily ducked their heads and giggled like schoolchildren.

On Friday afternoon they went to see Graham and Jenny's house. It was on a hill surrounded by seventy acres and part of the Springwater Estate. It was beautiful. They walked into the spacious, comfortable lounge, with a rose-pink carpet and light-grey velvet sofa and armchairs. The dining room had a

346

long mahogany table and ten chairs; they were planning to entertain, Jenny said. Upstairs there were six spacious bedrooms with en-suite bathrooms, though they were still waiting for the bathroom cabinets to arrive. They went downstairs again and looked out through the french windows. There was a small one-bedroom cottage halfway down the drive that had been built for a live-in housekeeper. Mrs Caldwell had already been contacted and she was willing to move in as soon as they were ready. At the bottom of the hill, near the entrance to the driveway, was the animal hospital, which was not furnished yet. They walked down to visit it. In the large waiting room was a large half-rounded reception desk with a polished mahogany top, which at the moment was covered in plastic to protect it from being scratched; there would be two receptionists. Filing cabinets would go here, and there would be a board up there on the wall for announcements about horse events and dog shows, and another on that side for wanted pets and puppies and kittens for sale. They walked through into the two large operating theatres with high wide windows for plenty of light. They would both have the very latest equipment, and there would be six nurses in attendance whom they had already contacted. There was a room at the side fitted with cages for sick dogs, and another for cats and other small animals, such as reptiles.

Graham said, 'Dad doesn't like handling reptiles. Morris Cutler has a snake and an iguana and on rare occasions they do need treatment, but not too often, thank goodness!'

'No, I don't think I would fancy treating them myself much either!' Dominic pulled a face.

They entered the two consulting rooms. The doors had frosted glass, and Dominic explained that when they got going they would each have their names painted in gold letters on the doors. Outside there were painted stables, which could house eight horses if need be, and also paddocks and plenty of grassland around.

Springwater Manor itself stood on a hill, set back into the trees, and was reached by a long tree-lined drive hidden from the road. It was a large Elizabethan hall with leaded windows, standing in two hundred acres of its own land. Most of the other seven hundred acres around the village were part of the

Springwater Estate owned by Lord Digby, including the land that Graham had bought to build the house and the animal hospital. Lord Robert Digby had passed away at least fifteen years ago, and Lady Digby, who was well into her eighties, lived in Springwater Manor alone with her staff. She was still quite active and on the village council, and had been chairwoman at the flower club for the third time last year. She still drove a little car around and had coffee mornings and church meetings at the manor. She had met Jenny and Graham, and told Jenny if she wanted any help to just call her. Jenny described her as tall and thin with lots of powdery make-up. A bit eccentric but charming, with bundles of energy. She had said that she was glad to have nice young neighbours, and that she liked young people because they kept her young.

On Saturday morning they were all at the Wickerbrook Show. Although early, it was already busy and the horse boxes were rolling in one after the other. There were horses and riders milling around everywhere; the ramps on the boxes were down, and horses were being groomed ready for their classes. Luckily the weather was sunny and bright, but there was a chill in the air as the early-morning wind blew across the fields. The usual sideshows were open for business; the hot-dog caravan and the ice-cream van already had long queues. There were people everywhere, many with children and dogs on leads, some of them there for the dog show later on that afternoon.

The girls came round to have a quick word with the boys who were helping Fred, Charlie Fenwick and the new guy, Bob Willis. They were each booked into a separate class. In the morning, Emily had ridden Pico. Then, in the afternoon, Tulip would be competing against Mary Clarke and Coolie, and Dominic, Graham Hadley and John Hopkins. When Emily and Dominic met at the entry gate for the class, they just acknowledged each other with a smile. There was no time for chitchat; this was business – they were about to go into battle.

Emily was determined to do her very best. Black Tulip had already jumped the perfect round, and the riders were now whittled down to just the two of them yet again, as had happened so many times before. When the announcement that there was to be a jump-off against the clock between Dominic Hadley and Silverspoon and Emily Peters and Black Tulip, the crowd clapped and someone cheered hooray. Emily was to go first. Dominic watched her carefully as Tulip took every jump with ease. Then it was his turn, and Silverspoon jumped to perfection as usual and won the day by only one second. The fence had been up to seven foot three.

The announcement came that the two riders were to go into the ring to receive their rosettes. The judge praised both Emily and Dominic for giving them all such a wonderfully entertaining performance, and the crowd clapped loudly as Dominic leaned over in the saddle to give Emily a kiss, taking her hand and holding it high for all to see. Then they filed out of the ring, Silverspoon following Black Tulip. For them, another Wickerbrook Show was over and there had not been one incident with Major.

30

Jenny and Graham had finally set a date – seriously discussing their wedding plans for the 20th of December. It would be a winter wedding. Jenny had found a dressmaker nearby, and Emily had gone with her. The dressmaker had designed a crinoline-style dress in cream velvet, with long sleeves and a high neckline, with a row of small pearl buttons down the front. The bridesmaids were to be Emily, chief bridesmaid of course, her cousin Jane, who lived in London, and Louise. Their dresses were to be similar – crimson-velvet affairs with fake-fur capes. They would carry posies of cream roses, and Jenny had ordered red for herself. She hoped it would snow.

Carol and Joe Ellis had arranged the reception in the Red Lion, where most of the village wedding receptions took place. There were to be over a hundred guests, and the tables were to be set out with white linen and red-and-white flower arrangements; very Christmassy. The three-tier wedding cake was to be made in Cambridge. The time would soon go, and there were lots of invitations to be written and posted. Jenny and Graham wanted everything to go out in good time, so that people could make arrangements to get to the church. Some of her family would have to travel by train If it snowed, as Jenny was hoping, things might be a bit more difficult!

John was in the yard as usual when Emily and Jenny came in from their ride. Liz saw them come past the kitchen window and automatically reached out for the pot to make fresh coffee. She had just switched on the machine when the phone rang: it was the police. She called out to Emily, who came in and picked up the receiver. It was Sergeant Bains. He thought that they had located her stolen tack, and could she please come down to the station and identify it.

Down at the police station Emily introduced Jenny to Sergeant Bains. A constable took them through to a large room crammed full of stolen articles. He showed them to one end of the room where he hoped that Emily could sort out her own gear. There must have been at least a hundred saddles, and there were two complete rails of bridles hanging tightly together. Velvet riding helmets were stacked in three piles from floor to ceiling.

'It won't be easy!' commented Constable John Robinson. 'But take your time; you are welcome to come back again another day.' He left the room, closing the door behind him.

Emily and Jenny were utterly bewildered. Where on earth could they start? Luckily, Emily's tack was almost new, which made it easier to identify, but it was still a taxing task. The bridle Emily was really interested in finding was made of very normal brown leather but she knew that it still had a few ginger hairs stuck in the buckle. The sorting-out took them the whole morning, but in the end it was Jenny who found it. She handed it to Emily, who took it and held it to her face, as if it was the most valuable thing in the whole world. They called to the constable to come in, and they said that they had found what they were looking for. They had to sign for the saddles, two old and two new, the bridles, and a box of brushes, which they took, though she knew John no longer needed them. There had been piles of green wellington boots in all sizes, and black velvet helmets, but without a name who could say? They all looked the same.

They put the stuff into the back of Emily's car, the constable helping them, and they drove home, pleased with themselves. From Emily's house, they phoned Dominic and Graham at college and told them about their success in finding the tack. The boys were due home again on Friday night: it was Emily's birthday, and there was to be another event at Foxhead Hall on Saturday.

For Emily's birthday, Dominic arranged a small dinner party in the Red Lion, after the Foxhead event. He had asked Jenny and Graham and Louise and Sir Simeon Hatch. They left the restaurant at a reasonable time, and Dominic kissed Emily goodnight in his car at her front gate. She thanked him again for the diamond bracelet he had given her and for planning the dinner party. He suggested that they go away on a holiday after the season was over; it could be part of her birthday present! Emily said it was a wonderful idea.

'You're worth it, my darling,' he smiled, and his eyes twinkled close to hers. 'I love you!' He kissed her again passionately, caressing her hair with his hand and taking her face in his strong hands. 'I think we should start planning our wedding. Shall we make it next July? What do you think?'

'Not July! What about the Goldsborough?'

He paused, a mischievous look on his face. 'I meant *after* I have beaten you at the Goldsborough, of course!' He broke into a devilish chuckle and winced, flinching away as she struck him playfully. 'Aren't you ever serious about anything?'

'Serious!' His voice rose in mock surprise, a smile playing around his mouth. 'I was never more serious about winning anything in my life.'

'I mean about the wedding.'

'Oh, *that!* Yeah! Well, I might let you win me over on that day. But the Goldsborough! *No way!*' He chuckled as she gave him a friendly slap on the shoulder and a quick kiss on the lips.

She turned quickly, getting out of the car. 'I'll see you tomorrow.'

He grabbed at her hand with a loving smile, not wanting to let go, but pulled away just before she shut the door. He opened the window. 'I love you, Em. Will you marry me next July?'

She looked in through the window. *'Only* if you let me win!'

He waved his hand, his handsome face grinning from ear to ear. 'I'll think about it!' Then, blowing her a kiss on his hand, he drove away with a mischievous chuckle.

She watched him go, a smile on her face. Next July! Wonderful! And she walked dreamily into the house.

The next morning Dominic phoned to say that he was coming over to Rosemary Lodge but he could not get there until eleven o'clock, so she suggested that he stay for Sunday lunch. She told her mother on the way through the kitchen and went on out into the yard where John had just finished saddling Black Tulip. She told him not to saddle Pico yet.

Emily was in the paddock jumping the poles. They were at

a good height, and Tulip jumped well. As much as she loved Dominic, she wanted to beat him, so she practised every minute she had. It wasn't hard work any more; she just loved to do it. After a while she rode into the yard and jumped down from the saddle. John took hold of Tulip, and she went into the tack room to get a Coke out of the fridge. She sat on the corner of the table and drank from the can.

John came into the tack room with the saddle and the bridle in hand and hung them both in the appropriate places.

'Nice mornin' out there, Miss. Should get a bit warmer later on. Although it ain't too bad now, is it?'

Emily took the can from her lips, holding her tongue tight against the roof of her mouth to quell the bubbles before swallowing, and then agreed with John that it was a nice morning.

'Do you want to take Pico out now, Miss?'

'No, not yet, John. Thanks! I'll wait now until Dominic comes, then I'll take him.' She slipped off the corner of the table, throwing the can into the bin, and went out to pat Pico and tell him she would come for him later. She went up to her room to brush her hair and renew her make-up, and be ready for when Dominic arrived.

She was ready now, in jodhpurs and a snow-white roll-necked sweater, standing looking out of the window at the sunny autumn scene. The breeze, although gentle, howled quietly through the treetops. She could just hear it faintly moaning through the closed windowpane. The breeze blew the long grass all one way, and it became a sea of silver rolling waves. Her mind drifted to Majorca and the sea... She imagined the warmth of the sun and she told herself that she would certainly ask Dominic if they could manage that week's holiday. She was staring into space, and suddenly, from across the fields out of the mist which was not even there, she saw Major. She blinked her eyes. Surely it was her imagination! She blinked again and again. He was still there. She stood looking, the mist was in her eyes now, and she saw Dominic riding him. He had that smile on his face. She blinked again, and they were gone! She must be in a sentimental mood.

She looked into the dressing-table mirror, checking her lipstick and her hair again, and spraying on some more perfume. She

353

imagined Dominic's handsome face looking back at her, and his voice echoed in her ears, 'I love you, Em!' She smiled at the twinkling brown eyes. 'You handsome devil, I love you, too!' she muttered with a smile and went out of her room and down the stairs into the yard, putting on her anorak as she went out of the kitchen door. Dominic would be arriving at any moment. Just as she turned into the yard, a horse box came up the drive. He was always pretty good for time, and now John could saddle Pico.

John had heard it and was coming out of the tack room, ready to help Dominic unload Silverspoon. As the box came to a standstill, he and Emily could see that it was not the Hadley box. Emily was surprised when Ben and George Mortimer got down from the cab, and she went forward to meet them. Ben and George both smiled, and Ben said that Dominic had phoned and told him that he would meet him here at eleven o'clock prompt.

'Oh, so he bought Stardust after all, did he?' She was beaming. 'We are riding out this morning, and I thought he was going to ride Silverspoon.'

Ben and George exchanged glances with a grin, and Ben looked at his watch. Two minutes to eleven. Dominic had said, 'Please don't open the box before I get there!'

'Could we have a look at your horses?' said George, thinking that it would fill up the two minutes' waiting time.

They walked with her to look at Black Tulip and Pico, talking to John about them. Emily looked at her watch. Where was Dominic? The time was getting on. Ten minutes past eleven.

'I don't know where Dominic has got to. I'll give him a ring.' She picked up the phone in the tack room, and it rang and rang. 'There's no answer,' she announced on coming back to join them. 'He must be on his way.'

Ben and George had coffee in the tack room. They had been waiting forty-five minutes. Ben looked at his watch. 'Look, I have a horse here,' he said. 'Dominic told me not to unload until he was here, but I don't think I can keep it shut up much longer.'

'No, of course not,' said Emily. 'I should unload if I were you.'

Ben went around to the back of the horse box. He let down

354

the ramp, and there was a clatter of hooves on the metal stays as he led the horse down. There stood the beautiful dapple-grey, Silver Lady, with a huge pale pink ribbon tied around her graceful neck and a big card attached to the front of it which said in large black letters, 'Happy Birthday, my darling, looking forward to the battle of the dapple-greys at the Goldsborough next July. All my love, Dominic xxxxxxxxxx'.

Emily was stunned. She smiled from ear to ear, then went to the horse and patted her neck and stroked her nose. She was beautiful, ready to ride with a brand-new saddle and bridle.

'Oh! Ben!' she squealed. 'What a wonderful surprise! I thought it was Stardust.' Her blue eyes lit up with excitement. 'Oh! I just can't believe it!' She turned to John. 'Oh! Just look at her, John. Can you believe it? Isn't she beautiful? Did you know?'

'No, Miss. I'm as surprised as you, but she is truly a beauty.' He came forward to pat the great mare on the neck.

'Oh, I must go and get Mum and Dad,' and she dashed off into the house. Both Liz and Mike came out, equally amazed at the sight of the beautiful mare, with the pink ribbon and the silver mane blowing gently in the breeze, moving her dainty hooves as they tapped on the cobblestones. Ben led her into the middle of the yard. Both Tulip and Pico whinnied, acknowledging the new arrival. Suddenly all three whinnied and Silver Lady shied and sidled as Major put his head over the his stable door. John hung on and shouted, 'Whoa there! Whoa!' But it was all over in a minute as Major disappeared.

Emily came forward, patting Silver Lady, and grimaced at John who patted her and talked to her, gently calming her. Emily walked across to where Ben and his father, George, were patting Pico, and Ben said that they were sorry if they had startled the horses. Emily smiled, telling them that they did get a bit agitated sometimes.

She looked at her watch again. 'I can't think where Dominic has got to. Are you sure he didn't tell you twelve o'clock? It's most unusual for him to be this late.'

'No! He told me to be here sharp at eleven, and not before. He wanted to be here to see your face when we unloaded.'

'Well, I don't know...' said Emily. 'I'll ring Packards Mill again.' She dashed off back into the tack room and dialled the number.

Ben and George stayed for an hour and a half, and still Dominic hadn't arrived. He must have broken down somewhere on the road. Emily knew what it was like on these country roads, if the car broke down. It had happened to her. There were no houses and no telephones, and all that faced you was a long walk, unless the odd passing car happened to give you a lift. She tried his mobile. It was ringing, but there was no answer. Where on earth could he be?

Ben said that they would have to leave as he had an appointment to go and look at another horse. He asked Emily to tell Dominic he was sorry that he could not wait any longer. She waved them goodbye, and thanked them again for coming, apologizing for Dominic.

She phoned Jenny to tell her the wonderful news about the silver-grey mare. 'You must come over and see her Jen; she's beautiful.' She asked her if she had spoken to Graham that morning as she could not get any answer from Packards Mill.

'No, I have been busy helping Anita all the morning, and have not had time to phone Graham, but he is coming over here for lunch.' Both girls thought it was strange that no one answered at Packards Mill. The nurses must be there; Packards Mill was always occupied.

'The phone must be out of order,' said Emily. 'When Graham gets there, give me a call, will you?'

John pulled down the stirrups, and Emily mounted the beautiful Silver Lady and rode her around the paddock, her parents and John, leaning over the fence watching.

'Isn't she wonderful, Mum?' she called as she sailed past. The mare cantered like a dream. She took her over a few jumps, Liz holding her breath, hoping that she would not fall, but Emily handled her like a champion. Liz knew that she would school her and take her to many shows. She certainly looked fantastic. Around she went again and then brought her to a stop by the gate. Both Liz and Mike leaned over to pat her.

The phone in the tack room was ringing. John left the group and went to answer it. It was Charlie Fenwick. He told John that there had been an accident, and Dominic and Graham were in hospital, and that was all he knew.

John came quickly off the phone, and called to Emily. She

356

brought the horse to the gate and, within a minute, she was off the horse, telling her mother to call Jenny and let her know. She was in her car and on the way to the hospital, speeding through the narrow country lanes and then up onto the motorway, her mind in a whirl wondering how bad it was, hoping that it was just a few scratches, hoping it wasn't a broken leg or something, hoping he had not smashed up his handsome face, hoping it was not something that would stop him riding...

It was hard finding somewhere to park. She went around twice and was just lucky enough to see a car backing out of a spot. She waited and then drove in, putting a pound coin in the machine and displaying the ticket on the windscreen. Dashing into the hospital, she asked the girl on the reception desk where she could find Dominic Hadley. He had had a car accident and had been brought in this morning. The girl gave her directions, and she walked quickly along the corridor looking for the sign that said 'B Ward'.

When she arrived, both Keith and Vivienne Hadley were there, their faces ashen. Vivienne stood holding his arm. She looked in a trance. Keith looked at Emily, tears glistening in his eyes. He shook his head gently, 'They were together,' then putting his arm around his wife he led her away.

Emily stood rooted to the ground. The loud racing sound in her ears was a silent scream. She knew it must be really bad. Her eyes darted from the floor to the ceiling to either side of the wall. She saw nothing. She felt slightly dizzy and was startled when a nurse touched her arm and asked her if she was all right and did she want to sit down? She turned slowly to face the nurse. The stark white of the uniform was a blur. She couldn't see her face, and she looked at her as if she had never seen a nurse in her life before, and then shook her head gently.

'I've come to see Dominic Hadley.' It was almost a whisper. 'How bad is it?'

'Are you a relation?' the nurse asked kindly.

'I'm his fiancé.'

'Oh! Sit down here for a minute, and I will get Doctor Yates.'

The doctor, a young, smart man in his thirties, took his hands out of the pockets of his white coat and sat beside her.

He spoke quietly and gently, holding her hand. There had been a car accident and death had been instantaneous.

Her heart panged violently, and she began to shake. Dr Yates held her hand tightly.

'And Graham?'

'The same. They would not have suffered.'

She swallowed hard, too devastated even to cry. 'Poor Jenny! May I see Dominic?' she asked in a gentle quick whisper.

'Well,' he hesitated, 'I don't think it's advisable just at the moment.' He could see the shocked look on her face, and she was near to collapse.

'Please!' Her eyes looked frightened. Her voice and her whole body were shaking.'

Keith had just come back to see the doctor. He had put Vivienne in the car. There was nothing they could do; they had been there for hours. He had overheard the doctor. 'Please, let her see Dominic.' He sounded as if he had not got the strength to speak. He looked sadly at Emily as she stood up. He nodded, 'They were together.' His lips trembled, as they fell into each other's arms and hugged for a minute. Then Keith quickly turned away and waited for the doctor.

Doctor Yates looked at Emily and nodded gently. 'Well, all right. Would you like a nurse to go in with you?'

She kept her eyes lowered and shook her head slowly. 'No, I'll be all right, thanks. I just want to see Dominic...' She almost choked on his name, but managed to sniff back the tears that were welling there and not break down. There would be plenty of time for crying later; she had to hold on.

The nurse opened the door. The private room was cool, the curtains closed and the room in semi-darkness. Emily entered quietly, standing by the door looking towards the figure in the bed, covered with a white sheet so still and silent. It was hard to believe that it was Dominic. She almost turned and felt like telling the nurse that it was all a mistake. Wringing her hands tightly together helped to steady her nerves, as she took a few steps to the bedside. Her head felt numb, and her teeth bit hard into her bottom lip. He was so still. His sun-bronzed face was badly scarred, and there were traces of congealed blood on his temple. The nurse closed the door quietly.

'Oh, my darling,' she whispered, with a quivering voice as

358

silent tears streamed down her cheeks. 'You promised that you would never leave me!' She held his cold and lifeless hand. She bent to kiss his bloodless lips, hoping that at any moment they would smile and say that it was all a joke, but knowing that they would never smile at her again. 'I had so much to say to you. I love you, I will always love you!' Her lips were trembling, and she covered them with her hand, but nothing would stop the hot tears that rolled down her cheeks. 'Thank you for sending me Silver Lady. We waited and waited and... You didn't come!' The silent tears stung her eyes, running down to her lips, and she felt their salty taste in her mouth. Wiping them away with her knuckles, she bent down beside the bed, putting her cheek gently against his, afraid of hurting him. He had lost that warmth, that pulsating vigour. She kissed his forehead, now cold and hard, brushing his dark hair with her hand. 'I have ridden Silver Lady in the paddock. She's lovely, but you will never see her in action at a show, will you?' She sniffed back the tears. 'I'll ride Silverspoon for you every day, I promise. I promise. I promise!' She took a breath, sobbing. 'Silverspoon will miss you, he will have his ears down, I know he will.' Her whispered voice trailed away, as the silent tears flowed uncontrollably as she bent to kiss him and she lay on the bed beside him, caressing his poor scarred face. She cried and cried; she had no idea how long she stayed there.

At the funeral, the whole of the horsey world turned out. Louise had phoned them all with the sad news, and the whole church had been packed to capacity, some not able to get inside. And now they stood in silence, three or four deep around the graveside in jodhpurs and black jackets, black helmets held in their hands. Emily and Jenny stood holding hands, both wearing black suits and hats, their eyes hidden behind their veils. All the parents stood in line together. Silverspoon and Skybright stood quietly by, held by Fred and Charlie Fenwick. Each wore a black rosette and black feather in his bridle.

The perfume from the hundreds of wreaths was almost overpowering. A huge life-size horse made up of hundreds of white carnations, contributed by friends and acquaintances from the equestrian world, stood majestically at the head of the double grave.

Emily, with tear-filled eyes, squeezed hard at the paper tissues in her hand. She shivered in the warmth of the October sun and looked up at the blue sky and the white fluffy clouds, hoping that Dominic was up there somewhere looking down on her. She noticed sunbeams shining through the leaves on the trees and heard the birds singing amongst them. She suddenly felt that she was standing here alone, but as the Reverent Saunders read the twenty-third psalm, she came back to reality and a terrible emptiness came over her. Dominic was gone out of her life for ever, and she saw again, through a misty glaze, his smile and twinkling brown eyes. They would haunt her, she knew, for the rest of her life. She looked around quickly as she felt a hand on her right shoulder and a hushed breath brushed close to her ear.

'Emily, I love you.'

There was a tingling coldness that ran all over her body. She lifted her shoulders, turning further round and smiling over her shoulder imagining him there, *knowing that he was*, as she put her hand to her shoulder covering his. She felt his arms enclose her, and she smiled warmly, resting her head back on his chest as she had done so many time before. Jenny gave her an enquiring look, and, with eyes wet and streaming, Emily gave her a faint and reassuring nod.

Two days after the funeral, the driver of the truck that had been involved in the accident, phoned and asked to come and see Keith Hadley. His name was Bernard Hemmings. He told Keith that he had been driving thirty years and he was so shocked at what had happened. He was used to driving through the country lanes and had driven this route many times before. Suddenly out of nowhere there came a horse. It was saddled – obviously it had thrown its rider – and it appeared so suddenly, right in front of him. It was ginger-brown and galloping at speed, and he swerved to miss it. He was sure he had hit it, it was so close to the bonnet of the truck, but he hadn't felt a bump. It had happened so fast and right on the blind corner. He remembered having a quick flash of the silver Mercedes, but it had been too late. He had been knocked out, and then the next thing he knew he was in the hospital with concussion. Later he had asked about the car and was told the tragic news, but no one knew or had seen anything of the horse; its rider had not come forward.

Keith listened to his story and nodded, saying that he understood. What else could he say? No one ever had an accident on purpose, and when he had mentioned a ginger-brown horse, Keith knew he meant chestnut, but he felt too devastated to start explaining about a ghost horse.

The day after, Keith phoned Emily, and she had gone to Packards Mill on her own. Vivienne and Keith told her the truck-driver's story, and she related it to Jenny the same afternoon, as Tulip and Henry walked slowly and quietly through the woods near Rosemary Lodge. For no matter what the tragedy, the horses still had to be exercised. The girls shed tears together almost every day. They had also been over to Packards Mill and rode Skybright and Silverspoon twice in the week, and they found it comforting. The horses had been so close to the boys they felt that they were part of them. And Emily made a silent vow, looking up into the cloudy sky, promising Dominic that she would look after Silverspoon, and the very thought made her cry out his name, and Jenny saw her and turned away, holding her breath.

31

A few months went by, and both the girls were surprised to receive letters from the solicitors Wilkinson, Babcock and Noble, inviting them to the reading of their fiancés' wills. That morning they were on the phone discussing the possibility that the boys had left them Silverspoon and Skybright.

On the Tuesday morning that they went with Keith and Vivienne to the solicitors' offices on the outskirts of Cambridge, Emily had butterflies in her stomach. To her, this was a frightening experience.

A middle-aged secretary with grey hair and a business-like grey suit greeted them and showed them into the office to the left of her desk. The room had a chilly feeling. The walls were wooden panelled, and there were pictures on the walls. In front of a large antique desk stood four cold black studded-leather armchairs. The room smelled strongly of polish and exuded an atmosphere of death.

'Good morning!' There was a quick smile from Mr Babcock as he came forward to shake them each by the hand. He was a plump little man with grey thinning hair, and he was dressed in a navy-blue suit, white shirt and dark-blue tie. He fitted into the dour atmosphere perfectly.

He looked over his silver-rimmed glasses and took them all in, with one grave sweep. 'Please, sit down.' He sat down behind the desk and shuffled some papers, they sat in silence, as if waiting for a death sentence. Emily was nervous. She kept swallowing hard and it was loud in her ears and she hoped that no one else could hear it.

Mr Babcock cleared his throat loudly, and it echoed in the quietness of the room, making Jenny jump. He looked over his specs. 'First, may I offer all of you my sincere and deepest sympathy. Your loss is so tragic.' Emily felt a surge of irritation. He had no idea how they all felt, and probably said the same thing several times a day. There was a pause as he gave them a moment to compose themselves. He looked down at the papers again. 'Well, I expect you are anxious to get on with this.' Taking the documents from a large buff envelope, he took a breath, looked up to see that they were all paying attention, and then looked down again and began to read:

'This is the last will and testament of Dominic Anthony Hadley.' He paused. 'I, Dominic Anthony Hadley, being of sound mind...' Dominic first said nice things about his parents; he had left them a few possessions he knew they would treasure, such as his cups and trophies he had won for riding. Mr Babcock went on, 'To Frederick John Mercer, the sum of ten thousand pounds and to Charles Benjamin Fenwick, the sum of ten thousand pounds...' Mr Babcock took a breath and gave a slight nod to Emily, as he read on:

'To Emily Anne Peters, I leave all my chattels, as of this moment, my horse, Silverspoon, or any other horses that I may possess at any given time. I am in no doubt that she will give them loving care, and I hope will keep them in training for competition, and to the said Emily Anne Peters, all money that I may possess, and the deeds to the Springwater Manor Estate. Signed. Dominic Anthony Hadley, this day June...'

Emily's loud gasp made Mr Babcock look up. She put her hands to her mouth, so shocked was she, that she almost fainted. Jenny turned and touched her hand, and both Keith and Vivienne looked at her with gentle smiles as she dug into her bag for a tissue. Dominic had told them about the house, but they had been sworn to secrecy. Vivienne's only regret now was that neither of these girls would become her daughters-in-law, and the thought saddened her. They would have made excellent wives for her sons.

Emily had had no idea about the Springwater Estate. Dominic had said that they would never have to worry again, but she had thought he was exaggerating, and the Springwater Estate must have cost him millions. She didn't even know what it was like, only that it was a big house on the hill opposite where Jenny and Graham had built their home. She hadn't even known it was for sale. She went cold all over. What was she to do with it? Could she live there alone, now that Dominic was gone? Jenny squeezed her hand.

363

Mr Babcock gave them a minute to digest what he had said. He then picked up another document. 'This is the last will and testament of Graham William Hadley.' Graham also said nice things about his parents, leaving them the things he knew they would treasure the most. 'To Jenny Carol Ellis...' It was almost the same as Dominic's will. Jenny sat there frozen to the cold leather seat, and at the mention of millions she almost collapsed. It was Emily's turn to comfort her, and Vivienne put a hand on her arm with a smile. But Emily was not really concentrating; all she could hear in her head was Dominic asking what kind of a house she would want, and her saying a big house, like Wickerbrook Hall. Her head felt dizzy, as if she were miles away. She could hear Mr Babcock shuffling papers, and it was like seeing him through frosted glass. He stood up and she remembered shaking his hand before they left the office.

The months that followed were difficult for them all. Keith and Vivienne tried to get on with their lives, but the loss of two sons was so great. Keith tried to get on with the job and still went out on visits – animals still needed attention. Some of his clients had not heard the news and had asked why Dominic or Graham had not come for a few months, and Keith had to explain. Once or twice he had broken down but he knew that the animals could not suffer for his misfortune, so he had taken on a young man by the name of Alan Granthem. Gradually, as the months went by, things got a little easier. Keith closed his practice and he and Alan moved in to the new premises. The sign on the door said D. and G. HADLEY CLINIC.

It had been six months and Emily had not yet set foot inside Springwater Manor. One day, when she was at Grays Hill, Jenny suggested that they walk over and have a look. Emily was a bit reluctant to go, but Jenny talked her into it, and phoned the housekeeper to let her know they were coming.

It was a cold dull day. Dressed in jeans, roll-necked sweaters and warm jackets, they walked up the gravel drive. Emily pulled the bell, and somewhere deep in the house they heard the faintest tinkle.

'I feel nervous,' said Emily.

'Well, don't be! It's your house,' Jenny reminded her.

'This reminds me of the first time we ever went to Wickerbrook Hall. Do you remember that day? I felt so nervous standing at the huge front door.'

'Don't start feeling nervous now!' Jenny gave her a little touch on the arm. 'This is your home, Em.'

Emily shook her head. 'No! It's not my home!'

Thomas Fielding, the butler, opened the door. He was a slight and dapper man, dressed in a smart black jacket and pin-striped trousers, a snow-white shirt and a dark-red tie. His face was pale and his light-blue eyes hard, his thinning grey hair brushed back, giving him a high forehead.

'Good afternoon, I'm Miss Peters!'

'Yes, Madam.' His voice was severe, but extremely polite. He gave a little bow. 'We were expecting you!' His face broke into many lines with a pleasant smile. 'Do come in, Madam. It's a pleasure to meet you.' He opened the door wider for them, as they stepped inside the spacious semicircular hall. Emily looked down at the cold black-and-white marble floor and shivered; it reminded her of the solicitor's office. In the centre of the hall was an oval mahogany table, with a huge fresh flower arrangement. He showed them into a small room to their left, opening a heavy oak-panelled door. The room was dull, with dark wood-panelled walls. To the left heavy dark-green drapes were open at the long casement window, which gave little light. There were two brown leather chairs either side of a low coffee table, on which was spread a few of the latest magazines. A roaring fire burned in a white marble fireplace; the aroma of applewood added warmth and comfort to the coolness of the dark-green furnishings.

'I will call Mrs Beckett, the housekeeper, for you, Madam. If you would please be seated for a moment. Would you like me to order some tea or coffee, Madam?' Emily declined.

A dense stillness seemed to fill the room as the door clicked shut. The house seemed silent, and empty. A moment went by, then another. The antique carriage clock on the mantelpiece ticked loudly, then the door opened and Mrs Dorothy Beckett appeared. Short and barrel-like, and dressed in a navy-blue suit and white silk blouse, she had short dark curly hair, a rosy face, and a big friendly smile. She appeared motherly but efficient, as she introduced herself with an outstretched hand, not knowing which was Miss Peters. Emily took the hand and Mrs Beckett shook it warmly. Emily introduced her friend, Miss Ellis, and Mrs Beckett shook her hand, too, with a smile.

'Oh, Miss Peters. It's a pleasure to meet you! We were all so sorry to hear of the tragedy.' She clasped her hands together and put her head on one side in a sympathetic gesture. 'But we have all been hoping that you would one day come to the house. It has been so dull here since Lady Digby moved away, you know. Were you thinking of taking possession soon, Madam? I do hope so, we all hope so.' She sounded quite motherly.

'Oh!' Emily was at a loss for words. 'Lady Digby has moved?' Emily thought perhaps she had passed away. And then she thought, what a silly question! Of course she would have moved if Dominic had bought the house.

'Oh yes, Madam. Lady Digby moved out last summer and went to live with her daughter in Yorkshire. The house has been empty, apart from the staff of course. We have seen no one since Mr Hadley.' She paused. 'Poor Mr Hadley came to interview us all. Fielding, his wife, and myself are the only ones, apart from the gardeners, of course, that he kept on. He said that we knew how to run the house, so we have been training all the new staff. They're a lot younger now, Madam, you understand; more your style, or so, poor Mr Hadley said.'

'Oh. How many staff do you have here, Mrs Beckett?'

'Twenty-two in all, Madam; that is, not counting Fielding and myself. Eighteen in the house and four gardeners.'

'Twenty-two!' What was she going to do with them all?

Mrs Beckett saw Emily sway a little. 'Would you like to sit down, Madam.' She indicated one of the armchairs.

Emily and Jenny sat either side of the fireplace. 'Thank you, Mrs Beckett. I'm sorry, but this is all so overwhelming for me. You see I had no idea. Dominic, my fiancé, Mr Hadley, said nothing to me. It's all such a big surprise. I knew nothing until I went to the solicitor's office.'

'Oh Madam, I am so sorry. Yes, it was supposed to be a surprise. He explained to both Fielding and myself, we were not to contact you. You were to be married...' She hesitated. '...And he was to bring you here after your honeymoon. I am so very sorry, Madam!' She looked sympathetically at Emily.

366

'The house has all been redecorated for you, madam. It was Mr Hadley, senior, who phoned to tell us the tragic news. He was here just a day or two ago just to check up. He has taken the veterinary clinic just down the road, opposite the drive.'

'Yes, I know!' Emily sat glassy eyed. Dominic had told her that when they were married, they would go on honeymoon to the Greek islands, and they would probably rent a small flat in Cambridge.

'How long has Mr Hadley actually owned this house, Mrs Beckett?'

'Oh!' Mrs Beckett had to think. 'It's over a year now, Madam; eighteen months. But he was kind enough to let Lady Digby stay on until she was ready to go to her daughter. They were having a small cottage built for her...'

'Oh! Please sit down, Mrs Beckett, and tell me more about the house.'

'Oh no, Madam!' Dorothy Beckett pulled herself up to her full height of five feet two inches.' Staff are not permitted to sit with the lady of the house. The staff are only permitted to sit in their own quarters, Madam! Would you like to see over the house, Madam? It does look lovely now it has all been redecorated. It really needed it, Madam, if you would permit me to make such a comment!'

Emily looked stunned. 'The lady of the house!' She looked up slowly as if in a dream. Mrs Beckett was waiting.

'Oh! Yes, please! Yes, please, Mrs Beckett, I should like to see the rest of the house. Wouldn't you, Jen?'

They followed her, stepping out into the chilled atmosphere of the marble hallway.

'The hallway is the only thing that Mr Hadley did not touch.' She opened the solid-oak double doors that were to the left.

'The house was built in the year 1600. This is the lounge. Mr Hadley had it redecorated, but the fireplaces in all the rooms are original, and of course we now have central heating!'

It was a large room carpeted in a rich rose-pink, with large easy chairs and two sofas either side of the stone fireplace where a log fire burned cheerfully. The furniture was old but charmingly elegant. The rich fabric of the curtains was of the palest green, their large golden tassels held back by bronze open-mouthed horses' heads. The room was warm and

367

comfortable, and Emily could imagine curling up in one of the big easy chairs to watch the television. But then she had the sad thought that she would be alone. Oh, Dominic, she sighed inwardly. 'It's beautiful, Mrs Beckett, just beautiful, isn't it, Jenny?' Dorothy Beckett nodded sadly. She could see the pain in the girl's face.

The dining room across the hall, past the sweeping staircase, was decorated in pale blue, the carpet a darker shade than the pale drapes at the windows and the covers of the twelve mahogany Chippendale chairs that surrounded the long mahogany table. In the centre stood a large ornament of a porcelain dapple-grey horse, its neck across that of a completely black horse. Emily saw this through misted eyes. She turned to Jenny, and they clasped hands secretly. Their eyes filled with tears.

'That is beautiful, Mrs Beckett,' said Jenny quietly.

'Yes, Madam! It came just a week ago. I believe Mr Hadley commissioned it in London. I mentioned that it had arrived to Mr Keith Hadley when he was here, and he told Fielding to unwrap it and stand it here. That's why he came just a few days ago.'

'So Dominic hadn't seen it then,' said Emily very quietly.

'No, Madam.'

Jenny gave her a tissue then dabbed at her own eyes.

'I'll get you some water, Madam.' Mrs Beckett, pulled the golden cord on the bell-pull near the fireplace, and almost immediately the door opened and a young maid in a narrow-striped pink-and-white dress and a small white starched pinafore appeared. 'Bring a jug of iced water and two glasses, please, Lily!' The maid bobbed a very small curtsey, and dashed away, coming back a few minutes later with a silver tray, a silver water jug and two glasses. She put it on the table and poured two half-glasses of ice-cold water, one for Emily and one for Jenny. Then again, giving a little bob, she left the room. Emily felt like a queen. She would have to get used to the curtseying.

They followed Mrs Beckett up the wide sweeping staircase, their feet sinking into thick silver-grey carpet; the old boards beneath them creaked under their tread. She showed them into the master suite. The carpet was creamy white, as was the counterpane, the curtains were of pale-blue silk with large golden tassels; the walls blushed with delicate apricot. An oak door to the side let into a spacious marbled bathroom with two showers and large mirrors that covered one side of the wall. Thick towels were of apricot, embroidered in white with the initials E and D. It took Emily's breath away. This was to be their room, but Dominic would never sleep in this bed.

'Mrs Beckett, I had no idea that Dominic...' Her voice broke at his name, and Jenny was there with a supportive arm. She looked at the bed, her thoughts that they would never share it together. She wiped a stray tear from her eye. 'I didn't know that he had been doing all this. It is truly beautiful. Isn't it, Jenny?' They walked in to all eight of the guest rooms, all beautifully furnished.

'How old did you say the house was, Mrs Beckett?' asked Jenny.

'Four hundred years, built in 1600, but as you can see it has been renovated at some time. The gardens and stable block are much the same, though, and the kitchen still has the original fireplace. Since Mr Hadley took over, the whole place has been transformed. I will show you the stable block. He was most proud of the stables, Madam!'

'Did Mr Hadley see the house finished, Mrs Beckett?'

'Oh, yes, Madam!' He was here a lot of the time, and he was here with his brother and his father on the morning of, of...' She saw the startled look in Emily's eyes, and left the sentence in the air, leaving a short uncomfortable pause. 'Come, I will show you the stable block.'

The stable block was large with solid flint walls and a raftered ceiling of solid-oak beams. 'There hasn't been a horse here for years,' said Mrs Beckett. There was an old pony trap standing in one corner. I don't know how old it is, but Mr Hadley kept this and had it painted to the original colours as you can see, black with a gold floral pattern. He even had the seat reupholstered. He said... She left another sentence in the air...

'I know what he said, Mrs Beckett. "It will be good for the kids to play on; my brother and I had one, and I used to whip an old bike for a horse." '

Mrs Beckett caught her breath. 'Yes!' 'And as you can see the woodwork has been treated and varnished...' She pointed to the rafters and the stable door. He said there would be about four horses in here to start with, but there would be

369

more. There is a staffroom for the grooms, but Mr Hadley hadn't yet employed any grooms, Madam.' She opened a door for them to see. It was fully fitted with a kitchen. 'And there is a new horse box outside this door...' She opened a door to the side onto a square bricked-in courtyard where there were three large carriage houses, in one stood a brand-new horse box. Both Emily's and Jenny's eyes lit up as they looked inside. It was of light wood and pale blue, big enough to take six horses. They looked at each other open-mouthed. There was nothing they could say.

'Well, thank you, Mrs Beckett, I think we have seen enough. Thank you for your time.' She walked round to the front of the house with them and Emily and Jenny shook her hand. Emily thanked her again and said she would be in touch, and they started to walk off down the long drive.

'Oh, did you walk, haven't you got a car?' Mrs Beckett sounded amazed.

'No, we walked. My friend Jenny owns the new house that was built up on the hill just opposite here.'

'Oh, I wondered who had moved in there,' said Mrs Beckett. 'I had not seen any movement over there, not that you can see much from here anyway, but of course I knew the builders were there. I didn't realize it was finished. When did you move in?'

Jenny smiled gently, 'I haven't yet, Mrs Beckett. You see, we are both in the same position, we were both planning on getting married. I was to be married in December, our fiancés were brothers...' She left it there. They saw Mrs Beckett's mouth drop; a surprised sadness come into her grey eyes. 'I'm so sorry,' it was a sincere whisper. She remembered the vet saying that he had lost two sons.

She watched them as they walked away together arm in arm, two lovely girls. Under her breath Mrs Beckett exclaimed, shaking her head in sorrow, 'Oh you poor, poor dears.'

Over the next few weeks they talked of nothing else but their houses. What were they to do? They both still had their jobs, although there was no need for either of them to work now, and they rode out together in the evenings and at weekends.

Then one evening, when they were at the Young Farmers Club, Emily's cousin Gavin said, 'Why don't both of you get together and open a riding school? You could employ someone to do the teaching. And the house sounds perfect!'

It seemed to be a good idea. It was something that she had always wanted to do, though she had imagined that Dominic would be there to help and advise her. Her parents encouraged her. She had sat around long enough mourning the loss of Dominic, and now, they said as gently as they could, she should do something with herself – and all that money.

Emily and Jenny thought more about it, discussed it this way and that, and in the end came up with the idea that they could each move into their own house, live their own lives and work together; that way neither of them would feel lonely, and they could have the riding school at Springwater Manor. Keith had the surgery at the end of Jenny's drive, which was very convenient when they ever needed a vet. They decided to do it.

Emily phoned Jenny at the end of the week. 'Hello, Jen. Look, I've had an idea. Before we move and start our new life, what do you think about going on holiday?' Jenny didn't have to consider, she thought it was a wonderful idea. It would do them both good.

'Where do you fancy going?' Emily could no doubt book something and get it half-price through the travel agency. They decided on Majorca, as Emily knew a little about it. Jenny said she would like to see where Emily had been for a year, so they booked into the Beverley Playa in Paguera. Emily had been in there for drinks and knew that it was a good place to stay.

Jenny moved first. Emily was there to help her move all her things into the new house. She stayed there a few nights, until Jenny was used to it. She contacted Mrs Doris Caldwell, who was pleased to take up her new post as housekeeper, and Pat Kimberly, daughter-in-law to Annie at Packards Mill, was employed as cook and proved to be very good. She and her husband, Bob, had moved into a cottage in the village and had given up his job as a farm labourer and taken on the job of driver and handyman

Emily phoned Mrs Beckett and said that she would be moving into Springwater Manor at the end of July, when they came back from Majorca. Mrs Beckett promised that the household staff would be ready.

'It must have been wonderful working here, Em.' Jenny was lying on a deckbed on the balcony at the hotel with her eyes closed against the brightness of the sun. 'I wouldn't have wanted to leave.'

'It's not the same when you are working, Jen. You don't get much time for sunbathing, and in the winter it's cold. That's why they sell all their leather jackets and coats!'

'I must get one of those leather jackets before I leave.' Jenny sat up. 'I saw a lovely cherry-red one!'

'Well, I've got to get some presents to take home.' They agreed to go shopping, but it was hot in the afternoon and they came back to the hotel exhausted.

That evening they went to the nightclub with Christine. It was the first time Emily had ever met Claudio. Christine had talked a lot about him, and she felt that she knew him already. She described him to Christine quietly as a 'handsome hunk', and wondered why they kept having rows and leaving each other! After two bottles of wine they were all dancing on the small crowded dance floor. Flashing lights dazzled their eyes, and everyone around them seemed to be jerking and suspended in mid-air. As they gradually danced towards the middle of the floor, Emily turned around and in a quick flash of the lights came face to face with Riccardo Calmanetti. It was as if time stood still. They both stopped dancing and stood facing each other. They couldn't speak for the noise, and then they got pushed apart by other dancers and she went back to her group with Jenny and Christine. It was hard to see, and he was gone!

Emily felt unsettled. The rest of the evening she spent scanning the people in the semi-darkness through the micro-spotlights that shone down from the star-studded ceiling like white rods. Beyond this it was total blackness.

Back at the hotel about three o'clock in the morning, she told Jenny about it.

'Why didn't you talk to him?'

'I couldn't. We were on the dance floor and then he was gone, I thought he might've come over to say hello but he didn't. Maybe he was with his wife. It's so strange, he usually isn't here in the summertime. The housekeeper told me they only come in the winter, because the house is rented most of the year.' They talked into the rest of the night and eventually fell asleep.

The holiday went by quickly. They sunbathed and shopped and wined and dined, and now it was the very last day and they had gone to Cordoba's restaurant for lunch, where Emily had gone quite often. Señor Cordoba recognized her and came over to shake her hand warmly. She introduced him to Jenny, and they ordered their food and a bottle of wine. Jenny thought it was a great place, the walls decorated with matador cloaks and hats and swords and posters of the bullring. She only wished the boys were there with them to enjoy it. Emily said they were there in spirit, that she could always feel Dominic around her, and it comforted her. Jenny said that she felt the same.

They were just getting the bill, and about to leave the table, when Riccardo and Jay Calmanetti walked through the door. Emily's heart missed a beat. He came over to the table with a flamboyant smile.

'Well, hello, Emily!' She stood up, and he hugged her and kissed her on both cheeks, and so did Jay. Suddenly she was all smiles, and introducing them to her best friend, Jenny.

'Mind if we sit with you?' Riccardo pulled out a chair. 'I remember hearing a lot about you, Jenny.'

'I hope it was only the good things,' she smiled, then hesitated. 'Well, we were just leaving.' She looked at Emily.

'Yes, we were just leaving.' Emily stood, picking up her bag.

'Oh, you can stay for a little while, can't you? It's good to see you again, Emily. I got a glimpse of you at the nightclub; you are still working here then.'

'No.' She sat down again. 'I left over a year ago, nearly two now. I'm back in England.'

'Sorry, I didn't call you. I had some business in the States.'

'Yes, your wife said you weren't there! How old is Lucia? She sounded very nice on the phone.' There was an awkward pause.

'Mmmmm.' He took a deep breath and leaned back in the chair, then leaned forward, his elbows on the table, clapping his hands softly and rubbing them together. 'Well, yes! Sorry about that. They arrived unexpectedly. Lucia is fourteen.' He took his elbows off the table as the waiter brought them a menu, easing the tension.

'Well, are you girls on vacation?' Jay changed the subject.

'Yes! 'Yes, we've been here two weeks.'

Riccardo was studying the menu and he looked up. 'Do you want to go riding? I've some horses here, the other side of Palma, just brought them over. That's why Jay and I are here. She's a great rider!' he said to Jenny.

Jenny nodded with a smile. 'Yes, I know.'

'So is she,' Emily smiled.

'Well then.' He slapped the menu down. 'What do you say? How about tomorrow?'

'Sorry!' Emily smiled. 'We're leaving tomorrow.'

'Oh!' he sounded diappointedly. 'Well, how about drinks tonight? Dinner? How about dinner? Just the four of us.'

Emily was about to refuse, but she looked at Jenny; she didn't want to spoil Jenny's last evening. 'What do you think, Jen?'

Jenny, like Emily, didn't want to spoil it for her friend either, but knowing Emily so well she knew she wasn't keen. 'Well, we *are* leaving tomorrow; we have to pack!'

'Well, you'll have time. Come on, it's your last night!' Riccardo coaxed. 'Come on, what do you say? Dinner?'

'Just dinner!' Jay chipped in.

Emily, knowing how persistent they could be, agreed. 'Dinner only! No nightclub.'

'No nightclub! We don't want to be too late.'

'OK! No nightclub. Cross my heart,' Riccardo grinned. 'We'll pick you up at eight.'

'No, Riccardo!' Emily was adamant. 'You tell us where, and we'll meet you, or we don't come.'

He smiled. He was losing the battle. 'OK, OK! You are very determined, Emily. How about Tortuga at the top of the hill?'

She agreed. They had been there before. It was a nice restaurant overlooking the sea, with a view of twinkling lights.

'We'll meet you there at eight,' said Emily. 'Now we have to go. Enjoy your lunch.' She gave them a sweet smile and stood up; Jenny followed her, saying goodbye.

They both stood politely as the girls left, and then sat down again, glancing at each other with smiles, then looked at the menu.

'So we got a date?' Jay looked across the table at his brother.

'No, not exactly, just dinner! Emily is a very determined young girl. If she says dinner, she sure means *dinner only*!'

Jay chuckled. 'If you say so. OK, dinner it is, and I won't push it.'

Outside, as they walked back along the street towards the hotel, Jenny asked why Emily seemed a bit aggressive with the men.

Emily told her. 'Riccardo seems a nice enough guy; there's no harm in him, but when he says dinner, it means three or four o'clock in the morning. It has happened twice before, so if they turn up at the hotel to pick us up, we are still going to take our car. I know the way to Tortuga, and I know the way he works. It's a nice restaurant, you'll like it.'

'Well, why did you say we would go?'

'Because it is our last night, and I didn't want to disappoint you, and we have to eat anyway, and we might as well have a little company, and believe me, they *are* nice company, but you can't trust men! Riccardo is married, after all.'

'Well, I don't suppose he will bring his wife!' Jenny chuckled.

32

Emily moved into Springwater Manor. George Fielding was there to open the car door for her.

'Good morning, Madam, and welcome to Springwater Manor.' He bowed his head politely.

She smiled and said, 'Good morning, Mr Fielding!'

'Just Fielding will do, Madam.'

He followed her in and closed the heavy oak front door.

Mrs Beckett was there. She came forward her hands clasped in front of her and bowed her head. 'Welcome again to Springwater Manor, Madam.' She had all the household staff, twenty-two strong, lined up in the hallway ready to greet her. The girls dressed in pale-pink pin-striped dresses, the men in a deep petrol blue. She introduced them in turn. Finally she said, 'This is Rosalie Miller! I've appointed Rosalie as your personal maid, Madam. I hope I haven't presumed too much, but I am sure Rosalie will be efficient and most discreet.'

'Rosalie; that's a nice name,' smiled Emily. 'It makes me think of the summer. I am sure we will get along well, Rosalie.'

The girl, aged about thirty gave a shy smile and a little dip of a curtsey. She was tall and slim with soft blonde hair rolled up neatly into a chignon at the nape of her neck. Her appearance was clean with no fuss. She was dressed differently from the rest of the staff, in a plain pale-pink short-sleeved dress with white collar and cuffs, a starched white organza apron, a small white tiara-like cap, black stockings and flat black shoes.

'I'll do my best, Madam. I live in, and am at your service at any time.' She was well-spoken and said quietly, 'I'm also trained as a beauty therapist, which includes make-up, hairdressing, and massage, should you require them, Mam.' She curtsied again.

Emily smiled. She would have to get used to the curtsey thing.

'That sounds very interesting, Rosalie, thank you.'

She told Jenny afterwards that it had been an ordeal, having to see so many staff, and she did not know how she would cope. Jenny laughed, telling her she wouldn't have to cope, they would do it all for her. And she was right, as the weeks went on, life got a lot easier, and now that the horses had been transferred from Rosemary Lodge, John and Susan came every day. John couldn't believe the size of the stables. They coped for three weeks, looking after Black Tulip, Pico, Silver Lady and Silverspoon, until Charlie Fenwick came to help John after he had finished in the stable yard at Grays Hill.

John and Charlie coped for another week with all six horses, Emily employed two new grooms, a young girl aged seventeen from the village called Caroline Jones, and Ray Washington, a young man in his twenties, a former stable lad in Newmarket. She also took on board Daniel Cameron, a Scotsman, horse trainer and tutor; he had been training people and horses for twenty years. Susan was appointed head groom, and they laughed because John was now working for her. And the riding school for professional horsemen and horsewomen was opened!

Jenny came up every day, and they had a few clients, mostly proficient young riders, and some who wanted eventually to turn professional. One of these was Alex Freemore, and another, Derek Milner, who brought their own horses for a lesson with Dan Cameron, who put them through their paces, timing them over the jumps and giving them sound advice. The school was beginning to get known in the area, and people came from miles around for training. It was special, the only one of its kind in the area. On occasions there were also special weekends where clients could bring their own horse or hire one, and stay at Springwater Manor for a whole training session from Friday morning to after Sunday lunchtime at three o'clock. Then, there were a few mothers who wanted their children to learn. Some had never sat on a horse. So Emily bought two ponies, and Emily and Jenny occasionally took them, but mostly they left it to Susan and the new girl, Caroline Jones. Fielding and Mrs Beckett said the house had never seen such happy times, with the phone ringing and people coming and going. It had been dull for so many years.

Louise had come over. She was amazed; she loved the house,

and the stable, and even came for a lesson with Dan, which she said was brilliant. She said she would get Simeon to come with her one weekend if she booked him a lesson. Poor Simeon, he had no choice. She stayed for lunch, and afterwards the three of them rode out together: Emily and Black Tulip, Jenny and Henry, and Louise and Pico. They rode over to Grays Hill, and Jenny showed her round the estate, the house and the stables.

'Why don't you send the ponies over here for the younger children to be trained?' said Louise. Both Emily and Jenny thought this was a good idea. It would be quieter for younger children, and Charlie Fenwick would be able to look after his own stable.

'Mystic Nights!' Louise went on. 'Are either of you interested? I kept him because Simeon has been riding him, and I will probably get something new, but he would be good for the riding school!'

Both Emily and Jenny said that they would think about it. Just at the moment they had enough on their hands.

As the years went on, both Emily and Jenny still rode in competitions, but their enthusiasm was dwindling. They spent a lot of time together, riding and occasionally going out for dinner, but still living their own separate lives. Jenny had had a couple of dates, which did not amount to much. They had been away on a cruise around the Greek islands; it had been a lot of fun with good food and wine, and they had made several friends, and danced the nights away, and came back with terrific tans.

Every morning John came in, and sometimes he would overhear Emily talking to Silverspoon about Dominic and asking him if he missed him as much as she did. She was in tears, the same as it had been when she had lost Major, but now she stood at Silverspoon's stable door, and the pain was much worse... On other days she would be bright and alive when John and Susan arrived, chatting and getting John to saddle Black Tulip and riding over to see Jenny.

The day came when Louise and Simeon got married. It was a big affair with three hundred guests, a lot of them VIPs, titled lords and ladies, and London dignitaries, everyone dressed to perfection. Although it was a lovely day and they enjoyed it, there was a certain sadness for Emily and Jenny, as they stood in the church, each with their own private thoughts, as the vicar said, 'Will you take this man...' Jenny caught Emily's hand and squeezed it. They glanced at each other with a sad smile.

Most days they tried to ride out together. It was nice to be alone and chat; they could say whatever they liked to each other, and neither of them thought the other silly or morbid. They knew each other so well. The conversation was about the boys, and they shed tears. As time went on, it didn't seem to get much better. They both felt lonely, even though they were together a lot. On occasions they went home to lunch with their parents, and about every two weeks they visited the Hadleys at Packards Mill, and there were more tears shed between them.

They had got to know Keith's new vet, Alan Grantham, very well. He was there this morning, checking on one of the ponies that was about to go over to Grays Hill. It had got a stone in its hoof and was limping. It was just a simple thing and the pony was right in a matter of a few minutes.

Emily stood near the stable door watching Alan. He had his back to her, but he was talking to her, and her mind suddenly flew back in time to when Keith was doing just the same thing and it was the first time that she had ever met Dominic. Her mind was miles away, and she was glassy-eyed, staring into space, not hearing a word Alan was saying.

'Shall I give these to John, to give to Sammy, Emily?' He looked up and got off his knees. 'Emily, are you all right? Emily?' He had his head on one side, looking up into her face.

She suddenly realized that Alan was talking to her and was holding out tablets for the pony.

'Shall I give these to John?'

'Yes...' She hesitated. 'Yes!' She looked up at him quickly, with a nod, but his face was in shadow, and she thought that she was talking to Dominic.

'Emily, are you OK?' Alan had his hands on her upper arms, and was giving her a little shake. 'Emily?'

'Oh, yes. Sorry, Alan, what were you saying?'

He frowned. 'Well, I was saying that Sammy needs this

379

medication, and should I give it to John? Are you really all right? You don't look too good.'

She still had that muzzy feeling. 'Yes, I am all right, Alan, thanks. It's just... It's just that sometimes, things trigger off things.' She was nodding. 'You know how it is.'

He said, 'Yes!' But he had no idea what she was talking about.

'I think I will go in and get some coffee.' She seemed in a bit of a trance. 'Do you want to come in for a cup of coffee, Alan?'

He hesitated for a minute, wondering if he should go or not, and then said, 'Yes, thanks, I wouldn't mind a cup!' and she just walked off and he followed her to the back door of the house, through a short hallway and into the morning room. He had never been into the house before. It was a pleasant and bright room decorated in pale green. The window looked out across the lawn to flowerbeds and shrubs. There was a table and six chairs in the centre of the room and a long sideboard on top of which were a few books and a telephone. Emily picked up the phone and talked to one of the kitchen staff, and then sat down, her elbow on the table, her head in her right hand. It was Lily who came in from the kitchen a few minutes later, with a silver coffee service on a tray and two cups and saucers.

Alan turned from the window. He had been watching Bill Stern, who was on his knees tending to the shrubs.

'Thank you, Lily! I will pour it.' Emily smiled. 'Do you want cream and sugar, Alan?'

'No thanks, just black.' It was the first time she had spoken to him since they had come in from the stables, and he thought she looked a little pale, but better after the first few sips of the coffee.

She knew that he was looking at her. 'I am sorry, Alan, you must think I'm quite mad. I'm sorry, but, as I said, some things just set me off. You see, it was you, poking around with Sammy's hoof. Have you ever had that feeling that it has all happened before? Well, that was what happened when I first met Dominic, he came with Keith...' She stared into space for a moment as the whole scene went before her eyes again, as it had done so many times before.

380

After she had told him the whole story of the way they had met, and then went on to tell him about the horseriding and the challenges, she seemed to become normal again.

'Well, you had me worried there for a moment. I thought you were going to faint.'

She smiled. 'No, I've never fainted. I'm sorry if I worried you, and I hope I haven't bored you too much with my silly reminiscing...' There was a pause. '...But I do miss him so!' She looked down to avoid his gaze and rubbed at her forehead, pushing her fringe back. 'It's nearly five and half years ago now.'

He looked at her, taking a deep breath. 'You know, Emily, you need to get out more, you can't stay around horses all the time. You have to get out and meet people.'

She smiled up at him. 'I know, that's what my father says, but I meet a lot of people who come here, and Jenny and I go out occasionally, but you know what animals are like. They take up all of the time. More coffee?' He shook his head. There was a pause. 'Anyway, I do enough to keep myself busy, but Dominic used to keep me on my toes, telling me when to get ready for this or that. "I'll pick you up at seven, don't be late" and that kind of thing.' She smiled thoughtfully. 'I used to get very frustrated with his arrogance, and his domineering ways.' She rested her elbows on the table, her chin in her hands. 'But I miss it all so much now.' She sighed, 'Oh, how I miss it! You didn't know Dominic, did you?'

'No, but I saw his picture in the paper many times, and yours. You used to do well at events, didn't you?'

'Yes...' She nodded vaguely. She had visions of Dominic on Silverspoon; she was going into one of the trances again.

'Do you still enter horse shows?'

She looked up. 'Oh, umm, yes...' She came back to reality. 'Jenny and I enter, but it's not like it used to be. We used to practise until we dropped.' She looked up at him and smiled. 'And if Dominic were here, I would be out there practising every minute of the day. He would say, "You have nothing to stop you now, you have a household full of staff and nothing to do, get out there and ride, make something of yourself. If you want to turn professional, now is the time."'

'Well, why don't you do it?'

381

'Why don't I do what! Turn professional?' She looked up at him in surprise. 'I have the riding school.'

'Get out there and ride. Give it all you've got! Don't relax and throw away all you had! Why teach everyone else to do what you really want to do yourself?' There was a pause. 'If you can't do it for yourself, do it for him; he wouldn't want you to fail, would he? Just because he is not here to egg you on.'

She looked at him thoughtfully, then took a deep breath. She smiled up at him, rubbing her hands together. 'You know, Alan, you have just made my day.' She seemed to have come alive before his very eyes. 'I will, I will. I'll do it for him. You're right, he wouldn't want me to be a failure! It was the one thing he lived for, to be successful! It was the only dream in his life to win at everything; he couldn't bear to fail.' She paused. 'I think you're right. I think I have done enough mooning around. It's time I really started to ride again!' Her blue eyes shone as they had not done for a long time. 'And I think I'll start right now. Thanks!' She left the table and started towards the door then turned. 'Do you ride, Alan?'

'Yes,' he nodded with a smile. 'I can ride, and I do when I get the time. A farmer I know has a horse and needs it exercised.'

'Do you want to come with me?'

He hesitated, unfolding his arms. 'What? Riding! What, now?' He sounded astounded. 'Well, I really have some house calls to make.'

'Oh!' She sounded disappointed. 'Oh, come on!' she coaxed, wrinkling her nose. 'Who is going to know? You can always say that you had an operation to do or something, and it made you late.' She stood for a moment, her hand on the door, a stupid smile on her face and feeling all girlish. This had all happened before, she was talking to Dominic, or was it Dominic putting words into her mouth. She waited, uncertain, wondering if she had done the right thing in asking him.

'Well, OK!' he smiled with a nod. 'You talked me into it.'

'Ha!' Her eyebrows rose. 'You didn't need much persuading.'

He smiled. 'But I really do have work to do.'

She smiled inwardly. This had all happened before. The same scene was being replayed; that was what Dominic had said.

And she had replied, 'Oh, you didn't want much persuading, did you?' It was uncanny. She gave Alan a mysterious smile, as he was about to follow her out of the door. He frowned, not understanding.

John was in the yard. She asked him to saddle Black Tulip and Pico, and they rode out together. In her heart it was the same, and yet so different. Alan rode well, but she saw Dominic before her eyes and they became glassy. She gripped the reins tightly in her hands. She must control her emotions. 'Come on, let's canter!' She clicked her heels, and Tulip took off, and Pico followed.

It all seemed to have happened too fast, but after that day she and Alan Grantham had ridden together a few times and he had taken her out to dinner. Emily still had her anxiety, depressions, moods, whatever you like to call them, but he was managing to understand her, and was able to snap her out of it with a kind word or a joke to take her mind off it. He was gentle and she liked him, and they got on well together.

Jenny was in the yard talking to Alex Freemore. He had just finished a lesson with Dan, and Derek Milner, while waiting for a lesson with Dan, was talking to Alan about Red Streak. He had bought him from Alex some months ago, and he had been going well. Alex had bought Mystic Nights and was pleased with the way he was shaping up, but he was concerned about Red Streak and was asking Derek what the problem was.

Derek, now talking to them both, was saying that Red Streak had a back problem, and asking Alan to come and look at him.

'Can't get out there today, Derek. Car broke down just about fifteen minutes ago. I had to leave it on the road. In any case, I couldn't make it until after five this afternoon. I'm operating.'

'I'll drop you over to Derek's if you like, Alan,' said Jenny, popping her head over the half stable door. 'I've got to go home, and it's not much out of my way. And perhaps Derek can drop you home.'

'Would you, Jenny? Thanks.' Alan seemed pleased. 'But I might get my car fixed by then, but well, if it's all right with you then, Derek, I will be there about six thirty. OK?'

Alan phoned the mechanics to come and look at his car. They towed it away, saying it would take a couple of days. Jenny

drove the Range Rover and waited while Alan checked Red
Streak. Jenny and Derek stood watching, and then Alan gave
him some medication and an injection, and told Derek not to
ride him. He would come back tomorrow if he got his car
fixed.

The car was not ready, and Jenny happened to be going that
way to have lunch with her parents. It was a bit out of her
way, but she dropped Alan off again at Foxhead Hall and said
that she would pick him up again in an hour and take him
back to the surgery. Alan checked Red Streak and advised
Derek still not to ride him at least for two weeks, and he was
disappointed. He had two other horses he could ride, but they
had not had the practice, and Red Streak was the best at
jumping anyway, and he had him booked into a show at Carling.

Jenny came back on the hour. Derek looked fed up. She
asked what was the matter, and he said he was going down
the pub to drown his sorrows because he didn't stand a chance
at the show without Red Streak.

'Well,' said Alan. 'Emily and I are going to the Red Lion for
a quiet meal, nothing special. Why don't you join us? It might
cheer you up.'

Derek thought for a minute, pursing his lips. 'Yeah, sounds
like a good idea, what time?'

'About seven thirty!'

Derek nodded. 'Do you want to come, Jenny?'

And that's how it all happened. Now, it was just like old
times. They became a foursome. On occasions, Emily and Jenny
were booked into a show, and they quite often met Derek
Milner, though for the girls the shows were getting fewer and
fewer, as running the riding school they had not got the time
to put in so much practice, and they were happy with what
they were doing. Derek came over more often for a lesson with
Dan, and occasionally popped over to Jenny's for lunch, and
sometimes all four of them had lunch at Springwater Manor.
The days went on, and they often just rode out together.

It had been a busy weekend, with six people booked in at
Springwater. They had had lunch with the guests, and now
Jenny had ridden Henry back to Grays Hill. Sunday afternoon

384

was quiet and Emily sat in her small TV room in a comfortable armchair. There was nothing worth watching, and she turned off the television. She was feeling in a sentimental mood, looking out onto the garden across the soft pinks and yellows, the last of the summer roses, and the neatly cut lawns. The day was dull, and it had been drizzling since the early hours of the morning. It was September and the leaves were turning to red and gold and falling, covering the lawn in a thick bronze carpet. It had been six and a half years now since Dominic and Graham had died, and it had happened in late September. It had been a bright sunny day then, the leaves had been falling then, and crackling under Silver Lady's feet in the paddock, when suddenly John had said that Dominic was in hospital. She put her hands up to her eyes, trying to blot out the awful feeling, that terrible scene when she first saw him in the hospital. He was near her now. She could feel him. She could still feel the touch of his hand on her shoulder, and she put her own hand on her shoulder as if to cover it, and tears pricked her eyes. She sniffed them back, when Rosalie came in, as she usually did on Sunday afternoon, with coffee and cook's fruitcake on a tray. She put it down on the side table. 'Will there be anything else, Madam?'

Emily didn't answer. She was deep in thought.

Rosalie waited. 'Madam?' She looked at her. 'Madam, are you all right?' Rosalie was used to Miss Peters. She had seen these depressions many times before.

Emily jumped, then turned slowly. She looked vague. 'Yes, thank you. I am all right.'

Rosalie stood for a moment, wondering if she should leave. She could see that she was upset and guessed it was about Mr Hadley. Rosalie had proved to be a good companion to Emily. They quite often talked, while she was laying out Emily's clothes, or bringing her coffee, as she was now. She had heard what had happened to the Hadley brothers years ago, and she had seen Miss Peters in tears before.

'It's fine, Rosalie.' She fingered her diamond engagement ring, and the gold bracelet that he had given her that very first Christmas. She had promised to wear it always. She sniffed, perking up with the slightest smile. 'I'm all right, Rosalie, really. Thank you! You may go.'

Emily rested back in the chair, taking the silver-framed photograph of Dominic off the side table. She smiled at him through misted eyes. She kissed the smiling mouth. 'Oh, Dominic, I need your tender touch. Where are you now, my darling? If only I could see you! If only, if only!' The tears flowed down her cheeks. 'I still miss you so. Silverspoon misses you, too. I know he does, and I keep him exercised, but he so often has his ears down. I talk to him about you, and he nods knowingly, and he is not swishing his tail.' She smiled gently. 'Do you remember saying that to me?' She smiled again and the smiling face smiled back, and she touched his lips again with her own. 'Oh, Dominic, she breathed, 'life will never be the same without you. I haven't seen anything of Major for ages. I guess you are having a word with him and exercising him. Oh, I do miss you so. I miss you, my darling, every minute of every day.'

There was a quiet tap on the door, and Rosalie came in. 'Oh, Madam, you have not drunk your coffee, are you all right? Can I get you anything more? Hot coffee?'

Emily did not turn round, but Rosalie saw her holding the silver frame and Rosalie knew she was crying.

'Please, Madam,' she gently whispered, 'try not to upset yourself. I know it is hard, I lost my brother three years ago in May, and my mother still walks round in a trance every May-time, but nothing is going to bring him back.' She spoke softly. 'It just makes her more upset, and I believe that my brother is still with us. We are a very close family. I talk to him sometimes, and my mother talks to his photograph, just like you, nearly every day when she is dusting the lounge. His photo is on the sideboard and she stands in front of it. I hear her asking him questions, and I'm sure she gets answers. It seems to satisfy her anyway, but nothing will bring him back; but talking seems to comfort her.' She paused. 'He, too, had a car crash. His girlfriend got away with just a few cuts and bruises, although she was in hospital for weeks, but I suppose we should be thankful for just that. She has another boyfriend now but still comes around to see my mother. She told us afterwards that they were just driving steadily, not speeding or anything, and this big chestnut horse just suddenly appeared in front of them, and my brother swerved to miss it. It happened on a bend and they ran into a tree and wrote the car off.'

386

Emily heard alarm bells ringing in her ears. As she turned round slowly, her mouth open in surprise, seeing Rosalie's face through blurred vision, she wiped a finger across her right eye and blinked to clear the mist.

'Oh, Rosalie.' It was a hushed and sympathetic sigh, as if she had not got the strength to speak. 'Oh, Rosalie,' she breathed deeply whispering, 'I am so very sorry to hear that, Rosalie, so very sorry. I have tried and tried,' she shook her head gently in despair. 'It was all my fault. I will have to speak to him again. It seems he has taken to the roads now.'

Rosalie frowned, looking puzzled. 'I beg your pardon, Madam?'

Emily sighed deeply again, dabbing her eyes with a tissue and shaking her head gently at her thoughts. She indicated an easy chair. 'Sit down, Rosalie, it's a long story.'